THE TOLLING

of

MERCEDES BELL

To Kristen
with warm regards
and many thanks
for your helping hand
to a fellow writer,
           Jennifer Dwight

Published 2016
Printed in the United States of America
ISBN: 978-1-63152-070-9 pbk
ISBN: 978-1-63152-086-0 hardcover
ISBN: 978-1-63152-071-6 ebk
Library of Congress Control Number: 2015954337

Cover design © Julie Metz, Ltd./metzdesign.com
Author photo by Mark Bennington
Formatting by Stacey Aaronson

For information, address:
She Writes Press
1563 Solano Ave #546
Berkeley, CA 94707

She Writes Press is a division of SparkPoint Studio, LLC.

For Laurel and Julian

The truth is incontrovertible.

Panic may resent it,

ignorance may deride it,

malice may distort it, but there it is.

—WINSTON CHURCHILL
May 17, 1916
Speech in the House of Commons

A KIND *of* TAROT

Dozens of index cards were laid out like a board game on the dining room table. The old manual typewriter and a ream of good bond paper were the tools of survival in her now-desperate campaign to find a job. Copies of letters already mailed sat in a thick stack next to the cards on which she'd written the name and address of every law firm within driving distance. Hundreds of calls and letters later, she was down to the end.

It has to be one of these, thought Mercedes Bell, arranging the last cards in front of her like some obfuscated Tarot reading. She stared out the open windows onto her neighbor's lawn and felt a hollow ache inside. Of all the many she had tried, there were only four law offices left to pursue for the elusive paralegal job.

Pull yourself together. It will be one of these four, she thought. She typed the letter she knew by heart, introducing herself, enclosing a résumé. There was something wonderfully satisfying about pounding out a letter. The table shook a little, the wood floor vibrated beneath her bare feet, and at the end of each line—*ding!*—the carriage return.

When she'd finished the letters, she sealed them and held them in her hand for a moment. *Please just give me a chance.*

She walked into the kitchen, stomach growling from not having eaten in hours, took an apple from the bowl, and went out back. The red paint peeling off the porch where she stood felt crinkly under her toes. She looked at the yard tools leaning against the house where Eddy had left them, and then at his work gloves on top of the wood pile. Strange, but she half expected him to come through the gate. In the weeks since his death, anxiety, sorrow, and anger had cloaked and choked her.

A soft breeze brought the scent of honeysuckle and jasmine and moved her long curly hair. She had hardly noticed the onset of spring. The plum trees budded and blossomed as though in a movie. The mourning doves returned to the bower outside the bedroom window where she'd lain sleepless, often holding Germaine. The daylight increased in length each day, a march of light toward some ineluctable end. The money was running out, and the full weight of what had happened lay heavily upon her.

Before Eddy died, she'd enrolled in a training program for paralegal work, a promising new career that was sprouting up all over the country. She wanted to have a means of support whenever the inevitable split-up occurred. She knew she couldn't endure his abuse indefinitely, and it would only be a matter of time until Germaine became his next target.

But here she was, only a few weeks from finishing the course, and Eddy had trumped her one last time. There was no time to study anymore. Her survival and her daughter's depended on finding work *now*. Mercedes relished the idea of breaking into something so new she could be one of the first—if she could just get her foot in the door.

Unfortunately, there were no paralegal job openings listed in any of the papers, and she had no paralegal certificate. But at least she'd have the jump on her classmates, who wouldn't be seeking jobs for another month. She smiled at the irony of that. She was hundreds of rejections ahead of them.

Germaine was the one saving grace of the whole fiasco. How such a sweet child could have been sired by the likes of Eddy was proof that anything was possible. How Mercedes could have been so blind about him, despite the ceaseless haranguing of her parents and the warnings of friends, was the haunting question of the decade. *Your gloves can just stay on the damn wood pile. They can lie there and rot,* she thought angrily.

Germaine would be home from school soon. She threw the apple core hard against the fence and went back into the kitchen. While she was making a snack for her little girl, she flicked on the radio and listened to the Journey song that was playing.

The back gate creaked, and Germaine climbed the wooden stairs to the kitchen. Her seven-year-old face was somber, with a pensive expression in her gray eyes. She made a beeline for her mother, put her arms around her waist, and pressed against her pink tee shirt, holding on tightly with eyes closed. Mercedes stroked her silky head, smoothed the Peter Pan collar on the flowered cotton dress, ran her hand down her little back, and felt her shoulder blades, thin and sharp. Mercedes knelt down and hugged her heart to heart.

"How was school today?"

"Okay," Germaine sighed with resignation. Her whimsy had departed the day she learned her father had died. Many things that had been interesting, if not fun, were now a struggle. She was all business and rarely smiled.

"But Miss Prentiss gave me a harder book to read." She wriggled out of her backpack, unzipped it, and pulled out a new book.

Mercedes looked at the book and nodded. Since age three, the

THE PINK PALACE

ardboard boxes were scattered all around the house. Mercedes knelt on the living room floor, quickly packing books. Her faded blue work shirt was rolled up to the elbows, her hands rough and dry from packing and cleaning. She was going to start making trips to the new place in the morning.

Their new landlord, a small Jewish man who had recently returned from India, had answered his door wearing a *dhoti*. After taking a look at Mercedes and Germaine, who stood holding hands on his stoop, he bowed and invited them into his tiny white house, behind the larger pink one he was renting out.

Mercedes looked out the window onto the small yard where blossoming sweet peas climbed a fence. Germaine stood attentively at her side, intrigued by the mandala on the wall. It looked like a big, pretty puzzle.

Mr. Friedman continued the conversation from the previous evening's phone call while Mercedes filled out the application. He read it over carefully and asked about her lack of employment.

"I'm changing careers and haven't found a job yet," Mercedes explained, "but I will."

He noticed the pale line on her left ring-finger, where the sun had not shone in some time.

"If you'd consider taking a chance on us, I don't think you'll be disappointed," she said earnestly. "I'll take good care of the house and will never be late on the rent."

He was quiet for a moment and then said, "Let's see if it's to your liking."

They followed him out through the little yard into the pink house. Just inside the back door there was a small bedroom with windows facing the yard, followed by a bathroom and then a nook for a washing machine. The kitchen floor was covered with new linoleum. Just off the kitchen were a second bedroom and a small living room that faced the street. A minuscule front yard rife with weeds and rocks was surrounded by a freshly painted white picket fence.

Mercedes looked up and down the street. Litter was strewn in the gutters and unfenced yards. There were bars on most of the windows, and no trees or bushes to be seen. They were just off the freeway in East Oakland, near a convenience store that was robbed several times a year. The cars parked in the street were battle scarred; Mercedes's rundown Beetle would fit right in.

She offered to pay the first month's rent and asked if she could wait until she got her first paycheck to pay the last month's and deposit. Mr. Friedman seemed unruffled by the request and agreed without hesitation. He smiled and handed her the keys. "Welcome to the neighborhood. I hope you and Germaine are happy in your new home," he said.

When they shook hands, Mercedes's eyes were moist. "I won't forget your kindness," she said.

⁂

"Tomorrow!"

"Our workday is from nine to five."

"I'll be there at nine."

"Well then, Mercedes, welcome to Crenshaw, Slayne & McDonough!"

Mercedes hung up the phone and burst into tears.

⁂

THAT AFTERNOON SHE WAITED IN front of Germaine's school in the car, enjoying the sun and marveling at how everything could be transformed by one conversation.

Germaine got into the car with her usual somber expression— one more tolerable day at school. Mercedes kissed her and patted her hand. When they pulled up in front of the ice cream parlor down the block from the newsstand, Germaine got out and went for the newspapers.

"Hold on a second, Honey," Mercedes called out. "I heard today they have free newspapers in here if you come by after two. Let's go in for a minute."

She opened the door to the ice cream parlor and found a table. Germaine trooped obediently along and slipped onto the banquette beside her.

"Will they let us wait here?" the girl asked.

A waitress approached and Mercedes broke into a broad smile. "Two hot fudge banana splits, please."

"Mama, you got a job! I was right!" She embraced her mother and kissed her cheek.

⁂

LATE THAT NIGHT, as Mercedes lay in bed, pictures of Eddy played in her mind—the interminable movie. She saw his mischievous face and the way he'd first looked at her, handsome and full of guile. She thought about his crazy sense of humor and how he'd made her laugh.

Then she saw him as he had been in their last moments together, enraged, inebriated, accusing her of taking money out of his wallet. There he was, bellowing that she should be glad he didn't leave her high and dry for another woman, as "useless" as she was. He seized the car keys and gave her a murderous glare, announcing he didn't know when or *if* he'd be back. The door slammed so hard it rattled the windowpanes. Her skin prickled and blood rushed in her ears as she relived the scene again.

Then she saw the dining room table, the stacks of index cards, the copies of letters she'd sent out, the countless rejections she'd received, the hundreds of newspapers she'd scoured, the last four pink cards against the dark wood, and the name that held her future: "Crenshaw, Slayne & McDonough."

Her tenacity had paid off. In the morning she would officially be a paralegal employed by a law firm, *no longer useless.* The thrilling promise of tomorrow made her smile in the dark.

Just then, car tires squealed loudly around a corner, followed by gunshots, men shouting, more tires squealing, and the roar of engines speeding away. *No, we don't live in Piedmont anymore.* Within moments, Germaine slipped into bed beside her. Mercedes curled around the child, calming her as quiet settled again over the neighborhood.

"Can you describe those incidents for us?"

She mentioned two exchanges in which Jason had slapped her and forced her down into a chair during an argument. He had never broken her skin, but she had felt terrified. Mercedes watched Emily's hands clinging to the chair. Her knuckles whitened, though she carried on with a steady voice.

"Did anyone ever slap you before these incidents?"

"No."

"Did anyone ever push you down in a chair before these incidents?"

"No."

"Were you afraid that Jason would do this again?"

"I don't know. I suppose so."

"Is there any history of violence in your family?"

Soutane objected and instructed his client not to answer.

"Jack, your client is claiming emotional distress damages. I think we have a right to know her background and history in this area."

"Yes, Darrel, but that doesn't entitle you to ask about every unpleasant experience she's had in her life," he replied flatly.

"Agreed, nor have I done so," Darrel snapped. Emily released her grip on the chair.

"Are you currently employed, Ms. Fredericks?"

"I was a bank teller," she said. "But after Jason left I had a lot of trouble concentrating, and sleeping, and getting to work on time. Eventually I was let go. I had a breakdown, I guess you could say."

"Have you worked at any other jobs since being fired?"

"No."

"Have you ever sought treatment by a mental health professional?"

Emily looked worriedly at Soutane, who kept a poker face.

"No," she said quietly.

Jason slapped her twice. Mercedes shook her head slightly as she wrote the words. *No longer able to work. Breakdown.* Mercedes had lost count of all the times Eddy screamed at her, smacked her, and terrorized her. If anything, her ability to concentrate on getting out had increased the more her marriage deteriorated. Something about Emily did not add up.

Noon recess was called. Darrel whispered that he'd talk to her after lunch, before the afternoon session. She felt Jack Soutane's eyes on her as she exited the room.

She went outside with her lunch and headed down toward a bench by the lake. The office building next door was being renovated; the carpenters on the roof were taking off their tool bags and opening their lunch boxes. Sunlight filtered through a thinning haze. She watched brown pelicans glide low across the surface of the lake. Joggers ran past as she ate her peanut butter sandwich.

Then she realized what it was about Emily Fredericks that had bothered her.

Darrel was on the phone when she returned to the office. He motioned for her to come in and take a seat.

"So," he said as he hung up the phone, "what do you think?"

"I noticed that every time you asked her about abuse, she stopped fidgeting with her handbag and gripped her chair. The subject of abuse obviously triggers something in her. I don't think she's faking. But I have a hard time believing that being slapped twice could be so traumatic that she wouldn't be able to hold a job."

"I agree, it seems disproportionate."

"What if she's hiding something so humiliating she's never admitted it to anyone before?"

"That would be interesting." He scratched his chin whiskers. "Not much gets past Soutane. This isn't our first case against each other. I want you to watch the afternoon session."

In the afternoon testimony, whenever Darrel attempted to learn

AT THE END OF THE DAY, she exited the back door of the building to the parking lot. Three shirtless carpenters were on the roof of the building next door. They were all wearing white hard hats and heavy leather tool bags strapped around their hips.

The summer she'd met Eddy in Colorado, he was working construction. The men at the sites were all young and tanned, hard-bodied and worked to loud rock 'n' roll blaring on a boom box, just like the three above her on the roof. Outdoor construction is seasonal in the Rockies, where the winters were too harsh for framing, siding, and roofing, so Eddy had pursued indoor work while they plotted their escape to California. She thought of his tanned skin and wild streak.

She turned away from the construction crew and found her car. A loud whistle pierced the air behind her. She didn't look up. Then came a second whistle, more prolonged and louder. She knew without looking that the three men had stopped work and were standing on the edge of the roof, waiting for her to react. She got into the car, rolled down the window, kicked off her heels, and started the engine. Glancing up, she saw them facing her with their tool bags swinging rhythmically, arms flailing, feet stomping like go-go girls in a review, dancing to a Bee Gees tune: *Whether you're a brother or whether you're a mother, you're stayin' alive, stayin' alive . . .*

She laughed out loud and waved at them as she backed out of the parking space. Yes, indeed, she was staying alive.

IN *the* COMPANY *of* WOLVES

"They're back," Julie, the receptionist, announced over the intercom. Lindsay and Simone stopped what they were doing and peered around the corners of their cubicles at Mercedes, who stood up and quickly applied some lipstick.

"Let's hope the news is tolerable," Mercedes said glumly. She had wanted so much for her first case to trial to be a winner, but that was not going to happen.

They joined the rest of the staff in the common area, just as Darrel and Stuart came around the corner, looking dour and carrying their big black trial briefcases. Darrel shook his head at Florida and stopped with Stuart in front of the assembled staff.

"I wish I had better news for you after all the hard work we've put in," he said, "but the jury handed down a stunning plaintiff's verdict. They awarded Emily Fredericks all the damages in her settlement demand and substantial punitive damages."

A wave of dismay went through the room. Mercedes stood in back. He caught her eye as he continued.

"I'm very grateful to all of you. We knew going in that it would be an uphill battle. We made that very clear to the carrier and did our best to settle the case, but things just don't always work out the way we'd like. We appreciate all your effort. Let's hope the next case turns out more to our liking." He nodded to the group and went into his office.

Mercedes headed for the kitchen, where Caroline, the family law associate and her friend, caught up with her.

"It's too bad Dailey's carrier wouldn't listen when they had the chance to settle," Caroline said. "Maybe next time they'll give Darrel more credence."

Mercedes acknowledged her observation with a look, but said nothing. She opened a cupboard and pulled out the peppermint tea. Her hunch about Emily Fredericks had now been validated by the evidence and by a jury. She poured hot water into her cup.

Stuart appeared in the doorway. He'd taken off his jacket and loosened his paisley tie. His boyish face made him look younger than he was, and concealed his deep exhaustion.

"So Stuart, what happened?" Caroline asked him.

"Jack Soutane is what happened," Stuart said wryly, shaking his head. "The guy has a silver tongue. He had the jury eating out of his hand from the opening statement."

Mercedes recalled Soutane's serene self-confidence in jousting with Darrel at the deposition. Not only did nothing faze him, he clearly relished the combat.

"And since our client is dying," Stuart said, "he couldn't attend the trial, couldn't testify, and would have been a terrible witness anyway. I think the jury felt they had an opportunity to correct a wrong, and took full advantage of it. The only questions were how much damage and how much money. And then there's Emily."

"What do you mean?" Caroline asked. She had not worked on the case or met the plaintiff.

"She was telling the truth," Mercedes said bluntly. "She was already badly damaged before her boyfriend ripped her off and terrorized her. She really *was* unable to work, and she needed Mr. Dailey to do right by her."

"That's it in a nutshell," Stuart said. "But you should have seen Soutane's closing argument. Oh, my God, what a performance! He had one juror crying, two others with their heads in their hands, and even the judge had to avert his eyes at one point. The guy could sell snow to Eskimos."

Mercedes felt bad for Darrel and Stuart, but glad for Emily Fredericks. Perhaps having money and vindication would help her make better decisions in the future, especially about men.

"We're going out for drinks, if you'd like to join us. Mercedes, you especially should come. You spotted this before anyone else, at Emily's deposition."

"Thanks, but I have to pick up Germaine. And she'll be all curious about what happened."

"Wait—you haven't told us how much the award was," Caroline said to Stuart.

"Would you believe $750,000? And that's tax-free."

"Wow," the women said in unison.

GERMAINE WAS WAITING AT THE door when Mercedes arrived at the small private school, which had recently awarded the child a full scholarship. They drove back to the little pink house, their palace, which now had flowers and blooming bushes in the front yard where only weeds had grown the year before. Wind chimes hung from the eaves and tinkled in the breeze.

The perimeter of their small living room was lined with open boxes of books. There was no money for bookcases yet, but Germaine had new glasses. Her dark brown hair was in pigtails and she looked very neat in her school uniform, none the worse for wear after a day at school. She skipped back to her room to change clothes. Mercedes bolted the front door, opened two windows, and retreated to her own room to change. She shed her heels, hung up her clothes, and pulled on jeans and a tee shirt.

Pink snapdragons from the front yard filled a mason jar on the kitchen table, where Germaine did her homework while Mercedes made dinner. She turned on the radio when Germaine finished her arithmetic; the driving energy of Michael Jackson's "Billy Jean" filled the room. Mercedes grinned and tried to moonwalk at the counter. Germaine, in socks, did several spins on the smooth linoleum floor as she set the table.

When the velvety black bean soup was hot, Mercedes ladled it into two bowls, spooned a generous dollop of yogurt onto each, and topped them with chopped green onions.

"Mama, is there really such a place as heaven?" Germaine asked between mouthfuls.

"I think what we have right here is pretty close," Mercedes answered. "Why do you ask?"

"I was thinking of Mr. Dailey. He's dying and now that the Fredericks lady is going to be rich, maybe he can go to heaven."

"It would be nice if things worked that way, but we really don't know, do we?"

"Do you think Daddy's in heaven?"

Not hardly. "Sweetness, I just don't know. But I do think that everything is connected somehow, and that the universe is full of love, even in the midst of life's sorrows. Just look at all that has happened to us, and how much help we've gotten since Daddy died, even from people who didn't know us—Mr. Friedman, Ms. Kinsey, the people at your school who gave you a scholarship. That's a lot of love."

Germaine put a spoonful of hot basmati rice in her mouth and chewed it pensively. "But what about the other people in our neighborhood? It doesn't look like there's much love for them."

"I agree, and I don't have an answer for that. But I do know there is true goodness all around, whenever we let ourselves see it. Things seem to happen for a reason, even really dreadful things."

Germaine was not convinced, but she contemplated what her mother said.

"Now how about you finish up your homework, and then we'll have another chapter of *Little House on the Prairie*." They had recently checked out Laura Ingalls Wilder's book from the library, and both were smitten.

Mercedes cleaned up the kitchen and pulled out the fixings for the next day's lunches from the old white refrigerator. There would be just enough groceries to make it to Saturday, the day after payday.

Germaine bent over her book, her left elbow anchored on the table, her hand cradling her head, her eyes glued to the page. The new school was far more demanding, but she seemed to thrive on it. Her glasses had slipped slightly down her nose. Her lips moved as she read. She took notes in her notebook now and then. Germaine was going to make something of herself someday, Mercedes knew, if she could help her stay strong.

"I'm ready for the test tomorrow," Germaine announced a short while later, closing her book with a flourish.

"Want me to test you a little?"

The girl shook her head. She was confident.

"Not at all?"

She shook her head again, more vehemently.

"Then the last little girl into the bath is a rotten egg!"

Germaine leapt to her feet and flew to her room to undress.

As they sat soaking in the tub, Mercedes thought of Stuart, Caroline, and Darrel, out celebrating the end of the trial, probably well lubricated with liquor by now, airing the details. She wished she could be hearing it all, but being around alcohol had lost its appeal after life with Eddy. She could get the lowdown from Caroline tomorrow.

Mother and daughter got into their nightclothes and curled up on the sofa. Germaine's clean pink face shone in the lamplight. She leaned her wet head against her mother's old terry-cloth bathrobe as Mercedes put her arm around her. *Little House on the Prairie* lay on Mercedes's lap, opened to the page where they had left off the night before. She read aloud, her voice rising and falling, speeding up and slowing down with the gripping story of Pa's encounter with a pack of wolves that had surrounded him and his terrified pony, Patty.

They imagined they were living in a small log cabin on the bank of a peaceful creek—a cabin exposed to the wide expanse of prairie all around it, with no shutters on the solitary window and no door in the doorway. Their roof was the sheet of canvas that had covered their wagon on the journey west. They slept on a floor of dirt made smooth with a homemade broom. Their nearest neighbor was a bachelor, who lived in a cabin several miles away.

They had no electricity. Nothing traveled faster than a horse. Food was grown or killed by those who ate it, and everything was made by hand. Out on the prairie, a child had no school or friends. Ma cooked on an open campfire, washing dishes and clothes with water hauled up from the creek in a tin tub. She spread the clean clothes on the prairie grass to dry. Her foremost desire was a clothesline, and Pa's was a well.

Suddenly, three loud cars roared around the corner near their house. One of the cars backfired. Or was it a gunshot? Germaine jumped at the sound. A neighbor's front door slammed, and people were yelling on the sidewalk as the cars sped away. From the next block, police sirens sounded. Germaine and Mercedes looked at each other, and then at the dead bolt on their locked front door.

CAPTIVE AUDIENCE

Mercedes and Simone worked together at the conference room table. Twelve black leather chairs surrounded it and a long credenza stood against the wall beneath a triptych of uninspiring abstract paintings.

Simone was a pleasant older woman with short salt-and-pepper hair. She wore pointy black spectacles attached to a chain that dangled on either side of her face when she looked down. The two women were immersed in stacks of files, their heads bent together in quiet concentration. The overhead light shone on the mahogany table and picked up the metallic flecks in Mercedes's sweater.

"There's news," a voice announced. The two paralegals looked up to see Caroline striding into the room. "We're going to have a new tenant," she said.

Why this news merited an interruption was lost on Mercedes, but an interruption was certainly welcome.

"Is it someone we know?" Simone asked.

"Someone we know *of*," Caroline replied obliquely.

"Richard Chamberlain? Sean Connery?" Mercedes mocked.

"Very funny. But close. You remember the silver-tongued devil from the Fredericks trial, the one who made jurors cry?"

"Indeed. How could I not?"

"Jack Soutane is moving into the empty office," Caroline said, pointing to the open door across the hall.

Mercedes looked Caroline in the eye. "My, that does put a different spin on things."

"You know what Darrel says." Caroline mimicked him, lowering her voice to the bottom of its register, "'Keep your friends close and your enemies closer.' Evidently he offered Soutane a deal on a sublease to lure him here."

"When is he coming?" Simone asked.

"At the end of the week."

"Do we know about his staff?" Simone, who was married to a doctor, wanted all the symptoms before making a diagnosis.

"No, that's all I've heard so far."

"Well, for the record, I don't give a fig *who* moves into that office," Mercedes stated.

"Sure you don't," Caroline replied sarcastically.

Simone and Caroline exchanged a look.

"Now, where were we?" Mercedes asked, looking at the stacks of files.

⁂

TWO MORNINGS LATER, Mercedes went to Stuart's office to deliver a project. His lamp was on and his briefcase was open, but he wasn't there, so she dropped the memo into his in-box. Outside the window, the lake was partially occluded by long arms of fog stretching across the water, dampening and darkening everything it touched.

She turned away from the view to see what all the commotion in the hallway was about. A tiny woman was leading a stocky fellow with a toolbox into the paralegal room. Mercedes's curiosity was roused, and she followed them.

"It's over here," the woman pointed authoritatively. "I can't get it to print. Something must be wrong with the connection."

The man nodded and put down his toolbox. They were setting up equipment in the unused cubicle at the end of the room. Mercedes groaned inwardly. It was already hard enough for the three paralegals to concentrate during the workday.

"Hi, I'm Mercedes Bell," she said when they emerged. She tried to look hospitable.

"I hope we haven't been bothering you. I'm Melanie Moran," the small woman offered. "I'm Jack Soutane's secretary, and this is Hank. He's helping us get everything installed. Ms. Kinsey said we could put the printer in here. I hope you don't mind."

When Melanie smiled, her whole face radiated happiness, especially her chestnut brown eyes, which were rimmed in dark eyeliner. Straight blond hair hung past her waist. She was lovely, poised, and obviously comfortable in her own skin.

"No problem. Welcome to the office. I'm sure we'll work it all out," Mercedes replied.

⋆⊱⋆

BY EARLY AFTERNOON THE FOG had cleared and bright sunshine warmed the Grand Lake neighborhood. Mercedes went out for her usual lunch-hour walk around the lake. Sea gulls circled over the water's surface, keening and flapping their white wings. She was listening to a cassette of Bach's Double Violin Concerto on the Sony Walkman that Darrel had given her for Christmas. With the ecstatic sound filling her ears, she walked the three-mile circumference, hands in pockets, deep in thought.

RAND TAYLOR

Mercedes wrote quickly, barely keeping up with Darrel's fountain of ideas. They sat in his office on a stormy October morning. Rain mixed with sleet pelted the windows. Darrel sat back with his legs stretched out, feet crossed at the ankles on the corner of the desk away from Mercedes. His fingertips formed a tent beneath his bearded chin while he instructed her. His wide brow and angular face were those of a thoughtful, smart man.

Stuart appeared in the doorway, his dark hair slicked back. He waited for Darrel to look up before speaking.

"Jack says he and Mr. Taylor can meet us at one o'clock," he announced.

"Okay, let's do it."

After Stuart left, Darrel said, "I'd like you to join us, too. Jack's bringing in a new litigation matter, and he's going out of the country soon for several weeks, so it'll be a working lunch. The new client will be with him. I want us all to hear his story simultaneously." Rain slammed against the window in a burst of wind. "Weather not-withstanding."

Her stomach tightened in a knot. "I hope we're not walking too far because my raincoat isn't up to this." Her raincoat was a sorry threadbare affair that should long ago have been replaced.

"I'll drive and I promise you will not get wet," he said kindly, smiling at her naïveté.

"Then I'd love to go," she forced herself to say.

Darrel drove his Jaguar with Mercedes and Emerson in the back and Stuart in front. As he navigated through the torrential weather, he shared what he knew of the case, a possible wrongful termination matter against a major hotel chain. Emerson leaned forward in the backseat, glancing at the back of Stuart's head and listening intently. Mercedes passively took in Darrel's account as she looked out the window at tall trees whipping violently and electrical power lines swinging with the force of the gale.

It was the first time she'd been in Darrel's car. Plush white leather seats caressed her back. She pictured the four of them driving in the blue Beetle with her at the wheel, the clutch slipping period-ically, the windshield seal leaking, and a fetid odor rising from the floor. She amused herself with the thought of the fastidious Emerson being gradually soaked as he sat crammed into the Beetle's impos-sible backseat next to Stuart.

Darrel turned left into the driveway of an immense white stone building with Doric columns supporting a domed roof. A valet took the car as Mercedes followed the men inside, into an elevator. The doors opened on the top floor, where they were greeted and their coats taken. A maître d' led them into the magnificent circular dining room, lined with arching windows in walls of Wedgwood blue. Quiet reigned all about them, save for the murmur of dinner-table con-versation, the clink of silverware against fine china, and the tinkling of ice in glasses. Thick rose-colored carpet absorbed the sounds of their footsteps as they were ushered to their table.

She caught Darrel watching her. Then he looked behind her across the room, watched for a moment, and stood up. She turned in time to see Jack, in a dark green suit, approach the table with a pale, brown-haired man of medium height and build. The waitstaff made way for them, all but bowing to Jack.

The pallid man took a seat between Darrel and Jack. On a signal from Darrel, a wood screen was positioned around the table to shield them from prying eyes.

Jack introduced Rand Taylor to the legal team. To Taylor, he introduced Darrel, his partner in the case, as a seasoned litigator in whom Rand could repose his full confidence. Emerson and Stuart, he told Taylor, were the associates who would do most of the legal research. "They are very skilled and hard-working," Jack said. "I know from personal experience what it's like to be up against them at trial." Emerson blushed. Stuart exchanged a look with Mercedes, remembering the Fredericks debacle.

"Which is how we came to be here," Darrel interjected. "We learned the advantage of staying on the same side as Jack."

Try as she might, Mercedes couldn't dispel the charm of Jack's regal manner or good looks, especially now that he was introducing her. "This is Mercedes Bell, Darrel's paralegal extraordinaire." He smiled into her face for the first time.

As her stomach rolled over in a slow somersault, she nodded to Jack and acknowledged Mr. Taylor. He seemed rather unprepossessing for someone who had supposedly held a high position in a major hotel chain. Everything about him seemed bland and pasty. Perhaps he was just not used to being surrounded by lawyers or "having a legal team."

"We'll do our best to help you," Mercedes replied, looking into his troubled eyes. "Please feel free to call me any time."

Rand sat forward in his chair and began speaking in a refined Southern accent, the words flowing out like satin ribbon from an endless internal coil.

"Immediately upon my graduation from Cornell University, I accepted a position at Franjipur Hotels International in New York." He looked around the table, making eye contact with each of them. "I was reared in Alabama, where my family has lived since the 1700s. I was brought up to respect the importance of the social aspects of life, so I learned all I could about the habits, preferences, and reporting relationships among the corporation's senior and middle management." He hesitated a moment and exchanged a look with Jack, who nodded for him to proceed.

"All companies have their idiosyncrasies, and I ascertained a few along the way, some of which came to me by way of confidences and others I learned independently. This knowledge was a contributing factor to my progress within the company."

"What sort of knowledge?" asked Darrel, stroking his beard.

Rand cleared his throat. "Personal information relating to individuals in positions of authority, but not related to finance or business or matters of that nature."

Darrel's index finger covered his lips and his brow furrowed.

"I was the youngest person ever in the history of the company to be given a position on the Quality Control Team. My duties there were to ensure that Franjipur's rigorous standards of customer service were consistently maintained throughout the chain.

"I was eventually assigned to the western region of the United States, where I traveled extensively and visited each facility to assess its quality of customer care. These assessments sometimes involved hiring outside consultants to assist in the evaluation process and in coaching teams to improve their performance.

"One of the consultants with whom I worked was a lovely

woman by the name of Anne-Charlotte Anderson, for whom I had the highest regard." He looked down for a moment and took a drink of water.

"That high regard blossomed, and we fell in love. We moved in together and seemed well suited to one another. We both traveled a great deal for our work, had similar career demands, and cherished our time at home together. Our families blessed the match. We became engaged, and wedding plans commenced."

He eyed Mercedes sorrowfully.

"However, as you may recall, the recession of 1982 was not kind to the hotel industry, and I can tell you it did not spare Franjipur. Profits took a dive and stock values declined. In reaction to this, the board of directors replaced the chief financial officer with another whom they had lured away from a competing chain.

"The new CFO reorganized several departments, one of which was Quality Control, and my position was eliminated. One Friday afternoon, I was abruptly and unceremoniously dismissed. I was given a modest severance package, paid by check on the spot, and was escorted by security from the building. It was a humiliation I hope never to repeat."

"How many years had you been employed at that point?" Darrel asked.

"Twelve."

Mercedes caught Stuart's eye. Questions were already forming in both their minds, which he dignified with a nod.

"The full impact of being terminated didn't register fully at first. Anne-Charlotte was away on business. I couldn't bear to tell her what had happened until she returned and I could do so in person. When I did, it was *not* a happy occasion.

"Since then, I've been unable to find a comparable position or *any* position in the hotel industry, despite Franjipur's promise of assistance. I have pursued employment using every available resource. My severance package has been depleted, my life savings are gone, and our engagement is over," he said, looking down at his hands and then at Jack.

In response to Darrel's questions, Rand reported that he had friends still at the company and also knew former employees who would be willing to help with the investigation. He had recently obtained a copy of his personnel file and he now believed his termination was retaliatory—that his difficulties in finding work were a result of being blackballed. Documents in his personnel file seemed to have been altered. He felt checkmated.

Jack, who knew the story, ate his salad while studying Rand's effect on the team.

Mercedes took notes in a small notebook. Jack buttered a piece of bread, bit into it, and stared at Mercedes's mouth while she wrote. His scrutiny raised her temperature and she shifted in her seat.

More food arrived as Rand's story drew to a close. A waft of lobster Newberg made Mercedes's mouth water. Darrel asked Rand several follow-up questions. Emerson and Stuart contemplated Darrel's questions while Jack's eyes fell on Mercedes's form-fitting turtleneck. She took notes between mouthfuls of the aromatic lobster dish, which she relished.

She met Jack's eyes, feeling pure satisfaction. Her hard work was paying off. Here she was, surrounded by beauty, intrigue, nice men, and amazing food. Jack tilted his head to the side and watched her swallow.

Darrel explained to Rand that if they did decide to file suit, it would be an uphill battle, would cost a lot, and would probably take a couple of years. They would have to decide within the next three months, due to the statute of limitations. Stuart looked at Mercedes. They both knew what that meant—fast work, and a lot of it.

Rand took their business cards and thanked them for lunch as well as their interest in his plight. On Darrel's signal the screen was pulled away.

Jack led their exodus through the now-empty dining room to the coat check. He retrieved Mercedes's weather-beaten raincoat first, grasped it by its frayed collar, and held it for her as though it were a floor-length sable. She slid one arm into a sleeve, and then the other. He settled the coat onto her shoulders, then slowly extracted her long French braid from beneath the collar, feeling every inch of hair. She caught her breath sharply, recovered her composure, and buckled her coat belt as Jack smoothed her collar protectively.

Stuart, who had been watching them, glanced over at Emerson, who looked away. Darrel was busy saying good-bye to Rand. Mercedes picked up her purse, thanked Jack nonchalantly, and followed Darrel through the double doors, the tip of her braid grazing her belt. She felt Jack's blue-eyed gaze still upon her until he climbed into his new Mercedes with Rand.

⊱⊰

"YOU HANDLED THAT JUST FINE," Jack reassured Rand as he drove away. "'Idiosyncrasies and knowledge' was a perfect way to couch it. Darrel and his crew will want you to be completely forthcoming, but there's no need to go into all the sordid details just yet. As I told you, there is much to be said for revealing only what you must, when you must."

Rand nodded assent. "I didn't know we would be in mixed company. It's hardly the subject matter for such a setting."

"I didn't know Darrel would be bringing his paralegal. She's very insightful, I'm told. She'll probably be quite good at getting information from your friends at Franjipur. Let's let nature take its course and see how far she gets with it. The less you're viewed as being culpable for what went on in the suite, the better. The fact that you knew *about* it is enough to make your case."

"*You're* the lawyer. I've told you everything. I place my fate in your hands," Rand said, staring out the window. He wrinkled his brow and bit his bottom lip.

Jack looked pleased. "Tell me, did you ever take part in the bacchanalian festivities yourself?"

"No, I have no taste for that sort of thing."

"The sex for hire, or sex with boys?"

"Either," he said, with a look of disdain. "I am a more private man than that, Mr. Soutane."

"But you understood the value of catering to your bosses' appetites."

"That is elementary if one wants to succeed in the hospitality business," he drawled. "It is not for me to judge the morality of others, but rather to see to their comforts. I was mistaken in thinking that my discretion would be rewarded."

"Yes, but it's a mistake that may prove very lucrative for you— and for us," Jack replied. He checked the time on his gold watch and stepped on the gas.

A TISKET, *a* TASKET

Germaine looked out her bedroom window at the crepuscular light of a November Sunday. Gold spider chrysanthemums bloomed along the fence in place of the sweet peas. The fiery red leaves of the maple tree shivered against a steel gray sky. The rains had darkened the long wood planks of the fence and the green patch of grass in the backyard, now scattered with red leaves.

Mercedes had just eased into a hot bubble bath after a strenuous hike with Caroline and their daughters. The phone rang, and Germaine ran to answer it, her shoes clattering on the kitchen floor. It was Eleanor, as predictable as the flooding of the Nile. Every week, without fail, she called to inject her little spurt of poison into their budding lives. Mercedes put a wet washcloth over her face and slid down into the water as far as possible. She ran more hot water into the tub to drown out Germaine's half of the conversation. But the exigencies of her mother's voice penetrated the bathroom wall like x-rays. Her relaxation in the bath was doomed.

"Grandmother wants to talk to you, Mama," Germaine announced from the doorway. "She says it's an emergency."

Mercedes pulled the plug, wrapped herself in a towel, and scurried to the kitchen. The air was chilly on her bare shoulders. The phone receiver lay on the table, its long twisted cord connected to the wall unit.

"Hello, Mother," Mercedes said. "What's the emergency?"

"I haven't talked to you all week!"

"*That's* the emergency?"

"We never decided about Thanksgiving."

"Hold on a minute, please." Mercedes put the phone down, threw off the wet towel, slipped into her robe, and sat in a chair. She took a deep breath and looked at Germaine with a resigned expression. Germaine shrugged her shoulders and ran to get her mother's slippers.

"There's nothing to decide. Germaine and I have plans already, as I told you last week."

"I insist you come home to Boston. Your father will pay the airfare."

"I'm already home."

"Germaine should be with her family at Thanksgiving, and whether you like it or not, we *are* your family."

Eleanor turned straightaway to whether Mercedes was dating anyone. Had she bought any new clothes recently? Was she taking care of her skin? Were there any attractive men in the office?

"You're just wasting your time out there, Mercedes. You would be much better off living here where we can find you a nice husband."

"I'm getting off now, Mother."

"For God's sake, Mercedes, you're thirty-two! *Think* about your future. Your looks will soon fade and then it's all downhill from there."

"Speak for yourself. Good-bye, and thank you for reminding me of a few things." Click went the receiver.

⸎

AFTER GERMAINE WAS IN BED, Mercedes set up the ironing board in the kitchen to press their clothes for the week. Trying to shake the miasma that Eleanor's calls gave her, she concentrated on the work at hand in the silent house. The hypnotic movement of the steam iron on small white cotton shirts relaxed her, and her mind fell back to an earlier time, when she was just a girl of seven, living in Texas with her parents.

On one particular day, after a bout of derision, she had fled the house and her mother into the surrounding woods. Down a dirt path among the cedar trees she ran, marking where the shadows fell on the ground so as not to lose track of time. Through a copse she scrambled, into a small clearing where she'd made her secret place. It was near where several paths intersected in a grove of pecan trees. The trees swayed in the breeze and occasionally dropped their beautiful brown nuts. Bright red cardinals sang on the branches of shaggy-barked cedars and ate their tiny blue-green berries.

She sat on a scrap of braided rug she'd found deeper in the woods amidst the ruins of a cabin. The hearth and chimney, built long ago of river stones, were still standing, but the cabin's walls were gone. There were all manner of treasures there—broken pieces of blue-patterned china, a shard of mirror, the head of an axe, and the remnants of the braided rug. She had dragged the rug to her spot and built a small fortress around it, piling branches on top of each other to form a low wall. Then she had fashioned a shelf from a plank and a few of the river stones, and on it assembled a collection of rose quartz, mica, and iron pyrite, some Indian arrowheads, and a rusty old coffee can full of cedar berries and pecan shells.

This was her haven. She sat, took off her shoes and socks, and gazed up at the trees, listening to the sound of the breeze rustling the branches, which seemed to be talking to each other. Shafts of sun-light filtered through the canopy to the forest floor, warming the cedar needles and scenting the air. A woodpecker's call rang out, followed by the staccato of his drilling beak.

She sat motionless, imagining herself invisible. She took a few deep breaths, wishing life could always be as it was in that moment, there in her private place. Birds chirped and squirrels leapt from branch to branch, while mice and an armadillo scuttled among the dried brown leaves. She'd seen pictures of the ocean and imagined that this was all a sea—that she was a little fish at the bottom and that the trees were kelp swaying in the currents. Tranquility de-scended upon her. All thoughts of Eleanor and home had ceased.

⟡

THE IRON WAS OUT OF water and was no longer steaming. Germaine's freshly pressed uniforms hung on the doorknob. The house was still and the neighborhood was unusually quiet. It was time for sleep.

⟡

NEXT MORNING SHE WAS IN the kitchen at the office putting her lunch into the refrigerator when Stuart appeared with his empty coffee mug in hand. His face was flushed, his wet hair neatly parted and combed. His dark eyes softened with a smile as Mercedes leaned into the refrigerator.

She straightened and turned toward him. "Looks like you've already been to the gym."

"I have a call with a witness in the Taylor case in five minutes. Why don't you stop by later so we can catch each other up?"

"Sure."

Mercedes headed for her desk past Jack's office and noted, for the first time in weeks, that the lights were on; the big man had been on a trip to Africa. In the paralegal room, Simone was already at work.

"You've had a visitor this morning," she said casually.

Mercedes spied a beautiful, colorful, finely woven basket on her desk. "Hmm," she replied, and put down her purse.

She picked it up to admire. It was about eight inches tall, with a circumference slightly larger than her palm and had a close-fitting lid. The fibers were woven in soft ridges of coral, brown, turquoise, ivory, and green. She lifted the lid, looked inside, and turned the basket over. On the center of the bottom was a tiny gold label: Made in Senegal. There was no note.

She felt herself blush. Simone had begun dictating on the other side of the cubicle half-wall. Mercedes brushed the surfaces of the basket with the palms of her hands, opened the deep bottom drawer of her desk, and placed the gift gently inside.

She left the paralegal room, walked the long way around the suite to avoid Jack's office, and slipped into the women's bathroom. She entered a stall for a few moments of solitude. When she emerged, Caroline was washing her hands at one of the sinks before the wide rectangular mirror.

"Are you okay?" Caroline could see she was flustered.

"I'm fine," she replied, unconvincingly.

They left the room together just in time to run into Jack and his startling blue eyes.

"Good morning, ladies," he said gallantly.

"Welcome back," Caroline said. "You must have been in the sun a lot."

He was deeply tanned; his teeth flashed white in a brilliant smile.

"Had a fantastic time, went on a safari in Kenya, and did a lot of touring. Got to run—client call in two minutes." He dashed down the hall. Caroline shook her head and looked down, keeping her thoughts to herself.

⁂

"I'VE CALLED ALL THE FORMER Franjipur employees on the list of names Rand gave us," Mercedes told Stuart. "They've confirmed what he said about his termination. Some of them knew Rand and Anne-Charlotte socially. They told me about how badly she took the fallout from Rand's termination. Here—I wrote a memo about each interview," she said, handing Stuart a file. "There are some interesting people here."

Stuart leafed through the file.

"Would they be willing to testify?" he asked.

"I think so, but we didn't really discuss that. I told them we were investigating the possibility of filing a lawsuit and it was too early to tell what would happen."

It was near noon. She sat back in the chair opposite Stuart and looked at the thick gray clouds gathering outside the window. She caught him sneaking a peek at her bodice.

"Others told me about how things changed after the new CFO was hired," she continued, fidgeting with her pen. "He tightened the budget on employee compensation and benefits and took away a lot of incentives. Jobs were eliminated and departments rearranged. The corporate culture became much more finance-driven."

"We should be able to corroborate that with documents from the corporation, once discovery gets going," he observed. "Anyway," he said, straightening his tie, "I've spoken with a few current employees, also on Rand's list, although I haven't written up all my notes yet. Guess I'll have to do that to keep up with you," he teased.

A slight grin broke her serious expression.

"But here's a promising nugget," Stuart continued. "One guy

mentioned rumors of a luxury suite at the New York facility that some of the senior executives used. Rand was initially hired to work as a concierge. Supposedly he knew what went on there."

Mercedes sat up in her chair.

"Like what?"

"I have no idea. The guy wouldn't tell me more than that. Perhaps a woman would have better luck getting it out of him." He looked into her eyes. "We need to get to the bottom of this one. Neither Rand nor Jack mentioned anything about a suite—and they certainly should have if Rand knew about it."

"Maybe it's just a rumor," Mercedes said. "When employees are disgruntled, they make up stories. Rand is gone, so he's an easy target. Or maybe it's true and Rand knows more than he's letting on. Maybe what he knows is the real reason he was fired."

"Now you're getting *way* ahead of things," Stuart said. "But one way or another, and sooner rather than later, we need to know." He handed her his pad of squiggly notes. "I think you should do the next round of calls. You've got a nose for this stuff, and I have to write a brief."

⌘

AT THE END OF THE day Mercedes looked into Jack's office as she passed. He was standing with his hands in his pockets looking out the window, but turned just in time to see her. He called out her name. No one else was in the hall, so she stopped and went back to the doorway.

"Thank you for the basket. It's very beautiful," she said. "I was going to write you a note."

"There's a story behind it, if you're interested." He knew he could count on her curiosity. He gestured for her to come in. His tie was slightly loosened, and his jacket hung on the back of a chair.

She hesitated.

"I won't bite you, I promise."

Her eyes narrowed slightly.

"Although it's not a bad idea," he quipped, with a smile.

She continued regarding him, now with a bemused expression.

"Oh, just a *little* bite." He laughed his infectious laugh.

She entered his office and sat down in one of his cushy high-backed guest chairs.

"I was in a marketplace in Senegal in a village near Dakar. It was almost the end of the trip. We got there fairly early in the morning, when all the goods were on display—everything from vegetables, grains, and farm implements to fabrics and handmade wares. Villagers were at their stalls, which are just brightly colored cloths spread out on the ground. Part of the market area was covered to provide some shade. I was listening to the haggling in French and other languages, watching the old women, and dodging the children running around —and then an unusual thing happened."

He looked away for an instant.

"I noticed the women—all these very graceful, dark-skinned, willowy women going about their business. Some were balancing great loads on their heads and carrying children in slings on their backs. They wear these long, brightly colored gowns with scarves wound around their heads and are most elegant, in spite of the poverty.

"I thought immediately of you—your carriage, your manner, your determination. Suddenly it was as though you were all around me in many different forms. I've never had an experience like that before, to be quite honest, and it surprised me."

She didn't know what to say, so she said nothing.

"There was a woman of the Wolof tribe, the predominant population in Senegal, selling baskets of all different colors and sizes that she and other women in her village had made. The fragile economy

Before she had time to get settled, Darrel dispatched her to the file room of the Alameda County Courthouse, a grand white Art Deco building on the other side of the lake from the office. The courthouse was humming with activity. Three elevator operators announced the incessant arrivals and departures of their cars. Footsteps clopped noisily on polished marble floors. Policemen, lawyers with their leather briefcases, clients, witnesses, law students, employees pushing carts of files, jurors, paralegals, and other people involved in the courts milled about everywhere. Mercedes loved the commotion.

She saw Jack emerge from an elevator, head and shoulders taller than everyone around him. He was escorting an elderly woman in a fur coat toward the exit. Catching sight of Mercedes, he nodded and waved as he held the door for his client.

Some hours later, her briefcase packed with file copies, she returned to the office building, where Jack happened to be waiting for the elevator in the lobby.

"Are you following me?" he asked in his low voice.

"No, I'm not," she said with a smirk. "Darrel sent me on a mission and it wasn't to follow *you*."

"Big mistake. Oh well. Did you get my note this morning?"

"You mean your valentine?"

"It was *not* a valentine. Valentines have hearts on them. Did you *read* it?"

"Yes, counselor, I did."

"Remind me never to put you on the witness stand. Was there a question in my note?"

The elevator arrived. "Yes, there was, and yes, I'd love to go." She leaned coquettishly against the wood paneling inside.

"Are you going to make things difficult?" he asked, grinning.

"Probably."

"Just as I suspected."

"You're the one who sent the valentine."

"It was *not* a valentine."

The doors opened. They stepped off together and walked past Julie at the front desk without saying another word.

ON SUNDAY MORNING SHE LAY wide awake at 6 a.m., despite her best efforts to sleep in. Germaine was at a slumber party and would be there until late afternoon. She gave up the pretense of luxuriating in bed and began the day's yoga. Soon her breathing and concentration quieted her thoughts.

As she was getting ready, she kept telling herself it was just another day, that she was just going to have a new experience with a nice guy from the office. She'd never been to Belvedere but knew its reputation for exclusivity. She pulled on her well-worn corduroy jacket and locked the door behind her.

Her car started on the second try. No one was out on the street yet and shades were drawn on most of the neighbors' windows. The sky was overcast. Surveying her surroundings, she was glad that she was taking the train into San Francisco to meet Jack instead of letting him pick her up, as he had offered. Although the round-trip train fare was possible only because of careful budgeting—something Jack probably could never imagine—concealing the fact that she lived in the ghetto was important.

The aftermath of a typical Saturday night was on display at the neighborhood "park"—a slab of concrete abutting a cinder-block wall, a sandbox full of dirt mixed with sand, bottle caps, pop tops, and probably a used syringe or two. Empty liquor bottles, some of them smashed to bits against the wall, littered the area, along with countless cigarette butts and assorted rubbish. A man in greasy clothes lay motionless on a park bench, his arm over his eyes to block the morning light. A collarless mongrel sniffed at the bench and lifted his leg.

⚬⚬

WHEN SHE EMERGED FROM THE train at Civic Center station, Jack was waiting for her at the top of the escalator. He reminded her of Cary Grant. He looked rested and ready for a date in his cobalt blue jacket, fine black slacks, and highly polished shoes.

She looked into his face and smiled. He guided her by the elbow to his shiny black Mercedes, which still had the new-car smell. He opened the sunroof, and they were off, heading north toward Tiburon and Belvedere. He popped a Joan Armatrading tape into the cassette player and music seemed to come from everywhere at once.

After they turned off the freeway, the traffic noise faded in the distance. The fog was in retreat; sunlight splashed on the roofs and roads in the hamlets they passed. They were on a small peninsula that jutted into San Francisco Bay, with idyllic coves for the yacht club marina and a ferry landing. The waterfront was both quaint and cosmopolitan, like pictures of the French Riviera. Jack snuck peeks at her profile as she stared out the window.

A paved walking trail hugged the shore. Passersby walked dogs and pushed strollers. Old people sat on the occasional bench to enjoy the view of the Golden Gate Bridge and sailboat traffic.

Jack turned left and the car began to climb a narrow roadway. Multimillion-dollar homes lined both sides of the street. Some were several stories high; all had decks facing the spellbinding panorama of the harbor below and the city of San Francisco.

Mercedes took stock of her boots, sweater and slacks, unpolished fingernails, and dry hands, roughened by housework. She considered how she would appear to her hosts. She smoothed the hair on the back of her head.

"Mercedes," he said, "you of all people shouldn't be worried about how you look. I can't imagine a setting that would not be improved by your presence."

She looked at him, shocked by the statement and embarrassed that her thoughts had been so transparent.

He parked at the top of the hill. She got out of the car and viewed the harbor below. Filling her lungs with fresh ocean air, she caught the scent of eucalyptus and wood smoke in the breeze. Jack came around, engulfed her hand in his and led her past a multiple-car garage built into the hill beneath a mansion. The touch of his hand guiding her up a wide stone staircase made her feel as though she were floating past all the colorful flowerpots lining the way. Stone lions stood on either side of the massive front door.

A boyish, ebullient man answered the door, and clapped Jack on the back. Gabe Harrow looked younger than Mercedes had expected, with thick ash-blond hair. He shook her hand and said graciously, "Welcome to our home, Mercedes."

Then a short woman appeared, in a salmon-colored top with lipstick to match. She opened her arms to Jack, who bent down to hug her and receive a gooey kiss on his cheek. Scanning Mercedes's figure from head to toe, she said, "Hi, I'm Kitty."

They were led into a grand drawing room flooded with light from numerous picture windows. Redwood beams ran the forty-foot length of the ceiling. Gabe poured a round of mimosas and asked Jack how his friend, Janine, was doing.

Kitty led Mercedes into a chef's kitchen with terracotta walls and exquisite cabinetry. There was generous work space on either side of an enormous six-burner gas stove, and there were sinks in two locations. A full set of the finest French copper cookware hung from a rack over a center island. Wood-framed windows faced the gardens and hillside.

My candle burns at both ends;
It will not last the night;
But ah, my foes, and oh, my friends—
It gives a lovely light!

Jack had a gleam in his eye. "We'd better get you away from that bookcase."

She reshelved the books and sighed. The library made her ache. "This *is* the best room," she said quietly.

"Let's go see whether Kitty and the kids have torched lunch or actually gotten it on the table," Gabe said brightly.

Mercedes helped Kitty carry the dishes to the table. Immediately the children abandoned their duties and began running in circles around Jack. Kitty yelled at them, to no effect. Gabe poured out the next round of mimosas. Jack grabbed a child under each arm, which made them both holler more loudly. He asked Gabe where the garbage can was. The children flailed and squealed with joy.

They sat at the rectangular dining room table, which was set with old, ornate sterling silver flatware. The food was delicious, although difficult to savor amidst the racket of the ill-behaved children and their mother's alternate cajoling and yelling. Jack and Gabe carried on, ignoring the noise, catching up on the news about their friends, especially Damon Vanderveer, a psychologist, and Murielle Hand, a psychiatrist.

Gabe told Mercedes about Jack in law school—how he hadn't been the best student in the class but had excelled at extracurricular activities, like making money in the foreign currency market, partying, and traveling in Europe.

Kitty piped up, "So, Mercedes, where did you go to college? Tell us a little about your family."

"I graduated from Colorado College, where I studied religion, philosophy, and English literature. Not the most practical education, I suppose, but it's what I'm interested in."

Gabe nodded and threw a look at Jack.

"My parents live in Boston now, but we moved around while I was growing up. My father is an engineer. My mother never worked outside the home. I have a nine-year-old daughter named Germaine Llewellyn."

Molly perked up. She looked at Mercedes and then at Jack, who winked at her.

"We live in Oakland. I met Jack at the office where I'm a paralegal."

The conversation turned to interests outside of work. "Kitty's got a new project," Gabe interjected. "She's been doing genealogical research so she can join the DAR—Daughters of the American Revolution." Mercedes thought she detected a taunt in his voice and wasn't sure at whom it was directed.

Kitty sat up a little straighter and stuck out her chin ever so slightly. Brandon slugged Molly, who had been baiting him. Gabe got up to intervene.

"Kitty, you've been holding out on me," Jack said. "I never knew you were a blueblood!"

"My ancestors have been here for many generations," Kitty said haughtily.

"Gabe's family was a bunch of horse thieves and grave robbers," Jack asserted.

Gabe laughed. "Oh, and no doubt yours were priests and poets!"

"You don't even want to know."

Kitty couldn't resist prodding Mercedes, whose circumspection and popularity with the men were getting on her nerves.

"Mercedes, what do you know about your family heritage?"

"Both of my grandmothers belonged to the DAR," she said quietly.

Jack turned his head, raising an eyebrow. Kitty sniffed.

"My ancestors were Dutch merchants who settled on Manhattan in the early 1600s. Another survived the *Mayflower* voyage and lived in the Plymouth Colony under William Bradford. Others came from England in 1627 and founded Dedham, Massachusetts. My father's ancestors were writers, artists, professors, and preachers. My mother's fought in the Revolutionary War, the Civil War, and both World Wars."

Jack and Gabe exchanged a knowing look. Kitty, trumped at her own game, got up to clear the dishes. Gabe ordered Molly to help her mother, which she did begrudgingly.

"So you come by your interest in religion and philosophy naturally," Gabe observed, "from the preachers and professors in your family."

"It's hard to imagine there's a gene for that," Mercedes answered.

"Jack's genes are highly suspect. I'd steer clear of them if I were you."

Jack feigned shock and offense. Mercedes laughed at him.

"Do they rub off?" she teased, touching the back of Jack's hand with her index finger and inspecting her fingertips.

"Now you've gone and done it," Jack said. "You're contaminated."

"Better go disinfect yourself, Mercedes. What he's got will probably kill you."

Brandon ran into the kitchen and returned with a spray bottle. They all laughed.

"Give her a squirt, Sport!" Gabe commanded.

Jack snatched the bottle and threw the boy over his shoulder. Brandon howled.

Kitty returned with a silver tray of fruit tarts. Molly brought in small plates and she distributed them to everyone but Brandon, who grabbed his out of her hands. She took her place next to Mercedes, licking her lips. Mercedes leaned over and asked her which tart was the best one, then pulled the tray over and put the chosen treat on Molly's plate.

Kitty couldn't help herself. "So with all that history, Mercedes, are you not a member of the DAR?"

"I'm not."

"I would think you would want to be, since your family has been so involved in the history of our country," she said in an unctuous tone.

Mercedes glanced at her watch under the table. She was getting tired of the inspection. A little of it went a long way when you were the daughter of Eleanor Bell.

"I hope you enjoy your family research and the DAR," Mercedes said to Kitty. She then looked up at Jack, who promptly changed the subject.

⚬⚬⚬

AS THEY RODE BACK TO San Francisco, Jack explained that Kitty had inherited an enormous fortune right after she and Gabe were married. Gabe had done well enough as a lawyer but didn't have to work, so he spent time on political interests. Mercedes said she liked Gabe, and meant it.

"May I drive you home?" Jack asked.

"I have to pick up Germaine and tend to a few things, but thanks for the offer."

"Is she with her father?" It was an innocent enough question.

Mercedes chuckled. "I certainly hope not, because he's dead."

Jack smiled at her drollness. "I'm sorry. I didn't realize you were a widow."

"That's okay. It's been a while now."

They turned off the freeway in San Francisco and wound through the streets into a parking space near the train station. Neither reached for the door handle. Jack admired the colors in Mercedes's hazel eyes. He lifted her long hand and interlaced their fingers. She felt the smooth texture of his palm—a lawyer's hand that had known no manual labor.

"It's nice spending time with you away from the office," he said, opening his palm. He laid her hand flat on top of his, matching their fingers. His were a full inch longer. He stroked the back of her hand. She withdrew it gingerly.

"Thanks for introducing me to your friends, and for a lovely lunch." She picked up her purse and put her hand on the door handle.

He leaned over, took her face into his hands, and kissed her squarely on the mouth for what seemed like an aeon. He kept holding her face for a moment more as they drank each other in. He kissed her one more time, and she felt it to her toes. She got out of the car and suddenly the pavement felt like sand, shifting in every direction.

⊷⧉⊷

IN OAKLAND, Mercedes picked up Germaine from the comfortable suburban home where her friend Cory lived. Driving into their own neighborhood afterwards, they saw the local drug dealer lurking at the edge of "the park," where a pickup game of basketball was under way.

Germaine was quiet and somber. Cory's wonderful home was near their school, not a car ride into hell away from it. Cory's father was a funny, affectionate, nice-looking man, who, with Cory's mom, had played many games with the girls, then driven them to the roller-skating rink and out for pizza afterwards. All the other girls at the slumber party had sleeping bags and fine clothes. They talked of trips to Disneyland, vacations in other countries, and adventures that Germaine could only dream about. She'd slept under a pink sateen quilt in one of the twin beds on the periphery of the group. They had done their best to include her and make her feel comfortable, which had only underscored the yawning chasm between their circumstances and hers.

As they pulled up to the house, Mercedes said, "I'll get us out of here as soon as I can, Honey."

"I know you will, Mama."

HIDDEN *in* PLAIN SIGHT

Mercedes hung up the phone at her desk and exclaimed, "Hot dog!" She hastened to Darrel's office and he motioned her in.

"I think we have a break in the Taylor case!" she announced.

"Tell me."

"You remember Percy Millner, the man Stuart found who worked in Human Resources while Rand was at Franjipur?"

"Yes."

"Well, he's jumped on the bandwagon. He gave Stuart the names of other employees in New York. One of them said he has a lot of information for us. He has details about the suite used by senior management. They had wild parties and God knows what else. He says he also knows who tampered with Rand's personnel file and why. He wants an in-person meeting with a lawyer."

"What's his name?"

"Lloyd Turner Strand."

"What ax is he grinding?"

"He says he's sick of covering up for people who are only interested in feathering their own nests. Also, he doesn't like the leaner, meaner corporate policies. He says Rand was a good guy, but I get the feeling it's not really about Rand. He wants to get even with senior management."

"I like it. Jack or I should meet with him. What's his availability?"

"He can meet you on any of his off days, but it has to be in New York."

"Good. Keep digging. We should meet with as many people as possible while we're there."

After lunch, a woman called and asked to speak with one of the lawyers on the Franjipur Hotels case. Julie put the call through to Mercedes.

"Hello, this is Mercedes Bell. I understand you've asked to speak with a lawyer, but they're all busy at the moment. May I help you? I'm a paralegal."

A sultry voice replied, "That depends. I may have some information of interest to you." Her voice had the raspy quality of a heavy smoker's.

"I'm listening."

"I work in the administrative offices at Franjipur. I heard you're going to sue the company. Maybe I can help."

"Why don't you start by giving me your name and telephone number?"

"I don't think that's a good idea."

"You're afraid of retaliation?"

"Something like that. But I can give you valuable information if you'll tell me the names of some of the people you've already spoken to."

"I'm sorry, all of our work is confidential."

"But you're investigating a case against Franjipur, aren't you? I know you contacted Percy Millner and that he's been helping you."

"Perhaps you'd like to speak with one of the lawyers. If you give me your name and number, I'll ask one of them to call you. Otherwise, I can give you our mailing address and you can write."

The phone went quiet and then the caller hung up.

Mercedes went again to Darrel's office and found Jack standing just inside the doorway, with his back to the hall. He was fresh from court, dressed in a perfectly tailored suit and white shirt. Mercedes reminded herself that two kisses should not be blown out of proportion.

She told them about the anonymous caller and also about people who wanted to meet with them in person. It was decided that Jack would go to New York.

"Oh, twist my arm and send me to Manhattan," Jack quipped. "I almost moved to New York once."

"Lucky San Francisco," Darrel said dryly. "Lucky me."

"I'll talk to Rand and find out more about these people," Jack said, waving the list of names Darrel had handed him. "I know a great private detective in New York, Tony Grey, who can ferret out all kinds of sordid details."

He turned to Mercedes. "We need to get our hands on as many documents and as much information as possible. We need to know everything about the corporate structure, the culture, and skeletons hidden in any closets. Tony has networks that we don't have access to. He can help us get the facts we need to launch this lawsuit."

Darrel added, "We may be exposing the executives of an international company to many embarrassing allegations, so we better be damn sure we're right before we light the fuse."

In Rand they had a sympathetic plaintiff, a southern gentleman, a loyal employee with excellent performance evaluations, and a man who had lost the love of his life in the bargain. The case had every ingredient of jury appeal. Darrel could not have asked for a more immediate return on his sublease to Jack.

⸻

AT HOME THAT EVENING, Germaine sat at the table with homework spread out before her. Mercedes hummed softly as she swept the floor in worn-out jeans and one of Eddy's shirts with the sleeves rolled up. She was tired and she looked it.

The phone rang and Germaine answered. She handed the phone to Mercedes.

"Hi. It's Jack. Your daughter has very nice phone manners."

Germaine watched her curiously.

"One of my friends from work," Mercedes whispered, her hand over the mouthpiece.

"I have something for you, from Gabe," Jack was saying.

"From Gabe?"

"Yes, he came over last night. Kitty's out of town with the kids, and the peace and quiet were too much for him."

She chuckled.

"He's been inspired to give you something and asked me to deliver it."

"Now I'm really curious."

"I could give it to you over dinner Saturday night, if you're free."

Blood rushed into her head. "I'll have to consult with my roommate about all this," she said, winking at Germaine.

"You have to arrange childcare."

"Yes."

"Okay, if not this Saturday, then perhaps another night before I go to New York."

"That sounds great."

Germaine waited expectantly as her mother hung up.

"That was Mr. Soutane, one of the lawyers at the firm."

"From the Fredericks case?"

"Good memory!"

"He asked you to go out with him?"

"He did."

"Mama, you have a date!"

"I guess I do," she said, not quite believing it.

⁓

LATE THAT NIGHT, the sound of a female screaming and a man raving in slurred Spanish woke Mercedes. They were out in the middle of the street under a lamppost.

She peeked through the blinds. A burly figure in jeans and a dark hooded sweatshirt was hauling a small woman toward an old Oldsmobile a few feet away—one hand clutching her long hair and the other gripping her armpit. The woman resisted with all her might: pulled at the arm that held her hair, dragged her feet, and kicked at his thick legs, all the while yelling desperately for help.

Mercedes sprinted to the kitchen, dialed 9-1-1, and gave the dispatcher a swift description. She was back at the window just in time to see him bash the woman's head against the car door and knock her unconscious. He opened the door and dumped her body on the seat like a bag of dirt, started the engine, and sped away. It was all over in a minute or two.

Shaken, Mercedes went back to check on Germaine, who was still asleep, breathing deeply. She climbed into bed beside her, pulled up the covers, and snuggled against her, inhaling her sweet smell. Germaine stirred and threw an arm over Mercedes's neck.

A host of memories flooded her mind—Eddy, roaring drunk, screaming in her face and slapping her.

It's over. Let it go. He's gone. You're safe, she told herself and thought of the woman outside. She hoped she was still alive, and that the police would catch them.

The world gradually slipped away. She saw giant trees swaying in a primordial forest. Sunlight filtered through the branches. Light fell in slanted shafts to a thick duff layer on the forest floor. The infinite layers of the past lay just below the surface of the present.

Words drifted through her fading consciousness: *The earth is a living being. All atoms are conscious and interdependent. No energy is ever lost. Everything is in plain sight for those with the eyes to see.*

CHAPTER TEN

March 1985

ONE MORE NIGHT

Caroline's normally Spartan office was cluttered with materials for the case going to arbitration. The white plastic model of a human spine sat perched on a corner of her desk. Mercedes examined it while her friend finished a phone conversation.

"Nice spine," she said, when Caroline was free.

"Why, thank you. I've grown rather attached to her," Caroline said, squaring her shoulders. She looked up at Mercedes. "Found any more smoking guns for us?"

"I still have a couple more boxes to go through. But I have to tell you something." She got up and closed the door.

Caroline raised her eyebrows. The pale pink of Caroline's sweater complemented her fair English complexion. She was a pretty woman with a dignified manner and an incisive mind.

"Are the girls still on for this Saturday?" Mercedes asked.

"I think Anne will expire if Germaine doesn't spend the night. She's so excited."

"So is Germaine! I just wanted to make sure because—I have a date that night."

"You *have* been acting a little mysterious lately."

Mercedes laughed.

"So who's the lucky guy?"

"Jack Soutane."

Caroline's eyes widened at the sound of his name, and she said conspiratorially, "Don't worry. I won't breathe a word to a soul."

"Thanks. I'll drop Germaine off around four if that's okay."

"Sure. We'll stock up the kitchen and get ready for that voracious daughter of yours. So how long has this been going on?"

"There is no 'this.' We've been out to lunch one time and that's it, unless you count the basket he brought me from Africa."

"He brought you a present? That trip was quite a while ago." Caroline assessed the timetable. "Where's he taking you?"

"I don't know. I hope nowhere too fancy. I don't have the wardrobe for that."

"Only you would say such a thing."

"It's the truth."

"Do you have any idea how any other woman in this office would feel about a date with Jack? Good grief!"

"I guess I have mixed emotions, considering my track record." Mercedes shifted in her seat and looked at her watch. "Listen, I'm supposed to see Stuart in half an hour, so can we talk about the arbitration?" Caroline gave her an amused look.

⚬⚬⚬

AFTER LEAVING GERMAINE AT CAROLINE'S on Saturday, Mercedes returned home to get ready for her date. She pulled out a short black skirt and the slinky top that Eleanor had sent her the previous Christmas. She abandoned the illusion of not being nervous.

This time he was waiting for her near the turnstile inside the subway station. The instant she passed through the gate, he was beside her with an arm around her shoulders.

He led her to a small restaurant near Davies Symphony Hall. They talked and laughed over glasses of wine and bowls of mushroom bisque. *What was it about Jack,* she wondered, *that seemed to put people at ease so quickly?* His looks were only part of his magnetism. Chameleon-like, he could adapt immediately to his audience. It was his genius. She watched him do it with everyone equally—with waiters, taxi drivers, clients, and peers.

He was gracious to all, always ready to laugh, perpetually appreciative. It was as though life had always been good to him and he was eager to return the favor from the abundant resources at his command.

They watched couples heading for the theater, the ballet, the symphony, and to nightclubs in the area. Like butterflies, bejeweled women in shimmering dresses of every color flitted by the windows accompanied by men in evening attire. Festively clad gay couples scurried past, many arm in arm or holding hands, talking animatedly. The whole world seemed to be in love.

As the dinner plates were cleared away, Jack reached into the inside pocket of his jacket and pulled out a slim, gift-wrapped package. He put it on the table in the circle of light cast by the small copper lantern between them.

"What's this?"

"From Gabe."

She picked it up and examined the wrapping, and the attempt to tie ribbon artfully around it.

"Aw, he even wrapped it himself," she said. She untied the ribbon and opened the paper where it was taped. It was *The Yoga Sutra of Patanjali,* the volume she had so reverently pulled off Gabe's library shelf. Her face lit up. Jack watched her.

"It appears the book has found its rightful owner," he observed.

"This is a great treasure to me and extremely generous of Gabe," she said quite seriously.

"Somehow I don't think he had the same appreciation for whatever is in that book as you do."

His eyes were shining. She watched his mouth and thought about kissing him.

Over chocolate mousse and cappuccino, their conversation turned to Germaine, to childhood, and to what life had been like for each of them when they were nine years old.

Jack's smile faded. His mother had been a nurse, but was institutionalized with multiple sclerosis when he was very young. He remembered her wheelchair but had no memories of her walking. She had died when he was nine.

Mercedes's childhood had not been marked by tragedy, although her small family was not particularly close. They had lived in different cities on the east coast, Texas and Colorado, according to the dictates of her father's engineering career. Her parents had been her world at nine.

She asked him, "Do you still see your father?"

"No. He died while I was in college. I had two older brothers, Patrick and Jeremy, but they're gone now, too—one to illness, the other to an accident in the military. Then there's Janine Reneau. I've known her since I was a little boy. She used to be a patient of my father's, when we lived in Atherton. When things went south for us, she was very kind to me. I used to take the train to San Francisco and Janine would meet me at the station. We'd go exploring and she'd take me to lunch, buy me clothes, take me to the museums, Golden Gate Park or wherever. Sometimes I stayed over in her apartment, where she still lives. She never had kids, so I take care of her."

After a moment, he asked, "What are you thinking?"

"That often life provides what we need, but not necessarily in

at their table before the next song could ensnare them. They sat laughing at each other and sipped their drinks.

Jack leaned over and kissed her damp cheek.

"Mmm, salty."

Mercedes took a long drink of water and returned his gaze.

"What time is it getting to be?"

He looked at his watch. "You've just missed the last train. Are you going to turn into a pumpkin?"

"That depends," she said.

"On what?"

"On whether you can drive me to my car."

"Of course I can."

Just then the sound of Phil Collins singing "One More Night" filled the room.

"Shall we?" Jack asked, holding out his arm. He led her out to the dance floor. Other couples joined them one by one. He held her eyes with a long penetrating look and began singing the words. *Please give me one more night . . . 'cause I can't wait forever . . .*

She rested her head on his broad chest, her ear on his heart, and felt the dampness of his shirt beneath her cheek. She closed her eyes and listened to his voice as he held her tightly, his big hand wrapped around hers, his other spread across the small of her back, pressing her waist against him, guiding her in a gentle swaying rhythm around the dance floor. When the song stopped he kissed her lips, the glittering reflections of the disco balls patterning them with flickering diamonds of color.

⁓⊘⁓

THE SPARKLING SKYSCRAPERS OF San Francisco receded in the rearview mirror. Soon they were on the freeway toward the East Bay train station where her car sat waiting in the deserted parking lot.

Yellow pools of light from light poles dotted the blacktop. East Oakland on a Sunday at 2:30 a.m. was not the safest place for a single woman. He pulled his car up beside hers and scanned the area warily.

"Do you have far to drive?"

"No, just ten minutes from here."

"Let me follow you then, please," he urged.

"It's probably not a good idea." She thought of the jarring appearance her neighborhood would make after such an enchanted evening.

"I'll wait until you're safely inside your house, then I'll drive away. I don't feel right about leaving you here. Indulge me." He was not negotiating.

She reflected for a moment, and acquiesced. There was no good reason to refuse his protection at this late hour.

He pulled her into his embrace, kissing her long and hungrily, stroking her hair. He kissed her again and put a hand around the curve of her hip. He felt the top of her lean thigh and ran his hand slowly up to her rib cage, just beneath her breast. She felt the side of his face and his muscular shoulder. Her hand came to rest over his heart. Her pulse raced.

"Got your book?" he murmured.

She patted her purse.

He kissed her once more, until she thought her head would explode. She gathered her things, pulled out her car keys, and looked into his eyes.

"Lock your doors," she said to him and exited his car.

The Beetle started with reluctance. She slipped it into gear and left the parking lot. He followed her closely onto the freeway, then east a few exits to her neighborhood. She turned down her street and parked in front of her house, the only one with its porch light still on. He pulled up behind her. She walked over to his car, and he rolled down the window.

"Now I know where to find you," he said with a smile. "Please go into your house and lock the door behind you before I break my word and get out of this car."

She kissed his delicious mouth one more time, then walked to her front door, floating.

⁕

THE NEXT MORNING SHE LAY in bed for a long while. She was in a waking dream, going over every detail of their date. She could see Jack's striking face at the dinner table and his quiet, genteel table manners. She recalled the light in his eyes when she spoke to him, his wicked sense of humor, and their frenzy on the dance floor.

Her feet ached from dancing. She could still see the flickering lights from the nightclub; her ears still rang from the music. A rush of desire and ecstatic wonder gripped her as she relived all of it.

⁕

WHEN SHE BROUGHT GERMAINE HOME later that afternoon, an unfamiliar white van was parked across the street from their house. An Asian man with a red baseball cap sat inside, staring at their front door. As Mercedes approached the house with her keys out, he sprang from the van, opened the back, and pulled out an enormous vase of long-stemmed red roses. Germaine gaped at him as he approached their door.

"You Mesadee Ber?" he asked in a heavy accent.

"Yes, I am," she replied, eyeing his cargo.

"My instruction say wait till you come. I been here over two hour!" he cried. Mercedes noticed the logo of a San Francisco florist on his hat.

She gave the keys to Germaine and reached out to receive the flowers, her face flushed. Germaine excitedly unlocked the door.

The delivery man bowed and scurried back to the van, looking uneasily up and down the street. Mercedes carried the heavy vase to the table. Germaine stood beside the luscious bouquet, gazing up at the velvety texture of the dark red petals. She had never seen anyone send flowers to her mother—certainly not her father.

Mercedes opened the envelope that accompanied them, held her breath and read.

Thinking of you today and
"One More Night."

Jack

"Mom!" Germaine exclaimed. "Are they from Mr. Soutane?"

"Yes, Babe." She sat down on a chair and pulled her daughter into her lap. Germaine took the note from her and read it.

"Wait till Anne hears about this! What's 'One More Night?'"

"It's just a song, Honey   a wonderful song."

No one was in the hallway when he closed the door behind them. He walked to where she stood, picked up her hand, and kissed it.

"You turn a good day into a beautiful day, Ms. Bell," he said.

"Do you think we'll actually be able to work on this case together?" she asked, with a furrowed brow.

"We're already doing it."

"You know what I mean."

"You worry too much."

"I just don't want to jeopardize my job. I've never—"

He leaned over and stopped her with a lingering kiss. It took her breath away.

"I can't think when you kiss me."

"Then don't."

He pushed her back gently, grasped both of her hands in his, stretched out her arms against the wall, and kissed her deeply.

"There now," he said.

Before she could speak, he kissed her again, longer, and pressed himself against her. For a moment she imagined they were horizontal.

"You said you practice yoga to still your mind," he said quietly.

"Somehow I don't think this is what the yoga masters have in mind."

He stepped back, took out a handkerchief, and wiped the smudge of lipstick from her face. Then he wiped his lips. He looked at the pink stain on the handkerchief.

"Now I'll have you with me all day. Are you free this weekend?" he asked.

She looked at him pensively, in a quandary about how she could possibly keep her concentration in the office when he was present. Her insides were in an uproar.

"I don't know."

"I'll call you tonight," he said.

She returned to the conference room and finished organizing the documents as prescribed by Jack before he had blown her concentration to smithereens. *Before I allowed him to,* she corrected herself. She heard him take a call and listened intently, just to hear the deep resonance of his voice. Rand Taylor was returning his call.

"Rand, I have good news." Jack closed his door with a shove and she could hear no more. She collected her wits, boxed up the documents, and carried them to the paralegal office.

Simone looked up as Mercedes entered, acknowledged her with a nod, and kept dictating. Lindsay was on the phone, trying valiantly to be understood by a non-native English speaker. She repeated her phrases several times, each more slowly than the previous. Mercedes set the box of documents on her desk, sat down, put on fresh lipstick, and deciphered the notes she had scrawled. The drone of voices and Lindsay's patience calmed her.

LATER THAT EVENING, she listened to a mockingbird on the lamp-post outside and noted that Jack had not called. It was actually a relief. He was a whirlpool, spinning her world, pulling her in, and she was tired of reacting to him.

If Jack were as sincere and smitten with her as he acted—a huge *if*—then the door might open to other possibilities. But if he wasn't, it was pure lunacy to submit to all the turmoil and to certain heartbreak. She might as well put her head back on the chopping block where she'd put it for Eddy.

She was in her bathrobe, brushing her teeth when the phone rang. On the fourth ring she picked it up.

"Hi. Sorry about calling so late, but I was with clients and time got away from us."

"It's an odd time to be with clients."

"It's a family I've known for many years. The father died this week. I prepared the estate plan and there's a lot of drama among the heirs over the will. Anyway, I did try calling before we got started, but the line was busy."

"I guess you get pretty entangled with families in estate planning. I never really thought about it."

"How was your day?"

"Germaine got the invitation of her lifetime, to Disneyland. She's out of her mind with excitement."

"That's like winning the lottery for a kid. How did this come about?"

"One of her friends from school invited her to go with their family. I can't believe their generosity."

"You'd do it if your fortunes were reversed."

"That's true."

"And Germaine is a special girl."

"You haven't even met her."

"I've seen the evidence." He was tired too and his voice was even deeper than usual.

"You see a lot of things."

"May I see *you* this weekend?"

"Why don't you come over for dinner on Saturday?"

"That'd be great. I don't know when I last ate a real home-cooked meal."

"Six o'clock Saturday then."

⁓

AT 6:05 ON SATURDAY NIGHT, Jack stood on the front stoop of the pink palace in a black golf shirt and khakis, holding a bouquet of blue irises in one hand and a cold bottle of champagne in the other.

Mercedes led him in through her modest living room. In the kitchen he spied a tantalizing confection on a flowered plate.

"Ooh, what's that?" he inquired.

"Decadent dark chocolate cake with raspberry filling," she replied. "I made it this morning."

"'Decadent?'"

"The name of the recipe," she grinned.

The table was set with cloth napkins, candlesticks and old sterling silver flatware, decidedly out of place in the ghetto. He picked up a fork, examined the monogram, turned it over, and put it back down on the table. 1916. Old family stuff.

He put the champagne in the refrigerator, taking the chance to snoop around the bags of fresh vegetables and jars of various home-made concoctions. Mercedes looked fresh in her ironed white shirt. Aside from the few nights Mr. Friedman had joined them for dinner, Jack was her first dinner guest.

Jack's ears tuned in to the neighborhood—the loud argument down the street, the noise of the young men playing basketball around the corner, dogs snarling at passersby, and freeway traffic. The classical station was playing the Beethoven violin concerto, so Mercedes left the dial there.

Without asking, he opened her cupboard and selected the only two wine glasses from her motley assortment of drinking vessels. He took the kitchen towel from her shoulder and opened the champagne.

"Here's to the culinary skill of my lovely hostess," he said. They clinked glasses and sipped the effervescent champagne, which burst on her tongue like ambrosia. Dinner not far from ready, he took the seat normally occupied by Germaine.

Mercedes sat down and drank the first glass with him. He mentioned again what a rarity a real home-cooked meal was in his life. There had been none at home, unless Janine Reneau had made him something in her tiny apartment. Once in college, he had always eaten out.

"You never learned to cook?"

He shook his head.

"But surely you've had girlfriends who cooked for you."

"No," he shrugged.

"No ex-wives?"

"Not one."

"Not one who could cook?"

"No ex-wives of any variety. What about you?"

"No ex-wives for me either," she laughed. "Only one late husband."

She served him a plate of oven-barbecued chicken basted with her special sauce, creamy scalloped potatoes, green beans mixed with toasted slivered almonds and tiny bits of bacon. Out of the oven, she pulled piping hot dinner rolls she had made from scratch. She split one, slathered it with butter, and handed it to him. He put it all in his mouth at once and closed his eyes. She watched bliss register on his face.

The setting sun ignited the sky into the colors of orange sherbet and rose pink, which gradually deepened and darkened. She lit the tapers and turned on the stovetop light. Stars gradually appeared and the moon rose through the bay window.

"So where *is* Germaine? I was hoping to get to meet her."

"Germaine Llewellyn is in demand. I'm afraid you will have to get in line."

"Like her mother. Then please give me a number."

"We'll see."

His eyebrows shot up in surprise.

"She's been through a lot, Jack. I'm going to do everything in my power to protect her and keep her world stable."

"Which includes not introducing her to . . ."

"To whom? What would you call yourself?"

"To someone who is courting her mother."

"Is that what this is?"

"What would *you* call it?"

"I'm not sure."

"How could you possibly not be sure?"

She rose and came around to clear away his dishes. He stopped her and pulled her down into his lap.

"I'm not dating any other women and I have no intention of doing so until . . ."

"Until what?"

"Until we see where this goes. Now it's your turn."

"You know I'm not seeing anyone else."

"Is that by choice or circumstance?"

"My circumstances *are* my choice. I don't want to waste my time if you're just playing with me. I'm quite content on my own."

"I can see that. And it's one of the most attractive things about you."

"I've learned to judge men by what they *do*, not what they say. Talk is cheap."

He pulled her down into the crook of his arm and kissed her, scooping up her long legs and cradling her against him.

"I don't want you going out with anyone but me," he said, "and I don't want to see anyone but you. You're an extraordinary woman. You have character, a good mind, and your feet are on the ground." He waited to see if she would say anything. "Plus I may be falling in love with you. Is that enough clarification?"

She smiled. "For now."

"Good, because I really want a big piece of that chocolate cake."

She extracted herself from his embrace, got up to brew coffee, and cut two pieces of the rich cake. They sat opposite each other in the candlelight. Jack slowly ate the enormous piece she had cut for him, savoring every bite in prayerful silence, worshiping in the temple of chocolate, and before the goddess who made such things possible.

They moved to the living room. He made himself as comfortable as he could on the small sofa and pulled Mercedes against him. He put his cheek on the top of her head, which leaned against his chest. She put her arm around his deeply satisfied belly. The rumble of his voice reverberated through her as he spoke about his visit to Janine earlier in the day and his trip to the San Francisco flower market, where he had found the irises.

"So tell me about Germaine's father," he said.

She sat up and faced him, leaning against the side arm of the couch, her feet up on the cushions between them.

"We met right after I finished college. Eddy was a carpenter working on a framing crew. I was a waitress in a nearby restaurant where the crew would congregate after work. He was good-looking, tan, and funny. I knew nothing about him except what I saw in his circle of friends, and I really didn't care. I was sick of family interference and just wanted my own life.

"We had an intense, immediate attraction for each other. His job came to an end and he decided to try his luck in California. He asked me to marry him and go with him. I'd always wanted to live in California and I was desperate to be free of my parents. I was thrilled to do something so bold and reckless. So we eloped."

Jack, the professional listener, nodded.

"Things deteriorated after only a few months. Eddy drank too much and became a control freak. He didn't like me talking to other people, going places on my own, or having a job, even though we needed the money. He changed careers and went to work in a retail chain, selling computers. I chalked up some of his weirdness to making so many changes at once. But then I got pregnant, and our marriage went from bad to worse.

"After Germaine was born and got past the infant stage, I decided to go to night school to become a paralegal. It was a new field and it looked interesting. But Eddy opposed the idea and hated any sign of my independence. I could see the writing on the wall. I went to school so I could support Germaine and me when the time came."

Jack reached for her hand.

"It was a good plan, but then he was killed in a drunk-driving accident."

Jack pulled her feet up into his lap and began massaging her soles.

For the first time with anyone, she spoke about the financial straits in which Eddy's death had left them—her struggle to find a job, to move, to find the right school for Germaine, to keep her parents at bay, and to make a new life.

"I've always wondered whether his death was an accident or suicide. Either way, the aftermath was not something I ever want to live through again."

Jack looked around her impoverished living room with enlightened appreciation.

"Death has a way of reprioritizing life," he said. "After my dad died I was a mess. At first I grieved being orphaned. Then I was relieved because he'd been such a bad father. Patrick, my oldest brother, had a family and was sort of a father figure, which made it easier. But then, three years after Dad died, Patrick died too—and soon after Patrick, my other brother, Jeremy, also died. I was devastated. I dropped out of school, bought a one-way ticket to Europe, and just wandered the streets."

"How old were you?"

"Twenty. And here I am, almost twenty years down the road with no family of my own."

She nodded. "What did you do in Europe?"

"I traveled. I had about ten thousand dollars the old man had left me. I learned to use the currency exchange rates to my advantage. After about a year, I decided to go to law school. I came back, finished college, and paid for law school with the money I made buying and selling currencies."

"I can't imagine what I would have done in your shoes," she said.

"I had friends."

"Why have you never married?"

"Never met the right person. Worried about whether I could really pull it off."

"What do you mean?"

"I didn't think I was cut out for family life. I never found anyone who really wanted the same things I did."

"And has that changed?"

"Maybe. I don't know what's going to happen, any more than you do," he said. "But I keep thinking about you and Germaine. Maybe possibilities are opening up that I never imagined."

"I could say the same thing," she admitted. "Pain and accepting responsibility for one's decisions can change a person."

"Life is giving us an opportunity. Let's see where it will go." Jack Soutane's handsome face broke into a soft smile.

Around midnight he got up to leave and held her in a long embrace. Her arms encircled him and she spread her hands across the muscles of his back. She inhaled his scent and kissed the black hair escaping his open collar.

He squeezed her gently in a long sensuous kiss, cupping her bottom in his hands.

FEET *in the* WATER

The long curving shoreline of Stinson Beach receded in the distance as they turned up the Panoramic Highway toward the city, with the sun low in the sky behind them. It had been a warm and windless day on the beach. The three had worn themselves out chasing the Frisbee, sprinting on the hard wet sand, running into the chilly water, and building a gigantic sand castle. Germaine had a pocket full of treasures from the water's edge—a sand dollar, shells, and a bit of mother-of-pearl from an abalone shell.

She was gazing out the side car window when Jack looked into the rearview mirror to check on her.

"Are you hungry?"

She turned and vehemently nodded yes, bright-eyed and suddenly not so sad to be leaving the beach.

"There's a great little restaurant right around the corner from my place, if it's okay with your mom. We can stop at my apartment first to clean up."

Germaine looked eagerly at her sunburned mother, whose braided hair was frizzed by the sea air.

"Fine with me."

"Oh, goody. I'm starving. Thank you so much!"

Germaine had easily warmed to Jack over the past few months. He'd gotten her the book of crossword puzzles she now pulled out from under a towel. He frequently brought her books to read when he came over or when they got together in San Francisco on weekends. She rummaged around for a pencil in her backpack. They drove the curving roads through cathedral-like eucalyptus groves to the highway. Germaine worked her puzzle, only half listening to the grown-ups talk.

Soon they were walking into Jack's apartment on Nob Hill. Bookcases lined the hall leading to the living room; a long Oriental runner carpeted their way. The girl's eyes were struck by the warm colors in the room and the enormous size of the furniture. An immense brown leather couch was positioned against the main wall and a low coffee table sat in front of it. Above the couch hung an African tapestry of big geometric designs in burnt orange, ocher, and dark brown. It covered all the space up to the high ceiling. Opposite the couch was a polished granite fireplace flanked by colorful African baskets full of firewood and kindling. At the end of the room, picture windows faced the city and sliding glass doors led out to a balcony.

Everywhere Germaine found artifacts and objects of art from Jack's travels. There were wooden side tables with curious hand-carved lamps on them; low-slung chairs with handwoven throw pillows in them. On the mantel, shelves, and tables were Egyptian boxes inlaid with ivory, stone figurines of animals, whimsical sculptures, hand-turned wood bowls, and beautiful picture books of places he had visited.

He showed them into the guest bedroom, which had thick carpet and an attached bathroom. Mercedes closed the door behind them and carried their bag into the bathroom, with Germaine following close behind. The floor and walls all around the walk-in shower were covered in small cobalt blue glass tiles. The vanity area was intimately lit and housed a dark blue porcelain sink. A large mirror was recessed into the wall, leaving a ledge upon which sat blue and gray hand-thrown pots of various sizes and shapes. Germaine lifted the lids and found every kind of toiletry they might need. Racks of Turkish towels hung beside a low, wide padded bench on a soft blue area rug. Another African basket with a lid sat on the floor for dirty laundry.

They kicked off their sandals and stepped down into the oversized shower area, divided from the rest of the room by a clear plate glass panel. They peeled off their sandy clothes and turned on both shower heads. Germaine stood under the gentle spray. It was like being in one of the swanky hotels she'd seen in the James Bond movie that she and Anne had snuck into. In fact, it was like being in James Bond's bathroom. She couldn't wait to tell Anne.

Soon they sat on Jack's gigantic couch, watching the city's lights come on in the distance. Germaine began inspecting the small stone animals on the coffee table—a pink quartz hippo, a green jade crocodile, an iron pyrite elephant, an obsidian gorilla. Jack came in, just out of the shower himself and in a starched white shirt. He handed the girl a crystal glass of sparkling apple juice and set a dish of cocktail snacks in front of her. She popped some of the salty mix into her mouth and swung her legs back and forth.

Jack invited her to see the rest of the apartment and she leapt to her feet. He led her first into the dining room, which held a majestic walnut table surrounded by eight chairs. The walls were an appetizing shade of melon. A remarkable copper chandelier hung from the high ceiling. Jack turned it on and adjusted the dimmer switch.

"I bought this light in Portugal several years ago. Do you know where Portugal is?" he asked her.

Germaine shook her head.

"C'mon, I'll show you."

He led her into his bedroom, where a world map hung on the bronze-colored wall opposite his massive bed. He pulled a chair over for Germaine to climb up on, and pointed to Portugal. It looked so far away from California. She was excited to think that the light in the next room had been bought there and brought here by the person standing next to her.

"Could you show me all the places you've been?"

"You mean on this map, or take you there?" he teased.

She giggled. "On the map, Silly!"

He began naming countries as he pointed to them: most of the countries in Europe, many in Asia, several in Africa and the Mediterranean, one or two in South America, plus Canada, Mexico, and numerous places in the United States.

"Where do you want to go next?" she asked.

"To dinner," he quipped, "but my next trip abroad will be to the Philippines—right there," he pointed.

He helped Germaine down from the chair, and she looked at the rest of his room, its elegant chest of drawers, bronze table lamps, and benign clutter.

"So what do you want to be when you grow up?" he asked.

"An architect," she said without hesitation.

"Have you heard of the Hearst Castle?"

She nodded. "One of the kids in my class went there."

"That was designed by a woman—Julia Morgan. Maybe we'll go there one weekend."

He led her into his white marble bathroom. Reposed in an alcove specially designed for her was a life-size marble statue of a Greek goddess on an imposing pedestal. Germaine gasped and went immediately to her. She looked up at the serene head and flowing gown; she bent down to touch her beautiful feet.

"Wow! She's so beautiful!" Germaine exclaimed.

"That's Athena. I brought her back from Greece a few years ago."

"She's the daughter of Zeus. She came out of Zeus's head!" Germaine exclaimed.

"Very good! How do you know that?"

"We have a book of Greek myths at home."

Jack beamed at his young protégé.

Germaine looked up at the ceiling, painted coral red, and all around the classical-styled room. The largest bathtub and highest shower she had ever seen were at the other end of the room. There was even a phone near the tub. She touched Athena's feet again on her way out.

In Jack's home office a photograph of Mercedes, taken in an unguarded moment at work, sat on his desk. Germaine picked it up and looked at Jack. Her mother had a whole life she knew very little about.

"I hope it's okay that I have a picture of your mom on my desk."

Germaine studied his handsome face and kept her thoughts to herself.

"What's *your* mother like?" she asked.

"I'll show you." He pulled a photograph down from the wall. A fragile woman with a sallow complexion and dark circles under her eyes peered out of it.

"Here's a picture of her when she was a little older than your mother."

"Is she sick?" the girl asked.

"Not anymore. She died when I was about your age."

The young girl's brow furrowed and she looked concerned.

He handed her a picture of a stern-looking man in a white coat. "That's my father. He brought me up. He was already old when I was born, so now he's gone, too."

Germaine looked at the man's face, his mean-looking mouth and sour expression. His thinning salt-and-pepper hair was slicked down and combed to the side. Jack didn't look anything like him but had his father's build.

"I'm sorry," she said.

"Don't be. It was a long time ago," he said. "Anyway, this is where I live and this is the chair I sit in when I call your house." He gestured at the leather-and-chrome swivel chair at his desk. "Want to check it out?"

Germaine plunked herself into the chair, which was too high for her feet to touch the floor, so she drew them up under her, cross-legged. Jack spun her around fast and she squealed with delight, hanging onto the padded arms.

"Faster!"

He spun her faster, and the chair was a blur. Mercedes followed her daughter's shriek to the office door and leaned against the doorway, holding her wine glass.

"Faster!" Germaine commanded.

"You've got a little thrill seeker here," he said to Mercedes.

"You have no idea," she replied.

When the chair came to a stop and Germaine could walk straight, he led them down a hallway lined with louvered doors.

The kitchen, just off the dining room, completed the circuit. It was a galley-style kitchen with a built-in wine rack, stainless steel refrigerator, and polished stone countertops. Jack showed Germaine some of the room's special features. She pushed her glass against the automatic ice dispenser and watched ice chips fill it. Jack opened the refrigerator to put the wine away. Germaine peeked and saw that the inside was all but bare.

⚬⚬⚬

THEY WALKED OUTSIDE AND AROUND the corner to a small Italian restaurant with a striped awning and flower boxes full of geraniums. The host greeted Jack by name and escorted the threesome to a corner booth. The white tablecloth hung down nearly to their laps.

Germaine surveyed the cozy interior and the other patrons. There were two well scrubbed teenage boys with their father and a young couple with a sleeping baby.

Mercedes ate her salad and met Jack's gaze. She was thinking of the ripples in his long back when he threw the Frisbee and the shape of his legs in swim trunks. He was thinking of her grace on the beach as she scooped up the Frisbee just above the sand and kept running, all in one smooth motion.

Their plates of steaming food appeared, and silence fell on the table.

A few minutes later, Jack said, "Germaine, you surprise me," nodding at her empty plate. She had also demolished a salad, a piece of garlic bread, and a glass of milk.

Mercedes chuckled. "She has a hollow leg."

When the waiter next appeared, Jack ordered Germaine a cannoli drizzled with chocolate. "If that doesn't fill you up, we're calling in the National Guard."

Mercedes slipped off a sandal and put her bare foot on top of Jack's shoe. He kept talking to Germaine as though nothing were out of the ordinary. Mercedes slipped off her other sandal and caressed his ankle with both feet. A slight smile played at the corners of his mouth. She slid a toe slowly up his long calf and pulled down the sock, baring his skin. He ignored her.

He was telling Germaine about the first time he'd had a cannoli.

Janine Reneau had taken him to a restaurant not unlike this one when he was eleven or twelve. Mercedes looked at Germaine and propped her head on her hand. She sipped the remainder of her wine and caressed Jack's calf with one foot while wedging her toe behind his knee with the other.

The cannoli arrived and Germaine's eyes brightened. She was enraptured by her first bite of the confection and closed her eyes.

Jack leaned back in the booth and dropped his hands into his lap. He seized one of Mercedes's bare feet and slowly pushed his index finger between her toes. Her foot was his captive, and color began to rise in her already pink face.

Germaine took another bite of the cannoli, trying to make it last as long as possible. Jack looked into Mercedes's reddening face, slid his finger out from between her toes, and asked her if she'd like her coffee warmed. He slid his finger back between her toes.

In a very controlled voice, she said she was fine.

Germaine was on her last bite. Jack played with Mercedes's toes, encompassed her narrow ankle with his hand, and wedged her foot between his thighs. He ran his hand up her silky calf. Mercedes watched Germaine, unable to think. Energy from Jack's body seemed to run up her legs and ignite her insides.

Germaine, having devoured the cannoli, took a long drink of milk—her second glass—and turned to Mercedes.

"Mom! You're so sunburned! Your face is way red!"

Mercedes choked on her coffee and coughed until her eyes were tearing. Germaine clapped her on her back, while Jack taunted her with a look.

He slowly extracted Mercedes's foot from between his thighs and ran a finger up her arch. Her reflex kicked in, and her knee banged the underside of the table. Germaine, startled, looked from Mercedes to Jack and back again.

Jack smiled and paid the check. Germaine crunched ice cubes, looking from one adult to the other. Something was going on that they were hiding from her.

⸱⸙⸱

AS MOTHER AND DAUGHTER DROVE out of the city onto the Bay Bridge, with the illuminated city skyline on their left, Mercedes let her hair loose and opened the window.

"So what do you think, Sweetness?"

"Mom, it's like a fairy tale."

"It kind of is, isn't it?"

TWO WORLDS

The sight of brown pelicans cruising low over the lake reminded Mercedes how close they were to the ocean. She and Caroline were out walking on their lunch hour. The morning's rain shower had subsided just in time. She cinched the belt tighter on her navy trench coat, thankful for the wool liner, and took a deep breath of the chilly salt air.

"Nice coat. You must be changing your image," Caroline remarked.

"I was very partial to that old rain coat, and there was certainly no need to worry about messing it up."

"Yes, plus it probably reminded Darrel how underpaid you are—never a bad thing. So may I assume the new model is a gift from our friend?"

"You may."

Caroline shook her head. "Tisk, tisk. Didn't your mother ever caution you about accepting expensive gifts from gentlemen?"

"You haven't met Eleanor. That thought is not part of her playbook. She's more in the take-what-you-can-get camp, and set your sights on the richest man in the room."

Caroline laughed. "So things are going well, then."

Mercedes sighed. "With Jack? I keep expecting to wake up."

"It's clear that Germaine's crazy about him," Caroline added. "Every time she comes over it's Jack this and Jack that. Very sweet."

"They're pals. Last time he came over they got into a heated checkers game. Before that it was Scrabble Junior, and of course the ubiquitous crossword puzzles. He drove us down to San Simeon so Germaine could see the Hearst Castle."

"She told us all about it." Caroline watched Mercedes's face. "Are you beyond the point of no return?"

"Not quite. We've managed not to go to bed together yet, but I don't know how much longer that will last."

"I'm impressed. That can't be Jack's idea, so it must be yours."

"I'm trying something new. It's called restraint."

"Must be difficult. But perhaps it makes it easier to accept gifts like gorgeous Burberry trench coats." She looked down. "And new boots—Ferragamos, no less. He must really be in dire anticipation."

Mercedes admired her footwear. "They are beautiful, aren't they? He does love to spend money. Took us shopping a couple of weekends ago, again. He bought Germaine a globe, as she always asks him about his trips. And he bought her new shoes. Which reminds me. Have you been able to find out anything from the lawyers Jack used to practice with?" Mercedes asked.

"I spoke with Martin Macey. He was pleasant and rather open about the group. They met in law school, decided to hang out their own shingle, shared overhead, and did a bunch of deals together. He praised Jack highly—just what you'd expect to hear, all the stuff we know already. He said he had the highest respect for Jack's skills as a lawyer. When I asked him the first word that came to mind when he thought of Jack, he said right off: 'Strategic.' And then he said: 'Just make sure you stay on his good side. He has a ruthless streak and does not suffer fools. People don't see it coming. They don't know what's hit them and it's over in an instant.'"

"That's a bit ominous."

"Martin said he'd known Jack for over twenty years and that the trail of broken hearts stretches around the block."

"I wonder why he's never mentioned any of them."

"Have you ever asked him?"

"I don't really care to know the details. But anyone who looks like that has got to have a past."

"I'll keep snooping. One thing more: I didn't get the feeling they're in touch or that Martin is particularly eager to see Jack. I didn't press it. Maybe they had a falling-out of some kind."

"I know I'm losing it, because I've been telling Eleanor about him and I don't even mind."

Caroline chuckled. "I have to meet your mother someday."

"Just go to a Joan Crawford movie. It's a lot easier."

"Any plans for the holidays?"

"Jack's going to the Philippines for some snazzy wedding. It must be some high-society shindig. The family is putting up all the guests at the swankiest hotel in Manila and paying all expenses."

"Has he asked you to go with him?"

"No. He knows I would never leave Germaine for that long, especially over the holidays."

"So have you met any of his friends, other than the Belvedere people?"

"I've met two. One of them is a close friend—a psychologist named Damon Vanderveer. He's a lot of fun. And a psychiatrist they both know, Murielle Hand, who has known Jack for many years. She has the most loving and perceptive eyes. When I met her, it was as though she immediately knew all about me."

"Jack probably told her about you. What's their relationship?"

"Maybe Jack used to see her professionally. They're friends, is all I know."

They returned to the office rosy-cheeked and refreshed from the brisk walk.

Darrel summoned Mercedes into his office when she passed by.

Jack and Stuart were in with Darrel. Jack acknowledged Mercedes without missing a beat. He reported that he had finally made contact with Rand Taylor's elusive former fiancée, Anne-Charlotte Anderson, PhD. She was now married and going by a different name, and was no longer a consultant at Franjipur. She had agreed to meet with Jack "off the record," but said she wouldn't testify.

"Why would she meet you at all?" Darrel asked.

"Because Jack asked her to," Stuart piped up, with a slight smirk.

"I'll fly to New York and take her to lunch as soon as we can get our schedules in sync. Since she was an independent contractor, she'll have a clear perspective on the company's management decisions. And of course she's our hook to punitive damages, based on Rand's emotional distress claims."

"Which is why you'll handle her with kid gloves," Darrel said. "Mercedes, please find me that research you did on Dr. Anderson a few weeks ago. Then I have another task for you. We received Franjipur's first response to our document requests late this morning. There are many boxes. You should get started on those right away."

"Sure thing."

Turning back to Jack, he asked, "So what's she doing now?"

"Teaching at NYU under her married name. Doesn't want us to rock the boat and made it clear she doesn't want her prior life to interfere with her present one."

Darrel nodded at Mercedes, who left the room. She retrieved her research for Darrel and began work on the boxes of documents stacked in the empty office. She was so absorbed by their contents that she hardly noticed the brilliant sunset.

Until Jack called her on the office line.

"Why don't you bring Germaine over on Saturday? I could hire a sitter for the evening, you and I can go out, and you two can stay over in the guest room."

"I thought we were 'taking it slow.'"

"And I want you to know you're doing an excellent job of that," he chuckled. "Damon's niece would be perfect as a sitter. I've known her since she was younger than Germaine, and she's now in high school. If she's free, we could go out and there would be no late-night drive back to Oakland. Germaine would have a great time."

"There would be no living with her after a night at James Bond's place. And I'm not sure I could fall asleep knowing you were in the next room."

"There's a remedy for that."

"That is *not* a remedy for sleeplessness!"

"Okay, an alternative."

"Let me think about it and I'll let you know."

She was hot all over when they hung up.

⟡

DAMON'S NIECE, GISELLE, WAS A rangy redheaded girl, athletic, with a freckled nose and a ready laugh. She and Damon had the same eyes. She had three little sisters and knew just how to take Germaine under her wing the moment she arrived.

Jack carried their overnight bag to the guest room and turned on a lamp.

"Please, make yourself at home," he said, kissing Mercedes's cheek. "You look absolutely gorgeous."

Her hair was wound up into a smooth French roll and she wore the crimson dress that Eleanor had recently sent her.

They left the girls bantering in the kitchen with rock 'n' roll blaring on the speakers. Germaine was shaking her little body to the music, while they decorated cookies with colored sugars. A rainbow of sparkles glistened on the countertop.

"Stay out as late as you like, Uncle Jack!" Giselle called out as he reached for the door.

"Yeah, Mom! We're watching a scary movie after this! Don't come back too soon!"

Jack looked at Mercedes. "She sounds heartbroken that you're leaving."

"Crushed."

⚬❦⚬

THEY SAT AT A SMALL candlelit table in a North Beach restaurant. Although the chef was a celebrity and the food five-star, they were scarcely aware of it. The aura of ease with which Jack surrounded himself now included her. He made her feel like an extension of himself, a queen, wherever they were, whatever they were doing.

"You're in a pensive mood tonight, Bella."

"I was just thinking that we could be dining at a truck stop in Bakersfield and I would be just as happy."

"The truckers would be a whole lot happier, too. You've turned my world inside out and upside down."

"You don't look it, Mr. Bond. A little stirred, perhaps, but definitely not shaken."

"And then there's your charming daughter."

Mercedes's large eyes glowed in the candlelight above the intense red of her dress.

He reached across the table for her left hand and spread it out on his palm. "It's a long hand," he said.

"Look who's talking."

"No nail polish, no frills." He turned it over and touched her calluses, then turned it over again. "It looks a little bare, though."

"Jewelry just catches on things and gets in the way."

"Very pragmatic."

"I'm a realist."

"So I've noticed. And how is that working out for you?"

Mercedes raised her eyebrows. "You tell me. We're here, aren't we? Not too bad."

"What if it could be better?" His eyes were soft in the candlelight.

"I'm just fine where I am."

After dinner they walked awhile in the crisp air and eventually arrived at his car. "My life was empty without you and I didn't even realize it," he said. "Now I can't imagine it without you."

She kissed him to stop the conversation.

"I don't want to live without you, Mercedes."

"Shhh. We have no control over that."

"We *do*. We could get married."

"You must have drunk more wine at dinner than I thought."

"I'm serious."

"It's too soon for this!"

"I'm almost forty and feel as though I just woke up from a deep sleep. I don't want to waste another year."

"You haven't wasted anything. You've been sorting out your past and becoming a great guy."

Now he kissed her to stop the conversation. "Just tell me you'll think about it."

"Okay," she whispered.

⸰⸰⸰

LOW LIGHTS ILLUMINATED JACK'S LIVING room when they
returned late in the evening. Giselle waved from the couch, where
she was watching the end of a movie on TV. She pulled on her
sneakers and gathered up her things, reporting to Mercedes on the
evening with Germaine.

Mercedes went in to check on her daughter. She lay sound asleep
in her cotton pajamas, sprawled out in the center of the bed, nestled
among the down pillows and comforter. The bathroom showed signs
of extravagant use. The lotions and powder were out, along with
Germaine's toothbrush and hairbrush. A damp Turkish bath sheet
was draped over the towel rack, and both shower heads were wet.
Mercedes laughed to herself, picturing her skinny little girl trying
out all the features of the bathroom, then engulfing herself in Jack's
dark blue towel.

She closed the guest room door behind her and followed the
sounds to the kitchen, where Jack was pouring drinks.

"Well?"

"Out like a light."

"Looks like they got on well."

She stood on the wood floor in her heels, with her back to the
dark granite counter. He took a step forward, facing her. She looked
up into his eyes and raised her arms in surrender. He put his arms
around her, held her tenderly, and kissed her. Then he reached
down, slowly lifted her skirt, grasped the backs of her thighs and
buttocks in his palms, and elevated her to the counter. She wrapped
her legs around him and crossed her ankles, her crimson dress
splayed out all around her like the petals of a giant red blossom. He
kissed her passionately, tasting her, feeling her ribs with both hands,
and moving up her back, to the clasp of her bra.

She was pulling the hairpins out of her hair, releasing the French roll into a cascade, when in the back of her mind an alarm faintly sounded. She unlocked her legs and broke away from his kiss to catch her breath. She had to get off the flow of hot lava they were riding.

"Jack, you will set us both on fire."

"Bella, I want you right here, right now."

She moved back on the countertop, picked up her glass of water, and put her left hand on his chest, pushing him back a few inches. She looked down at his trousers, distended enormously, then up at the sheepish expression on his face. Jack was no more in possession of his faculties than she was of hers, nor did he care. She scooted back a few more inches until she rested against the wall, the edge of the counter behind her knees. He removed her shoes and grasped her feet in his palms. His hands ran up the silky hosiery to her knees, then toward her inner thighs. She drank the rest of her water and asked for a second glass, handing him the empty one.

When he turned to fill it she slipped down and out of the room, into the guest room and into the bathroom, closing doors behind her. She looked in the mirror to see a flushed woman in a red dress whom she barely recognized. Love made her look younger. Desire made her look more desirable. She could not remember the last time she'd felt such a craving for a man. She washed her hands, put her cold wet fingers on the back of her neck, and concentrated on the sensation of the cold tile beneath her feet.

Jack was reclined on the couch when she returned, her full water glass on the coffee table before him. The lights of the city sparkled like a vast galaxy. His eyes followed her as she approached.

"Hope I didn't scare you off." He had removed his shoes. The full length of the splendid man was prone, the sleeves of his fine white shirt rolled up to the elbows. She imagined unbuttoning the rest of his shirt, then quickly redirected her thoughts.

"I don't think *scare* is quite the word," she said, taking the chair next to the couch. She sipped her water. "We did make a deal before I agreed to spend the night. You could still wake up tomorrow, realize I'm just a girl you like to dance with, and that would be that. Poof. Dream over."

"It's not going to happen."

"We'll see. There's no rush, is there?"

"There is, Bella!"

"I know, I know, you're turning forty and you have sixteen gray hairs and your clock is ticking. It feels like the middle of the night," she said, to change the subject.

"I think it is. I hope you have everything you need," he said, nodding toward the guest room.

"Of course we do."

Soon she padded into the guest room and closed the door solidly behind her. Jack turned off the lights and the music, and gazed out at the city from his darkened fortress.

⸎

WHEN MERCEDES AWOKE, she was alone. The room was so dark she had no sense of the time and was shocked to see 10:30 on the illuminated clock. She lay in the soft bed and listened. She could hear the low rumble of Jack's voice and Germaine's high one out in the living room. She warmed at the thought of the two of them, working on the morning crossword puzzle.

She opened the shutters to a foggy morning. Her heart leapt with excitement when she recalled their last conversation. While she showered and puttered around in the bathroom, she imagined living this way for the rest of her life—with a loving husband who enjoyed Germaine's company in such a kind and paternal way, someone who thought of them as giving purpose to his existence, never taking them for granted.

Germaine came in with a glass of fresh-squeezed orange juice and a mile-wide grin. Jack had shown her how to work the juicer. They had warmed up cinnamon rolls and made coffee, and had been busy planning the day. She hugged her mother.

Could life really become so easy? Mercedes wondered. Jack had always made his life *look* easy, but she knew now that he had suffered greatly and worked hard to overcome many obstacles. Despite a sad childhood, he had been able to capitalize on adversity.

She pulled on jeans, a rose-colored sweater he'd given her, and the Ferragamo boots. She emerged feeling rested, hungry, and eager to see him. He stood up when she entered the room, then kissed her tenderly on the cheek.

⁂

THEY WENT TO BRUNCH AND then to the aquarium in Golden Gate Park. While Germaine was watching the fish in one of the darkened rooms, Jack came up behind Mercedes and embraced her, pulling her back toward him, nibbling her ear.

"I came very close to kidnapping you from your sleep last night," he whispered. "I kept thinking of you lying under my roof at last, and what I would like to do to you."

They separated just in time to see Germaine turn, looking for them, pointing at iridescent blue-and-yellow-striped fish in one of the tanks. Jack bent over to approximate her height and silently mimicked the fish, opening and closing his mouth. She laughed and clapped her hand over it. He fluttered his long arms behind him as though they were fins and "swam" past Germaine, who was in giggles at his antics.

⁂

LATER, AS THEY PARTED, Jack bowed and kissed Germaine's hand as he always did when saying good-bye, and held the door of the Beetle for her. She threw her arms around him in a burst of affection. He closed his eyes, patting the back of the sweet, gawky little girl in glasses and pigtails who had won his heart. Then he made his fish face, and she swatted his arm.

⸱⸰⸱

THEY PULLED UP TO THE pink palace in the waning daylight. Mr. Friedman's car was gone. When Mercedes unlocked the front door, Saturday's mail lay on the floor inside, beneath the mail slot, as usual. But something was terribly wrong with the desk. All of its drawers were either standing open or overturned on the floor, with their contents scattered everywhere. Letters were removed from envelopes, photos and desk supplies were strewn all over the floor. Germaine clutched her mother's arm. Mercedes scanned the room. The TV was missing. A lamp was gone. The Venetian blinds were bent and the windows were still locked from the inside. She signaled to Germaine to remain silent as they crept into the kitchen, listening for any sound from the back of the house.

The kitchen drawers were all open. Mercedes went immediately to the drawer where she had kept her grandmother's silver. The drawer was empty. Food remnants were on the counter and the table; an empty milk carton sat on top of the refrigerator. All the kitchen knives were missing. The cooking sherry and her only bottle of wine were gone, too.

They walked together into Mercedes's room, which looked as though it had been hit by a storm. All of her underwear had been taken out of the drawer and scattered across her now-rumpled bed. Each pair of panties and every bra had been handled by a stranger.

She winced. Her small jewelry box was missing and the dresser drawers were all open, thoroughly rifled.

She remained silent, on high alert. Her bedroom windows were still locked. The closet door was open, its contents ransacked, hangers and clothes dumped on the floor, her other purse turned inside out. Only one item remained undisturbed: the basket from Senegal.

Together they walked back through the kitchen toward Germaine's room, where a window was wide open. A screen had been forced off and the curtains fluttered in the breeze. The closet door was open, but nothing seemed to be missing. Her little single bed looked untouched, along with her toys and schoolbooks. The beautiful new globe still sat on a small desk.

In the bathroom, the toilet seat was up. Urine ran down the front of the bowl and onto the floor. One of Mercedes's lipsticks lay uncapped beside the sink. "BICH!" was scrawled in pink letters covering the mirror. The towels were rumpled and the shower curtain had been thrown back. Dirt was tracked in throughout the house.

When they were certain no one was lurking anywhere inside, Mercedes carefully closed and locked Germaine's window, taking precautions not to disturb any fingerprints. The back door was unlocked, so they looked outside. There were muddy footprints under Germaine's window.

Mercedes turned on the wall heater, phoned the police, and sat down on a kitchen chair. Germaine curled up in her lap and remained there while they waited. The front doorbell rang. Mercedes felt queasy recalling the last time two policemen had stood at her door.

The officers walked all through the house and dusted for fingerprints. They sat with mother and daughter in the living room and made a list of all the items Mercedes could identify as missing. There was little hope of retrieving the stolen property, they said, and the officers were surprised the house had not been burglarized before. There were no security bars, no alarm system, or menacing dog to protect it. They assured Mercedes they would check the pawn shops, but it was a low-priority crime.

Feeling dejected, they began putting their things back in order. Mercedes felt as though she'd been kicked in the stomach. She was repulsed by the thought of strangers in their house, eating their food, fouling their bathroom, playing with her underwear, leaving profanity on her mirror—as if *that* were really necessary to make the point.

Germaine went back to her room. The window sills were now blackened with the powder used to dust for fingerprints. It gave her the creeps to think of unknown men breaking into her private space. She went to help Mercedes put the desk back in order.

"I guess they were hoping to find money in these old letters," Mercedes muttered.

"Mom, aren't you going to call Jack?"

"Not right now. This is our business and something we have to take care of. Jack loves us, but we must always stand on our own feet. Nothing truly valuable can be stolen. The real things are inside here," she said, lightly tapping Germaine's heart. The girl grasped her mother's meaning; but while some things could never be stolen, it also seemed true that other things could never be repaired.

Mercedes's bedroom was by far the most ransacked room in the house. She collected all her undergarments and put them in the laundry. The bald audacity of anyone doing this made her furious. She smoothed her bed where a mocking stranger had lain. She picked up all the clothes from the floor and hung them in the closet.

She thought about her lost jewelry and realized it included Eddy's and her wedding rings, which she'd been planning to give

Germaine when she was older. She looked at the basket from Senegal where it sat, unmolested.

Germaine left Mercedes alone and went into the bathroom, which stank of urine. She felt scared and sad, and wished they could call Jack. She wanted him to come over. He'd be able to reach the mirror, which she couldn't, for one thing. She looked at the disgusting word. The stupid person who'd written it couldn't even spell. The thought of anyone calling her mother that name filled her with rage.

She dragged in a chair from the kitchen along with window cleaner and a rag. She climbed up on the chair, sprayed the lipstick, and rubbed vigorously. The lipstick smeared and covered an even greater portion of the mirror, but at least the letters of the word were blurred beyond recognition. She kept spraying and rubbing harder, her little pink tongue sticking out, her brow furrowed in a scowl, her full determination on the target. Finally the glass came clean. She felt like scrubbing the entire room, the whole house, and the neighborhood too.

She went into her room and sprayed the blackened window sill. When Mercedes came to check on her, Germaine was sobbing, wiping the tears from her eyes angrily with the back of one hand and scrubbing furiously at the window sill with the other. Mercedes stood behind her and gently touched her daughter's shoulders until the girl was ready to turn around. They looked at each other with the same expression, tears in their eyes, lips pursed. Once again life had thrown them a curveball.

ELEANOR

Mercedes stood in the office kitchen reading an article that Simone had just handed her. It was a tribute to Rock Hudson, who had just died of AIDS after thirty years as one of Hollywood's favorite leading men. She filled her cup and returned to the spare office, where she was indexing Franjipur documents. Julie buzzed her on the intercom.

"Your father's on the line," she said. He seldom called her, and neither parent had ever called her at work.

"Dad?"

"Hi, Kid. Sorry to have to call you at the office, but your grandmother's had an accident, and we thought you should know right away."

"Is she okay?"

"She fell in the dining room, either early yesterday or maybe even the day before, according to the doctors. The housekeeper found her this morning and called an ambulance. She's in the hospital in Riverside."

"Poor Granny," she said mournfully.

"She has a broken hip and a head injury. She's unconscious and dehydrated, so they have her on an IV. It looks like we'll be flying out as soon as possible. Could you get away and come down?"

"I'll work it out," she said, filled with dread. "Love you, Dad."

"Love you too, Kid. See you soon."

She went over to the window and looked out. Suddenly everything seemed so dark. Poor Granny! She tried to imagine what it must have been like for her lying there on the floor hour after hour in pain, unable to get up, hoping for help to come.

Then the prospect of spending a few days with Eleanor infiltrated her thoughts.

Florida told her to take as much time as she needed. She wished her and her grandmother well.

When she resumed work on the Franjipur documents, the phone rang again. This time it was Jack, inviting her to lunch. It was a relief to hear his voice. Soon they were seated at their favorite Japanese restaurant. He was coughing a little and intermittently held a handkerchief to his mouth. Their late-night phone calls seemed to be taking a toll on him. By the time the red lacquered bento boxes arrived, she had filled him in on the news about her grandmother.

"You don't seem in any rush to see your family," Jack observed dryly. Then added, "What if I went down there with you?"

She looked up to see if he was joking. "Why would you want to?"

"Guess."

"I'd hate to ask you. You'd have to run the gauntlet."

"You're not asking me, I'm volunteering. Perhaps I can help. And I'd like to meet your parents."

She hesitated. He reached across the table and took her hand.

"We are not responsible for who our parents are or how they act. Trust me on this one. I'll go with you, and we'll make the best of it."

So it was settled.

WITHIN TWENTY-FOUR HOURS THEY were on their way to the hospital in a rental car driven by Jack. During the drive from the Ontario airport, as Germaine listened in the backseat, Mercedes recounted the history of her grandparents settling in Riverside. The old place had once been surrounded by orange groves, and no smog had obscured the view of the mountains. Some of Mercedes's happiest childhood memories were of visiting there and hearing the mourning doves cooing in the eaves.

Germaine was on an adventure. She loved riding on the airplane. The prospect of seeing her grandparents filled her with joy. She had no clear memory of her great-grandmother though, and didn't know what to expect. She had never met anyone so old before.

Philip Bell was waiting for them in the hospital's reception area. He was a lean, patrician man with harmonious features, thinning silver hair, and bushy white eyebrows. He held out his arms, and Mercedes and Germaine ran into them. His eyes were moist when Mercedes kissed him on the cheek and introduced him to Jack.

As they shook hands, Philip looked up into the younger man's face and took his measure. Jack looked into the older man's face and saw Mercedes's angular features and hazel eyes.

"This is a pleasant surprise," Philip said. "I hope you haven't been inconvenienced on our account."

"Not at all, sir. I've been looking for an opportunity to meet you. I hope my being here isn't an imposition."

Philip and Mercedes exchanged a meaningful look and hugged again.

"It's so good to see you, Kid. Glad you brought some reinforcements."

They checked in at the nurses' station and walked to the room where Elizabeth Stearn lay. An overdressed, perfectly coiffed woman in her late fifties stood at the bedside, holding forth with the staff. Heavy gold jewelry adorned her neck and ears, dangled from her wrists, and encircled several fingers. The scent of her French perfume filled the room. She wore an elaborate purple silk dress and impatiently tapped the toe of her designer pump as the nurse meekly recounted their efforts to awaken Elizabeth.

The frail, white-haired patient looked no larger than Germaine. She was propped up on pillows with IVs running into both arms. The heart monitor made quiet beeping noises. Her eyes were closed, her expression peaceful. The other bed in the room was empty and the curtain between the beds pulled back, exposing a picture window that faced the parking lot.

The commanding woman turned with a start when Philip cleared his throat and announced, "Eleanor, we have visitors."

"Grandmother!" Germaine exclaimed and ran to Eleanor, who hugged her fiercely. Mercedes gave her mother a quick peck on the cheek, but Eleanor was already looking past her to the gentleman in a charcoal gray suit and royal blue tie who seemed to fill the doorway.

Jack smiled and fixed his gaze on Eleanor, who let go of her granddaughter and took a step in Jack's direction, holding out her right hand to be kissed.

Philip said, "Eleanor, this is Mercedes's friend, Mr. Jack Soutane, who has been kind enough to leave his law practice and join us."

Ever gallant, Jack bowed and kissed the bejeweled hand. "Mrs. Bell, it is an honor."

"Oh please, call me Eleanor," she said, clearly stunned by his looks.

Mercedes crossed her arms. Watching her parents' thinly veiled astonishment, she basked in the satisfaction of having been underestimated yet again, and by such a wide margin.

Germaine turned her attention to the tiny woman in the hospital bed. She stared at her aged, oval face. She hesitated, then held her great-grandmother's hand, which was nearly as white as the bedding. Even the fingertips had wrinkles. Germaine watched her with fascination and wished she would wake up.

Mercedes bent over her grandmother and lifted her other hand a few inches off the blanket to kiss it. Elizabeth's eyes fluttered in her sleep. Mercedes bent over farther and kissed the old woman's cheek, then began talking softly into her ear.

Eleanor glowered at Mercedes. "She can't hear anything. You're wasting your breath."

Mercedes ignored her mother. Eleanor sniffed, and asked a new nurse who had entered the room about the medication schedule. She then announced, without discussion, that they should all go to "the house" at once. She gave Jack a beatific smile, then held out her hand for Germaine. The girl left the bedside and thrust her small hand into Eleanor's. As they filed out of the room, Jack put his hand on Mercedes's back and stroked gently downward, as if smoothing ruffled fur.

In the parking lot, Germaine climbed into the back of the red Cadillac her grandparents were driving and waved to Mercedes, who winked at her. Jack and Mercedes took a moment just to sit in the rental car as the Cadillac pulled out of the driveway. He put his arm around her shoulders with an amused expression on his face and kissed her cheek.

He said, "Now I know."

"Now you know what?"

"Now I know why you're so reserved."

They broke out laughing.

AN IVY-COVERED EMBANKMENT CREATED a barrier between the tree-lined road and the old estate at the foot of Mount Rubidoux. A long, curving brick walkway led through dappled shade across the well-maintained grounds. Gardenia bushes surrounded the mansion and its deep veranda. Freshly painted green shutters flanked the large windows. Jack and Mercedes walked hand in hand toward the open front door, where Philip was waiting for them. Eleanor was not in view, but her bold voice could be plainly heard instructing the housekeeper.

They entered a high-ceilinged drawing room, carpeted with oriental rugs and furnished with exquisite antiques. There was a massive brick fireplace in the center, with an oil painting of the Hudson River Valley hanging over the mantelpiece. A grandfather clock stood off to the side and chimed the hour. There were three separate sitting areas in the stately room. Two double doorways led to other rooms.

Entirely oblivious to Eleanor, Philip struck up an easy conversation with Jack, while Mercedes went off to find Germaine. The curious child was wandering down the hallway, exploring. Eleanor summoned them to the kitchen, in a voice that raised the hair on Mercedes's arms.

"If the old gal can no longer live on her own here, I guess we'll have to arrange home care or move her," Philip was saying to Jack.

"There are a lot of options, particularly when one has assets," Jack assured him. "I'm a probate and estate planning lawyer, and my clients deal with this all the time. As I'm sure you realize, a lot depends on whether Elizabeth has already made arrangements or put anything in writing, and how mentally competent she is."

Philip invited Jack into the study. They crossed the hallway and entered a spacious wallpapered room overlooking the back gardens. An oak rolltop desk with an old manual typewriter on it faced the windows. Philip poured himself some scotch from a crystal decanter and served Jack a drink.

They talked about the superpower summit in progress in Geneva, expressing admiration for both Reagan and Gorbachev. Philip was pleased that Jack seemed to share his views on foreign policy. The younger man was extremely well informed. Moreover, he was respectful and elicited Philip's opinions. Philip felt as though he'd met a younger version of himself.

They sat in wing back chairs, looking out through a portico covered by trumpet vines to a small grove of citrus trees. Jack admired the bounty of green fruit on the trees and watched the gardeners at work.

"All of this was acquired by Eleanor's father in another era. This room was his. Mercedes can give you the full tour. Enormous place—five bedrooms upstairs and two more down here. How long can you stay?"

"Just a few days. If I can be of any assistance, I'm at your service."

Philip said confidentially, "Mercedes isn't one to talk much about herself, as you may have noticed, but she has mentioned you. We've been very happy to hear her sounding so much more positive about life this last year or so, after the trouble she's been through."

"I find her to be quite fascinating."

"The Kid is all right," Philip said proudly.

"I'm a subtenant of the Crenshaw firm. She's working on a case I brought in last year."

"She seems to enjoy her work."

"She's insightful and unconventional. She's done some investigating and writing, which have altered the direction of our inquiry. I'm happy for any time she gives me."

"You're a shrewd man."

Germaine appeared in the doorway, curious about what the men were up to. She ran in, plunked herself onto her grandfather's lap and petted the front of his soft gray cashmere sweater. He meowed loudly, and she giggled.

"Would you like a Shirley Temple?" Philip offered. "I have everything to make you one, just the way you like it."

"Oh, yes!" she exclaimed, leaping off his lap.

Philip hoisted himself to his feet and ambled toward the bar. A few moments later Mercedes quietly entered the room.

"Looks like you've found a peaceful spot amidst the storm," she said to the men.

"I was telling Jack here that you should give him a tour of the place. Maybe he'd like to meet the ghosts in daylight."

Jack rose from the chair and gave one of Germaine's pigtails a tug. She playfully swatted his hand.

"When you finish your drink with Grandpa, come find us, Sweetness," Mercedes told her.

She led Jack out of the study to the far end of the drawing room, where she recounted her grandparents' history. They had met in 1916, when he was twenty and she only sixteen. He had enlisted in the military before the beginning of World War I with an unquench-able desire to see the world and learn to fly. He became one of the country's first airmen. She showed Jack photographs of her grand-father standing beside an open-cockpit bi-wing airplane. There were pictures of him with his young bride, of the house when they first bought it, and of Eleanor as a young girl.

By the time World War II broke out, he had been promoted to general and was later given a European command. She showed Jack photographs of General Stearn in his uniform, seated at a com-mander's desk, surrounded by officers. Jack looked down at the floor and examined the colorful Turkish carpet, no doubt acquired by the general during his travels.

"It's too bad you'll never get to meet my grandfather," Mercedes said. "He was intensely interested in people and traveled more than anyone I've ever known. His stories could fill any evening with adventure. Grandmother's passion was antiquing," she gestured toward the furniture that filled the room. "Wherever they traveled, she made forays into the countryside and went to auctions in search of old things."

"Gabe and Kitty would be so interested in all this," Jack said.

⁂

MERCEDES LED HIM INTO THE formal dining room, where a sterling silver tea service sat on a long sideboard. An immense walnut table was surrounded by sixteen chairs under a chandelier dripping with crystals.

"We had some big dinners here when I was growing up. Grandfather sat at the head of the table there, and Granny sat here."

Eleanor appeared in the doorway. Her voluminous bangles, gold chains, and heavy bracelets announced her approach, so Mercedes had already stopped speaking. Eleanor stared at Mercedes, curious about the conversation she had just missed, and turned a doting eye on Jack. Her full lips were painted red and her large, beautiful eyes were outlined in black. Her arching eyebrows gave her a permanent expression of imperiousness, never to be surprised by the failings of others. Eleanor spared neither time nor expense on her appearance and felt superior to women who did otherwise—a category that invariably included her daughter.

Jack, insouciant as always, turned his loving gaze away from Mercedes and looked kindly upon her mother. Whatever her flaws, Eleanor had married a fine man and given birth to his beloved.

"I just got off the phone with the doctor in charge," she announced. "Granny has broken her pelvis and fractured her femur.

She is alarmingly malnourished and may be in the early stages of dementia. She will need twenty-four-hour care, probably in a convalescent hospital. It's worse than we thought."

You always expect the worst, thought Mercedes.

"How unfortunate," Jack said. "I hope they've made her comfortable. Mercedes has been telling me some of your family history. Mrs. Stearn seems to have led a fascinating life."

Mercedes reached out to comfort her mother but was promptly rebuffed. "There's no need for that," Eleanor said. "I'm perfectly fine."

Jack raised an eyebrow and checked Mercedes, who remained cool.

"If you like, I can investigate assisted living facilities while we're here," Mercedes offered.

"We'll see if that's really necessary."

Eleanor squinted at her diamond watch. "You finish showing Jack around, and I'll make some dinner reservations."

Mercedes resumed the tour she was giving Jack. Germaine left the study to join them as they mounted the winding staircase. Mercedes's luggage had been placed in a charming room with a pitched ceiling at the top of the stairs where she had always stayed as a child. A four-poster bed stood in the center of the room, covered in a vibrant handmade quilt nearly identical to the one on her bed in Oakland.

Next door, prepared for Germaine, was a room with two single beds and a great variety of antique dolls in handmade clothes, sitting in a cradle that had once held Eleanor. The dolls had been Eleanor's as well, and looked as though they'd traveled the world.

The three other bedrooms on the floor had not been inhabited in many years. In each of them, time seemed to have been suspended. Mercedes felt unseen eyes upon them and closed each door behind her as they exited, knowing that Germaine would feel better for her having done so.

"Closing this place up will be no small undertaking," Jack said.

"I think that's what's weighing on Mother," Mercedes said as they descended the staircase. Jack followed last and, seeing the backs of their heads, thought of the many female antecedents whose pictures hung in the drawing room.

Downstairs, Philip and Eleanor's suitcases were in what had once been General Stearn's bedroom. Elizabeth's room was on the other side of the bathroom, just as she had left it only a couple of days earlier on her fateful trek into the dining room. A marble-topped vanity with a gilt-framed oval mirror, worthy of any film star of Elizabeth's day, was positioned between the two windows. Elizabeth's legendary beauty had been preserved for as long as nature permitted.

Germaine opened the door to the walk-in closet and stood there with her mouth agape. It was nearly as big as her whole bedroom at home, and was packed with hat boxes, garment bags, handbags, countless racks of clothes, and shoes in every imaginable color.

THEY ALL DROVE TO THE hospital in the Cadillac, which belonged to Elizabeth. Philip talked to Jack about the history of the area and General Stearn's last post as commander of the nearby Air Force base. The visitors took turns at Elizabeth's bedside. She was groggy from medication, confused by her surroundings; her pale eyes squinted to focus on their faces. She struggled to recognize them and to understand why they were there.

Eleanor's impatience grew by the minute. She fidgeted with her jewelry and interrogated the nurse further about the prognosis. She wanted the situation to be resolved immediately.

Jack extended his arm to Eleanor and invited her to go for a walk with him. He didn't wait for a response, but hooked her hand onto his arm, put his other hand on top of hers, and guided her out of the room. Philip exchanged a look of understanding with Mercedes. Then he watched his daughter and granddaughter as they gently coaxed a smile from the ancient one in bed.

"We love you, Granny," Mercedes told her. "We'll come back to see you tomorrow and every day we're here. We're staying at the house. Everything is fine there. I have my old room at the top of the stairs and Germaine is staying in Mother's old room. Mother and Dad are staying in Grandpa's room while you're recovering from your fall. My friend Jack is staying in a hotel."

The more she spoke, the more Elizabeth seemed to grasp what was going on. She followed Mercedes's eyes and lips and looked between her and Germaine. She looked over at Philip, who waved at her. Signs of progress.

Jack and Eleanor returned in a jovial mood. Eleanor was expounding on the cruise from which she and Philip had recently returned. Her impatience temporarily abated, she was happy to see Elizabeth more responsive. She seemed, for the first time that day, actually happy to be in the company of her family.

⁂

DINNER WAS IN A NOISY Mexican restaurant that had been a family favorite since the general had befriended the owner more than thirty years earlier. There was a photograph of the two men in the entryway, which Jack spied instantly. When Señor Martinez heard that Eleanor Stearn and her family had arrived, he came out to greet them personally and made a sweeping bow before kissing Eleanor's hand. Germaine was ravenously hungry, excited by all the fanfare, and fascinated by the oversized sombreros and serapes on the walls.

Not long into the meal, after Señor Martínez had ceased fawning over her, Eleanor looked over at Jack and Mercedes, who were teasing each other a little too softly to be overheard. Philip was talking to Germaine, who was telling him all about school, the field trip planned for the spring, and the work they were doing in class to prepare for it. Entrees were served all around and still no one engaged Eleanor in conversation. Jack put a bite of the beef enchilada in his mouth and continued listening to Mercedes. Eleanor could bear it no longer.

She picked up her fork, reached across Jack's arm, and pierced his chile *relleño*, jabbing deeply into it to get a large bite onto her fork. The *relleño* squirted ingloriously onto the tablecloth and enchilada sauce spilled over the side of the plate, narrowly missing Jack's sleeve. Philip, Germaine, and Mercedes all stopped in mid-sentence and watched as Eleanor put the gigantic bite into her mouth. She stared defiantly into Jack's surprised face. He removed his left hand from the table and placed it in his lap.

"Grandmother!" Germaine cried out.

Mercedes flushed red hot but said nothing.

Jack looked down at his plate as Eleanor carved off another forkful of his beef enchilada, loaded with cheese and sauce, dripping more onto the tablecloth between them as she brought the fork to her gaping mouth. Mercedes put her face into her hands. Jack looked into Eleanor's face, held her eyes with his, and slid his plate toward her.

"Please, help yourself."

"I wanted to see if it was good enough for you."

"And is it?"

"I don't know. I may have to have another bite." She looked away from him and stared challengingly at her daughter without blinking. Mercedes excused herself from the table and fled to the ladies' room.

"That's all I wanted," she replied, dismissively, and pushed the plate back toward Jack.

Germaine looked at her grandfather, shocked. He shrugged his shoulders and poured himself another margarita.

S E A L E D *with a* K I S S

Mercedes walked up the path to the old house alone, heavy of heart. Philip and Eleanor had dropped her off after a discouraging visit to the hospital and had taken Germaine on an excursion.

Once Elizabeth's condition stabilized, she would be moved to a convalescent hospital, and when her bones were healed from the fall, she would be moved to an assisted living facility. She was not able to care for herself any longer, and had suffered neglect enough over the past few years. Her days in the grand home were over.

Eleanor had directed Mercedes to begin purging old clothes from her grandmother's bedroom, starting with the campaign chest at the foot of the canopy bed. The trunk was full of the tiny woman's hand-knitted dresses and silk shawls, along with memorabilia dating back to the 1940s. Like every cupboard and cabinet in the house, it would have to be sorted through. *But not immediately,* Mercedes thought.

She walked into Elizabeth's bedroom, sat down in the soft pink chair, pulled out a phone book, and began researching elder care facilities in the area. She made many calls and filled several pages with notes her parents could use. Next she called the airlines. There was room on the return flight that Jack was taking the following day, so she changed their reservations.

Both parents had vied for Jack's attention the last two days. Philip had taken him under his wing and the two seemed to be old friends already. Eleanor was hell-bent on learning every detail of his personal life. She'd been ecstatic to hear that both his parents had graduated from Stanford, and that his father had been a high-society physician.

Jack parked under a royal palm on the side of the house and came in through the kitchen door. The lovely old estate had begun to feel like home. He liked the grandeur of its many rooms and the pastoral beauty of the grounds. It was a big man's house.

Mercedes ran to greet him and he leaned over to kiss her, pulling her arms around him. The resonant silence of the house enveloped them.

"Where is everybody?"

"On an outing."

"What do you want to do?"

"Let's go for a walk," she said.

High clouds and thick haze obscured the sun. The light seemed to come from everywhere at once, leaving no shadows.

They walked steadily up the inclining road, amidst the warning calls of the quail in the brush and mockingbirds perched on posts. Neighborhood cats skulked in the undergrowth. How remote the affairs of the office now felt; how long it seemed they'd been gone. And to think, on the other hand, that Elizabeth had lost her home in an instant!

They reached an overlook where a sturdy wood bench had been installed on the edge of a steep drop, sequestered from the road by a thicket. They sat down to take in the view of the populous valley below, dotted with swimming pools, transected by roads and freeways. A small airplane flew past, towing a glider. The sun became faintly visible through the overcast, like a silver dollar suspended over the scored and cratered landscape. They leaned back to rest in the cool, fragrant air. Jack put his arm around Mercedes's shoulders. A soft breeze rustled the leaves and her hair.

"I'm really glad I came with you," he said quietly. "Now more than ever I believe we're right for each other. You have every quality I could possibly want in a life partner. You're kind, dependable, intelligent, beautiful, and a lovely mother. And you have a great deal of forbearance."

She chuckled.

"You have character and you come from a fine family. Every time we go out, I'm proud to be by your side. I know I'll never get tired of talking to you, of looking at you, of enjoying your sense of humor. I'm a very lucky man and I know it."

"I think I can provide well for you and Germaine," he offered. "I want to make you happy. I want to be a worthwhile stepfather to Germaine. She certainly deserves one. I want to show her the world. I want to help her reach for the stars. You've made my life magical and I love you as I have never loved another human being. I cannot imagine the future without you."

"Mercedes, will you marry me?"

He looked at her beseechingly, while she cast her eyes over the valley. The sun broke through the overcast. She felt doors opening all around her and inside her.

"Of course I'll marry you. I'd be thrilled to be your wife! Besides, Germaine would kill me if I said no."

He took her face in his hands and kissed her squarely on the mouth, just as he had the first time.

How different the world looked when she opened her eyes. Jack was studying her face. He was hers now, forever, and she was his. They would be by each other's side through middle age into old age, as their hair turned gray and they became wrinkled with the years like Elizabeth.

Her heart raced as they clutched each other, laughing and kissing and crying with joy. It was a miracle, the answer to her prayers, reparations for all her suffering. Life as she and Germaine had known it was forever changed.

"Oh, we're going to have such a great life together," he proclaimed.

Mercedes envisioned waking up next to Jack every morning and finally being able to make love to him. As if reading her mind, he pulled her up onto his lap and wrapped his hands around her, feeling muscle and bone, and the soft places where a husband's hands might freely roam. She would soon be his entirely, one heart and one flesh.

Three crows landed in the branches overhead. One cawed, another croaked, and the third chortled deep in the back of his throat. Mercedes looked up. The third crow turned his head sideways and looked at her with a shiny black eye, his blue-black feathers as smooth as oiled wood.

Jack kissed her neck, buried his face in her hair, and inhaled her womanly scent as if he would never get enough.

"Bella, you're going to be my wife! I just can't believe it."

"I can't believe it either," she murmured.

Presently the crow chortled again and took flight, followed by his two companions.

Jack and Mercedes descended the mountain and entered the house. She fixed a plate of food, which they were sharing on the couch in the living room when Germaine bounded through the door. She was hauling two large shopping bags and was dressed entirely in new clothes. Mercedes clapped her hands over her mouth. Nearly all of her daughter's long, thick, glossy hair was gone. What remained was a pixie haircut, shorter by far than Eleanor's.

Next through the door came Eleanor, wearing gray cotton gloves and a broad-brimmed magenta hat that matched her dress. A magenta-and-gray handbag was draped over her arm, which she held out at an angle for maximum effect. The ever-patient Philip followed, laden with more bags, which he set down on the carpet. He greeted them and headed straight for the study to make himself a cocktail.

Germaine spun around to show her new navy blue polka-dot dress, red petticoat, and beautifully tailored navy blue coat, patent leather shoes, white leggings, and, of course, the haircut. The gawky little girl who left the house in braids and loafers had returned a chic young lady. Her long, beautiful neck was now visible beneath the short hair. Mercedes was speechless. Jack smiled at Germaine's obvious delirium.

"Mama, Grandmother took me to a real beauty salon and had all my hair cut off! Then she took me shopping and bought me all these new clothes!"

"So I see! That was very . . . generous of your grandmother—and of Grandpa," Mercedes said without looking at Eleanor.

Eleanor, for her part, focused a taunting stare at Mercedes.

"*Someone* had to do *something*. The poor child looked like a vagabond. I couldn't have her running around town that way any longer. People must be wondering what in the world has become of me to allow my only grandchild to . . ."

Seeing Jack's eyes narrow and his smile fade, Eleanor stopped talking, reclined on a nearby chaise, and sighed. The spikes of her gray suede high heels protruded like ice picks. Jack looked at Mercedes and Germaine, and felt a new appreciation for Philip's love of alcohol.

Germaine frowned and deposited her bags near her mother. Mercedes put her hands on Germaine's fragile shoulders. The child looked into her mother's eyes, the frown intensifying into a scowl.

In a soft voice Mercedes said, "I think you always look nice, and you looked fine this morning when you left the house. You're always neat and clean and well mannered and nice to people. You're a smart, good girl. Other people's opinions of you don't matter nearly as much as what you think of yourself. And your grandparents love you, you know that. Grandmother didn't mean there's anything *wrong* with you. She just wanted you to have prettier clothes and a haircut *she* liked. Now why don't you show us what's in all these bags? It looks like Christmas in here!"

Mercedes stroked the back of her daughter's newly shorn head. She contained her fury and reminded herself they would be leaving the next day—a fact she could spring on Eleanor whenever she felt like it.

One by one Germaine went through the bags, pulling out lovely dresses, sweaters, shoes, slacks, blouses, pajamas, and even a navy purse —practically a new wardrobe. Eleanor's comments now forgotten, Germaine was her old exuberant self. Eleanor watched from the chaise, her seat of victory, enjoying her granddaughter's excitement and knowing that the new clothes would always remind them of her.

She kicked off her spiked heels and removed her enormous hat, which she carefully placed on the end of the chaise. In a shrill voice, she directed Philip to bring her a drink. Jack left the room and headed for the study.

Mercedes helped Germaine fold and gather all the new clothes and carry them upstairs to her room. When they were alone together, she asked, "So was the haircut something you wanted?"

"No, but Grandmother didn't give me any choice. She just took me to the salon and told them to do it. I said we should ask you first."

"How do you like it?"

"It feels kind of weird," she said, rubbing her exposed neck, "but Grandmother likes it. She says 'no girl with any style has long hair,'" imitating Eleanor, with her hands on her skinny hips, which she swung from side to side like Mae West.

Mercedes laughed. "I know, I know. I've heard it all my life. But it *does* make you look older, and it's very stylish. Your hair will grow, if that's what you want. I know you had a good time. What a lot of beautiful clothes you have!"

When they descended the staircase, the men's voices could be heard from the study. A discussion of Elizabeth Stearn's estate was under way. Ever the scrupulous lawyer, Jack always seemed to be working.

When the men emerged, Jack caught Mercedes's eye and a bolt of electricity passed between then. Now was the time to let their secret out of the bag.

Jack asked Germaine to come outside with them for a minute. She was immediately suspicious. She looked to her mother and then back to Jack, who put his finger to his mouth to indicate secrecy. This only heightened her suspense.

He led them to a bench in a copse of orange trees, in a far corner of the yard that couldn't be seen from the house. They sat down on the bench with Germaine in the middle.

"Your mom and I have some important news to tell you, before we tell anyone else."

Wide-eyed, the girl nodded and squeezed Mercedes's hand.

"What I've been hoping for a long time is that the three of us could be a real family. So today I asked your mother to marry me."

Germaine looked at Mercedes with wild expectation.

"And I said yes!" Mercedes exclaimed.

Germaine cried out and hugged her mother. Then she jumped

into Jack's lap, threw her arms around him, and exclaimed, "I knew it! I can't wait! You'll be my dad!"

Mercedes scooted over, Jack reached out his long arms to encircle them both, and Mercedes began to cry.

Germaine wiggled free. "Yippee!" she shouted, flinging her arms into the air. "Jack's going to be my dad!" She spun around on her tiptoes with her skinny little arms extended, a swirl of polka dots and red petticoats.

Jack started laughing and pulled out his handkerchief. He wiped Mercedes's face, which was streaming with tears even as she laughed at Germaine's antics.

"When will the wedding be?" Germaine asked. "I can't wait to tell Anne!"

Jack grinned. "As soon as your mother and I can plan it the way we want."

"Can I go tell Grandpa and Grandmother?"

"Absolutely," Mercedes replied.

Jack and Mercedes watched Germaine fly into the house as quickly as her legs could carry her, threading her way through the orange trees. She clattered up the steps to the kitchen, threw open the door, and shouted out the news at the top of her lungs.

They stayed behind, kissing on the bench beneath the bountiful trees. Jack slipped his hands beneath her sweater to touch the silky skin of her lean back.

"I just can't wait to make you mine," he whispered, "one hundred percent—*after* there is just the right ring on that finger." He ran two fingers up and down her ring finger. "It's a shame I can't just drag you upstairs right now and have my way with you." He collected a handful of her hair and gave it a yank. Mercedes laughed out loud.

"Oh, you don't know how tempting that is," she said, imagining her mother's horror at such behavior.

"Bella, my love," he said, "I think I do."

The minute they got back to the house, Philip vigorously shook Jack's hand, clapped him on the back, and welcomed him to the family. He swept Mercedes into his arms and kissed her cheek noisily.

"Everything's going to work out for you now, Kid, and your old man just couldn't be happier!"

Eleanor inclined her cheek for Jack to kiss and patted his arm patronizingly. Nothing much about Mercedes pleased her, but Jack was undeniably a catch. Her friends would be very envious of this son-in-law, who looked like a movie star and exuded charm. They would also be perplexed at how Mercedes had ever managed it, in light of all the scurrilous things Eleanor had reported about her over the years. There would be some explaining to do, but never mind that. First there was the wedding to think about: the guest list, what to wear, and innumerable arrangements that she must supervise.

Then, to her daughter, she gave a perfunctory hug. Embracing Eleanor was like caressing an armadillo, and just as much fun. Today she had fastened to her dress an especially large and prickly brooch. While Mercedes averted impalement, Eleanor barked at Germaine to settle down. The girl, who simply could not restrain her joy, ran off into the living room and threw herself, enthralled, upon the couch. Mercedes laughed and looked up at Jack, who was also laughing at Germaine's irrepressible glee.

Philip nodded his head. "That says it all."

Jack invited everyone to be his guests for dinner at a new restaurant. Philip, who had just poured his third drink, happily accepted.

⸙

AT THE RESTAURANT, Eleanor looked askance at her surroundings. Instead of a traditional place where she was sure to be recognized,

Jack had invited them to a sleek, modern restaurant, popular with a hip young crowd that favored its California nouvelle cuisine. Eleanor didn't know what to make of the spare, modern decor—the absence of tablecloths, carpets, and elaborate window coverings. Instead, there were exotic lighting fixtures suspended over polished wood tables and sleek black chairs. Eleanor glowered at the gay couple who sat at a nearby table, shamelessly holding hands. She scrutinized her menu and shot Philip more than one disgruntled look.

Philip, now three sheets to the wind, toasted the happy couple and winked at Germaine. He started to get up, presumably to make a speech, but Eleanor seized his hand and gave him a kick under the table. He sat down and emptied his glass.

LONG AFTER JACK HAD RETURNED to his hotel and everyone had retired, Mercedes lay curled up in the soft covers of the four-poster bed, in the soothing stillness of the night.

She was ascending a wide staircase a few steps behind Eleanor, several steps behind Elizabeth and a few ahead of Germaine. Elizabeth followed an infinite line of women whose shapes faded into the distance. Mercedes, on a landing, looked to the left, then to the right, then down.

The smooth marble of the stairs was cool under her bare feet. All four women wore loose white robes. Elizabeth looked as she had when a young bride. Her hair was blond again, and all her wrinkles had vanished. She beckoned them to follow. Eleanor, also young, had glossy brunette hair and full red lips. She went up the stairs reluctantly and looked back at Mercedes, as if to warn her. Tree branches hung over the banister. Germaine stooped to pick up a pecan shell and gestured to Mercedes. They looked over the banister at the adjacent forest. Then they were in the forest, following Elizabeth and Eleanor through the majestic trees, whose leaves shimmered in the breeze. Sunlight slanted through the branches to the forest floor.

Mercedes sat cross-legged in her special spot and inhaled the cedar-scented air, transfixed by the branches swaying high up in the canopy.

"All of life is one continuous flow of energy, of which you are an integral part," a voice said. "All parts are interconnected, interdependent, and conscious. Energy never dies, cannot be disturbed or harmed. This truth is innate in every human being and is eternally accessible to those who wish to find it."

A great horned owl glided silently past Mercedes's window as she slept. The light of the full moon shone on the bird's back, making its silhouette visible below. Another owl hooted from a nearby magnolia tree as it circled in the cool air. The quiet earth was awash in moonlight. A large rat darted out of the ivy into the street and down the gutter. The vault of heaven above was filled with stars, billions and billions of stars that shone even during the day, when they could not be seen by the creatures of the earth.

THE DOOR CLOSES BEHIND

Mercedes let out a sigh when the front door of the pink palace closed behind her. They were back to the ghetto's tumult. Mercedes thought wistfully about how quickly they had acclimated to the bucolic setting of her grandmother's home, where the loudest sounds came from the gardeners' tools and from Eleanor. She missed its surroundings and their little house seemed so empty without the men.

Philip had slipped a roll of cash into her pocket when they parted. "Put some meat on those bones," he said, "and let us know how we can help with the wedding. It's about time things straightened out for you. Your mother and I just couldn't be happier with Jack. He's an excellent addition to the family."

Germaine ran to phone Anne with the news. Mercedes began unpacking and fitting Germaine's new wardrobe into her small closet. The delight she heard in Germaine's voice made her smile. As she hung up the polka-dot dress, she envisioned the child again, twirling with joy, shouting that Jack was going to be her dad.

They left the house to go to the big, new grocery store in Piedmont, near their old neighborhood. They took their time and filled the shopping cart to the brim. They parked in the driveway and brought the bags in through the side door, to avoid notice in the neighborhood, lest it prompt another burglary. They sang along with the radio as they unloaded the bounty, stuffing their cupboards with food and supplies.

After Germaine was tucked in, Jack called.

"I'm getting addicted to you," he said. "I want you here with me."

She twisted the phone cord around her finger.

"Listen," he continued, "I know just the place to take you ring shopping. It's the store where my father bought my mother's engagement ring, which I still have, actually. But it would be lost on your hand."

"I'd be happy to wear your mother's ring."

"I know you would, but it's small, and I can't have my friends thinking I'm a cheap bastard. I wonder if you'd mind not telling anyone at the office just yet."

"Germaine just called Anne. She's so excited. So Caroline will know, but she's discreet. When Germaine goes back to school, it'll be very tempting for her to share her news."

"They're going to be quite surprised by her transformation."

Mercedes laughed. "It's fine with me if you make the announcement—then you can answer all the questions."

"I'll be your mouthpiece," he chuckled.

"Then be careful what you say."

"I've had an excellent teacher."

"Your training hasn't even begun," she teased.

"I could say the same to you, my love."

⊷⧓⊶

DURING MERCEDES'S ABSENCE, the Taylor case had been set for trial in early summer and had taken some interesting turns. Darrel was relieved to have her back and rattled off several assignments to be done as soon as possible.

Later in the day she walked into Caroline's office, where her friend sat immersed in reading. She looked up into Mercedes's eyes and said gleefully, "Anne told me your news. I want to hear everything!"

She told Caroline about her grandmother's condition, and about Jack meeting her parents. She gave a detailed account of the proposal and Germaine's ecstatic reaction to it. Caroline got to her feet, came around the desk, and hugged her.

"Isn't that wonderful! I'm so happy for both of you. When are you going to tell people?"

"Jack wants to take me ring shopping next Saturday, and make an announcement after that."

"Of course he does. Perhaps I should call you 'Your Highness' now."

"Oh please! Germaine is half out of her mind. My mother bought her a new wardrobe and had all of her hair cut off."

"That's radical."

"I hope you recognize her."

"It's easy to recognize your daughter. All I have to do is put a plate of food in front of her. If the food disappears instantly, it's Germaine." Mercedes laughed.

"Anyway, your secret is safe with us. And we would love it if Germaine could come over next Saturday, so take all the time you want ring shopping."

EVERY EVENING THAT WEEK, Germaine pored over her studies to catch up with her classes. She read intently, worked math problems, and mouthed words as she wrote a book report for English. She recited French vocabulary, searched the globe that Jack had bought her to locate the Congo, memorized a poem by Robert Frost, and clipped news articles for a social studies project.

The haircut had brought stillness to her. She no longer tossed her head to get hair out of her eyes; nor did she have a braid to twirl in her fingers or bite as she read. It was easier now to picture her as an architect, a journalist, or a lawyer.

Every night Jack called with ideas for the wedding. After his calls, Mercedes tossed and turned. He was a man on a mission, and they were steamrolling down the expressway to an elaborate wedding. He wanted her, and it, more than he had ever wanted anything, he said, and his perseverance showed it.

⚬∙≼∙⚬

FINALLY THE DAY FOR RING shopping arrived. Jack waited in front of Shreve & Company with his hands in the pockets of his black vicuña topcoat, a Black Watch tartan scarf around his neck. He was whistling happily and smiled when his fiancée approached.

"Hi, Beautiful! I see the old jalopy got you here in one piece."

She stood on her tiptoes to kiss him. "Don't start insulting my car just because we're engaged. Anyway, it adds soul to the streets of San Francisco."

"Yes, and with any luck it will be towed. Now come this way, *Madame*," he said with a grin and led her into the store.

He brought her over to a glass display case where a pleasant brunette sales clerk stood waiting. She was about Mercedes's age and introduced herself as Minette.

At Jack's signal, Minette pulled out a large diamond ring.

Mercedes slid it onto her finger as far as it would go and examined it closely.

A sudden panic set in and she felt the urge to run out the door, to escape all the wedding planning and commotion before them. What had come over her? She wanted to remain independent, to be free, and to preserve the peace she had fought so hard to create. Her heart throbbed, and she could scarcely breathe.

But then she looked at Jack's deadly handsome face, saw him watching her and maintaining his great poise. She saw his joy and charm, and she calmed herself. What was she thinking? A chance like this would never come her way again. She resolved to stay in the present, to think practically, and to evaluate the ring.

It was heavy and the design was unnecessarily complicated. She supposed it would get in the way when she was working. No doubt women who wore such rings had housekeepers and secretaries. She could not see herself becoming a woman like that. What was she getting herself into?

"Proportion is important. You have big hands and long fingers," he was saying. "If you choose something more typical, like a one-carat solitaire, it'll be lost on you." Minette drew a one-carat diamond ring from a nearby case. It was simple and, to Mercedes, stunningly beautiful—far beyond anything she would have presumed to pick out on her own. She put it on and admired it.

"This ring is beautiful. I would be very content with it. It's simple, classic—"

"And far too small," he interrupted.

"Oh, it is not," she protested. The stone was exquisite and sparkled in the light. It fit her finger perfectly and suited her taste.

"I like the sapphires," Jack said matter-of-factly. "They're different and show a little more imagination than diamonds. Let's have a look."

Again, Minette responded to his signal. She pulled out a lovely two-carat sapphire set with a small diamond on either side. Mercedes hesitantly pulled the diamond ring off her finger and slid the sapphire on. It was different, for sure, and she loved the brilliant blue.

Minette explained the difference between heat-treated and natural sapphires. This was a heat-treated sapphire, less expensive than it might be. Mercedes liked that and admired the ring. It was definitely striking, and the design was interesting.

"It's the color of your eyes," she said. Jack smiled and pointed to three much larger sapphire rings in an adjacent case.

"Let's have a look at those," he said. "I want to see a ring on your hand that will thrill you every time you look at it—something that will tell people about this great love we have, and about how your husband takes care of you."

He looked at her tenderly. Inside her, a million butterflies were in a frenzy.

She took off the sapphire ring and handed it back to Minette, who put it away and withdrew one of the enormous rings from the adjacent case.

"*Now* we're getting somewhere," Jack said.

Minette repeated these steps until Mercedes had tried on all three. They were all eye-poppingly beautiful, but the designs did not suit her. They seemed outlandish, like something a rock star would wear.

"Really, I prefer the diamond solitaire to any of these three rings," she said, "although the sapphires themselves are amazing."

Jack nodded to Minette, who walked down to a display case at the far end of the room. When she returned, she placed a closed ring box in front of Mercedes.

"This is a natural sapphire," Minette said, "one of the finest in our possession."

Mercedes opened the box and gasped. Inside was an extraordinary six-carat cushion-cut sapphire set in a bezel surrounded by brilliant pavé diamonds. She blinked her eyes and pulled it out of the box, turning it around to look at each angle before she slipped it onto her finger. It was the most exquisite piece of jewelry she had ever seen. It was neither oval nor square but something in between. Instead of being suspended on prongs, the bezel and surrounding stones were held in a platinum V-shaped basket. At the points of the V on either side were half-carat diamonds. Running down the shoulders of the ring were more diamonds. All told, there were forty-four diamonds and one perfect, glorious natural sapphire—pure magnificence from every angle, just like Jack. The ring was too loose, but the design and dimensions of the jewels precisely suited her hand.

She turned over the price tag and was stunned. It was a number greater than her annual gross salary, the price of a new luxury car. Jack immediately put his hand on hers.

"Forget about that," he said. "So what do you think?"

"I don't know! I can't believe my eyes," she stammered. "I've never seen a ring this beautiful before. It's too expensive. Oh, my Lord."

"I think this is it," Jack said. He looked up at the beaming clerk and told her: "We'll take it."

Mercedes gasped again and threw her arms around him.

"That's the reaction I was hoping for!" he exclaimed. He kissed her and winked at the clerk over Mercedes's shoulder. "How long will it take to get it properly sized?" he asked.

"It usually only takes a couple of days. I'll check with the jeweler to be sure."

Mercedes stared at the ring on her finger and held out her arm to see it from a distance. Jack drew her close while she gaped at the ring, completely astonished. He kissed her cheek, which was flushed bright red.

Reluctantly she removed the ring and put it back in the box. She stared at it a short while longer before closing the lid and nodding to Minette, who sized Mercedes's finger and then took the ring to the back room.

Mercedes looked at Jack and tears filled her eyes.

"Oh, Bella," he said softly, "I've wanted to do this for the longest time. I saw this ring awhile ago and hoped it would still be here if I could entice you into the store. It's perfect for you. I want you to remember this day and to know, regardless of what the future may hold, that I will love you forever."

"I don't know what to say," she stammered. "I'm flabbergasted." She looked at her fiancé. How was it possible for a man to be so perfect and to love her this way? He returned her gaze and said nothing.

Minette returned momentarily. The ring would be ready by Wednesday. Mercedes put it on one last time, feeling its weight, studying its captivating design further while Jack and Minette took care of business.

Afterwards, they strolled arm in arm toward Union Square and the gigantic Christmas tree bedecked with grand ornaments and lights. Holiday shoppers and excited children scurried across the square. All the display windows were decorated for Christmas. Santa Clauses stood in artificial snow drifts, their reindeer-borne sleds laden with packages and toys; mannequins in gorgeous holiday apparel watched the crowds pass by.

They walked through the double doors into the lobby of the St. Francis Hotel, turned left, and ascended the carpeted stairway into the lounge area. Two-story black marble pillars supported the ornate ceiling; all around the walnut paneling were antique furnishings.

They were escorted to a corner table where they sat, euphoric. The waiter brought menus, which they only pretended to examine.

"Jack, there's something else we need to do soon."

"Find a place for Germaine to stay overnight, you mean?" Beneath the tablecloth, his hand was advancing up her thigh.

"That too," she smiled, taking his wandering hand into both of hers. "But we need to take the HIV test."

His eyebrows shot up. "Is there something I need to know?"

"No more than I do about you. Face it, we've both been with other people and we don't know about the others those people have been with. We'd be crazy not to take the test, now that there is one."

"Good point. I just hadn't thought about it, Bella. I was thinking about next weekend, and how lovely you will look—dressed only in your engagement ring." He looked at her with the eyes of a hunter. "And right now I'm also thinking about what's on this menu. Sapphires always make me hungry."

"Then you have a lot of hungry years in front of you. You may become a fat old geezer yet."

"I'm counting on you to be part of my exercise plan."

"So what about the HIV test? We should have it done this week, don't you think?" she persisted.

He looked back down at the menu without changing expression.

"Yes, I'll have an HIV test and a bowl of chowder please," he joked. "And a glass of something alcoholic to celebrate the new car—I mean ring—we'll be putting on your finger. But seriously—you have no idea how relieved I feel now that we're engaged. I thought I was going to be an old fart who would die all alone, and now the future looks just smashing—absolutely smashing."

She laughed at his imitation of an English accent.

"You could have had any woman you wanted. But back to my suggestion—if we got tested in the next couple of days, we might have the results back by next weekend. I don't know how long it takes."

"I have to be in court on Monday, but I can take care of it beforehand. And as to your first comment, I never really wanted any woman before you. Not enough to marry. I didn't have the best role model for marriage, so it's never been a goal of mine."

"You can hardly say I've had a very good role model for marriage. Good grief!"

"At least Philip and Eleanor are still together. Your father is a nice man, who clearly loves you. You were well taught, whether you liked the methods or not."

"My father endures because of three things: his work, booze, and me. If he tried to leave, Eleanor would take him for all he's worth, out of pure spite."

"He must get something out of it. But let's not get into that. I don't want our marriage to be anything short of fabulous and, need I say, extremely rich in earthly delights." He kissed her hand again.

After they had eaten, Jack asked, "Why don't you come with me on a quick errand? I have to stop by Janine's apartment to take care of some things, and it's the perfect day to introduce you to each other— if you have time."

The legendary Janine Reneau, at last! "I'd love to."

THE TEMPERATURE WAS DROPPING OUTSIDE. Jack coughed into his handkerchief. A storm was brewing when they got out of his car in front of an unremarkable building. Mercedes was surprised. She'd imagined Janine living in a swanky apartment like Jack's, or in Pacific Heights, not in a rundown dwelling with a metal security gate instead of a doorman.

"She's lived in this same apartment for over forty years, if you can believe it."

He had keys, and led the way to the elevator lobby. They entered the small elevator and secured the metal accordion gate before the slow, rickety ascent began. When they reached Janine's apartment on the third floor, Jack rapped on the door and a slight, young Filipino man answered. As soon as he saw Jack he bowed, averted his gaze, and backed away. Jack introduced Mercedes to him—Enrique, Janine's current caregiver. He looked from her to Jack with great deference. Jack called out Janine's name and the door was quietly closed behind them.

The apartment was a small four-room unit with high ceilings, an ancient light fixture in the center of the entryway and faded flowered wallpaper. The ornate baseboard molding was thick with dust. None of the woodwork had been painted in a decade. Mercedes could see into a second room that appeared to be a living room. She glimpsed a settee covered in worn green mohair with crocheted doilies draped over its arms. An old-fashioned black phone, exactly like Elizabeth's, sat on a small table against the wall. The radiator hissed and poured more heat into the stuffy room. Enrique scurried across the faded carpet to the tiny kitchen to put on the kettle. Jack called Janine's name again, and a faint voice answered.

"Janine, I have a special visitor with me. Can you guess who it might be?"

Janine named a few names, none of which was Mercedes.

They entered the doorway together, hand in hand. The frail old woman sat in a rocking chair with a black shawl around her shoulders, squinting at them. Her snow-white hair was short, thin, and wavy; her skin had the pallor of one who was seldom outdoors. Her eyes were cloudy and pale blue. She wore round wire-rimmed spectacles, a flowered skirt, and matching blouse.

"Come closer, so I can see." Her hands gripped the wood arms of the rocker and she leaned forward. As Jack drew near, she smiled. He bent down and kissed her powdery cheek. He lowered his voice and took one of her hands, while still holding onto Mercedes.

"I've brought Mercedes to meet you, Janine." The old woman looked confused and her smile vanished. She looked up at the strange younger woman.

"You remember, last time I was here I told you about her?"

Janine nodded reluctantly.

"Well, last weekend I proposed to Mercedes, and she said yes!" His face was bright and expectant, like that of a young boy who had just done well and was waiting for praise. "I've been anxious for you to meet each other."

Mercedes, who was glowing from the day's events, leaned closer so the tiny old woman could see her more clearly.

"I'm very pleased to meet you, Miss Reneau. Jack has told me so many lovely things about you."

Janine nodded, said nothing, and pointed to a nearby chair for Mercedes to sit. The old lady turned to Jack as if to say: *Next topic, please. We'll pretend that never happened.*

Jack explained that he'd come by to check her mail and to make sure she was staying out of trouble.

She replied with a jest, "The coppers haven't come by to pick me up yet." She observed Mercedes, who shifted in her seat.

"Is Enrique doing his job okay?" Jack inquired.

She nodded affirmatively. Enrique came in with a tea tray and set it down on the small table. He poured each of them a cup, mixed Janine's the way she liked it, and brought it to her.

Jack excused himself, took his tea, and followed Enrique into the next room. The men spoke in soft voices for a few moments. Mercedes tried to engage Janine in small talk, but the old lady gazed vacantly forward, her eyes seemingly disconnected from the reality surrounding her.

Mercedes abandoned the effort, stood up, removed her coat, and walked around the room. On the wall was an old photograph of a severe-looking man in a stiff collar and dark coat. His dark hair was slicked down and parted in the middle. Beside him stood a fretful-looking little girl with pale eyes, possibly Janine as a child.

As she walked slowly around the room, Mercedes noticed that the old lady's eyes were on her. She complimented Janine on the brooch she wore. The old lady touched it, muttering that it had been her mother's. Mercedes volunteered that she had a young daughter to whom Jack would soon be a stepfather. Janine only squinted, and a worried look descended on her features.

Jack returned with his topcoat unbuttoned, holding a small stack of mail and a list. Janine brightened immediately. He sat beside her and took her hand. He said he'd come back to see her soon, before his trip to the Philippines, and bring her a Christmas present. She squeezed his hand.

"We just came from Shreve's, and you'll never guess what we bought there."

"Oh, what?" asked Janine, wide-eyed.

"A big, beautiful sapphire engagement ring for Mercedes. Next time we come, she'll have it on and you can see it."

Janine looked a little crestfallen. He mentioned that they were going to be married within the next year, that they would make sure Enrique brought her to the wedding and that she had a new dress for the occasion. She responded with a faint smile and nod.

"There are loads of things we need to do before the wedding," he said. Noting her lack of enthusiasm at the prospect, he added, "Janine, please don't worry. You're a very important part of our family. I'll look after you as always—nothing about us is going to change. You'll get to know Mercedes and her little girl, Germaine, who is a very well-mannered young lady. We'll bring you to our home, and you can enjoy Mercedes's wonderful cooking. But right now we've got to go. I'll pay these bills and bring you the items on your list." He stooped over and kissed her forehead.

Mercedes stood and clasped Janine's cold hand to say good-bye, thinking that Janine was only a few years younger than Elizabeth and fragile as an egg. Jack slipped the bills into his inside coat pocket and led Mercedes out of the building.

"Poor old thing," he said. "I'm not sure she's really fully aware of what's going on. She's losing her faculties a bit."

"It's natural that she'd be reticent. You're the gallant knight, not someone she wants to share."

"Janine was my refuge when I was a boy. She taught me many things. When I needed my mother the most, Janine was there." Changing tone, he asked: "Is there time for you to come up to my place? We could do some wedding planning." A mischievous grin on his face betrayed his motives instantly.

"You mean rehearse our wedding night. Very funny. Not until we get tested, my love."

"And not until my lady has her ring." *The ring.* The vivid image of it popped into her mind's eye and a new rush of excitement filled her. She threw her arms around his neck, and he swept her off the ground.

"Next weekend," he said.

"Next weekend," she replied.

He drove her to the parking garage where her car was parked and pulled over to the curb.

"There's something I'd like to show you and Germaine to-morrow. Are you doing anything in the afternoon? I'll come over and pick you up."

"Later in the afternoon we'll have some time."

"Okay, I'll pick you up around four then." His expression gave her no clues, nor did his lingering good-bye kiss.

THE NEXT AFTERNOON GERMAINE WAS waiting by the window when Jack pulled up. She ran outside to greet him as if he had been gone for months. Mercedes watched from the doorway. Jack took Germaine's hand, bowed, and kissed her fingertips.

"*Mademoiselle*," he said. She giggled. Behind his back he had a bouquet of flowers, which he presented to her.

"Perhaps you and your mother would like these."

Germaine played along. "Perhaps. Won't you come in, *Monsieur*?"

He entered the house and hugged Mercedes. He kissed the top of her head and looked around the living room. He scrutinized the furnishings, as if sizing them up at a garage sale.

"What are you doing?" she asked pointedly.

"Nothing! Can't a guy just admire your homey living room?"

"I know what you're doing. Now that we're engaged, you're thinking about how we're going to merge our households, in particular our sketchy furniture with your lovely things."

"Not much gets by your mother," he said to Germaine.

"No, *Monsieur*—nothing gets by her. Some things might get by her for a little while, but eventually she figures them out."

"I see. Well then, I consider myself duly warned. And where are your pigtails when I need to yank on one of them?" Germaine scooted out of his reach.

Mercedes arranged the flowers in the vase she had pulled down from the shelf, then helped Germaine into her coat.

"Thank you for the flowers. They're very beautiful," she said to Jack.

"You're welcome. And you're very perceptive," he said sheepishly. "I *was* sizing up your furniture, and soon you'll see why."

In a few minutes they were jetting down the freeway. They

turned up toward the hills of Oakland and into the beautiful Montclair district.

Mercedes knew the area well, for she and Germaine frequented the park in Montclair and the laundromat a few blocks away.

Jack had a sly smile on his face as he drove up past the shopping district, turned down a side street, and wound his way around the curves of the road. A canopy of trees overhung the road, and dense shrubbery partially concealed the homes.

He parked in front of a grand Mediterranean-style house with a red tile roof and white stucco exterior. There were hibiscus bushes on either side of a low wooden gate, which opened into a shaded courtyard with moss growing between the bricks. He unlocked the door of the house and ushered them into a spacious living room with a high open-beamed ceiling. The floor was polished wood covered with area rugs. A fireplace and brick hearth were in the center of one wall. Late-afternoon light flooded into the room from many leaded glass windows, which looked out onto a wild garden enclosed by an ivy-covered fence. The house was furnished and apparently inhabited, but no one was there.

"Welcome to one of my properties," Jack said simply. "I've been thinking about where we should live and it occurred to me that this might be a nice place to begin our lives together."

Germaine, whose eyes were filled with wonder, was silent. She clasped her mother's hand and stood close to her. Mercedes looked admiringly around the room and curiously at Jack. So many surprises lately! She waited for him to explain further.

"I bought this house about ten years ago and lived here for a couple of years, but it was sort of lonely for a bachelor. I missed the energy of San Francisco. So I've been renting it out ever since. The tenants have given me permission to come in, so don't worry. They know I'm deciding whether to renew the lease, which is up in April."

He led them down a hallway to the master suite on the right and other bedrooms on the left, facing the backyard. Each room had French doors that opened onto a redwood deck. Mercedes noticed the beautiful woodwork of the house, the arched doorways between the living room and dining room and the hall leading to the bedrooms. Germaine let go of her hand and went in to inspect a large bathroom opposite the bedrooms. Then she walked carefully through one of the bedrooms, opened a French door, and stepped out onto the deck. Mercedes and Jack followed her as she explored, admiring the sylvan view and breathing in the moist, cool air.

In the corner of the deck was a hot tub, screened by wood lattice covered with ivy and wisteria. The house was on a downward-sloping lot that contained a yard carpeted with thick, soft grass surrounded by trees. The neighbors' homes on either side were completely obscured by trees. It was like being in a tree house. Mercedes thought of her secret place in the woods as a child. She followed Germaine silently, like a doe with her fawn. Jack watched them both.

They proceeded along the deck to another pair of doors, which opened into the dining room. It would easily accommodate Jack's dining table and chairs and even his chandelier, should he decide to bring it.

Next they walked into the spacious kitchen. There was a breakfast nook in the corner, with windows that looked out onto the deck and yard. There were plenty of cupboards, a big gas range, ample counters, and a pantry. Another door led downstairs into the basement. Jack flicked on the light and led them into the somewhat dank utility room. It had its own door to the backyard, and another internal door leading to a spacious unused room beneath the deck. Its exterior wall was also lined with windows facing the verdant yard.

"I've never quite figured out the logic of this room, but it would be great for storage, I suppose," he said.

Germaine sprinted into the yard and was checking out the toolshed, blackberry bushes, and every tree within reach. One had a limb perfectly situated to hold the ropes of a long swing. There was a precipitous drop at the end of the yard, which was guarded by an eight-foot high wood fence.

"Be careful back there," Jack warned. "We don't want you to fall off the hill or get pestered by some varmint." The warning only excited Germaine further. She picked up steam as she circled the yard and ran all the faster.

"What a beautiful house!" Mercedes exclaimed. "Do I dare ask about your other properties?"

"Well, let's see, there's a condo up in Lake Tahoe, a rental property in Huntington Beach, a share in an office building, a couple of lots, this and that." He smiled like the Cheshire cat in *Alice in Wonderland*. "You see, we'll be very comfortable." He put his arm around her and pulled her close.

"I really don't know what to say. It makes me wonder what else you've got up your sleeve."

"I didn't want to scare you off."

He contemplated her pensive expression. They walked a turn around the yard and went back up the wooden steps to the deck.

"This patio furniture is ours too, as is the gas grill. And the hot tub works." He shot her a look that needed no interpretation. Germaine came flying up the stairs and asked if she could go back into the house. She wiped her feet on the doormat and tiptoed into the dining room, followed by the adults. The heat kicked on. She walked over to a floor grate and stood over it to bask in the warm air.

"A couple of the kids in my class live up here," she said cheerily. "Oh, it's so pretty!" She scampered down the hall to look at the bedrooms again, and to speculate on which might become hers.

"So what do you think?" Jack asked Mercedes. "Should we move in here? We don't have to, you know. We can do whatever we want."

"Such as?"

"We could buy another house and live somewhere else. We could even move down the peninsula if you like."

"Your house is exquisite. I have no objections to moving here. How could I possibly?"

Even now she wondered if he had any idea what it had been like for her and Germaine the last three years. Perhaps it just was not possible to step into others' shoes and imagine their lives—even when great love had bloomed. Even when two were taking each other as one flesh and one blood.

TAKE ME DOWN

When she hugged Germaine good-bye at Caroline's house, she held her for an extra few seconds. Germaine had seen Mercedes's overnight bag in the backseat next to her own. She knew her mother was meeting Jack.

"Mom, are you okay? You're acting kind of weird."

"I'll be fine. Our time together as a twosome is short. I want to make sure you know that no one, not even Jack, could ever possibly take your place in my heart. You will always be my Number One."

"I know that, Mom! And I love you—even when you act weird."

Caroline walked Mercedes out to her car. "Don't do anything I wouldn't do," Caroline teased. Seeing her friend's apprehension, she added, "Listen, you've waited, you've done everything you could to keep your head and make the right decision. You've shown great restraint, and Jack has been a gentleman. He's given Germaine time to get used to him, and he's begun a very nice relationship with her. He's met your parents and received their blessing. He's given you a commitment, has a house waiting for you to move into, an engagement ring ready to slip onto your finger, and I have to say he does look overjoyed. I don't know what else you have to do to be sure. We've checked him out. Darrel thinks the world of him—and his former business associates have great respect for him. So relax and enjoy yourself! It's about time," Caroline pronounced confidently.

"It means a lot to hear you say so," replied Mercedes.

"I'll be here with Germaine and Anne when you get back tomorrow," Caroline reassured her.

⸎

MERCEDES DROVE TO JACK'S APARTMENT building and parked on the street. The doorman tipped his hat to her and held the door. The concierge greeted her.

She felt herself walking into the next world; the doors to the old one closed behind her.

Jack opened the door to his apartment before she could even ring the bell. He was somewhat formally attired in a black-and-white-striped dress shirt, which had his initials monogrammed in tiny red letters on the pocket. His trousers were perfectly creased and his black wing tips highly polished, like everything else about him. He looked at her as though he could devour her. He took the overnight bag out of her hand and kissed her mouth and both cheeks.

She went to freshen up. In the bathroom stood regal Athena, her beautiful form in marble, her strong features staring bravely forward with a goddess's self-assurance. Mercedes looked into the mirror and straightened one of the pearl earrings Eleanor had given her from Elizabeth's collection. Suddenly she felt she was exactly where she should be, doing just what she was supposed to be doing.

⸎

SOON THEY WERE WALKING INTO Shreve & Company, where Minette was just finishing with a customer. She brought the blue velvet box over to them. Mercedes's heart leapt. Jack removed the radiant sapphire ring, took Mercedes's left hand, and reverently slid the ring down her finger without a word. It had been sized perfectly.

"It's even more beautiful than I remembered," Jack said. "This ring must have been made for you, for us." She turned to face him as he put his arms around her and held her. Soon they were on their way out of the store.

Although the weather was chilly and damp, Mercedes had worn no gloves so she could look at the gorgeous jewel on her finger while she walked beside the gorgeous jewel of a husband she was soon to have. They were jostled by other shoppers, admiring Christmas decorations and elaborate window displays. Magic seemed to have enveloped them entirely.

Full of energy, with the whole afternoon and night in front of them, they teased each other playfully and picked out presents for Germaine, Janine, Melanie, Philip, and Eleanor. When their bags grew heavy, they stopped at a café just off Union Square. It was late afternoon, and the dinner crowd had yet to appear. Jack ordered food for both of them.

"Bella, you have to build up your strength. We have a long night ahead of us."

She tore off a piece of sourdough, buttered it, and pushed it into his mouth. He nibbled at her fingers and eyed her.

"So, are there any other hurdles you're going to make me leap over?" he asked. "The clock is ticking. In a matter of moments I'm going to throw you over my shoulder and haul you back to my cave."

She laughed.

"Germaine has given me her stamp of approval. I survived Eleanor, made friends with your dad, your boss, your landlord, took the HIV test, and passed through the gauntlet of East Oakland to get to you."

"My compliments on your tenacity." She spread out her left hand on the white tablecloth so they could both admire the dazzling ring.

"Although it has been a bit torturous to wait, honestly I admire your self-control. You're not one to be hurried to judgment. You make up your own mind. I like that. My wife will be her own person and stand on her own two feet." He signaled the waiter for the check.

"No dessert?" she asked. She knew he had seen the chocolate cake touted on the menu.

"We'll have dessert at my place." He looked steadily into her eyes. "It will be the sweetest thing you've ever tasted."

⌖

NIGHT WAS FALLING WHEN THEY got to his apartment. He unlocked the door and ushered her in. They put their bags down in the entryway. He turned on a light and hung their coats. She walked into the living room, where the lights of the city were beginning to twinkle against a backdrop of deep blue. Fog drifted in from the bay. Jack took off his shoes and tread silently across the carpets. She turned from the view to face him.

He scooped up her face into his hands and kissed her lips hungrily. He kissed her eyes, her nose, and again her mouth and held her tightly in his arms. She felt his shoulder blades through the satiny shirt, felt his well-muscled back and slid her hands down his backside. His hands wandered down her neck and across her shoulders. The city lights shone in the darkening room. The only sounds were their breathing, and the traffic in the distance.

His hands caressed her breasts gently, then her narrow ribcage and her waist. He slipped his hands beneath her blue sweater. He kissed her deeply, exploring her mouth with his tongue. He ran his fingers up her back and unfastened her bra. His hands moved around to the front, to feel her breasts beneath the loosened bra. Her nipples responded to his touch. Suddenly she craved his touch all over her.

He took her by the hand and led her into his darkened bedroom. He turned down the duvet on his king-sized bed and lit a candle lantern on his bureau. A dozen long-stemmed roses were arranged in a vase on the lovely dark dresser. She walked over and put her face into the center of the blossoms, inhaling their fragrance deeply. He looked at her and smiled. He turned on the sound system with a remote switch. Glenn Gould began to play Bach's *Goldberg Variations* on the piano. Mercedes stood there with her eyes closed for a few moments as the notes entered her body and moved up and down her spine.

Jack stood behind her and ran his fingers beneath her sweater to her breasts again. She turned, and he pulled her toward him with another long kiss. He gently led her over to the bed and sat her down on the corner. He knelt on the floor in front of her and slowly raised one of her legs. He unzipped her boot and carefully peeled off her thin sock. When he had done the same with the other one, and her trousers, he ran his hands up her smooth legs, spread them apart, and pulled her closer so she was straddling him. He pulled up her sweater and undressed her as if she were a child, carefully removing her arms from each sleeve. He gathered all her hair in his hands and pulled the sweater over her head. He let her hair down tenderly.

She unbuckled his belt, pulled it out of its loops in one firm motion, and unfastened the top of his trousers. She extricated the long tail of his shirt. The black and white stripes were vivid in the dim light. Mercedes smiled, even as Glenn Gould held part of her attention.

"You look like a skunk," she murmured as she kissed him.

"I finally get you in my bedroom and that's what you have to say?" He feigned distress.

She unbuttoned his shirt and ran her fingers down his undershirt. She kissed his big beautiful mouth. She removed his cuff links and set them down, then pushed the shirt back on his shoulders until he had taken it off. He stood up and pulled his undershirt over his head and dropped it to the floor.

His bare shoulders and silky black-haired chest were a sight for her hungry eyes. She had longed for this moment and imagined it countless times. She unzipped his loosened trousers and pulled them down. She grazed the tormented bulge with the top of her head, her long hair brushing his thighs.

He stepped out of his trousers and pushed her backward onto the soft bedding. She looked up at the classical proportions of the statuesque Jack Soutane, his long muscular arms, wide shoulders, and long neck. Holding her gaze, he stripped off his underwear, put his arms down by his sides, and let her inspect him for a moment where he stood.

"I'm all yours," he said.

He climbed onto the bed and hovered over her. He kissed her neck and inhaled her perfume, pressed her breasts together softly with both hands, burying his face between them. She ran her fingers through his thick hair and succumbed to his explorations—his lips on her nipples, his tongue in her navel, and his removal of her underwear. The world began to vanish, the edges of reality blurred, leaving only Jack, the music, and the vortex into which they were falling.

He lay in bed beside her and scooped her into his arms. He encircled her body with his legs, reeling her in, pulling her on top of him, and draping her lithe form over himself like a velvet cloak. There were neither words nor thoughts—only an infinite now. He kissed her mouth with unbridled desire and ran his hand up the curve of her back. He felt each vertebra. He explored her mouth with his tongue. She spread her legs around his hips, pressing against him, stretching out her torso on the great expanse of his chest. She felt home at last, with his heat radiating into her heart. Eventually he rolled her over. She sank into the soft bed and let go. Something inside her relaxed completely for the first time since they had met.

⚬⚬⚬

HUNGER AND THIRST EVENTUALLY DROVE them to the kitchen. She wore his now-wrinkled striped shirt with its sleeves rolled up to her wrists. It was longer than most of her dresses, grazing her knees. She pushed hair away from her face. The ring, still a stranger to her hand, caught in her curls. She looked at it in the kitchen light. It was proof that this night was not a dream.

He was in a thick black chenille robe tied at the waist, barefoot, his hair disheveled, his five-o'clock shadow tolling midnight and sprinkled with silver. Mercedes drank in the sight of him, the real Jack, as no one ever saw him in the outside world. He stood in front of the open refrigerator and began pulling out things to eat. She retrieved a water glass from one of the kitchen cabinets and filled it from the dispenser on the refrigerator door. She guzzled the glass in two gulps.

He watched her, raised an eyebrow, and shook his head. "I'm not surprised you're that thirsty. You should have warned me."

"Some things are best kept to oneself," she said. She raised one foot and pressed it against the opposite knee, stork fashion, and leaned against the counter where food was accumulating.

"That they are, Mrs. Skunk."

She looked at her ring again and spread her hand out on the counter. "I can't imagine I'll ever get used to seeing this on my finger."

He brought over the last food items, put them on the counter, and looked at Mercedes. He lifted her left hand, kissed the fingertips, and sucked on her index finger.

"May it always remind us of this night."

He washed his hands, got down a gold-rimmed plate, and began arranging food on it—cheeses, olives, crackers, dried figs, and prosciutto.

He poured wine and led her out to the living room to sit on the leather couch. He lit a fire in the fireplace, put on Miles Davis's *Kind of Blue* album and sat down next to her. She snuggled into the deep cushions and pulled her bare legs up beneath her. He covered her with an afghan and popped an olive into her mouth. He wrapped a piece of prosciutto around a dried fig and a piece of cheese and put the bundle on her thigh, then took a drink of wine. The fire crackled in the dark room. The city lights glimmered in the rain, and the light from the fire flickered. The rain increased in intensity on the deck outside the glass doors. They sat silently, basking in the glow.

After a while, sated with wine and food, Jack put his arm around her and unbuttoned the striped shirt, exposing her breasts. He bent over and kissed a nipple, then her mouth. She held his head in her hands.

"I will never ever get enough of you," he said.

"Nor I of you."

He scooped her into his arms and carried her back to bed, where he lay her down gently and took off his robe.

⚬⊂⊛⊃⚬

LATER, DEEP IN THE NIGHT, they lay awake in each other's arms. Her ear was pressed against his heart, listening to the rhythmical sound of the great pump circulating her beloved's blood. He collected and smoothed her voluminous mane.

"We could elope, you know." His deep voice reverberated in her ear.

"I thought you wanted a snazzy wedding and a grand party to celebrate the loss of your virginity," she teased.

"It's about a quarter century too late for that, I'm afraid. I just want you, from this day forward, until death us do part—Mrs. Soutane. Doesn't that have a lovely sound?" He caressed her behind and with an index finger stroked the hollow at the base of her spine.

"Actually, I'm rather attached to my own name," she said quietly. "I've been carrying it around for an awfully long time."

"You don't want to take my name?"

"It's not that I don't *want* your name. It's that I already have one. My identity isn't going to change, is it?"

He said nothing.

"Why don't you change yours to Mr. Bell?" she asked with a laugh.

"Too risky," he replied. "Your mother might get confused and move in with us, and then I would starve to death, because she'd eat all the food off my plate."

Mercedes laughed out loud.

"Eloping would eliminate the Eleanor factor in the wedding," she added.

"But Philip couldn't walk you down the aisle, and Germaine would miss out on all the pageantry. We can't deprive her of that."

"Perhaps you forget that I eloped once already. It didn't work out so well." She fingered the sapphire engagement ring and then ran her hand across the silken pelt on his chest.

"I wouldn't say that, my love. It's worked out very well for me," he replied. "Everything happens for a reason."

He rolled her over onto her back and lay lightly on top of her, supporting his upper body on his elbows. He kissed her tenderly, nuzzling her neck and rejoicing in the unquenchable harmony of their bodies, something very new to him.

She luxuriated in the great warmth of him from the top of her head to her toes. They fell asleep listening to the rain streaming down the windowpanes.

⚬⚓⚬

LATE THE NEXT MORNING, Mercedes went into the kitchen to make coffee. Jack brought in the Sunday paper and started filling the bathtub. He brought the roses in from the bedroom and placed them on the marble ledge beside the tub. He sprinkled turquoise bath salts and the petals of a rose into the water. He put Mercedes's black lace bra on Athena and draped her blue sweater over the goddess's shoulders. Mercedes brought in a tray holding coffee mugs and warmed scones. Jack took it from her and set it on the ledge. Mercedes noticed Athena and burst out laughing. Then she took one of the roses and placed it at the goddess's feet.

They slid into the tub facing each other, their legs stretched out. Mercedes lay back and stared at the coral ceiling and the white crown molding all around it. Jack lay back and took in the sight of Mercedes's face and shoulders and long bejeweled hand holding her coffee mug. They drank and let the beautiful hot water work its magic. He put a hot washcloth over his face and rested his head against the rim of the tub. After a few moments of silence he peeked out, like a snake coming out from beneath a rock, and took another sip of coffee. Mercedes laughed. He put the washcloth back on his head and tickled her ribs with his toe. They drank the coffee slowly and listened to the rain.

"We're in heaven right now," she said.

"We are," he said, "with a goddess standing watch."

THE ANNOUNCEMENT

The office holiday party was the following Saturday evening at the club where they had hosted the luncheon for Rand Taylor just fourteen months earlier. The Doric columns surrounding the white stone building were lit from below by red and green floodlights, visible from several blocks away. Mercedes thought of the first time she'd been driven there, sitting in the rear seat of Darrel's car, and how Emerson, next to her, leaned forward like a Doberman on high alert, staring at the back of Stuart's head.

Jack was coming down with a cold and coughed into his handkerchief. In spite of this, he was in an exultant mood, resplendent in his tuxedo. Her left hand, heavy with the sapphire and diamond ring to be seen in public for the first time, rested on his taut thigh as he downshifted.

After leaving his car with the valet, Jack draped his arm lightly around the back of Mercedes's evening coat as they walked through the lobby. In the elevator, he admired his fiancée's profile, her long neck, and the smooth chignon into which she had coaxed her hair.

They made their entrance. Mercedes stepped out of her coat in the emerald satin gown he'd bought her, dazzling and enchanted like Cinderella at the ball.

A towering noble fir decorated with globes of colored glass and hundreds of tiny lights stood in the center of the circular room. She gazed upward at the angels painted on the high domed ceiling. She remembered Jack helping her into her tattered raincoat that first fateful day and freeing her long braid an inch at a time.

Darrel and his partners, John Slayne and Peter McDonough, stood together in a receiving line. Their wives stood beside them, all brunettes, about the same height and all in lovely holiday gowns of purple, gold, and cranberry red.

McDonough was a silver-haired gentleman, rather like Philip Bell. He was lean, and taller than his partners by a few inches; a temperate, circumspect man who listened more than he spoke. This evening he wore a red-and-white-striped stocking cap on his head. He clasped Mercedes's hand and greeted Jack warmly.

Darrel had donned an elf's hat and had pinned a sprig of mistletoe on his lapel. When Jack and Mercedes approached, he kissed his paralegal on the cheek. "I'm glad to see you're making an honest man of Jack," he told her quietly. "Somebody had to do it."

"That's easy for *you* to say," Jack replied.

Simone and Lindsay spied Mercedes from across the room. They hurried over to hug her, grasped her hand to inspect her ring, then gasped and embraced her again.

"Tonight must be the night," Caroline said from over Mercedes's shoulder.

On a nod, Darrel, his wife Marguerite, Jack, and Mercedes moved toward the softly lit dining area. Darrel and Jack selected seats with Mercedes between them. Oohs and ahs could be heard as people took their seats. Each table was covered by a white tablecloth, with glitter and sequins and a multitude of votive candles in small red glasses. The centerpieces were tall pedestaled vases of evergreen boughs decorated with tiny lights and holly stems. Beside each plate was a box of Belgian chocolates wrapped in gold paper.

The table decorations created a magical effect in the low light. It was as if everyone were sitting in a forest with starlight twinkling overhead, surrounded by sparkling snow. Mercedes placed her left hand on the table beside Darrel and looked at him with the eyes of a child on Christmas morning. He spied her hand and did a double take.

"Don't let Marguerite see that thing, whatever you do," he whispered to Mercedes. "And I hope you plan to stay on at the firm after you marry."

"Of course I do. You rescued me, remember?"

"You rescued yourself. I'm glad things worked out."

Mercedes looked across at the table where Emerson was seated with Stuart and his wife. Emerson was staring across at them, but averted his eyes the instant Mercedes noticed. He picked up his steak knife and slit the roast beef on his plate with more vigor than necessary, carved off a hunk, and shoved it gracelessly into his mouth. Jack, behind his cupped hand, nibbled Mercedes's ear.

Darrel glanced at them happily, and kissed his wife's cheek.

After dishes were cleared from the main course, Jack rose to his feet. There was no need to signal for attention. His voice, even deeper than usual due to his cold, carried easily.

"Friends, this has truly been the most wonderful year of my life. When I went to Africa last year, for some reason I couldn't get Mercedes off my mind, although I barely knew her. So when I got back, I asked her to go to lunch with me. The more I got to know her, the more I wanted to know. I discovered what an interesting, multifaceted, capable person she is and also what a great mother she is. Many of you have met her daughter, Germaine, so you know what I mean. I was smitten, to say the least. I am the most fortunate man tonight, because Mercedes has graciously agreed to marry me."

Jack raised her hand in the air while everyone applauded and cheered. He encouraged her upward, and she stood. She saw Caroline, who was radiant. Stuart had his arm around his wife and squeezed her shoulder. Melanie wiped a tear from her eye. Florida, just across the table, nodded with approval. Emerson grew pale and turned away.

Darrel stood and raised his glass. "To Jack and Mercedes, all the happiness in the world. It is well deserved." Darrel touched his glass to Mercedes's.

After the toasts, Darrel gestured toward a large stack of envelopes on the table in front of him. "In recognition of this very profitable year, Peter, John, and I will be bringing each of you your bonus check."

He cast a sardonic grin at Jack and said under his breath, "You don't get one. You've already received far more than you deserve."

Mercedes caught a movement out of the corner of her eye. She was startled to see Emerson bolt from his chair, which he left in a waiter's path, and abruptly exit the room. She exchanged a questioning expression with Caroline, who shrugged in surprise. The partners, acting as though nothing were amiss, fanned out among the tables, handing each person an envelope and thanking them for their service.

⁓⬥⁓

"HOW EXACTLY DOES ALL THAT hair go up so neatly?" Jack asked as he unlocked the door of his apartment. "I've been wondering all night. It must come down like a waterfall." He pulled out one hair pin, then another. Soon a cascade of hair tumbled into his hands. He pulled her toward him.

"How do you feel being officially engaged?" she asked.

"Like a king." He kissed her neck. "It went off perfectly. I couldn't have asked for a better night."

"Did you see Emerson leave?"

"I did."

"He seemed almost offended."

"We all have our baggage, Bella. Right now I'm very interested in unwrapping the beautiful package in front of me." He slowly unzipped her dress and slid it off her shoulders to kiss them.

"Did we do something to upset him?" she asked as he unfastened her bra and stroked the length of her spine.

"I doubt it. Some people just can't tolerate very much happiness."

She revolved to face him. "Can you?" She turned up his collar and unfastened his bow tie.

"I think I already answered that question last weekend, although you very nearly did kill me," he said as he kissed her slowly.

"Perhaps you're out of your depth," she answered, working the studs out from the front of his shirt, "which would be rather surprising for such a tall man."

He chuckled. "Not likely. But we can test your hypothesis. Perhaps last weekend was an anomaly." He took her by the hand and led her into the guest bedroom. "Change of venue. Must make the housekeeper earn her pay."

BREAKING *the* CODE

Documents had swamped the office like a flash flood. The New York firm representing Franjipur had let loose the floodgates. The paralegals were awash in paper, searching for information to be used in the imminent depositions of several corporate executives. There was much work to be done in a short time and the atmosphere was charged with the adrenaline that accompanies a crucial deadline.

Lindsay sat on the floor, cross-legged in her wool trousers, sorting a collection of documents into piles all around her. Mercedes moved quickly about the office in her skirt and stocking feet, sifting through pages in the open box on her desk. Simone used the shelving unit against the wall to sort stacks of paper. Piles were everywhere. Mercedes cleared off the bulletin board where they planned to post any hot documents that might turn up. They were creating files for each witness and working together to share their discoveries. A picture of life in Franjipur's corporate headquarters was slowly emerging.

Darrel and Stuart would soon be flying to New York to take the depositions. If they were successful, the witnesses would be forced to commit themselves on many issues they had so far avoided—in particular, whether Rand had gained knowledge of something that he was never supposed to know, the knowing of which would have made him a liability to upper management and explained his removal from the company.

Mercedes was reviewing documents for Emerson. He had given her precious little guidance and seemed to be avoiding her like the plague. She was on her own to get things right, or face the consequences.

Defendants, after losing a protracted court fight, had recently produced the personal calendars of the executives and phone message logbooks. Meanwhile, the friendly snitches at Franjipur had sent them security logs, reservation data, and correspondence about a particular suite in the New York facility. Mercedes hunted through all of it—but for what exactly, she did not know.

There were odd symbols on some of the dates in reservation logs for the suite—but no names were associated with those reservations. She wondered if there was a correlation, and showed them to Lindsay and Simone. They checked personal calendars for various individuals and found "Out of Town" written on some of the dates. There was nothing incriminating about any of it, but neither was there any explanation—no flight information, nothing about destination or the purpose of the trip, as was the case for other entries.

Mercedes tacked a copy of the organizational chart for the New York facility on the board. Photographs of all the top management were there by their titles: all white males in their forties and fifties. Which of them had used the suite and what went on there? She felt edgy and her intuition nagged her. One of their informants had given them the name of an escort service frequently called by a trusted few. She felt that somewhere in the maze were the keys to Rand's case and that nearly every piece of the puzzle was right under her nose. She had only to fit them together.

⋯

JACK'S DISTINCTIVE HANDWRITING COVERED A large picture postcard that was lying beneath the mail slot at home. Germaine scooped it up when they opened the door at the end of the day, and they read his words together.

Far from having the ideal vacation, he wrote, he was sick in bed with a bad cold, unable to go out. Room service was supplying all his sustenance; he was bored and missed them. He still planned to attend his friend's wedding the next day, but his ill health had definitely put a damper on the trip. He'd been thinking about their wedding. How were his girls doing?

"Behave yourselves," he wrote, "at least until we can misbehave together."

The front of the card showed the palatial Manila Hotel, host to heads of state and famous for exquisite luxury. *Leave it to Jack even to get sick in style,* Mercedes thought. For the tiniest instant she wondered what illicit delights room service in the Philippines might provide a wealthy American. She imagined him laid out on a bank of pillows, his nose red from blowing, his eyes puffy, his feet sticking out at the end of the bed. At least he was in a place where he could rest. She wondered what she would do if he were in San Francisco.

What was he like when he was sick? *In sickness and in health, until death us do part.* She envisioned him as he had been on the night of the holiday party, glorious in his tuxedo. Even though he had not felt well, no one discerned it. Her pulse lurched at the thought of his return on Christmas Eve. Then she saw Germaine studying her, and gave her daughter a hug.

"He'll be home soon. He's just tired and caught a bug. So let's have a good supper, and you can read me your book report."

⁓

SHORTLY BEFORE LUNCH THE NEXT DAY, Emerson sent his secretary, Lorraine, into the paralegal room to retrieve the documents that he presumed Mercedes had organized. Mercedes told Lorraine she would deliver them herself.

His office was next to Caroline's, on the opposite side of the floor from Jack's. Rarely had she been in it, but it was the brunt of many jokes. Every item on his desk had a designated position with precise coordinates. The tape dispenser, stapler, pencil holder, paper clips, and telephone were arranged exactly an inch apart along the edge of his desk. The game the staff played at his expense was to rearrange these objects when he was out for lunch. A prisoner of his obsessions, he corrected any minute deviation the moment he returned. A secretary or a file clerk would happen to pass by while he did it, and a few moments later snickering would erupt from the secretaries' cubicles.

He sat primly in his big chair, nervously stroking his thin moustache, brooding intently, when Mercedes appeared in his doorway with an accordion file of documents. He jumped slightly and tried to assume a more commanding pose.

"Lorraine came to get these, but I thought I'd bring them to you," she said confidently. "I wonder if you have a moment to talk." She didn't wait for a response, but flipped the door closed behind her and sat down across from him.

"I suppose," he said dismissively.

She placed the documents in the center of his blotter. He corrected their position to parallel the blotter edges exactly.

"Just a couple of ideas," she said. "I think there's some kind of code used in the reservation log for the suite. I'm not sure why, but maybe it was to let certain people on the staff know which of the managers would be there or what the plans were for that particular day. There are symbols on the reservation log we're trying to figure out. We've started a chart and I'm hoping to decipher the pattern before Darrel and Stuart go to New York, or before you get much further with the outline."

"Humph," he sniffed, unimpressed.

"I just thought you'd like to know my suspicions, since you're working on the prep with Darrel."

"Got it."

"And there's something else," she said, fingering her engagement ring. Emerson sat up even more stiffly.

"I hope Jack's announcement of our engagement at the party didn't make you uncomfortable. I saw you leave."

He flushed and pursed his lips. "Why would I care about that?"

"I just wanted to be sure we hadn't done anything to offend you," she said, trying unsuccessfully to look him in the eye. "It was such a happy occasion, and we were sorry you left."

"Did Jack say that?" he asked caustically.

"I'm sure I speak for both of us."

He glared at her. "And I'm sure you haven't a clue."

"About what?"

"About Mr. Perfect Bridegroom-To-Be." He gestured toward the door, flicking his fingers at her. "I have work to do, if you don't mind."

Mercedes searched his face for a long moment. At her leisure she stood up and went out, leaving the door open behind her.

᳐᳐

THAT NIGHT A LETTER IN a Manila Hotel envelope arrived in the mail, along with another picture postcard for Germaine. It showed the Manila marketplace, a crowded scene of vendors' tables shaded by colorful awnings and palm trees. Filipino women with glossy blue-black hair carried children on their hips as they milled about tables piled high with mangos, coconuts, and vegetables that Germaine couldn't identify. Everyone wore loose, short-sleeved clothes, and many children were barefoot.

The hotel stationery was heavy and embossed, and Jack's bold script had been written with his blunt-tip fountain pen. He had attended the wedding, in spite of his health, and was effusive in his praise. Splendor had been on display in every detail. A seated dinner for more than four hundred guests had followed the service. He'd met all the family members of both the bride and groom and enjoyed all the pomp and ceremony, down to the horse-drawn carriage bedecked with flowers that carried the newlyweds from the church to the reception. But he had been forced to turn in early and hadn't left his room since. He wished she'd been there with him, but was glad she was not being further exposed to whatever he had. His symptoms had moved into his lungs, and he was waiting to be seen by the house doctor.

> It's a shame this big gorgeous bed is going to waste, Bella. But it's making me think about our honeymoon. Where shall we go? What about Tuscany? Have you been there? We could spend a few days in Florence. I love every inch of you!
>
> Jack

She held the paper to her nose, trying to detect some scent of her beloved. Emerson's comments stuck in her mind and pricked like nettles. Whatever he thought he knew was irrelevant. Mr. Perfect Bridegroom-To-Be was a prince. Emerson was the one who didn't have a clue. She folded the letter and slid it back into its envelope. Uneasily she wondered what the doctor would say. When Jack came home everything would be all right again. She was sure of it.

"Well, what did he say?" Germaine asked.

"He wants me to keep his seat warm at the gaming table," she grinned at her bright child, "so his Scrabble partner isn't too restless." She smoothed Germaine's hair and touched her chin. "Soon you'll have a very nice stepfather."

Germaine grinned. "I know!"

⚬⊂⊃⚬

AT THE OFFICE, the hunt continued. Mercedes focused on comparing entries on calendars to entries on the reservation logs for the suite, reading phone messages, and digging more deeply into the identities of the witnesses. Page by page she sifted until she spied an incongruous page from a telephone memo pad stuck in the middle of the typed minutes from an executive committee meeting. The handwriting on it was feminine. The author's rounded letters formed curlicues at the end of each word, and there were tiny circles for the dots of the i's. At the bottom of the page were several symbols, identical to those she had found in the reservation log. Beside each symbol was the name of a senior manager of the corporation. Four symbols, four names.

"I found it!" she exclaimed.

Lindsay and Simone dropped what they were doing and came to see. Mercedes pinned the small piece of paper to the bulletin board next to the list of dates. She rummaged through the papers on her desk and pulled out the reservation log. She flipped to various dates on the list and showed them the symbols—symbols which they now could match up to names.

They excitedly looked at each other and said, almost in unison, "We have to find out who wrote the memo."

Lindsay reached for the photocopies of handwritten calendars for several of the company's executives, maintained by their secretaries. Somewhere in those pages they would find more of the mystery woman's handwriting.

In addition to calendars, there were voluminous amounts of typewritten correspondence signed by the four men. Simone compiled a list of the typists, whose initials appeared at the foot of each letter, and the dates of the letters.

Mercedes put in a call to Percy Millner, the employee in Human Resources who had been so helpful.

"I'm in a meeting," he whispered. "I'll call you right back."

Mercedes made copies of several of the reservation log pages, each of which showed a different symbol, and pinned them up on the bulletin board. She added copies of pages from the reservation log that showed the same symbols, each written on a different date. Simone added pages from the personal calendars for the same dates, from each of the men whose names had been assigned a symbol. The entries matched. Where the reservation log showed that man's symbol, his personal calendar said, "out of town."

When Percy called back, Mercedes was ready. She gave him a range of dates showing when the correspondence had been typed, and a list of the typists' initials. With that information he was able to identify the secretaries who had worked in the Franjipur executive offices during the times in question. Two of the women were still employed by the company. Mercedes wrote names beside her list of initials and added them to the growing collage on the bulletin board. Now there were more witnesses to interview.

The paralegals searched through the calendars for other samples of the handwriting with curlicues and circles for the dots of i's. Lindsay made the discovery—on phone messages for one of the men whose deposition Darrel would be taking. Thanks to Percy, they could now match a name to the handwriting, and they added it to their wall: Shirley Idol.

Lindsay, Mercedes, and Simone exchanged exuberant high-fives. They had decoded part of the mystery: they knew who had used the executive suite, at what times, and the names of the staff who had assisted them.

Mercedes practically sprinted to Darrel's office. He looked up from his reading, surprised by her sudden appearance and the expression on her face.

"What is it?"

"We have something to show you on the Taylor case. I think you'll like it," she said, beaming.

In short order they were standing before the agglomerate of documents.

"According to this note," Mercedes said, pointing, "which we've been able to determine is in the handwriting of a secretary named Shirley Idol, each symbol represents one of the managers at Franjipur's New York facility. We've matched entries on their calendars with dates on the reservation log for the executive suite. See their symbols on the log?"

He nodded his head and scrutinized the documents on the wall.

"We found correspondence sent out under each of their signatures, and we called Percy Millner. He was able to give us this list of names," she said, pointing to another page pinned to the wall. "And these are the names of all the secretaries they had working for them at the time. Maybe they have some knowledge of what went on in the suite and why there was such a need for secrecy. If not, why did they have to use symbols in the reservation log?"

"I like it. This is great!" Darrel's eyes were quick with excitement as he praised his paralegals.

"Maybe Tony Grey, our private investigator, can track down the secretaries who've left the company. And now that we have specific dates, maybe he can get his contact at the escort service to open up about whether any of their employees were sent to the suite on those nights, who visited, and what they did."

Darrel agreed. "We need to know exactly what Rand knew about all this, when he knew it and who at Franjipur knew that he knew. Has Emerson seen this?"

"No. We just now put it together. I told him about my idea yesterday, but he wasn't terribly enthused."

"I want him to get this into the outline."

"I don't think he welcomes my suggestions, to put it mildly."

Darrel looked annoyed. "Okay, make sure Stuart sees this right away. I want him to get in touch with Tony immediately and to come see me as soon as he's gone over it. Please write a memo about this and circulate it. And draft a notice of deposition for Shirley Idol. We need to get it on calendar ASAP. This is excellent work—all of you. Thank you very much!"

Stuart was all ears when Mercedes went to his office. When she'd finished, he grinned at her. "You may have done it again, just like you did in Fredericks."

"Let's not get ahead of ourselves."

"When will Jack be back? He's the one with the client's ear."

"Not until next week. But we can call him in the Philippines, or send him a telex."

"What's keeping him there?"

"He's sick with a bad cold," she said, fingering her engagement ring.

"It's probably the first time he's been able to catch his breath in a while," Stuart teased.

She sighed, thinking of their insatiable, sleepless nights together and longing for the next one.

THE TEAM WAS SEATED AROUND Darrel's desk late the next day when Melanie put the call through.

"Jack, I hope it's not too early for you. We're sorry to interrupt your vacation," Darrel began.

A fit of coughing was the reply. Mercedes winced.

Then, in a gravelly voice, Jack said, "I'm happy to have a distraction. Is my fiancée there?"

"She is indeed," Darrel responded. "And it's because of her that we're calling."

If Emerson had been a cat, his ears would have gone back on his head.

"I knew if I left there'd be trouble," Jack joked.

"She solved a riddle, or part of a riddle." Darrel explained their recent discovery and how the paralegals had cross-referenced the documents to put it all together.

More coughing erupted on the other end of the phone. "You've been busy," he sputtered. "Good work. How's Tony?"

"He's pretty certain he can get us what we need before the depositions, which is why we're calling. We need you to get in touch with Rand and have a heart-to-heart. He needs to be completely forthcoming with us."

Emerson shot a hostile look at Mercedes.

"I think he has been," Jack replied. "He had suspicions, but that's all. That and the hope that we would find out what it was all about. I'll call him again to be sure there's nothing more he can tell us." His voice cracked and he cleared his throat.

After the business portion of the call was done, Mercedes went to Jack's office and closed the door so they could speak privately.

"Jack, you sound awful."

"It sounds worse than it is."

"I'm glad you have room service and a doctor. What did he say?"

"He said it's bronchitis and a sinus infection and gave me anti-biotics. I'm supposed to feel much better in a day or so. I've been lying here scheming about our future and what I'm going to do to you the next time I get my hands on you."

"I'd love to go to Florence on our honeymoon! Were you serious about that?"

"Absolutely." He broke into another fit of coughing, which went on for some seconds.

"I wish I were there to take care of you."

"There will be time enough for that," he whispered hoarsely. "Give my Scrabble partner a hug for me."

She sat in Jack's enormous chair and took stock of the room. She tried to imagine being him, with a law practice, facing marriage and parenthood for the first time at age thirty-nine. She looked out his windows toward the lake. Now that darkness had fallen, the path around it was lit by a necklace of lights.

Jack's desk was the antithesis of Emerson's. On top was a snow-storm of paper, which had a suggestion of order only thanks to Melanie. Mercedes opened the top drawer. Loose papers filled it to the brim. She opened the drawer farther. The top document had a fax cover sheet addressed to an insurance company. She turned the page and saw an application for insurance in Jack's handwriting. Her name was there, too.

Someone knocked on the door. She quickly closed the drawer and called out, "Come in!"

Melanie entered with the day's mail. She spied Mercedes, who was dwarfed by Jack's chair and desk. "Is he as sick as he sounds?"

"I think so. He lost his voice completely during the call and was coughing horribly."

"Lying in bed will drive that man crazy," Melanie said, as she carefully deposited the newest mail.

"He's been planning the honeymoon, though," Mercedes said gently.

Melanie looked at her sweetly.

"You know, I've worked for Jack for many years. He has a moody streak and can be . . . difficult at times, but I've never seen him so content. I think you and Germaine give him ballast, a sense of purpose. It's the family life he's always wanted, and being accepted for who he really is."

"What's *not* to love? He's Prince Charming."

Melanie's face softened. "He is with you."

⌐⌐⌐

JACK LAY BACK ON HIS pile of pillows, coughing strenuously, his face vermilion and his hair disheveled. During a brief respite he forced himself upright on the edge of the bed. He struggled to his feet and teetered in his rumpled pajamas, only to be hit by a new bout of coughing. He reached for the glass of water on the night-stand, then moved toward the desk, sipping as he stepped carefully over the clothes, magazines, and dirty towels that littered the floor of the luxurious suite. He rummaged through his opened briefcase until he found his address book and picked up the phone. In a moment the international call went through. He sat down in the upholstered chair and mopped his forehead with a handkerchief.

"Hello? Rand Taylor speaking," the voice drawled.

"Rand, it's Jack," he wheezed, then took a gulp of water.

"My goodness, counselor, you sound a bit under the weather."

Jack coughed violently for a few seconds. "We have to talk," he croaked. "I just got off the phone with Darrel. The paralegals are beginning to piece together the details about the suite—who in management used it and when, and who their secretaries were. They're getting down to brass tacks."

"Very enterprising of them," Rand commented dryly, "but you know what I know."

"Darrel is concerned. His instincts are—" Jack broke into a violent cough. "I reassured him that you'd already told everything you knew, and that you only had suspicions of what went on. No direct personal knowledge." His voice was growing hoarser with each phrase. He took another drink of water.

"So what happens next?"

"Tony will work with his contact at the escort service to try to find out who went to the suite and what went on there, and who at Franjipur they were in touch with. So far your name has not come up directly."

"And if it does?" Rand drawled, sounding more casual than circumstances warranted.

"You just let me handle it. You know the depositions start next week, right?"

"Yes."

"Tony will try to ferret out the facts before then so Darrel and Stuart can get the witnesses on record. Tony's connection may even give up the names of the boys."

"Oh dear."

"Did you ever meet them? Would they be able to identify you?"

"Certainly not. As I told you, I have no taste for that sort of thing. My sole concern was the pleasure of my employers and to ensure they got what they wanted."

"Could anyone at the escort service identify you?"

"No. I never met any of them."

"Good," Jack said with relief. "And that's the way it must stay, do you understand? No matter how bright a spotlight they shine on you,

you were in no way instrumental in arranging the events that transpired in the suite." He stood and steadied himself by gripping the back of the chair between coughs. "Your only sin was surmising what went on and keeping it to yourself. They had to *suspect* you knew or we can't get to retaliation. This is critical for your case."

"You are quite a chess player, Mr. Soutane. My lips are sealed."

THIEF *in the* NIGHT

Caroline and Mercedes sat on the redwood deck overlooking the wooded hillside behind Jack's house in Montclair, drinking lemonade at the outdoor table. Anne and Germaine were inside. Profuse giggling spilled out of the open French doors.

"Those two! Always laughing," Mercedes said. She slid back in her cushioned chair and extended her legs across the edge of the table. Deep blue lobelia and bright yellow marigolds filled all the pots along the deck and down the wooden stairs to the yard. The wisteria cloaking the canopy over the hot tub was beginning to show its lush violet blossoms. It was a warm, languorous Sunday afternoon for late April.

"How's the wedding planning going? Only eight weeks away, right?"

"Just about there. We're down to the details now. I'm probably the first bride in history whose fiancé has done most of the wedding planning." She put on her sunglasses with satisfaction. Caroline poked her.

"What about your gown?

"Eleanor flew in on a shopping blitz a few weeks ago. Our dresses are being finished as we speak."

"She must be overjoyed about Jack."

"She's happy, for sure, but she's equally thrilled about being on center stage at a big wedding her friends will be attending."

"Her approval must be a relief."

"It won't last. I know how this works."

"What do you mean?"

"As long as she's in the spotlight, she'll be pleasant and strive with all her might to remain the center of attention. As soon as the focus shifts, forget about it."

Caroline looked at her friend in disbelief.

"The minute we're back from our honeymoon, things will change, mark my words."

"I hope you're mistaken. Has she seen the house?"

"Not the inside. Jack's tenants were still in here when she was in town. But we drove by it, and she liked the neighborhood."

"Well, I love your house." More laughter pealed out of the open doors.

"The scenery is definitely refreshing," Mercedes remarked, "although I do miss the gunshots and the neighborhood fights."

"Oh, you do not!"

"The used condoms and empty liquor bottles in the park—they were special."

"Oh my God!"

"And let's not forget the occasional home invasion—those I probably miss the most."

Caroline laughed.

"Seriously, I feel like nothing anyone could do will ever upset me again. I know this state can't last, but whoever would have imagined things would turn out like this?"

Caroline nodded. "It is pretty amazing."

"Jack had this whole house painted inside and out as soon as it was vacated. Then he hired movers to come to our little place, pack everything, and move us in here. It only took a few hours. We hardly lifted a finger."

Just then Germaine came running out, with Anne hot on her heels. The two raced past their mothers and clambered down the stairs onto the lawn. Anne overtook Germaine and beat her to the swing, then scrambled onto it.

"The house is great, whatever it took you to get here. What a yard."

"It's all Jack's doing. I guess he plans to move in right before the wedding. I just can't wait to live with him. He is the kindest, sexiest, most generous man. He asks almost nothing of me and is grateful for anything I do. I can't believe my good fortune."

"You're not living together before the wedding?"

"Evidently not, although *I* would. He wants to wait, since we've done everything else 'by the book.' My parents are coming to stay in the house with Germaine while we're on our honeymoon—to Tuscany!" She clapped her hands together. "Germaine is delirious. Many of her friends from school live up here, and the neighbors have been very welcoming." They looked down at the two girls. Germaine was pushing Anne, whose feet almost reached the branches at the top of her arc in the swing. Her blond braids flew behind her head and her purple hair ribbons fluttered in the wind.

⁂

WHEN MERCEDES PASSED BY JACK'S office the next day, he was speaking quickly into his Dictaphone, head down, with pages of his scrawl all over the top of his desk. She heard Germaine's name, so she stopped and backed up to listen. Germaine Llewellyn, residing in Oakland, California, was to be the beneficiary of the Soutane Family Trust.

Mercedes's heart quickened. She listened a moment longer until Melanie came around the corner and spied her. She motioned Mercedes into the conference room and closed the door.

"What's he up to?" Mercedes whispered.

"I'm sure he'll tell you. He's working on his estate plan to take care of you and Germaine. Don't tell him I told you. He's been revising his will."

"Why?"

"Because you're about to be his wife, Silly."

Mercedes scratched her head. "I wonder why he hasn't mentioned it."

"I don't know, but when he does, please act surprised."

"Of course."

Later that afternoon, after Simone and Lindsay had both gone, Mercedes was standing at her desk organizing summaries of the New York depositions in the Taylor case for Darrel. She sensed Jack nearby before he entered the room and turned to meet his gaze.

"Bella, that's a beautiful dress on you."

It was a simple black sheath with a bateau neckline.

"Say, would you mind marrying me?" he said, kissing her.

"Oh, if you insist," she retorted, and returned his kiss, buffing her ring on the soft surface of his dress shirt. "You've been busy all day, dictating away every time I've been by. Are you coming up for dinner? As your rent-free tenant that's the very least I can offer."

He kissed her again. "And what's the most?"

"Come up and find out."

"Actually, I need to finish up some work here. I wonder if you'd mind going over some papers for me and filling out a form."

She followed him to his office, where his desk was even more buried in paper than it had been earlier.

"What's going on in here? It looks like you're in charge of some major acquisition."

He smiled. "In a way that's true. The acquisition is you—and vice versa."

"Is this what happens when lawyers get married? A tide of yellow paper is unleashed upon the world?"

"I wouldn't know. It's a first for me." He turned suddenly serious. "I'm making arrangements to protect you and Germaine should anything happen to me once we're married. You've been through it once, so you know what happens when there's no plan."

"And no assets. And no job."

"Exactly. I'll explain it all to you when I'm done, but it would be very helpful if you'd fill out this application for life insurance." He handed her a long multipage document. "Germaine will be the beneficiary."

"You mean *would* be *if* something happened."

"Someday, something will. No one lives forever, my love. And when that day comes, the life insurance proceeds will be held in a trust for Germaine."

"How very thoughtful of you."

He waved off her compliment. "I'm applying for one too. Before we fly off to Europe, I want to know that she's protected. And there's something else. I'm drafting a separate property agreement."

"Okay," she said hesitantly.

"It's not what you think. Let me explain."

"You don't have to explain anything. I'm not marrying you for your money or your property. That's not what life is about for me, and I can take care of myself."

"I know that. But here's the deal. I've done some things in

business I'm not exactly proud of, and I don't want you and Germaine to be in any jeopardy if I should die prematurely and someone decides to come after my assets. It's been known to happen."

"What are you talking about? What things?"

"I'd rather not go into it right now and it doesn't concern you. I promise I'll tell you about it sometime. For now I'm setting up a trust, so I need you to review these documents and fill out the form and sign before a witness."

She searched his face, but he looked down at the documents in his hand. On top was a draft prenuptial agreement.

What have you done that you're not exactly proud of? "Everything about you concerns me. Don't you know that?" she asked.

"Well, it needn't—not the unpleasant things."

"What unpleasant things?"

Color rose in Jack's face, and he set his jaw. She could see she was getting nowhere and only adding to his distress. Perhaps there was the tiniest glint of anger in his eye, which only roused her curiosity further. His Majesty's dark side—unexplored territory.

"Look, I appreciate your consideration for Germaine and me, and I love it that you're working on an estate plan before we're even married. Of course I'll do whatever you wish." She took the documents out of his hand and put her arms around his waist. He drew her close and put his head on top of hers. He seemed hot and his heart was beating faster than usual.

"Whatever you've done, whoever you've been, I don't care. I'm not afraid and I want you to tell me," she offered. "Whatever you want to know about me, I will tell you. Our marriage should be completely frank and based on truth, and we should go into it with our eyes wide open. I love all of you—freckles, warts, gray hairs, and all."

"I'm not used to this—this—closeness, this trust. Bella, I *will* tell you—just not right now. I really do want to finish this work tonight." He raised his head. "Remember the night at your house when you told me what you'd gone through after Eddy died and left you high and dry?"

"Of course."

"Well, that preys on my mind. I can't imagine a more horrific thing for a young mother to go through, and it was unforgivable for that asshole to be so irresponsible—especially when it was avoidable."

"We had no money for a lawyer, and we were very young."

He stared at her, unmoved.

"I'm not making excuses for Eddy. It's just that having a will and life insurance is not at the top of your list when you're poor—and one of you is an alcoholic."

"So we're not going to have that situation in our family, okay?"

"Okay! I'll leave you to your work. I have to go pick up Germaine now."

Why did she feel she'd done something wrong by questioning him on a topic he'd raised in the first place? She slipped the papers into her briefcase and tried to put them out of her mind as she drove to Germaine's school. Whatever it was could wait. But Mr. Perfect-Bridegroom-To-Be was indeed concealing something—and the less she kidded herself about it, the better.

⌒⌒⌒

GERMAINE WAS GNAWING ON AN apple with her nose in a book when Mercedes pulled up in front of the school. Her short haircut was now a smart chin-length pageboy. As she walked to the car, Mercedes realized that her daughter had grown noticeably in just a few months. She saw the teenager who was about to burst forth from a girl's gangly body.

They ate dinner at the kitchen table, which was nestled into the nook they both loved, with its view of the house's sylvan setting. As the sun set, a young doe stepped into the yard and began nibbling flowers from the pot at the bottom of the stairs. In moments her fawn appeared and followed its mother's example. The bright white spots of the young one made it easily visible in the dusk. Mercedes and Germaine sat transfixed, knowing they should save the flowers, but unwilling to disturb the enchantment of the moment.

"You'd think with all the lush grass in the yard they would be too busy to notice the flowers," Mercedes said.

"But why eat grass when you can have flowers?" Germaine asked sweetly. At that, the doe bit off a hibiscus and raised her head, a red flower protruding from her mouth.

"She agrees with you. Why eat grass indeed?" Mercedes thought of the lawyers at the office with their elaborate luncheons at the club and their fine suits, and all the poor people in her former neighbor-hood. It was obvious who ate the flowers.

"Do you think we'll forget what it was like living in the pink palace?" Germaine asked, as if reading her mother's thoughts.

"Perhaps some things, but not the overall experience. We're not going to forget who we are or what we went through. What do you think?"

"I hope we remember the good things about it. Reading *Little House on the Prairie* and Mr. Friedman, and the day you got your job and when I got the scholarship to my school."

"And I hope we remember the suffering of our neighbors and never take our good fortune for granted."

The sky turned tangerine with the sunset; the deer crept down the yard to the bush of sweetheart roses near the swing.

Germaine cleared away the plates to make room for her books. Even though she had a desk in her room, she still preferred to do her homework at the kitchen table, while her mother packed their lunches for the next day and washed dishes.

Mercedes brought in her briefcase and sat across from her. Night had fallen. The lamp sitting between them cast a circle of light on the blue and white checkered tablecloth. A screech owl made his presence known in the trees and was soon answered by another. The tranquility of evening up in the Oakland hills was a balm to both of them. Germaine caught her mother's eye, smiled, and resumed reading her textbook. Soon she was back to writing, fully absorbed in the Civil War.

Mercedes pulled out the papers Jack had given her and began to read. The insurance policy application was straightforward. It was an application for a $300,000 whole life policy. There was a draft will he had drawn up for her, a power of attorney, and the prenuptial agreement. The last, she could see, was complicated and something she would need legal advice about.

She read the list of Jack's assets disclosed there. He owned far more property than he had let on. He had investments worth more than $2 million, many thousands of dollars in personal bank accounts, a lucrative law practice, cars, and furnishings he had had appraised. He had done well with his small inheritance. What was it he'd said? His father had left him $10,000, which he'd learned to increase while he was in Europe, buying and selling currencies on the foreign exchange. But she sensed there was more than met the eye, and she needed to understand all of it.

After Germaine was asleep, Mercedes was in the master bathroom getting ready for bed when she heard familiar steps in the courtyard and then a key turning in the lock. Jack entered the foyer and removed his shoes. She dried her face and slipped into the midnight blue satin nightgown he'd bought her for Christmas. In moments his arms were around her, his tie loosened and his shirt pulled out from his slacks.

"God, you feel so good in that gown," he murmured.

She ran her hands over the rough stubble of his cheeks and pulled his face down for a long kiss. Dark circles were beginning to form under his eyes.

"I thought you weren't coming up tonight."

"I wasn't, but I changed my mind."

"Did you finish all the paperwork?"

"Oh, it's never done—you know that."

She viewed him skeptically.

"You look awfully tired to me, sir." He was too busy kissing her neck to listen. His hands explored her contours.

There was something disquieting about him. She wondered if it had anything to do with the prenuptial agreement he'd given her to sign, or the momentary tension in his office.

She tried to see his eyes, but he was ardent and insistent and scooped her up into his arms. Her own words came back to her. *Whatever you have done, whoever you have been, I don't care. I'm not afraid.* They were past the point of no return. He gently laid her head and neck on the pillows and settled the rest of her on the duvet. His precious Mercedes. Trusting, supple Mercedes. He laid his head upon her womb and kissed her there, almost worshipfully.

In great haste, without even removing his trousers all the way, he parted her legs and climbed into her. She wrapped her arms around his back and clung to his broad shoulders, lost to desire—that great slayer of reason, annihilator of patience, and obliterator of prudence. Jack had awakened desires in her that she'd never known existed, and now her most cloistered cravings haunted her daily, sometimes hourly. Thoughts of him roused her constantly and gave her no peace.

In wave upon wave they rose, riding the crest. She wrapped her legs around his muscular thighs and breathed in his scent, completely abandoned herself, and hung on for dear life. The roof could have caved in on them without their having the first inkling. And when at last the tidal wave broke, they were thrown out with blinding force onto shore. The waters pooled around them and gradually receded. Mercedes came yet again, one last surge remaining, until her spirit itself seemed to have emptied.

"You're so incredible," he whispered into her ear, feeling her tremble slightly with an aftershock. "You're just too much."

Her mind was completely still and blank. No thought formed. A great pellucid joy overcame her, and she felt both of them inside a great ball of energy, as if all their molecules were melded together, all distinction between them gone. She could neither move nor speak, so profound was her rapture.

Slowly Jack disengaged himself and made order of his clothing. He helped Mercedes slide beneath the covers and curled himself around her. He stroked her hair and kissed her again, the sultry kiss of spent love, before he stole away into the night.

CHAPTER TWENTY-ONE

June 1986

FLORENCE

She dozed in her seat on the airplane, her body turned toward Jack. The shades were pulled down throughout the first-class cabin. The only light was that which seeped out of the steward's galley. A gentleman in the row behind snored softly. Jack stirred, reached out for her hand, and pulled it to his mouth. She leaned in close. He peered at her out of slits between his eyelids, like a guard dog keeping his eyes on the prize. She kissed him, and he tugged on her hair, which had fallen onto his chest. He pulled it around their faces, like curtains, and kissed her again, then closed his eyes, unable to resist the call of slumber.

Mercedes shifted in her seat restlessly. Images of the wedding drifted into her mind. The gorgeous church decked out in flowers. Rows of eager faces turning to watch her proceed on Philip's arm. Germaine and Anne, the jubilant flower girls, behind her. The groomsmen, splendid in their morning coats. Gabe, the best man, smiling as she approached. Jack at the altar, waiting for her in serene confidence. She felt the wedding ring on her finger, a band of sapphires and diamonds to complement the engagement ring. She relived the moments at the altar, Jack's eyes full of love for her as he proclaimed his wedding vows. She felt like running down the aisle, yelling at the top of her lungs in ecstasy, instead of walking with stately grace holding her husband's arm past aisle after aisle of guests.

At the hotel, in the receiving line, she met them one by one, many for the first time. There were the family members: Janine Reneau in a new frock, her wheelchair pushed by Enrique; Eleanor and Philip and their retinue of wealthy friends, who had known Mercedes most of her life; and darling Germaine. How sweet she looked with her crown of flowers, transformed from the waif of four years past. Never again would she question whether miracles happen.

The noise of the reception rang in her ears. A mountain of gifts had been deposited on a table near the entrance. She saw herself sitting at the center of the long table on the dais, with Germaine and Anne sitting nearby, thrilled by the pomp and ceremony, whispering to each other excitedly. The groomsmen treated them like princesses and escorted them to the dance floor again and again.

She heard the toasts and tasted the wedding cake. She saw Jack tenderly feeding her the first bite, and the affection in his eyes as she savored the buttercream frosting.

Jack raised his glass to Eleanor and Philip. All eyes turned toward the elated parents. It was a moment Mercedes never had imagined possible: the salve on old wounds, uniting her family. Eleanor even looked at her approvingly, as though she meant it.

After Germaine had eaten her cake and danced one more time with Jack's good friend Damon, Mercedes took her aside.

"It's time to say good-bye, Sweetness. Three weeks is the longest we've ever been apart. But I'll write you every day and send you lots of postcards. Your grandparents will take good care of you and keep you busy, and Caroline has promised many overnights for you and Anne. We'll be back before you know it."

The reality of being without her mother for so long struck Germaine forcefully, and she burst into tears. Mercedes calmed her as best she could. Then Jack appeared and seized the moment, lifting Germaine up into his arms and holding her higher than she had ever been held in her life. She looked into her stepfather's handsome face and blue, blue eyes.

"You're my girl now, and I'm counting on you," he said quietly. Her sobs subsided. She rubbed her eyes and looked at him with her lips pursed.

"Hold the fort while your mom and I are in Italy, and keep track of where we are on that map I gave you, okay?"

She nodded.

"We'll bring you lots of interesting treasures and think about you every day. Next time we go to Europe, you're coming with us, okay?"

She nodded and hugged him.

"And one more thing—don't let your grandmother take you to any beauty salons." Germaine laughed. "I don't want to come home to a stepdaughter I can't recognize. You're fine just the way you are, and we're a family now." He set her down gently and wiped her tears away with his handkerchief.

After many farewells to friends, they ascended the hotel's grand curving staircase, pulling the long train of Mercedes's gown around them in the elevator, kissing all the way up to the bridal suite.

At the door, Jack gathered her up into his arms, carried her over the threshold, and lowered her onto the white silk divan.

"Mercedes, my lovely wife, we did it."

He sank into the cushions next to her and let out a loud sigh. Her dress was a sea of heavy ecru satin all around them. Jack pulled some of her skirts across the front of his morning coat. He closed his eyes, stroked the silky fabric, and smiled.

The following afternoon, a limousine took them to the airport for their overnight flight. They would see the Swiss Alps in summer, roam the storied streets of Florence, and explore the hill towns of Italy with not a care in the world.

Now on the plane, Mercedes closed her eyes. Her heart beat more quickly recalling the hours of passion of their wedding night, the consummation of their vows. Jack played her body like a song, methodically drawing out the raging desire he had taught her to feel. They peeled each other away, layer by layer, hour by hour, until husband and wife sounded one chord. They fell asleep entwined, her head upon his all-protecting chest, his arms wrapped around her. Never had she felt so safe or so loved by anyone.

⁘

THE BELLS IN THE OLD church tower were pealing again. A friar tugged on the thick rope with dissipating energy. A wooden cart creaked as it was being pulled and pushed along a curving lane in the ancient town. The rough cloth of her hood scratched her head and the edges of her face. She drew a filthy sleeve over her nose and mouth. The overwhelming stench of death made breathing difficult.

Along the lane she trudged. The dead were dragged out of their dwellings by any family members who still had the strength to do so. Those who were strong enough took care of distributing what food and water there was to the sick. Others removed corpses from the street, loading them onto wooden carts.

A haggard woman carried the body of a young girl out of a multistory building, one of several along the lane. From the limpness of the girl's body it was evident that she was either unconscious or dead. A black pustule protruding from her neck testified to her malady. Mercedes again covered her nose with her sleeve and cast her eyes down. There seemed to be nowhere in sight where death was not impatiently waiting.

A black rat darted across the lane in front of her in the dusky light. She flinched and looked up at the heavy gray sky, searching for any sign of change or relief from the suffering that this plague had spread across the land. There had not been enough people to harvest the crops that season, nor would there be enough to plant next year's.

She rounded a corner. Another multifamily dwelling house, with an arched lintel and walls aged to a dark gold color, came into view. The air was humid due to the proximity to the river. A chill ran up her legs beneath the hooded robe. Two young men stood beneath the arch in the open doorway. The taller one, sandy-haired, draped his arm around the shoulders of a shorter, swarthy fellow and said something into his ear. Who were they? She knew several families in the area, but these faces she could not quite place.

The church bells grew louder and louder. A large pile of corpses was being burned in the fallow field outside the town wall. This, no doubt, was the destination of the heavy-laden cart she followed. She wept as she walked, unsure how much longer she could continue. She covered her ears with her grimy hands to muffle the sound of the deafening bells.

⚬⚭⚬

"BELLA, WAKE UP," a faraway voice said. She slowly became aware of someone embracing her. With a start she awoke. Church bells were announcing morning mass. It was June in Florence, and with profound relief she remembered that she and Jack were on their honeymoon.

"Oh!" she exclaimed. She burrowed into him, and he rocked her in his arms. The horrific smells and sights she had just left were still vivid. She inhaled Jack's sweet scent while the ghastly visions played at the edges of her consciousness.

"That must have been a doozy, the way you were thrashing around," he said, stroking her back and running his hands down the curves he loved so well.

"It was the same dream again, only much more graphic this time. Ugh!" She shuddered.

Jack brushed her tangled hair away from her face.

"My lady, let me help you forget that terrible dream."

A soft, warm breeze fluttered the curtains and wafted over them. Fine bed linens covered their intertwined legs. The bells had stopped, and Mercedes pushed herself deeper into her husband's tender embrace, feeling his hardness and his softness both, and his magnificent size. How comforting he was. How lucky and clean she felt after the misery and bleakness of the dream. He rocked her in his arms for a few more moments before spreading her legs with a gentle nudge and rolling her onto her back. The dream evaporated as they became engulfed, his fingers threading through hers.

⁂

THAT AFTERNOON AFTER A GALLERY TOUR, they explored one of the city's historic quarters. The past was around them and beneath them, on every wall, bridge, and abutment. The work of ancient hands and their designs were woven into every architectural form they saw, in the statuary and sumptuous stone urns and tiered gardens overflowing with flowers. Italian cypress and myrtle hedges lined roadways, edged properties, outlined the hills and provided the backdrop for their wandering, as in so many Renaissance paintings. Quietly they walked the cobbled streets between darkened stucco walls. It was like being in a living painting.

They turned up a little lane, following two small boys, who were kicking a ball. Mercedes watched their little sandaled feet as they nimbly passed the ball back and forth. The lane narrowed and curved. Multistoried buildings on either side impeded the daylight. She looked up at the apartment houses with shuttered windows and strings of laundry stretching across overhead. Jack pulled out his camera to capture the scene, but found it impossible to frame artfully in such a narrow space. He snapped pictures of Mercedes instead.

She pointed. "Around there is a church and up on the left will be a two-story apartment house with an arched beam over the doorway. This place here," she said gesturing toward the building on the left, "was where the woman came out carrying her daughter. This is the place I dreamed!" She felt her hair standing on end.

Church bells began to toll, and Jack jumped with a start.

"Bella, you didn't tell me you were psychic."

"I'm not. It was just all in the dream."

As they approached the house with the curved lintel, she pointed at it and said, "That's where two men stood, one with his arm around the other. I couldn't make out what they were saying. Jack, this is eerie."

"The ghosts are talking to you." He scratched his head and observed the scene. The lane was too narrow for cars to pass through. It had been constructed in an era when nothing moved faster than a horse, when cities were like nations. Yet children continued to play in the very places where piles of corpses had lain—where death had snatched away so many.

"Everything is exactly as I dreamed it," she said. "What do you think it means?"

"I don't know. Does it have to mean something?"

She frowned and said, "Look. I've had that dream twice now, and by chance we find ourselves in the exact spot where it takes place. Could you ignore that if it happened to you?"

"Only if I were hungry," he said, "which I am." He held out his hand. "Mrs. Soutane, *you* are an adventure."

She took his hand and pulled him in the direction of the bells. "Let's go see the church," she said. The boys with their ball ran into a doorway just ahead of them, and the lane soon led to a plaza adjacent to an old, but well-maintained, church. An elderly priest stood next to its open doors, welcoming parishioners to evening mass. His black cassock touched the tops of his shoes. He looked across the plaza past a large fountain at the two people in the distance. Water spouted out of the mouth of the lion that seemed to roar mightily at the pinnacle of the fountain.

Shops and a small market surrounded the plaza. A few tables sat outside a café with a striped awning. People greeted the priest and entered the church.

"Inside the doors to the church, on the right, there's a stairway to the belfry. There is a thick rope that one of the priests pulls to ring the bells. That was in the dream, too. All this area was bare ground— no plaza, no paving stones, no fountain, no businesses. There was a stable, I think. The dead were burned outside a wall that was over there," she said, gesturing. "This used to be one of the exterior walls of Florence."

Jack listened intently, looking unsettled. She walked around the plaza slowly, as if communing with the spirit of the place. The twilight seemed to blur the boundaries between present and past, dream and reality. When he saw that she was finally ready to go, he hailed a cab. The sun sank into the west, bloody fingers of light streaking through the billowy gray clouds that had gathered on the horizon. Mercedes withdrew into herself. She looked out at the gathering darkness, strangely possessed by foreboding and sadness. She could not guess what it all meant, but she had an uneasy feeling.

⌁

AT DINNER A BOISTEROUS FAMILY sat at a round table nearby. Among them, in a tomato-red pinafore, was a lively girl with beautiful dark eyes, perched on her knees in her chair. Mercedes peeked at the girl while she also tried to decipher the menu. She missed Germaine keenly. She thought of her daughter's bright eyes and of how she would have enjoyed seeing Michelangelo's *David* earlier in the day. She imagined her here at the table, next to her Italian counterpart.

Jack noticed the girl and asked, "Is she making you homesick?"

"Yes. What do you think Germaine's doing right now?"

"Probably giving Eleanor a run for her money."

"I'm not sure anyone ever gives Eleanor a run for her money," Mercedes said.

"You underestimate Germaine. She'll probably have another new wardrobe when we get back, and she'll have won the swimming competition at the pool."

Mercedes knew she didn't underestimate her daughter one bit.

Jack's attention went to a table of men across the room. They were young and sharply dressed—out for a night on the town.

"Bachelors," Mercedes said.

"Perhaps. You never know."

She looked more closely. Beneath the table two sat leg to leg, their feet touching. They reminded her of Damon and one of the other groomsmen.

⁕

AFTER DINNER THEY WAITED FOR a cab. The family had left shortly before, the young girl skipping behind her father, avoiding the seams in the paving stones. Her pigtails bounced with each hop, and her wrists were daintily angled upward. Mercedes noticed one of the men nod ever so slightly toward Jack. A look passed between them. Jack took her hand and led her outside to stand in the soft evening air in front of the restaurant window. A cab rounded the corner.

"Now, my love, let's go do what honeymooners do best." He

grasped her rib cage with both hands and kissed her tenderly on the lips. "You're pretty sleek for someone who has just eaten a mountain of spaghetti carbonara."

He looked over her head into the restaurant window and met the gaze of the interested stranger.

They returned to their room, where maids had turned down the bed, left chocolates on the pillows, and opened windows to the evening breeze. Jack walked out onto the balcony over the quaint street below. He stood with his hands in his pockets, turning something over in his mind.

Mercedes happily peeled off the day's clothes and walked into the shower. When he heard the water running he drew the shades. It was time to get down to more serious matters. He had played nice long enough. There was much his new wife had to learn. He had his needs, and it was high time she began to gratify them. Every smooth stone was once a jagged one whose surfaces have been worn down by time and the elements. Since he couldn't have what he wanted, he would do the best he could with what he had.

He stripped off his clothes and headed for the bathroom, caught Mercedes from behind, grabbed her hair in his right hand, and forced her against the shower wall. It was the beginning of a night in which boudoir niceties were superseded by a more gritty aspect of male lust: not pleasant, not tender, and not at all personal.

⁓◦⊱⊰◦⁓

SHE TRUDGED ALONG THE ROAD. *Dirt caked her feet and ankles, and the remnants of sandals were just visible beneath the rough brown hooded robe. She looked down, careful not to step on any of the dead. In the distance behind her, smoke rose from a pyre and vultures circled overhead.*

Her errand completed, she walked back toward the village, wondering where to search next for food. She covered her nose with her sleeve. There was the ashen body of the little brown-haired girl she had seen the woman carry out of a building a short while earlier. The horrible blue-black buboes of the plague showed on her face.

Ahead on the right was the building with the arch over the doorway. The two men stood just outside the door, the sandy-haired one still with his arm around the other. They shared some private joke. Amidst the ravages of death they had found some source of amusement. As she approached, the sandy-haired man noticed her and spoke into his friend's ear. She drew closer, straining to hear. He stood up straight and stared at her.

"It'll be your turn soon, you'll see," he said. "You think you've escaped, but you walked right into it." He laughed wickedly.

Mercedes panicked and began to run. She was hungry and tired and weak but felt desperate to separate herself from everything around her. A rat scuttled across her path. She ran as hard as she could, her heart thundering, the man's words ringing in her ears. She dodged many impediments and ran until sweat trickled down her back.

"Whoa!" A man's deep voice seemed to come from out of nowhere. "I don't know where you've been but I know you've been running from something," he said. She felt arms constrain her and lift her off the ground. She beat on the man's chest with both fists, impuissant to make him put her down.

⌖

"BELLA, WAKE UP! You're dreaming. Honey, wake up!"

She was breathing heavily when she awoke. Jack's arms held her tightly in the dark bedroom. She felt disoriented and frantic to free herself. She broke out of his embrace and quickly sat up in bed to regain her bearings. She looked around the room. The bathroom door was slightly ajar and let a narrow column of morning light into the room. Jack's clothes were heaped on the floor where he'd left them. The wardrobe door was open. Her garments hung there like so many silent witnesses. She sat up, naked and shaken and sore from rough sex. She slipped on her negligee, pulled up her legs and propped her chin on her knees. Jack gently stroked her back. She bristled and moved out of his reach.

"I don't know what it is about Florence that disturbs your sleep so," he said. "You were kicking furiously. Perhaps tomorrow we should move on to another city. Remind me to stay on your good side."

She glared at him. "How can you say that after last night?"

He lay back in bed, unperturbed. She'd get over it. Her training had only just begun.

The wood floor was cool under her feet. She walked delicately to the bathroom. After splashing water on her face, she poured a glass of water and drank it all.

This is the twentieth century. The Black Plague is over, and my bright new life has begun, hasn't it?

FISSURES

She parked the red Alfa and walked briskly through the front doors of the elegant office building where Jack had relocated his practice. The glass door with Soutane & Associates painted in gold letters opened into a swanky reception area. Melanie looked up from transcribing to greet the new arrival. Her desk faced the entrance so she could be both receptionist and secretary. Large pearl drop earrings gleamed on either side of her pleasant face.

"He's in there," she said, nodding in the direction of Jack's office.

Around the corner, the bookkeeper, an Asian woman named Rose, was crunching numbers on the adding machine with consternation written all over her face. Emerson appeared in a doorway, caught a glimpse of Mercedes, and retreated as she spotted him. *Sneaky little bastard*, she thought, as she placed a tin of cookies on the corner of Melanie's desk and patted her shoulder.

"These are for the office. Germaine and I made them last night."

Melanie pulled off her headset and pried open the tin, releasing the fragrance of ginger and spice. She bit into a chewy cookie and beckoned to Rose. Mercedes walked past the long row of file cabinets toward her husband's office.

He sat dictating quickly, his paisley tie loosened in the collar of his forest-green shirt. His lean face was darkening with new beard despite the early hour, and his navy blazer was slung over one end of the couch. He sorted through the papers on his desk as he spoke, and nodded in her direction without pausing.

"Bella."

She sat down in a guest chair across from the desk. Though tired, he was as courtly as ever. He located the document he'd been searching for and put down the microphone. His smile deepened the dark circles under his eyes.

"I have documents for you from Darrel," she said. "Since the Franjipur trial was postponed, he thinks we should augment the witness list and get Tony to try to find those two former employees." She plunked the file down on his desk.

"He does, does he? I'll take a look. Sorry I had to work so late last night. I feel as though I haven't seen you in days."

"You haven't. Maybe I should call Melanie and get on your calendar."

"As soon as I finish putting this deal together," he said, gesturing, "things should ease up. We'll get our lives back."

I still have my life. It hasn't gone anywhere.

"There's a Clive Morrissey on the line," Melanie's voice announced. "He's been referred for an estate planning consultation." Jack looked at Mercedes pleadingly and picked up the receiver. She nodded and got up, closing his door behind her.

⚬⚬⚬

AFTER SUPPER, Germaine and Mercedes lingered over their empty plates at the dining room table.

"There are ways to inform the school without broadcasting it, you know—although I suspect they'll call both sets of parents as soon as you say what you saw."

"Oh I hate this!" Germaine exclaimed. "Judy has everything. You should see her clothes and how the boys gape at her. She didn't have to steal that wallet and plant it in Amy's backpack."

"People misbehave for lots of reasons. Look at the Harrow kids. Their parents are loaded, the children have ten of everything they could possibly want, and they act like little monsters."

Germaine's expression was glum. "Why is it on *me* then? I didn't do anything!"

"It's on you because you *know* and because you're an honest person. If you don't come forward, an innocent girl will be wrongly blamed and Judy may very well get away with it, which will only invite a repeat performance."

"But it'll make me into a tattletale."

"How will you feel a month from now if you keep silent and Amy can't prove her innocence? You have a lot of power in this situation. Better use it wisely."

Germaine pondered her mother's words and looked around. Their house was rich with Jack's furnishings and those Mercedes had inherited from Elizabeth. The chandelier from his apartment hung over the walnut table where they sat; his African tapestry covered the wall nearby. One of Elizabeth's Persian carpets filled the living room. Antique floor lamps on either end of the leather couch gave the living room a warm glow. A long wall was lined with dark wood bookcases, filled with their combined libraries. Outside, the statue of Athena stood watch in the brick courtyard.

Just then the metal gates clanged and familiar footsteps approached the front door. As soon as Jack had one foot over the threshold he smiled. The aromas of Mercedes's cooking enveloped him. Germaine bounded over to greet him. He bent over to receive her kiss on his cheek and gave her a fatherly hug.

"You grew an inch today. Did you save me some dinner or did it all go down that hollow leg of yours?"

Mercedes helped him out of his coat, and he kissed her. Soon he was at the table with them, digging into large helpings of shepherd's pie and spinach salad. He ate unhurriedly and closed his eyes to take in the flavors.

"Bella," he murmured. She and Germaine looked knowingly at each other. Food was one of the currencies of love they had always spent freely.

After answering Jack's questions about school, and carefully omitting the crime she'd witnessed, Germaine left the table. Soon the sound of water running in the tub could be heard over Thelonious Monk on the jazz station. Mercedes poured two glasses of wine and brought them to the table.

"So, how is Emerson working out?" she asked.

Jack finished chewing. "He's catching on quickly. We're getting a lot of referrals right now. I'm trying to peel off as much of the work as I can so I can concentrate on client development. Isn't that a good thing?"

"Of course it is," she said with concern. "I just always feel that Emerson has an agenda and no one knows what it is, that's all. Darrel certainly didn't seem all that sorry to see him go."

He looked at her darkly. "I have some accounts to settle, okay? I needed help and I hired Emerson. The business that stands still is dead in the water. That's how it works. We have to start planning for Germaine's college, among other things. We have to plan for the future or it will come at us like a shark attack."

"You don't have to talk to me that way," she bristled. "I'm only expressing my concern."

She went into her daughter's room and stayed with her while she got ready for sleep. Although uneasy, Germaine had resolved to report what she'd seen at school. She chewed her bottom lip and turned onto her side, apprehensive about the fallout that would come from her peers. None of her mother's reassurances assuaged her misgivings. She was still wide awake when Mercedes said good night.

In the large walk-in closet of the master bedroom she pulled off her clothes, brooding over some of Jack's remarks. She slipped on a nightgown and turned with a start to see him standing there watching her every move. No smile softened his expression when they made eye contact.

"What is it?" she asked.

He said nothing.

She tried again. "How was your day?"

"Not bad."

He was in his pajamas leaning against the doorway, his shirt tossed into the pile for the laundry, his suit pants hung carefully from the cuffs. His clothes surrounded them. There were rows of Jack's suits, shirts of every hue, racks of ties, stacks of sweaters, shelves of shoes, and more shoes on the carpeted floor. The intimate room smelled faintly of his cologne, shoe polish, wood, and wool.

"Do you like your new life?" he asked. "Have you forgotten your life before?" He seemed to be getting at something, but she didn't feel like engaging in a guessing game.

"Of course I do—most of it, anyway. But I'll never forget my life before you came along, nor do I want to." She glowered at him. "Is something the matter? A shark attack on the horizon?"

"Nothing you need to worry about."

"I'd like to be the judge of that."

He said nothing.

She persisted. "You said you had accounts to settle. What accounts?"

He looked at her steadily and kept his own countenance. He touched her shoulders and ran his hands down the front of her satin nightgown, then lifted its hem.

She reached down inside his pajama bottoms, which soon lay around his ankles.

"You're evading my question," she said, roused by his erection and their tension.

He seized her by the thighs, picked her up effortlessly, and slammed her back against the wall. She clung to him in the face of ferocious desire, digging her fingertips into his shoulders. He thrust against her as hard as he pleased, not caring how much noise they made or whether her back would be bruised by the assault. She gasped at the force of him, but her body responded with hunger just the same. He let her down the minute he was finished, humored by her stunned expression.

"It's time for bed, Mrs. Soutane," he announced, pulling up his pajama bottoms. He grinned as he watched her straighten her gown. "Don't forget what side your bread is buttered on."

"I could say the same to you," she said with a glare. "And don't threaten me."

❦

THE ROOM WAS STILL DARK when the alarm went off and kept sounding until she clambered over Jack to shut it off. He stirred only slightly. It was a moment or two until she became aware of the dampness of her nightgown. She lay back down, still groggy, and felt the bottom sheet around her. Then she spread her hand toward Jack. The closer to him she felt, the wetter the sheet. She touched his back. His pajamas were soaked. She smelled the salty scent of sweat. He lazily rolled over on his back and reached out his arm to hold her, as he did most mornings, but she was not in the mood. She was chilly and sat up.

"Jack, you're all wet, and the bed is soaked."

He felt his torso with a start and sat up too. After a moment and without a word, he swung his legs around and sat on the edge of the bed. He held his head in his hands, then rose and marched into the bathroom, peeling off his pajamas as he went. He stood naked before the shower while the water warmed up, his bare back to her. She beheld her complicated husband, poised as if he were a statue. He rubbed his eye with the back of a hand and ran his fingers through his hair, then stepped under the hot water.

She pushed back the covers, pulled off her nightgown, and slipped on her winter bathrobe and slippers. She got out Jack's and left them for him outside the shower. He ignored her, scrubbing himself under the torrent.

She removed the top layers of bedding. The sheets were drenched through to the mattress pad. She peeled them all off and felt the mattress, which also was damp. The down duvet was obviously too hot for him, even in winter. She turned up the thermostat and went to make coffee.

An hour later, Jack was shaved and dressed in a bronze shirt and the burgundy and gold baroque tie from their shopping spree in Milan. He was drinking coffee and reading *The New York Times* at the kitchen table when Mercedes returned to the kitchen in jeans and a flannel shirt. Germaine sat beside him finishing the breakfast he'd fixed for her and simultaneously studying the crossword puzzle folded on the table between them. "Oh!" she exclaimed, grabbing the pencil to write in a word, then resumed chomping her cereal and bananas in milk. Jack took note of her entry and nodded.

"Germaine, it's time to get ready for school," Mercedes announced. "You'll have plenty of time for crosswords over Thanksgiving."

When the girl was out of earshot, Mercedes asked, "Jack, are you all right?"

"Of course," he said nonchalantly and continued reading the newspaper.

"I've never seen you sweat like that, not even last summer in Italy."

He shrugged. "It's just stress from work. We have a lot going on. Lots to juggle." He looked up and blazed his most dazzling smile into her face. "Bella, don't worry."

"That's more easily said than done, I'm afraid."

He put the newspaper down and took her hand.

"Right now things are hectic, but after I get better situated at work we'll go away somewhere on vacation. Maybe we'll take Germaine to Hawaii or go skiing. This is only temporary."

"You changed the subject. I'm worried about your health. I don't think it's normal to sweat like that."

Just then Germaine came back in to ask for help with a zipper.

"Are you turning in your science project today?" he asked.

"Yeah."

"You did a great job on that. Good work."

He carried his coffee cup to the sink, patted Mercedes on the bottom, and bade them both a happy day. He was off to the races. Mercedes was taking the day off to begin cooking the feast for the following day.

When she dropped Germaine off at school she said, "Remember who you are and just tell the truth. It will all work out, Sweetness."

"I hope so, Mom, but it still makes me mad that I have to do this."

⬥

THE THANKSGIVING TABLE WAS SET with sterling silver and crystal, and dressed in elegant linens that had once belonged to Mercedes's grandparents. A cornucopia of gourds and autumn leaves was artistically arranged in the center. Janine Reneau, tiny and fragile, sat in a chair to Jack's right, with velvet cushions cradling her frail body. As always, she wore her mother's brooch. She squinted to make out the objects in her immediate vicinity and the many colorful, aromatic foods on her plate. She spoke little, but beamed with pleasure and kept touching Jack's arm.

Germaine sat next to Mercedes, fidgeting excitedly over the beautiful feast and their first Thanksgiving as a family. Seeing Janine squint at her plate, she tried to help her by describing the various foods that she and her mother had prepared. This seemed to agitate the old lady, who stopped smiling and leaned toward Jack.

"You remember Germaine, don't you?" he said. "Flower girl at the wedding? Wicked at crossword puzzles, student par excellence, daughter of the loveliest mother in the world?"

Mercedes sat across from them. She couldn't blame Janine for wanting Jack to herself. He proceeded to cut her turkey, feed her small bites, and tenderly wipe her mouth with the cloth napkin.

Germaine noted the old woman's wrinkles and birdlike hands. Janine had shrunk even more since the wedding, and her pale eyes looked cloudier.

When Germaine had eaten all the food on her plate, she asked their guest what Jack had been like when he was a boy.

Janine brightened. "Well, he wasn't very happy, but he was always a good boy," she began.

Jack pretended to ignore the conversation.

"After his mother died and his brothers were gone I tried to help out."

Jack shifted uneasily in his seat.

"What was he like when he was my age?" Germaine asked. "Did you meet his friends?"

"He was—he was—lonely, I think. He was home alone much of the time. No, I didn't meet his friends. He was such a thin, sad little boy when I first got to know him, but then he was forever out-growing his clothes."

"Mercedes, I think we're about ready for dessert, don't you?" Jack interjected.

His attempt to disrupt the conversation only piqued Germaine's interest.

"What was Dr. Soutane like?" she asked.

"Oh, he was a lovely man. Very dedicated to his work and an excellent physician. Went to Stanford, you know. He was unlucky financially, though."

"Underinsured and irresponsible, you mean," Jack said. He abruptly got up from the table and uncharacteristically busied himself clearing plates. Mercedes sat still, drank wine, and watched Germaine in action.

"How old was Jack when you first met him?"

"He was younger than you. He missed his brothers, who were grown and gone, and of course he was so young to lose his mother. He had to fend for himself without a lot of guidance."

Plates clattered in the kitchen. Mercedes remained where she was.

"Jack takes after his mother in his facial features, but his father was very tall," she said wistfully. "I was one of his patients and was very ill for a time, so I had much occasion to see him. He saved my life. Then I found out his wife was in an institution and that he had a little boy." Janine turned her clouded eyes in Mercedes's direction.

"Jack has always spoken of you with the utmost affection and respect," Mercedes said in her low voice. "I think you *are* his mother in many ways, Janine. In his heart, most certainly."

Janine smiled. "I never knew Mrs. Soutane. She died not long after I found out about her. Unfortunately, there had already been some financial reverses. They had to sell their nice home in Atherton to pay for her medical care, and they moved to a small apartment in Burlingame, not far from the hospital where Dr. Soutane had privileges. Jack had to go directly to the apartment after school and wait alone until his father got home from work, which was often very late."

Germaine's face darkened and she wrinkled her brow. She imagined herself alone in the pink palace day after day, waiting for Mercedes to come home from work—no dinner hour, no company, no reading together or help with schoolwork.

"That's when Jack and I began to go on our adventures," Janine said. "Sometimes I picked him up from the apartment and we'd visit a museum or go shopping or just have a meal together."

Jack entered and set one of Mercedes's beautiful pies on the table with four china plates. He disappeared into the kitchen. The aroma of pumpkin pie made Germaine's mouth water.

"After a while he used to come see me in San Francisco and stay over," Janine continued.

"Why didn't Jack go to an after-school program, or have someone taking care of him?" Germaine couldn't understand why a little boy would be abandoned like that.

Janine hesitated before replying, "I can't answer that."

"Did Dr. Soutane marry again?"

"I don't think he wanted to."

"Why not?"

"He had his reasons."

"What happened to him then?" Germaine asked. Pain flickered across Janine's face.

"He died when I was in college, Sweetie," Jack said, returning from the kitchen, "and left my brothers and me a mess to straighten out. But enough about the old man." He placed a pecan pie on the table and handed the ornate silver pie server to the chef. Mercedes could tell a speech was imminent, so she waited.

"Janine, I'm a very thankful man today. I never imagined that you would live to see me with a happy family of my own, living in a beautiful home. I had no idea I would find a woman like Mercedes, or that there *were* women like Mercedes, who is so skilled in so many ways and so kind and down-to-earth."

Mercedes looked into Janine's face and wondered what she was thinking.

"I never imagined I would have a daughter, so smart and brave and inquisitive, and so much fun." Germaine swung her legs under the table and grinned. He continued, "I am happiest of all that you're here to share our first Thanksgiving with us. May many more follow! Mercedes and Germaine, thank you for this incredible feast."

⁕

LATE THAT NIGHT, after Jack had driven Janine back to her apartment and Germaine was in bed asleep, husband and wife sat opposite each other on the long leather sofa facing the fire that crackled in the hearth.

"Did it make you uneasy hearing Janine talk about you that way?" she asked.

"No more than you'd expect. Those years are best forgotten."

"There's something I'm curious about. Was Janine in love with your father?"

"God, I hope not. He was a mean son of a bitch."

"But she gets so soft-eyed when she speaks of him."

"Yes, well, we all have many facets to our personalities. When he wanted something from you, he could charm the shirt off your back."

He picked up Mercedes's foot and began caressing it.

"What did he want from Janine?"

"Female companionship, I suppose."

"But not enough to marry her?"

"He must have known he was unfit. I suppose he was afraid to ruin a good thing. I never asked about their relationship. Her love was enough for me. Without Janine, I would never have survived. And I wouldn't have found you." He rubbed her other foot. "I just couldn't live without you now, Bella, now that I know what I've been missing all these years."

She scrutinized his face, freshly reminded about the cold sex of the previous night and his mention of "accounts to settle."

"I hope you mean that," she said. "I'm very sorry about your unhappy childhood."

"And I'm sorry that Eleanor has been such a rough ride for you."

"You can't always get what you want," she replied softly. "But then sometimes you get it when you're not even trying to."

CHAPTER TWENTY-THREE

April 1987

GETTING AWAY

The surf roiled and swelled and flung glistening spray as it ran onto the white sand of Waikiki. It crept up toward Mercedes, but then pulled back into the ocean before it could touch her. The thunder of the surf rumbled deep down inside her. She lay on her stomach on a turquoise beach towel, soaking in the sun's heat from above and the sand's warmth below. The cares of daily life ebbed with each wave.

Jack moved her hair to the side, drizzled suntan oil on her, and smoothed it over her browning back and thighs. The feel of his touch, the smell of coconut oil mixed with sea breeze, and the sound of the surf lulled her into bliss.

"Don't ever stop," she mumbled.

He slipped his finger under the elastic of her sleek black swimsuit and ran it slowly around her behind.

"Very tempting," he said, "but this is a public beach." He finished working in the oil, then lay back on his towel.

"That was pure genius to bring Anne for Germaine to play with and Giselle to babysit them," she said.

"You're easily pleased."

Seagulls marauded along the beach, squabbling over an abandoned potato chip bag as the booming surf rolled into shore.

Jack raised himself up on his elbows at the passage of two perfectly groomed young men wearing Speedos. One turned to look at Jack over his shoulder, pointed at him in a taunting gesture over the oblivious Mercedes, and made a face.

"It's amazing how some people can read your mind," Jack murmured.

"Uh-huh," she said, too relaxed to think.

"I think I'll go get a cold drink," he said.

To the soundtrack of seagulls' cries and pounding surf, she sank into slumber.

⌐◦⌐

THE BEACH WAS NEARLY DESERTED when she awoke. There was no sign of Jack. The afternoon sun was low in the sky. She rolled over and sat up with a start, reflexively jerking up her legs. Her back stung, her legs too, and one side of her face was on fire.

She gathered up their belongings and lugged the beach bag toward the hotel. Why hadn't Jack come back for her? Where were Germaine and Anne?

She checked the pool area, the outdoor bar, the lobby. On the second floor she found Germaine and Anne playing shuffleboard on the linoleum of the game room. Giselle was lying on a nearby couch, reading a novel. Germaine gave a start and ran toward her.

"Mom! You're so red! Half your face is burnt!" She kissed her mother's face on the unburned side and cautiously inspected the backs of her arms, legs, and shoulders, which were hot and scarlet.

"I fell asleep. What have you all been up to?"

The girls excitedly recounted their afternoon with Giselle, who joined in the conversation. They'd explored many shops and swum in the hotel pool.

"I should have gone with you. I wouldn't be a lobster if I had. Are you hungry?"

They nodded eagerly.

"Silly question I guess. Jack must be up in the room. I'll just go clean up for dinner. I'll be back soon." She kissed Germaine again, smoothed Anne's hair, and patted her shoulder. The girls were having a fine time without her; that was plain to see.

When she unlocked the door to the suite she heard the shower running. She saw herself in the mirror over the bureau. Half her face was harlequin red; her back and thighs looked freshly broiled. This burn would be with her for some time.

She tapped on the bathroom door. No answer. She opened the door and called out. Jack stuck his head out of the shower stall, did a double take and said nothing.

"That's an interesting reaction," she said caustically.

"I'll be out in a second."

"Where did you go?" she asked. "And why didn't you come back?"

With care, she began to peel the bathing suit off her scorched body.

He stepped out of the shower, grabbed a towel, and wrapped it around his lower half. As he was not usually shy about his body, his use of the towel did not go unnoticed.

"Jesus," he said, seeing her skin.

She scowled at him. He touched her chin with his fingertips and turned her face to ascertain the damage, as if she were a doll. She tossed her head away from his touch.

"That's a second-degree burn," he remarked. "We should get something on it right away."

"You haven't answered my questions."

"We're on vacation, remember? Save the cross-examination for home."

"Forgive me, but it doesn't *feel* like a vacation right now. I don't appreciate being abandoned on the beach. If you'd said you weren't returning, that would've been fine. I wouldn't have let myself fall asleep like that. So where were you that was so damned important?"

"I went to get a drink and one thing led to another," he said casually. "Guess I lost track of time. Sorry," he shrugged.

"A lawyer losing track of time! That'll be the day." She pushed past him and stepped into the shower. She turned on cool water in a gentle spray and walked beneath it. It stung like fire. Half her face was boiling hot and the backs of her legs screamed.

Jack left the bathroom to dress. He stepped into boxers and donned a fresh white golf shirt and shorts. He combed his glossy salt-and-pepper hair and smiled into the mirror, whistling to himself. His tan was progressing nicely. He dabbed on cologne, collected his wallet and room key, and called out to Mercedes that he was going down to get something for her sunburn.

On his way back up he spotted the girls in the game room. "Come up with me and help your mom take care of her sunburn," he said to Germaine.

The girls ran to meet him, and each took hold of an arm. Germaine grabbed the paper bag from him and pulled out the spray can of Solarcaine.

"You think of everything," she said.

"Glad you think so, my friend."

⟡

LATE THAT NIGHT JACK SLUMBERED peacefully while Mercedes suffered. The sunburn was raw against the sheets, yet it had her shivering. She tried to arrange the covers in some tolerable position and find a way to fall asleep. Compounding the misery, an unpleasant after-dinner scene replayed in her head. Jack's inexplicable moodiness had turned to cold indifference once they were alone in their rooms. She got up to find the Solarcaine and reapply it.

He moaned in his sleep. He lay on his back with his arms pressed against his sides, clenching his fists and vigorously rolled his head from side to side. He tensed and pressed his ankles together, as if writhing against invisible restraints.

"No! No, Daddy! Jackie's a good boy! No!" he protested pitifully. Mercedes turned on the light in the bathroom and left the door open so she could see him. His agitation increased and he began whimpering. His fists struggled to leave his sides and he bent his knees slightly. His head jerked to the side and he cringed, as if dodging a blow.

"Jack," she said, touching his shoulder.

"No! Jackie will be good!" he shouted.

She hovered over him and shook both his shoulders.

He gasped and was suddenly quiet. His eyes opened, but he seemed not to recognize his whereabouts for a few seconds.

"Jack, you're having a bad dream," she said. "Everything's okay."

"No!" he said. Then he looked up at her suspiciously.

"You've had a nightmare."

"Were you spying on me?" He recoiled from her touch.

"You were very upset."

He sat up, again sweating profusely.

"What were you dreaming?"

He straightened out his hands and shook them, giving her no answer.

"You seemed to be constrained in some way. You clenched your fists."

"I haven't had one of those in a while."

"One of what?"

"They're dreams, but they're really more than that. They're memories I can't seem to shake."

"Memories of what?"

"My childhood." He regarded her darkly. She waited for him to continue.

"Sometimes my father tied me to my bed for hours on end. Days, maybe. I can't be sure. I was very young."

"Why on earth would he do such a thing?"

"I was a toddler and my mother was in a wheelchair and evidently he thought I was a pain in the ass. Then he'd beat me when I wet the bed. He never showed me anything but contempt, unless other people were around."

She began reaching out to comfort him, to touch him, but something held her back.

"He used to tell me that having me was what made my mother get sick—that it was my fault. When she died, he blamed it on me, and I felt responsible."

He swung his legs around and sat on the edge of the bed. Mercedes walked over to the open window with a blanket loosely draped about her burned body.

"I'm so sorry. I had no idea."

"Some things are best kept to oneself, as you say."

"Not something of this magnitude."

"I've been in psychiatric treatment for years," he blurted out.

"What?"

"Don't tell me you're surprised."

"Of course I'm surprised."

"You've met Dr. Hand. Did you think she was just an acquaintance?"

"She's not the only doctor we socialize with. Why didn't you tell me this before?"

"I thought it would complicate things."

"I see. And did it ever cross your mind that I had a right to know and decide for myself?"

"What difference would it have made," he said snidely, "after I put that fat rock on your finger?"

"Oh, you think you own me? Am I hearing this right?" Now her blood was boiling along with her skin.

"Spare me your offended feelings! I've lived a fucking nightmare, okay?"

He stormed into the bathroom. She turned her gaze toward the balcony, then walked out into the night to hear the ocean and feel the flower-scented air of Hawaii.

For better or for worse, until death us do part. She thought of him as a small child, strapped to a bed, terrified, alone, hungry, lying in his own waste, dreading the sound of his father's footsteps coming toward his room. How he had survived to become such a polished man was a marvel.

He walked out onto the balcony and stood beside her. He took her left hand into his and stared at the sea. He bit his lip.

"I'm sorry," he said. "I should have told you, but I was afraid you'd head for the hills if you knew. And I know you can't be bought. I was the one who insisted on this ring, because I wanted you to have it." He kissed her hand.

"Thank you," she said quietly. "You just don't know how much I love you or you would never have doubted me. I can appreciate how you'd have a hard time believing in love like that, after what you've been through."

He stroked her hair and the unburned side of her face, and kissed her. The sea breeze caressed them.

"I'm not going to bail on you," she said. "I promised to stay with you no matter what. Remember?"

He kissed her again. She put her arms around him and felt him shaking. She realized he was crying. She could feel the little boy locked away in the big man's body. She wondered if he had ever let another person this close.

"What's been wrong today? You haven't been yourself," she asked softly.

"It's hard to explain. I've been a bachelor for so long and messed up so many relationships, I wonder if I'm capable of being a good husband. When I'm working I don't have time to think about it. But now we're on vacation, and I'm a bit unmoored."

"You're a fine husband and stepfather. A little mysterious sometimes, but that's okay."

"It's too soon to tell."

"Then just hang onto me," she replied. "Let no man put asunder what God hath joined together, and that includes the groom. I'm new at this, too. If you don't level with me and I can't trust you, we're doomed."

⎯⎯⎯⎯

AFTER BRUNCH WITH THE GIRLS, Jack went to the business center of the hotel to receive a telex from Melanie, while the female contingent went to find a better treatment for Mercedes's raging sunburn.

When they returned, Mercedes found Jack in a state of great agitation.

"Rose quit and one of our deals just came apart. I have to go back," he blurted out.

"I thought Rose loved her job. She seemed so diligent every time I've been to your office."

"I don't know all the facts, but she walked out yesterday. We've got to get the billing out and Melanie is swamped."

"What deal fell through?"

"It's not one you know about and—I can't really talk about it."

She examined his face for a moment before responding. "So much for our carefree getaway! Are we all going back?" She hated the thought of telling the girls.

"No—you should all stay. I'll catch a flight. Come up to the room with me while I pack."

She watched him closely in the mirrored wall of the elevator. His mind was already working on the problems he faced. He pursed his lips and looked down at his feet, holding her hand.

"At least you got a few days," she offered. "I just don't see why it all couldn't wait a few more."

"I think I can salvage the deal with a personal visit. These are people I've known a long time. They trust me. It's the lawyer on the other side who's the problem."

"And Rose? Why is her quitting such a calamity?"

"It's not. It's just that on top of everything else, Melanie is— challenged a bit too much."

Melanie is hard to rattle, thought Mercedes, but held her tongue. It was Jack's practice, and really none of her business.

Soon they were all out in front of the hotel saying good-bye. A few days alone with the girls would be fun, although watching Jack climb into the taxi filled Mercedes with inexplicable anxiety. Telling herself she was sleep-deprived and being overdramatic, she blew one last kiss to her dashing husband.

CHAPTER TWENTY-FOUR

Summer 1987

R A I N

The deposition testimony, which all three paralegals had summarized, was bothering her. Mercedes reexamined what had been said about the executive suite. She could hear Jack's voice as she read his examination. She could picture him sitting near the court reporter and counsel, his big hands on the table, drumming his fingers. She could see him handing documents across to the witness, holding his gaze like a serpent hypnotizing his prey.

What if the turnkey to the case wasn't what someone had said, but what had been omitted from the testimony? She wondered. Amidst vociferous objections to the relevance of his questions, Jack had persisted, switching topics frequently and unpredictably. The objections were most strenuous when he broached issues related to the individual defendants' families.

Mercedes asked herself: *What did the wives know? Or suspect?*

Tony had spent hours interviewing his contacts at the escort service, researching the backgrounds of the defendants, their present circumstances and marital histories. He'd reviewed divorce files, family birth and death records, voting histories, property ownership, and more. On impulse, she picked up the phone. He answered on the second ring.

"Tony, it's Mercedes. Listen, do you know if anyone has tried to contact any of the spouses of those managers at Franjipur?"

"No, but I know a couple of people who'd love nothing better."

"Your anonymous informants at the escort service?"

"You got it. But no one from the plaintiff's legal team can do it. You know that. It's improper for us to contact an opposing party to a lawsuit directly, once they have an attorney—and that includes family members of parties. Darrel would have a hissy fit." After a moment, he added, "but Jack, not so much."

"What do you mean?"

"If Jack wanted to get in touch with them, he'd make sure it happened, but in a way not directly traceable to him."

She chuckled. "Do you think your informants would get cold feet if we wanted them to testify?" she asked.

"Don't really know. The two who left have an ax to grind, and there would be some credibility problems. They're not exactly choir-boys."

"That's my point. It's one thing to suspect your husband of having the occasional tryst with a younger woman. It's quite another if it's with a man, let alone a boy. Once that kind of trouble hits home, Defendants may want to settle rather quickly. The corporation would want to avoid criminal prosecution and the scandal of divorces with nasty secrets exposed. It's reasonable to think that the corporation would terminate any culpable employees. And from the executives' or employees' perspectives, losing your job is better than going to prison."

"You're starting to sound like Jack. You'll have to get Darrel to go along with it before anybody contacts the wives. Those two young chaps will probably be more than happy to make a few calls and give the women just enough information to hang their husbands out to dry on."

"I'll see what I can do."

She called Jack, who saw where she was going before she even finished the preliminaries.

"Tony could definitely orchestrate this," he said. "It would be like dominoes. The next settlement conference is next month. I think this just might work. It would give them a reason to settle the case before the damage snowballs, and keep our little snitches off the stand where they can be impugned all to hell. Bella, you're a genius."

She smiled. "Darrel won't like it."

"If he resists, I'll call him."

Darrel, as expected, was hesitant. "I suppose that spouses of defendants are not off-limits to third parties over whom we have no control, but I still don't like it." He sat behind his desk and reclined in his leather chair.

"Tony thinks his informants would be willing to call the wives and give them just enough information to start the ball rolling," Mercedes explained. "No one will force anyone else to talk. If the women don't want to know the sordid details, they don't have to listen. They can hang up. But seeds will have been planted that may bear fruit in time."

"It's very risky and could backfire." He made a tent with his fingers, to which he pressed his lips. "But a good settlement sure beats a plaintiff verdict that spends years tied up on appeal."

"It's the catalyst we need, and it's the truth," she urged. "Those women have a right to know and Rand has a right to a good settlement. The corporation won't stand for sponsoring illegal activity, at least not overtly. Think of all the good that will come of it."

He nodded reluctantly. "I get your point, although our concern is not what people *deserve*. Advocating for Rand is our concern." He looked at her intently. "Tell Tony not to screw this up."

JACK WAS IN A JOVIAL mood when he came home. She was relieved to see a glimmer of the old Jack and watch him banter with Germaine over dinner.

After Germaine had gone to bed, he sat at the table reviewing work he'd brought home. Mercedes washed dishes and hummed, happy to have him home at a reasonable hour even if the workday was not done. Documents were spread all over the table, and he held several in each hand. He broke into a coughing fit and pulled a handkerchief out of his trouser pocket. The persistent cough had developed a high wheeze.

She was reminded of his sudden exodus from Hawaii.

"Honey, whatever happened to that deal you came back from Hawaii to rescue?"

"We came up with an interim solution."

"You still need the break you missed."

He stared at the paper in front of him. "Emerson put the finishing touches on something else that we've been working on for months."

"I'm glad he's working out," she lied. Her dislike for Emerson increased every time she was forced to lay eyes on him. "I meant to tell you—Darrel gave the green light for Tony to proceed."

He was rearranging papers and scratched his head in puzzlement. "Proceed on what?" he asked vacantly.

"You know, the Franjipur thing—about having those former escort people contact the wives and volunteer a little information. Dominoes, you called it."

Jack glowered at the documents and then absently said, "I'm afraid I don't know what you're talking about."

His shirttail hung out on one side, and she noticed a food stain down the front of his loosened necktie. In all the time she had known him, His Majesty had never worn a stained necktie. He coughed again and turned his head away from the papers, shielding his mouth with the handkerchief.

"That idea I called you about this morning—the one I had while going through the deposition testimony."

"No, you didn't."

"Jack, I most certainly did. You thought it was a great idea. You even told me I was a genius!"

"If I'd said that, don't you think I'd remember it?"

"I certainly think you *should* remember it. Melanie put the call through. If you don't believe me, why don't you call her at home and ask her?"

"Now you're just being insulting." He glared at her malevolently, then burst into another coughing fit.

"Jack, what is the matter with you?"

He turned his back and continued coughing.

She left the room and went down the basement stairs to tend to the laundry she'd started before dinner. The humid darkness of the basement, usually creepy, was calming. She switched on the lights, which shone on the boxes of Jack's business records at the far end of the room. The smell of laundry detergent pleased her, as did the sight of Germaine's many beautiful clothes.

She folded jeans and hung up dresses and blouses on a rack, remembering a time not long ago when Germaine's entire wardrobe would not have filled a dryer. She moved a load of wet clothes into the dryer and tried to count her blessings.

The basement was directly below the kitchen. She heard the chair legs creak as Jack leaned back, then slide on the wood floor as he pushed back the chair and stood up. She heard him pace, walk into the living room, and make a phone call.

Was he playing some kind of mind game with her? He seemed sincere, but how could he possibly not remember her call? And why was he so belligerent all of a sudden? She began to iron a blouse.

The Beatles' song "Rain" came on the radio. She turned up the volume. John Lennon's nasal baritone struck her directly in the heart, as if he were singing only to her.

> If the rain comes,
> They run and hide their heads,
> They might as well be dead . . .

She ironed a while longer, then switched off the iron, and carried the garments upstairs. It was very late. Jack had gone to bed. She tiptoed into Germaine's room and hung up the freshly pressed clothes in her closet. She loved seeing her daughter in her great-grandmother's bed. She kissed her and pulled the covers up around her shoulders.

⌖

THE SOUND OF JACK'S SHOWER woke her in the morning. She rubbed her eyes and focused on the numbers on the radio alarm clock. It was nearly two hours earlier than he usually got up. She was tired and closed her eyes again.

Out of nowhere she remembered his words: "I've done some things in business I'm not exactly proud of." Hadn't he said that to her when they were dating? She wondered if he was in some kind of trouble she didn't know about. She put a pillow over her head. She pictured all the boxes of Jack's business documents on the shelves in the basement. She hadn't given them much thought, but last night they seemed to jump out at her. The paralegal in her wanted to go through them.

The shower stopped, and she heard all the familiar sounds of his getting ready for work. She hoped he would just leave and close the door behind him. But when he was fully dressed he sat down beside her on the bed. He placed his hand on the curve of her hip. She warily pulled the pillow off her head.

"Good morning, Bella." His voice was soft and low.

"Why so early today?"

"Client meeting. Have to prepare for it."

"Jack?"

"Yes?"

"Are you okay? Don't you think you should call your doctor?"

"I'm fine," he said too quickly. "There's nothing for you to worry about."

"I'm asking you to go see your doctor and get checked out."

"I'll see you tonight."

She rolled back over and put the pillow over her head. She heard John Lennon's voice.

> *If the rain comes,*
> *They run and hide their heads,*
> *They might as well be dead . . .*

She pulled the pillow off. She was not going to hide her head— not from this, whatever it was.

⚬❈⚬

A FEW WEEKS LATER, Louise buzzed Mercedes's phone.

"Mercedes, Darrel said to let you know we just got a settlement offer in the Franjipur case. He seems very happy about it."

"Is he in his office?"

"Yes, and he's alone."

"I'll be right there."

Darrel had just returned from the settlement conference. He grinned from ear to ear when she entered the room.

"We're getting somewhere. The defendants definitely don't want to try this case and have made a very generous offer. It amounts to three times Rand's salary at the time he was terminated. I think your domino theory worked, or is working, I should say."

"What did Jack say about all this?"

"He wasn't there and I haven't called him yet. I wanted to tell you first, since this was your brainchild."

She smiled slightly, but then her brow furrowed. "I thought Jack was going today. He told me he was planning on it."

"He said he had some urgent business and couldn't make it."

"When did he tell you that?"

"Late yesterday."

"Oh, I see," she said. She felt her stomach clench. She had discussed the settlement conference with Jack that very morning and he had been determined to go.

"Well, I'm sure he'll be very pleased," she said. "And so will Rand."

"This is only the initial offer. There's bargaining room."

◦⸰⸰◦

THAT NIGHT SHE AND GERMAINE were working on the girl's lines for a play the local theater group was putting on at the end of the summer. Mercedes sat cross-legged on the couch with the script in her lap while Germaine marched back and forth on the carpet, gesticulating wildly and reciting her soliloquy. Mercedes looked down to shield her amusement at her daughter's dramatic flailing of arms and exaggerated voice modulation.

It was well past eight o'clock when they heard Jack's car pull up and the garage door open. He burst through the front door, which slammed behind him. He flicked his fingers in their direction, as if to wave, and stomped down the hall to the master bedroom, closing that door loudly, too. Germaine, who had paused in mid-speech and mid-gesture looked at her mother in bewilderment. Mercedes was equally astonished.

"What's the matter with him?" the girl asked.

"I have no idea. It must be something from the office. Let's just leave him alone. You were saying?"

Germaine resumed her impassioned speech to the citizens of Rome.

A short while later he emerged from the bedroom in his nightclothes. He stopped at the console where Mercedes always put the day's mail. He leafed through it, looked up into the large round mirror, and saw their reflections. As though repeating memorized lines of his own, he acknowledged them and tramped into the kitchen in search of the hot meal he hoped to find in the oven.

After Germaine retired, still perplexed, Mercedes went into the kitchen and closed the pocket door behind her. Jack was finishing his dinner in the breakfast nook while staring at pictures in *National Geographic*. She kissed him on the cheek, pulled out a chair, and sat down. He took a handkerchief out of his pocket and coughed into it, pushed the magazine aside, and regarded her in silence.

"Hard day?"

"I guess so." He eyed her suspiciously.

"How were the chicken and mashed potatoes?"

He relaxed slightly. "Very good."

She clasped his limp hand and looked at his wedding band. "Want some peach cobbler?"

He brightened and nodded eagerly.

She cleared away his dishes and brought him a bowl of cobbler and a glass of cold milk. She sat and watched as he ate it in silence.

"We had a big day in the Taylor case. Did you hear?"

He thought for a moment and took another bite.

"Darrel was going to call you, but I guess he hasn't yet. He said you couldn't make it to the settlement conference."

He said nothing, apparently focused on the flavors in his mouth. She decided to drop it.

When he finished eating, he made no move to leave the table. She held his hand again. She told him about Germaine's work on the play and watched his face change. He seemed to soften as she spoke, but only listened. Then the realization struck her forcefully: the man before her was five-year-old Jackie Soutane, Jackie who wanted to be a good boy. Jackie who wanted his mommy. Jackie who had been brutalized, confined, abandoned, starved, reviled, and blamed for his mother's illness and death. The hair rose on her arms.

She knew how to take care of a five-year-old. She stroked his arm soothingly and asked him if he'd like help getting ready for bed. He nodded obediently. She stood and led him by the hand to their bathroom. She spread toothpaste on his toothbrush, which he dutifully took and used. She helped him out of his robe and slippers and guided him to use the toilet. She led him to the bed. She turned down the covers and watched him meekly climb in. She pulled up the duvet. He closed his eyes and sighed. She turned out the light and sat down on the edge of the bed beside him. She laid her head on his chest. He wrapped his arms around her and smoothed her hair. Her throat constricted and her heart ached. She stifled the urge to cry. She concentrated on the warmth of his arms around her and the affection in his hands, tenderly stroking her as if she were his kitty. She listened to his breathing as it grew deeper and slower, and to the rattle in his chest. His hand stilled and rested on her head; he fell asleep. She put her arms around him and wept.

NEXT MORNING SHE PASSED BY Darrel's office in time to hear him exclaim, "Jack, you're way off base on this. We have a legal obligation to tell Rand *all* the details of the settlement offer, and to abide by his wishes if he chooses to accept it." Silence. "I know you have the client's ear. You've made that abundantly clear since the beginning of the case. . . ."

She stood outside the door, out of sight, and tried to divine Jack's half of the conversation.

"What are you *talking* about?" Darrel asked incredulously. "This is *precisely* the sort of offer we were hoping to get. In fact, it's higher than we imagined their opening might be. We discussed this in detail. Don't you remember?"

Mercedes winced.

"We *can* get them to come up. There's no doubt about that."

Darrel was exasperated in a way she'd not heard before.

"I am asking you to evaluate it and I am *insisting* you communicate it to Rand, or I *will*. Louise will fax Melanie the document the moment we get it."

More silence, while he listened to Jack.

"That makes no sense, Jack. We've said all along that we want to avoid a trial, which neither side wants. . . . Yes I'm well aware of that, but you're not a trial lawyer, remember?"

More silence.

"But we are *light-years* away from punitive damages, with the evidence and the witnesses we have—"

"Just hold it right there. My firm has already sunk far more time into this thing than we think is justifiable."

More silence.

"Jack, listen to me—we *have* to tell Rand. This is not your decision to make." Darrel's voice had gotten louder with each salvo and now he was practically shouting.

Mercedes could stand it no more. She continued on down the hall, past the paralegal office where Simone and Lindsay were immersed in their projects for the morning. She ducked into Jack's old office, now furnished with a bare-bones desk and chair, to be occupied by some future associate. She closed the door behind her and sat in the quiet to collect herself. Her heart was throbbing. She felt hot and thoroughly shaken.

She picked up the phone and dialed the number she'd memorized.

"Doctor's office," a kind voice answered.

"Good morning," she replied. "My name is Mercedes Bell, and I'd like to make an appointment to see Dr. Hand as soon as possible."

NEW FRIENDS

It was midafternoon when Mercedes arrived home from her appointment with Dr. Murielle Hand, the kindly doctor who had once been Jack's psychiatrist and who had now agreed to see his wife in a time of crisis.

The house was quiet. Mercedes changed clothes and began her yoga practice on the carpet in the living room. With Dr. Hand to guide her she felt fortified. She began to concentrate on the postures and her breathing; she focused her mind.

At the end, she lay on her back with her eyes closed. She heard birdsong and wind in the trees, the brushing of branches on the roof. She thought about how alone she was. It had ever been so. Marriage never really changed that. It offered the illusion that one was not alone. *Solitude can be solace, if one appreciates it properly.*

She got up and walked out onto the deck. The tops of the trees were swaying in the breeze high overhead, like willowy women arm in arm, moving to some ethereal music, whispering among themselves. The late afternoon sunlight cast shadows in the bushes surrounding the emerald grass below. Everything around her seemed to be breathing. She became acutely aware of the movement of the bushes as the breeze ruffled the leaves and birds hopped from twig to branch.

Suddenly there was a great flutter and flap and commotion. An enormous pheasant, half leaping and half flying, landed on the deck just a few feet from where she stood. The bird regarded her warily, tilting his iridescent green-and-blue head with its bold scarlet patches around the eyes. Then he spread his brilliant plumage and pirouetted in front of her, stepping carefully as if he were performing in the queen's court. He turned his back so she could admire his feathers, speckled in gold, rust, and black. He turned to face her and dipped his head, as if nodding to her. The ring of white feathers around his throat reminded her of the starched white collar on a tuxedo shirt. He puffed out his breast feathers and stood perfectly still for a long moment. Then, as mysteriously as he had appeared, he flapped his wings and leapt back down to the ground.

Mercedes peered over the railing and saw the bushes quiver where he had vanished. She looked up at the trees and watched them.

The phone rang. She ran into the house to catch it on the third ring.

"Hi. It's Melanie. Jack asked me to let you know he'll be dining with clients tonight and won't be home until late."

"Is he there?" Mercedes asked.

"Yes, but he's in a meeting and will be leaving right afterwards."

"Mel, is everything all right? He always calls me himself."

"Everything's fine. Just busy, that's all."

Mercedes was not convinced. "Did he say which clients?" There was an awkward silence. "Never mind, sorry I asked."

"Have a pleasant evening and be sure to say hi to Germaine for me."

As Mercedes hung up the phone, some of the optimism she had just mustered drained out of her.

She decided to put him out of her mind for the time being. It was time to take the upper hand and make the most of the situation. She changed clothes and drove down the hill, with music blaring, to pick up her daughter from her after-school activities. Their first stop was a shoe store. Then they walked to a nearby bookstore. Nothing took her mind away from life like a good novel. She bought three, plus two new books for them to read aloud together. Finally they drove to one of their favorite places, a natural foods restaurant in Berkeley. The waiters were cheerful students with big hair, beads, and Birkenstocks.

Between mouthfuls, and completely off the subject of their conversation, Germaine blurted out, "Mom, what's the matter with Jack?"

Mercedes looked into her daughter's sad gray eyes. "I'm not really sure."

"He's been so weird lately. He doesn't remember stuff and he's grouchy and he's just no fun like he used to be."

"I think he's having some trouble getting used to living with a family. It's new to him."

"Well, he's new to us, too! Jeez!"

Mercedes nodded.

"It's like he's becoming a different person. He's kind of mean to me when you're in another room." Germaine scowled and stuck out her chin.

"Mean to you? Like how?"

"I can't ask him a simple question without him getting all huffy about it. And sometimes he looks at me like he wants me to get lost. He's just not nice like he used to be. It really makes me mad. I haven't done anything to him."

"Germaine, I know he loves you very much. And I agree he's not been himself lately. He's got too much going on at work, and I don't think he's feeling well."

Germaine shook her head, rejecting her mother's explanation. She pressed her feet down hard into the new shoes and appreciated the room her toes now had. Then she looked down into her plate and quietly confessed, "Mom, sometimes I wish it was just you and me again."

Mercedes dared not ask herself if she felt the same way. "We'll *always* have you and me. That's permanent," she reassured her daughter. "Things will get better, you'll see. By the way, I think we have a new friend living in the neighborhood. He's a very colorful fellow, who loves to show off. . . ." And she told Germaine all about the pheasant.

⚬⚬

LATE THAT NIGHT MERCEDES AWOKE to an empty bed. She thought she'd heard Jack's car pull in earlier, but he was not beside her. She heard a cough in the living room. She got up and slipped on her robe. He was sitting on the couch with his legs stretched out, still clothed in his black gabardine suit pants, with the necktie loosened in his collar. The shock of silver at his temples was more pronounced than it had been a few months earlier. He was reading *The Economist* with a drink in his hand. A small fire was dying down in the grate. He smiled up at her.

"I didn't want to wake you," he said calmly. "I was coming in in a moment."

He set his drink down on the floor as she bent over to kiss him. He pulled her down on top of him and cradled her in his arms. He switched off the reading light. The firelight flickered and the tree branches scraped against the side of the house in the wind. Shadows danced on the opposite wall. She settled her head on him and listened to his heart beat. She was too tired to tell him about the day or ask about his. She closed her eyes and felt small in his arms. She desperately wanted to believe that all her worries would go away as mysteriously as they had come.

When they walked down the hall toward the bedroom, Jack stepped into his stepdaughter's room to check on her. He pulled up her covers, checked that the door to the outside was locked, and took a look at the books on her desk and nightstand. Mercedes watched from the doorway. These were not the contrived gestures of a man who regretted having become a stepfather. He loved Germaine and was protective of her.

She climbed back into bed. When he joined her he held her again, smelled her neck, and kissed her as though he meant it.

"I'm so glad I married you, Bella," he whispered.

Then go back to being the man I married.

She closed her eyes and let go of all thoughts of him. She felt relieved, as though a weight had been lifted. She contemplated her options and recalled Germaine's troubled eyes and stern expression at dinner.

⁂

THEY WERE SELECTING BOOKS IN the bookstore. She saw Germaine's feet in her beautiful new shoes. Next to them were the pheasant's. She heard his strutting steps on the carpet of the bookstore as he promenaded around both of them, then down the aisle, his wings tucked up close to his sides, leading them away from the store.

Then they were out in the forest of her childhood, among the shaggy cedars and pecan trees. She and Germaine scrambled through the underbrush after the pheasant. He turned his iridescent head to see them, his curious eyes circled in red. He looked at them knowingly and spread his brilliant plumage in full display. He stepped proudly into a small clearing, illuminated by the slanted shafts of sunlight that penetrated the forest canopy. He let out a piercing call, spread his wings, and took flight.

THE NEW REGIME

J ack stormed out of the living room toward the master bedroom, presumably to get ready for bed. His relentless bickering had left Mercedes in a black mood, furious, and sick of him. She was grateful it was spring break and Germaine was away at Yosemite because she could take refuge in her daughter's bed. She was at the end of her rope.

A strange rhythmical thumping sound came from the master bedroom, like the sound of a dog's tail wagging against the floor. When she went to investigate, she was surprised to see the bed still made. The bedside lamp was on, but Jack was nowhere to be seen. Then she spotted his feet protruding from the closet, jerking uncontrollably. The thump-thump-thump came from his body banging against the floor. She caught her breath and raced to the closet.

Jack was on his back where he'd fallen. His arms were flailing and his right leg was at an unnatural angle. His eyes were open, but revolved to show only white; his body convulsed vigorously. Waves of energy coursed through him as he foamed at the mouth. His tongue rolled back in his throat, and he made gurgling sounds. She froze in horror.

Momentarily his convulsions subsided and his eyes rolled back around. He lay there stunned, as if in a trance, staring vacantly ahead, unaware of his surroundings.

She put two fingers into his mouth and flattened out his tongue. She examined his head for blood, and found none. She grabbed a towel from the laundry basket and wiped the saliva from his face and neck. She straightened his limbs as best she could, with his clothes all twisted around his body. He must have been in the act of un-dressing when he'd fallen and started convulsing. He focused and stared at her as if she were a stranger.

"Jack, can you understand me? Can you feel your hands and feet?"

He moaned and tried using his arms to maneuver his unre-sponsive body. He struggled to get up. Soon he was sitting, holding his head in his hands. With a monumental effort, he got on all fours and crawled slowly to the bed. He pulled himself up and climbed onto it.

"How do you feel?"

"Fine," he said abruptly.

"Jack, you just had a seizure!"

"No, I fainted."

"Fainting would be bad enough! But I saw you. You were having a seizure."

He gave her a nasty look. "Ridiculous," he spat out. "My head hurts. I just want to sleep."

"Jack, you need to see a doctor *tonight*."

"No."

He broke into a coughing fit, which forced him to sit up and then nearly toppled him. He sat up again and tried to take off his socks but couldn't manage it, so he gave up and struggled with the buttons on his shirt. She knelt in front of him, gently pulled his hands away, and placed them on his thighs. He looked into her eyes with such a forlorn expression that she hugged him. He leaned into her and buried his face in her neck and hair.

She unbuttoned the shirt and took his clothes off, while he coughed continually. She helped him into his nightclothes. He gave a sigh of relief and lay down when it seemed to be over.

"Jack, I should take you to the hospital or call 9-1-1 or something."

"No," he mumbled, "just let me sleep, please."

He closed his eyes and exhaled, then erupted into coughing. He seemed thoroughly drained of energy, all reserves depleted. She listened to his wheezing between coughs, the perpetual wheeze he had brought back from Hawaii.

She debated. If she called for an ambulance, how would the paramedics deal with a huge man who refused to cooperate? She pictured them trying to strap him to a gurney. Being tied to a bed would push every button Jack had. They would go to the ER in the morning. She covered him and turned out the lamp on his bedside table.

She had to find out who his doctor was and get to the bottom of it. She rummaged through his drawers in the bathroom, through the writing desk and his bureau. She had never opened the small drawers on top. They were full of pens, business cards, and random keys, but no clues to his medical care. She searched his wallet, to no avail. He slept on, wheezing and coughing, unaware of anything.

It was after 1:00 a.m. when she climbed into Germaine's bed. She told herself the doctors would find an explanation for all this and treat it. But then she wondered what would happen if Jack were seriously ill. How would she care for him and hold down her job? How would she keep things afloat?

You're getting ahead of yourself. Jack is sleeping. Germaine is with her friends. Tomorrow will take care of itself.

She slept fitfully and was awake when daylight broke. The first image in her mind was Jack's body convulsing, his eyes rolled back in his head, gagging on his own tongue.

When had she become afraid of him, his mood swings, and his vicious streak? She recalled his last verbal assault before the seizure, and it repelled her all over again.

She got up to get a drink of water from the bathroom. She looked into the mirror. She'd lost weight from all the stress in recent months. Her face, angular by nature, was much more so now. Her eyes showed exhaustion and anxiety. She washed her hands and went into their bedroom. Jack lay on his side, breathing with difficulty and wheezing, as though a war now raged in his lungs.

She slipped into bed behind him. She felt the warmth of his body, the comfort of his big back, damp with perspiration, and closed her eyes. She sank into a black dreamless sleep, an abyss devoid of images.

Sometime later, she became dimly aware of his coughing. Then something jerked her into consciousness. He was sitting on the edge of the bed, wheezing and coughing violently. She touched his back, thinking to reassure him, but he jumped in a fright, shocked by her touch. The face that turned to her was not one she had ever seen. He was beet red and wild-eyed, drooling at the corners of his mouth, his hair sticking out all over his head. At first he seemed shocked to see her, and leered at her maniacally.

"Jack!" she cried out. "We've got to get you to a hospital!" She jumped out of bed and hurried around to his side.

He looked at his hands and pulled up the sleeves of his pajamas. His hands, arms, neck, and head were covered with a brilliant red rash. He looked down. His feet, too, were swollen with the rash. His face was puffy. He coughed uncontrollably. She felt the back of his neck. He was burning up. He slapped her hand away.

She ran into the closet, ripped off her nightgown, and pulled on the first clothes her hands could seize. She chose Jack's clothes and took them out to the bed. He had not moved from where he sat. She gave her hair a few violent brush strokes and jammed it into a ponytail on her way to the bathroom.

She grabbed a washcloth and dampened it under warm water. Jack was struggling for air. Between the bouts of coughing, she gently wiped his face. This calmed him. His eyes looked bluer than possible, peering sadly out of a bright red face, now with an expression of bewilderment.

"I can't breathe," he sputtered, and launched into another round of coughing.

"Jack, we're going to get you dressed. Then we're going to get help."

"No," he whined. "Don't want to. Want to go home."

"This is home, Baby."

"Jackie's a good boy."

"Yes, he is. Jackie's a very good boy."

Yet another spasm of coughing erupted. She quickly unbuttoned his pajamas. His entire upper body was red, puffy, and boiling hot. He cooperated with having an undershirt and a soft polo shirt pulled over his head.

She took his hands when he was again quiet from coughing and helped him stand on uncertain legs. He listed right and left, as though tipsy, and grabbed the top of the doorjamb with both hands to keep from falling. She guided him to the toilet. She pulled down his pajama pants and seated him firmly. He complied without objection. He seemed relieved to be sitting. Walking was scary. She put his feet into his underwear and pulled them up to his knees.

Suddenly he thundered, "Just what the hell do you think you're doing?" There was the Jack from last night.

"I'm taking care of you."

"I don't need taking care of. What's going on here?" he demanded, with the frantic look of a captured bird.

"We're just getting dressed for the day," she said reassuringly. His eyes flitted here and there, as though wild animals were about to leap out from the shower.

"Am I going to work?"

"Not just yet." She helped him into his socks and trousers, then stood him up. She fastened his pants, moving as quickly as she could lest he become uncontrollable.

"We're going on an adventure."

"An adventure?" A delirious, manic grin spread across his face. An adventure meant travel, and travel always made him happy.

"Yes, Honey. Do you want anything to eat?" It was going to be a long day.

"Not hungry." He shook his head, which made him dizzy and prompted another coughing fit. She put a handkerchief in his hand, grabbed her purse, and shoved his wallet into it, along with his car keys. While he coughed more, she retrieved a jacket for him. Soon they were ready to walk through the front door.

She prayed that he wouldn't balk, and led the way with confidence. He followed on uncertain feet, concentrating on his balance. Soon she was helping him into the passenger side of his big black Mercedes, which she had never driven.

"I'll drive," he announced, although he was already belted in on the passenger side.

"Not right now. I have a surprise for you."

He nodded, obviously confused. His hair was uncombed, his face unshaven and red as the hibiscus blossoms on their bush. Never before had the elegant Jack Soutane left the house without show-ering, shaving, and tending meticulously to his appearance.

By the time they crossed the bridge, he had stopped coughing and was dozing.

Mercedes's mind was flying. She had opted for a San Francisco hospital because Jack had lived in the city for so many years. His doctor or doctors might have privileges there. They were soon parked near the entrance to the emergency room.

He looked up with sleepy eyes, coughing.

"I'll be right back," she said, taking the keys. "There's something I have to do."

He was too feeble to object. She got out of the car and marched into the intake area. A few minutes later she emerged with a Samoan orderly and a wheelchair. She tapped on Jack's window and opened the door.

"Jack, Honey, we need you to come with us."

He looked skeptical.

She took his hand and encouraged him to stand. He complied as the orderly took his other arm, settled him into the wheelchair, and pushed him into the hospital.

After Jack was taken into an examination room, Mercedes filled out forms at the desk, her hands shaking. She forced herself to find Jack's health insurance card in his wallet. She felt hollow inside.

A dark-haired doctor named Sinclair appeared. He sat down beside her and questioned her about Jack's symptoms. She told him everything she could think of.

"Why don't you go to the cafeteria and have some breakfast?" he suggested. "I think we'll run some tests right away and see what turns up. We're going to admit your husband. He's a pretty sick fellow." He looked at her compassionately.

She wished she felt surprised, but it was as if all the weirdness of the past few months had been leading ineludibly to this day. She went to the cafeteria and tried to compose herself with a cup of coffee. She stared out the window, looking but not seeing.

⁕

SOMETIME LATER SHE WAS SITTING in the lobby when the doctor reappeared. She tried to read his face, but he was practiced at shielding his emotions. How much bad news had he delivered in his career? She felt pure dread when he led her into a private room and sat down beside her.

"The preliminary tests show that Jack has pneumonia. His oxygen level is quite low, which might explain some of his memory problems," Dr. Sinclair began.

"He's been coughing for months and I've been trying to get him to go to his doctor. I have no idea who his doctor is or even if he's been to see him. We've had so many cross words over it. I've been very worried."

"*I'm* his doctor. I thought that's why you brought him here."

"You? Dr. Sinclair?"

"Yes. Jack's been my patient for many years. I'm not always here, so it's coincidental, to say the least, that you brought him when I happened to be making rounds."

Tears filled her eyes. He put his hand on her shoulder.

"Let me tell you what's going on with Jack. First of all, the rash is an allergic reaction of some kind, possibly to medication. But the greater concern is pneumonia. The strain Jack has is called pneumocystis. Have you ever heard of it?"

She shook her head.

"Fortunately we are well prepared to treat it because it's become more common in recent years. We've already put him on oxygen and medication, including a steroid. He'll have to remain in the hospital for now."

She was having a déjà vu. It was like watching the events unfold through a plate glass window, as after Eddy's death.

"Your husband is fighting for his life," he said. "We have the lab and MRI results. We think we know the cause of his convulsions." He placed his hand on her forearm. "Jack has tested positive for HIV and has a colony of the AIDS virus in his brain." She gasped and covered her mouth with her hands. "That explains last night's convulsions, the erratic behavior, mood swings, night sweats, and so on. I'm afraid this does not bode well for his future." He waited a moment, but she could not form a response. "And I'm sorry to say that you are at risk," he continued. "You must take an HIV test as soon as possible."

She covered her ears with her hands and bent over. Not another word. She couldn't bear another word.

"There is no cure yet, but research is going on all over the world. We have drugs to boost the immune system and suppress infection, but none to kill this virus yet. I'm very sorry."

"How long does it usually take for HIV to show up on a test?" Her pulse raced. *Germaine! Oh God, no!*

"Anywhere from six weeks to six months. If your test comes back negative that'll be good news, but temporary. I don't want you to have any false hope. Take another test in three months."

"Does anyone who's exposed ever escape getting it?"

"I personally don't know of a case, but there is a tiny percentage of people reported in the literature." He paced himself, attuned to her reactions. "Less than one percent."

She stared at his face. She wanted to scream. She wanted to run upstairs and throw herself into Jack's arms. She wanted to flee the hospital and pretend that none of this was happening. A vision of Germaine's gray eyes flashed in her mind. She felt as though a knife had just been shoved into her heart.

"Use this time wisely. You do have some time. Jack has less. Get your affairs in order." After a moment's silence he said, "Now let me tell you what to expect with Jack. AIDS is an unforgiving illness that can take many different courses. Unfortunately, Jack is already very ill. Depending on the degree to which his immune system has been compromised, he may have an uphill battle with the pneumonia. We must keep him here where we can closely monitor him."

"You mean he could—die—soon?" She was horrified.

"We should know within a couple of weeks. But that's not all. If he survives the pneumonia and we release him, he'll be homebound for a good while. He'll need a home-care nurse. He's in a significantly compromised mental state."

He let Mercedes catch her breath. "I know this is a lot to hear all at once. I wish I could do something to mitigate the bad news."

"Just tell me everything." She held her head in her hands, to keep it from exploding.

"As the virus replicates and moves around in his brain, there will be many changes—to his mental capacity, his appearance, his personality, and eventually motor functions. You've already seen some of that. But there will also be periods of lucidity when he seems almost normal. Take advantage of those. Get his business affairs organized. Find out what insurance you have, whether he has a will, and make provisions for your daughter."

"Will he be able to resume his law practice?"

"Certainly not—even if he recovers from pneumonia. He's on the road to dementia, and his judgment is no longer reliable. Since the virus is in his brain, it's not likely to leave. Obviously there will be a lot of business for you to attend to."

"Do you know how he got it? I mean, we had the HIV test before we were married and we were both negative."

"Has either of you had any blood transfusions or taken any drugs intravenously since then?"

"No."

"Then one of you has exchanged bodily fluids with an infected person."

"That just doesn't make any sense to me. Isn't it a gay man's disease?"

"That's the public perception, but this virus doesn't discriminate. It's not exclusive to the gay population by any means. We're in the middle of an epidemic that's becoming a pandemic."

"But Jack's not gay, and we love each other. He wouldn't cheat on me," she said in bewilderment. "I haven't been with anyone but him since we first fell in love—in fact, for a lot longer than that."

"Perhaps how he got it isn't so important right now," Dr. Sinclair said. "You have quite enough to deal with without worrying about that. You're welcome to go up and see him now. Please bear in mind that he's on the floor with our other AIDS patients, all of whom have depressed immune systems. Consequently, we limit visitors to immediate family and only during visiting hours. No children."

Our other AIDS patients. Was this all just a nightmare? Would she wake up soon? Afternoon light poured into the windows of the room in which they'd been sitting. The whole day was passing by in a procession of horrors. Life as she had known it was suddenly gone. Nothing would ever be the same. Not one thing.

"Yes, I'll go see him now, unless you have anything else to tell me."

"Just that I'm very sorry," he said.

Dr. Sinclair's dark brown eyes were rimmed with long black lashes, she noticed, like Jack's. He was obviously a kind man with great endurance. He shook her hand and said he would call her soon with updates.

THE AIDS WARD, as it was called, was full. Jack had a semiprivate room, shared with a deranged-looking wraith, who was probably in his early thirties. A thin blue curtain separated the two beds; both patients were under oxygen tents with IVs in their arms.

The roommate gaped at Mercedes as she walked past. He was a skeletal figure, like a concentration camp refugee.

Jack's eyes were closed. His feet extended beyond the end of the bed and had been carefully wrapped in a blanket by one of the nurses. She touched them with both hands as she rounded the bed, staring in disbelief at this kingly man, felled by a form of life too tiny to see with the naked eye.

Despite having his upper body elevated, he fought for breath and continued to cough frequently. He seemed relieved to be in the hospital and had taken to it without complaint. She sat in a chair beside him and slid her hand beneath his left hand.

She held his long, well-formed fingers and the large square fingernails so dear to her—fingers which had stroked every inch of her body, fingers she had nibbled playfully, fingers which had pulled her long braid out from beneath her tattered raincoat on that fateful day. She bent over and kissed those fingers, which had soothed Germaine, made her breakfast, applied Band-Aids to her scrapes, helped her with math, and thrown the Frisbee when they played on the beach. These were the fingers that drummed on the desk when he was thinking intently.

She felt his wedding ring and remembered putting it on him. She saw him looking down into her eyes at the altar, as though she were the most delectable being in the world, mumbling "Bella" softly as she moved the gold band down his long finger. Tears welled up in her eyes and spilled down her face. How could everything deteriorate in such a catastrophic fashion after such a perfect beginning?

When she left his room, she crossed the path of three patients, who were walking the length of the hall, pushing their IV towers. They were deathly apparitions with sallow, mottled skin stretched over their shrinking bones. Their hollow cheeks accentuated their protruding eyes. One of the men had dark purple splotches all over his face and neck. He smiled at her, revealing the absence of several teeth. She nodded respectfully toward him, and realized with a shock that he was probably in his twenties. This was how Jack would eventually look, if he was lucky enough to survive the pneumocystis. This was the future, both his and hers.

She walked out to the parking lot, slid into the driver's seat of Jack's car and sat for a moment. Suddenly his scent enveloped her, and she exploded in tears. She clung to the steering wheel, her shoulders shaking with the first torrent of sobbing, the tears contained all day behind a dam of incredulity. The magnitude of what lay before her was nearly incomprehensible. Was she up to the challenge? Could she handle it? No, it was impossible, out of the question. God was asking too much. She *couldn't* lose Jack. She *couldn't* get AIDS. How could she care for him if she got sick? How could she stand knowing that Germaine was going to be an orphan? How could she stand seeing her child watch the suffering, knowing her mother would be next?

She had to protect Germaine somehow. She had to keep her from finding out about Jack as long as possible, which meant she couldn't tell anyone who might tell Germaine. She had to be tested as soon as possible and keep it together at the office. She couldn't tell her parents either. Eleanor would become hysterical, and the news would kill Philip. She would protect them from knowing as long as she could, since their knowing would serve no purpose, as yet.

These sobering thoughts slowed her tears. For Germaine she had to be stoical and dignified, so they could make the most of the time they had left. For Jack she would be clearheaded and strong. She had to, she told herself.

When the crying stopped, she turned the key in the ignition and drove straight home. She wondered why she'd never driven Jack's sensational panther of a car before.

⁖

ATHENA STOOD WAITING IN THEIR brick courtyard. Shadows from the house fell on her white marble form, darkening her face. She gazed down at Mercedes in the quiet of the late Sunday afternoon. Flowers bloomed in the stone urns inside the courtyard. Mercedes stopped and looked all around at the brilliant colors of the flowers against the white stucco, inhaling the fragrance of eucalyptus in the breeze. How many times had she walked through here on her way to the door without feeling the fresh air on her skin, without seeing the pattern of shadows on brick, without noticing the goddess?

She unlocked the front door and walked into the entryway, with its high-beamed ceiling. Everything in the house appeared transformed, suddenly ephemeral. She felt the sharp and immediate contraction of time that comes with a death sentence. There would be no old age, no mellowing with time, no gray hair, no lines forming around their eyes. She would never know these furnishings to show wear. There would be no seeing Germaine off to college.

She walked to the middle of the living room, where she and Jack had spent their last evening bickering—their last few hours under the old regime. Now there was a new one. The newspapers and magazines of yesterday, piled on the coffee table, might as well have been from the last century.

She went into their bedroom, to the unmade bed out of which she had coaxed her desperately ill husband that morning. It was a movie set from another life in which a healthy couple had made love, and then lain awake talking of the future.

She walked into the closet, where the shoes on the floor were still jumbled from the movements of Jack's legs during the seizure. With a shock she realized that only yesterday afternoon they had been getting along amiably. Jack had seemed relatively normal. He had patted her bottom and kissed her, and told her how good the house smelled from the cooking she'd been doing all afternoon. Tears welled up in her eyes again. Would there ever be any more exchanges like those—those simple niceties of marriage, ordinary expressions of gratitude and affection, which are worth far more than the sapphire ring on her finger?

If only I had known when he left that night that I would never see him again, I would have stopped him, she remembered thinking after Eddy's sudden death. But this time . . . How many women are widowed twice before they reach forty?

She slowly took off her clothes and looked down at her body. Not yet thirty-six and very fit. Her stomach was taut and flat, her long legs lithe and muscular, her arms strong and well-defined. She'd always taken her health and strength for granted. She had *assumed* they were hers by right and had thought very little about what a gift her body was—her body that never lied and always told her just what it needed. It worked as hard as she pushed it, even amidst its messages of fatigue. This body of hers had always resisted illness fiercely. She had taken it all for granted—recklessly, foolishly.

Would she make it to forty-five? To forty? She took a long shower, as if death and decay could be rinsed away. She pulled on pajamas and wrapped herself in her bathrobe. She buffed her sapphire ring and gave her hair a thorough brushing for the first time that day. She became aware of how long it had been since she'd eaten or drunk anything. Even today, of all days, she had neglected her body. That was a luxury she could no longer afford.

She reheated leftovers and poured a glass of wine. She mustn't think with fear about her own death. In fact, she realized, if the advent of death delivered her fully to the present moment, it was her friend.

She lit the candelabra and sat down at the dining room table in the waning daylight. She smelled her food deeply and filled her mouth with homemade chili and hot toasted cornbread. She looked all around her at the home they had made, so full of color and warmth and beauty from around the world.

Jack must stop practicing law. What did that mean? How exactly would that come about? She ate her salad and finished the bowl of chili, thinking about the next day. She would stop at Planned Parenthood and take an HIV test on the way. And while she was at the office she would spend some time at Jack's desk to find out, at the very least, when the mortgage was due. Maybe if she went during Melanie's lunch hour she could get away with more time at his desk and less explaining.

She cut herself a big chewy brownie from the pan in the kitchen and licked the powdered sugar off her fingers. She felt a trickle of strength, and then she hit a wall of overwhelming fatigue.

For the second night she climbed into Germaine's bed. She wondered if her grandmother, in the darkest hour of her long, fortunate life, had ever felt as utterly hopeless and alone as she now did. One thing was certain: no one had ever told Elizabeth that the great General Stearn was going to lose his mind. She clutched her daughter's pillow to her stomach and wept.

EPIPHANIES

J ack was buying her a plane ticket and had the playful twinkle in his eye he'd had at the jewelry store the day he'd bought her engagement ring. She looked down and saw that his shoes were missing, along with his socks and his flesh. Long white skeletal feet protruded from his trouser legs. The clacking of his bones on the floor of the travel agency didn't seem to bother him. Nor did it concern the travel agent, an emaciated man with mulberry-colored blotches on his neck and left cheek. Jack bent over and kissed her mouth passionately. "I just can't leave without you," he said. "It wouldn't be any fun."

MOURNING DOVES COOING OUTSIDE SUMMONED her from sleep. The memory of Jack's kiss lay sweet and deadly on her lips. She ached as the memory of the previous day possessed her mind. Her heart pumped pain and sorrow and grief through every vein.

She opened the doors to the back and felt the cool night air. Her eyes burned from crying. She got back into bed and looked out at the treetops. She didn't want to get up but knew she was awake for the day. She couldn't face her coworkers in this wretched state. She must keep her secret tightly wrapped. She would call in sick, because she was—sick at heart.

She wondered if Jack was awake. Did he know where he was? Did he remember his trip to the hospital? Did he understand what was happening to him—to them?

The sky grew brighter. She closed her eyes and slid down farther into the covers. Her throat tightened. In her mind she heard the shrill edge of Jack's cough. He'd been coughing for so long. When was the first time she'd made note of it? She cringed. He was sick in the Philippines the December before they were married. He was coughing the night he announced their engagement at the Christmas party. *Could he possibly have been sick with . . . ?*

She silenced the thought. They'd been tested for HIV before they married. Her head swam with unanswered questions and with visions of AIDS patients: their young, forlorn faces, their wasted bodies, their sunken eyes.

Germaine would know something was going on, even if she told her nothing. She had to come up with a plausible explanation. Jack was hospitalized with pneumonia and had oxygen deprivation, which was what had been causing him to act so strangely these past months. It was true, just not the whole truth. That's what she could tell anyone who needed to know.

She dragged herself out of bed and took her coffee out to the deck. The bougainvillea draped around the hot-tub trellis would burst with color soon. The marigolds and lobelia spilling out of the planters were beginning to bloom. Small songbirds chirped and sang at her birdfeeders. A low morning mist was lifting from the Oakland hills. The sun rose over the ridge and filled all the droplets of dew with light, turning them into pearls and diamonds glistening in the grass, dangling from each leaf and petal, darkening the trunks of eucalyptus, redwood, and pine. Every droplet sparkled with light. The dazzling beauty stopped her thoughts and enthralled her. The sun rose higher and the ephemeral spectacle passed. How was it that she'd lived there so many mornings and never taken notice of such moments?

She called in sick to the office, then looked up the address of the Planned Parenthood clinic. The doctor's words rushed through her head: *I don't want you to have any false hope.*

She forced herself to walk into their bedroom, which unfortunately had not cleaned itself up. She knelt in the closet and straightened the jumbled shoes. In her mind she heard the rhythmic thumping of his body during the seizure. She put his dirty clothes into the hamper. Holding them, she smelled him and pictured him crawling toward the bed, his pants unzipped and twisted on his hips. As she stripped the bed, she visualized Jack sitting on the corner, holding his head, wracked with coughing. She made order in the bathroom and packed his shaving kit. She put together a valise of things he might need in the hospital.

She suddenly thought of her mother. What would Eleanor do in this situation? She examined herself in the bathroom mirror and heard her voice. *Pull yourself together, Mercedes, for God's sake! Self-pity will get you nowhere!* She knew exactly what Eleanor would do. She would put on makeup, lots of it, then elegant clothes, the most expensive shoes she owned, enough gold jewelry to sink a battleship, and a double dose of heavy perfume. She would act as though nothing at all were amiss, until she found out exactly what she needed to know and had manipulated every last detail to suit her purposes. No one could match Eleanor for confidence or command of circumstances, even when the deck was stacked against her—even when her ship might be sinking.

Use this time wisely.

She applied makeup and outlined her eyes in black. Her final journey had commenced. A dirge played in her spirit. She had begun to see through the glass darkly and felt trepidation about what lay ahead.

She pulled on an indigo gabardine sheath and heels. She put on the gold earrings Jack had bought her in Florence in atonement for the brutal sex he'd visited upon her.

She applied blood-red lipstick. She put her hair up. She filled her costly red handbag, another consolation prize from Jack, and picked up the keys to the Alfa. He was all around her. He was on her finger, in her hand, on her person, in her mind, and in her blood, where he had left his dark surprise.

⚬⚬⚬

AT PLANNED PARENTHOOD SHE LEARNED more about HIV, and none of it was good. At least there would be no way for anyone to trace her test. The nurse wished her the best, but they both knew that the odds could hardly be worse.

She drove to Jack's office. The bell on the front door of the suite tinkled as she entered. Melanie looked up at her in surprise.

"Hi. I wasn't expecting to see you this morning."

"I wasn't expecting to be here this morning either, Mel. What's happening?"

"Emerson's with a client in San Mateo, and I'm not sure where Jack is."

"I can tell you where he is," she said. "He's in the hospital with pneumonia."

"What?"

"He collapsed at home this weekend and I took him to the emergency room. They admitted him right away. He's under an oxygen tent being pumped full of antibiotics."

Melanie was shocked into silence. Mercedes looked into her sweet face a moment longer.

"Mel, he's very sick. They said he'll be there at least two weeks."

"Two *weeks*?" She looked horrified. "All that coughing—"

"Yeah. All that coughing."

"But he's going to be okay, isn't he?"

"I wish I could say yes, but he has a big battle ahead of him. His oxygen level is very low."

"No wonder he's been so . . . ," she trailed off, unable to say the word to Mercedes. "Oh, this is wretched! What can I do to help?"

"I need to find some things, and I'd like to start with his desk, if you don't mind."

"Of course."

"Do you have any idea how Jack pays the mortgage? I don't even know the name of the bank."

Melanie led her to the credenza in his office where he kept his personal files. Mercedes was welcome to search.

"I feel like such a numbskull. I'm not on any of his accounts and I have no idea how our finances work, other than what I pay for."

"I'm sure it's all straightforward. Since Rose left last year, he's been handling all the accounting. I get the bills out every month, but he handles the money. I can sign checks on the operating account, in case he's away and we have to pay a bill."

"Thank God for that."

"Mercedes, I just can't believe this. And it was under our noses the whole time."

"I don't want to believe it. Germaine doesn't even know. She gets back from Yosemite tomorrow."

The sudden thought of Germaine as an orphan pierced her again. She shook her head to hold the emotion at bay. Then she turned to the business at hand.

The desk's tidy surface, with opened mail stacked in organized piles, was belied entirely by its contents. The top drawer could hardly be opened, so jammed was it with papers. She took her time and sifted through them, searching for anything from a bank. Near the bottom there were photographs she'd never seen before.

The first was a photo of Jack as a very young man, perhaps in his twenties, posing with Damon. They were bare-chested, standing close together, with Jack's arm around Damon's shoulders. It looked like a picture Jack had taken of them with his other hand. Damon's head rested on Jack's shoulder; his beautiful eyes were full of love and sweetness.

She swallowed hard. There were other photos—Jack in a disco club, dancing with a man she didn't recognize; Jack and Gabe in law school; photos with Martin, to whom Caroline had spoken before their engagement, and one of the groomsmen in a bar; another of them in a hot tub. A terrible panic set in. She closed the drawer and took a deep breath.

She forced herself to open the next drawer. There were check-books for two accounts in Janine's name. With horror she realized she hadn't even given a thought to poor Janine. Who would look after her now? Who would tell her about Jack?

The next drawer contained the ledger for the client trust account, another for the Soutane & Associates operating account, checkbooks bearing the names of various partnerships, and one for a personal checking account of Jack's. Her mind was reeling. She would have to figure out how all this worked in order to keep things going while they decided what to do. Jack's sudden death would be a cataclysm.

The deepest drawer of the desk was locked. She asked Melanie about it, but Melanie didn't know where the key was. She had never been inside the drawer, and had no idea what was in it.

The credenza was full of tax records, bank records, household and credit card information for their household and Janine's. Jack, the money manager. She found the payment coupons for the mortgage and was shocked by the size of the monthly payment, especially on a house Jack had allegedly owned for so many years. It was far greater than her gross monthly income. Her pulse raced when she scanned Jack's checkbook. The house payment was dwarfed by the total amount of money leaving the account every month. Almost as much went to insurance companies, and more went to credit card companies. The numbers swam before her eyes. She put the checkbook in her purse. At least a house payment wasn't due for some time, and his income seemed to be adequate for the amount of it—while he was working. She felt like a little girl turned loose in an adult's world, where much more was expected of her than she was equipped to handle.

She sat back in Jack's chair and looked at his silver-framed photograph of her and Germaine, which sat on the credenza. Jack, the family man.

She opened the top drawer again and took out the photos. Suddenly they all made sense. How could she not have realized? He had no pictures of previous girlfriends because there *weren't* any. They were *men*. With a clunk, another piece fell into place. Emerson's weird behavior was *jealousy*.

Church bells began to toll in the distance. Someone had just gotten married or was about to be buried. She closed her eyes. The ringing of the bells took her back to their honeymoon, waking up next to Jack in Florence, the white curtain fluttering in the breeze, the bells clanging in a nearby church.

Her scalp prickled. The dream. Of course! It was Emerson in the dream with his arm draped around Martin, whispering into Martin's ear, taunting her.

You think you've escaped, but you've walked right into it.

She looked down at the photographs in her hand. Dr. Sinclair must know. *Perhaps how he got it isn't so important right now.* She dialed his office number, but he was with a patient. She left a message. She needed to stay focused, but now there were so many things to focus *on.*

Top priorities: Germaine and survival. Today she needed to buy groceries for Germaine's return, get the house in order, and go to the hospital. Then she needed to find the key to that drawer.

Tomorrow she'd speak with Darrel. Jack's illness put all the burden of the Taylor case squarely on her boss's shoulders. The new date for trial was only six weeks away. How she could assist in a trial with all this going on, she did not know, but she was getting ahead of herself. When two days had taken fifty years off her life, six weeks were an eternity.

Melanie stood up to give her a hug on her way out. She said she'd tell Emerson that Jack was in the hospital. She had already started rescheduling appointments and reprioritizing the mail.

⊸⊱⊰⊷

MERCEDES DROVE TO THE GROCERY STORE. Everything had a truncated feeling to it now. The number of times she would buy groceries was finite. It had always been so, but she had never been cognizant of it. The number of times she would drive her beloved Alfa was limited.

She wanted to slow down her mind, to stop taking things for granted, to get all of the negativity in her life away from her. Time was too precious. Everything was too precious. Feeling all this was an exquisite torture that she would never be able to convey to anyone; but at least she had lived long enough to realize it.

She pushed a cart into the produce department. The flood of colors and shapes that greeted her was breathtaking: orange, yellow, ivory, red, purple, red-brown, tan, and greens of every hue, all vibrant. It was as though she'd never seen fruits and vegetables before. She noticed the other shoppers. They were all going about their business as though they were sleepwalking, except the toddler in the cart next to hers, who also appeared to be enchanted by the pageant in which he found himself. His mother fed him a small piece of banana, and he wiggled with pleasure, his tiny teeth gleaming like pearls. He slapped his hands together and squealed in delight.

Every carton of milk, every sack of flour, every bag of lentils, every object in sight was alive. The awareness of death was working some kind of magic on her. She felt fully, crazily, inexplicably alive as she had after she'd given birth to Germaine, fallen head over heels in love with Eddy, and first laid eyes on Jack. Whatever had she been waiting for? How could she possibly have been so unaware?

The very act of breathing was new. So was all this life around her. It was new because of its rapid and constant change. Every molecule, with expiration and birth embedded in its electrons, was fleeing past, dying and being born, dying and being born, dying and being born. And now that she was dying, she also was being born.

⋅⋅⋅

SHE MADE THE HOUSE READY for Germaine. She filled a big crystal vase with daisies and put them in the center of the table. She put the food away. She put fresh sheets on Germaine's bed. Soon her darling daughter would be back. In this foreshortened life, everything true and beautiful must be freed from its hiding place.

Hiding places. The key to Jack's bottom desk drawer had to be in the house, and readily accessible. She must have seen it without realizing what it was. She remembered her frantic search for the name of Jack's doctor after the seizure. She'd hunted through every drawer in . . .

She went to Jack's bureau and opened one of the small drawers on top. Beneath the business cards and clutter in the back corner was a small gold key. She examined it carefully, wondering if it would fit the lock. She slipped it into her coin purse.

⸎

AFTER RUSH HOUR, she drove Jack's car to San Francisco, listening to the Joan Armatrading tape he loved so much, the one with "Show Some Emotion" on it. She was getting the hang of driving his big sleek car; it kept her from thinking much about where she was going until she crossed the bridge and saw the steel and glass skyscrapers of the city looming on the right. Apprehension steadily crept up her back and gripped her neck in its cold fingers. Her mood of the early morning had returned. She dreaded seeing the patients on the ward, dreaded the hospital smell, dreaded the dejected eyes of the visitors, and, most of all, dreaded seeing Jack.

She parked in the hospital parking lot and remained in the car. She smoothed her hair, put on more lipstick, and spied the glove compartment—another place she had not yet explored. *No more hiding places!* In it she found another jumble of papers, some maps, a tire-pressure gauge, several plastic vials of medicine, and an inhaler. She read the labels. One was an antibiotic she'd heard of, but all the other drugs were foreign to her and came from a pharmacy in San Francisco. She scooped them up and deposited them into her handbag. *Why in the world would he keep his meds in his car? Why hide an inhaler when it was so obvious he had respiratory problems? Why so many secrets?*

Jack's roommate's bed was empty and all his personal effects had been removed. She walked to the far side of Jack's bed and pulled up a chair next to him. He lay exactly as she had left him the previous afternoon—on the inclined mattress with his mouth open, struggling for air, his head rolled to the side. He was oblivious to her. Paul, the big blond nurse assigned to monitor him, came in to check vital signs. He smiled at Mercedes, who was a refreshing sight in the ward, and shook her hand.

She pointed at the empty bed with a question in her eyes. Paul shook his head sadly.

He said Jack had been awake a little earlier and had gotten agitated, but they were able to calm him.

"Did he understand where he was?"

"No," Paul said, "and his speech was quite . . . garbled."

She stared at Jack and took his hand, while Paul busied himself checking the equipment and making notes on the clipboard at the foot of the bed. Only two nights ago they'd been arguing. She would gladly trade an argument for this. She kissed his hand and held it with both of hers against her cheek, under a stream of tears. She thought her insides could not withstand the pressure of the grief in her heart. Paul patted her back, which only made her cry harder.

Who will take care of Germaine when I'm the one lying in the hospital bed? Will her last memories of me be like this?

Paul tried to reassure her. "The first onset of illness is not often fatal," he said. "I think Jack will rally and you'll have more time together."

"How much time?"

"They're improving the treatments all the time."

"Ten years?"

He didn't want to say.

"Eight years?"

"Not likely, from what we've seen here."

"Five years then? Could we have five years?"

"I wish I could tell you, but we just don't know."

Jack began to moan and move his legs. He opened his eyes and looked through the clear plastic tent at the woman in the chair. He stared at her without blinking and tried to form words, but nonsense came out instead. Mercedes stood up and leaned over him, hoping that the sight of her would comfort him, but he only grew more agitated. She put her hand on his leg, and he recoiled.

Paul observed, "You might look rather odd to him through the oxygen tent. His reaction is fairly typical for patients where the virus has moved into the brain, but it can change as rapidly as it starts. It all depends on where the colony has set up camp that day."

Jack stared at her and inched his way to the bed rails farthest from her. She could comfort neither him nor herself.

"What can I do to help him?" she asked.

"In this state, not much. Be patient and take care of things at home. Take care of all the things he can't do right now."

Tears filled her eyes again. "What good does it even do for me to come here?"

"You can call the nurse's station about him at any time. Why don't you do that, and not plan on coming every day?"

"But he's my husband!"

"You have a child. You're lucky. Spend time with her. We'll keep you posted."

Jack moved his head from side to side, as if trying to convey his disagreement.

Mercedes looked right at him and said, "Jack, I found your medication and gave it to your nurse. He's going to give it to your doctor. We're trying to help you get well."

He stared at her wild-eyed. Her throat tightened. Somewhere in that tent was the man with whom she had fallen in love. Would she ever see him again?

"Honestly, it's as if I agitate him. I don't get this," Mercedes said.

Paul said, "Try not to take anything he does or says personally. He's not in his right mind, and I'm sure he loves you very much. This is not an easy place for anyone to visit. You're a brave woman."

"I'm not brave, Paul. I'm next."

She felt repulsed by the hospital ward, by the patients, by her prospects. As she walked down the narrow corridor to the elevator, she felt herself in an updated version of her honeymoon dream, following a cart loaded with the dead.

Before turning the corner she looked back. Two skeletal patients stood in a doorway, one with his arm around the other. They both watched her, and she remembered the men in the doorway from her dream. She could almost hear the wooden cartwheels creak, their crunch on the hard, rocky ground, the squeal of a rat. She pushed the button for the elevator and the down arrow lit up.

PUTTING TWO *and* TWO TOGETHER

"Mercedes, is everything all right?" Darrel asked.

"I've been better."

"That's what I thought."

"I've been meaning to tell you. Now is as good a time as any." She got up and closed the conference room door. "It's Jack. He's very ill. He collapsed on Sunday at home. He'd been having a lot of trouble breathing."

She had Darrel's complete attention.

"I took him to the ER and they wound up admitting him. He's been diagnosed with pneumonia. He's fighting for his life." The words caught in her throat. "He's apparently had it for some time, but we weren't aware that's what it was. You know, he's had that cough. They told me he hasn't been getting enough oxygen for quite a while . . . which may explain why he hasn't been himself . . . and . . ."

Her voice cracked. She covered her mouth with her hand.

"And anyway, I'm afraid you'll be on your own at trial. Jack is totally incapacitated and the prognosis is very guarded."

Darrel sat for a moment, thinking about the news.

"Mercedes, that's terrible. I'm so sorry . . . for you and for him." He looked troubled, but not surprised. "I'm sure you have him in the best possible hands. Jack's a force of nature, and I know he'll pull out of it. Please take all the time you need and let us know if there's anything we can do to help."

"The doctors say that even if he recovers well enough to come home, he'll be out of commission for some time. You should consider the Taylor case yours. If you decide to settle it, there'll be nothing to stop you. I'm afraid Jack is beyond consultation."

"What about you? How are you handling all this?" His gaze seemed to penetrate her façade.

"I don't think it's really sunk in yet. You're the only person I've told, except for Melanie."

Just then the phone intercom buzzed. It was Julie, from reception. "Tony Grey is on the line. He says it's urgent."

Darrel and Mercedes exchanged a surprised look as Darrel pressed the speaker-phone button.

"Tony, what's up? I'm here with Mercedes, and we have you on speaker."

"An unsettling turn of events, I'm afraid." Mercedes looked down into her lap. He continued, "Our boy Rand may not be so lily white after all. I was able to track down a young fellow who used to turn tricks at Franjipur. He did a stint in the executive suite. I got quite an earful."

Darrel sat forward in his chair and braced himself.

"I've been trying to nail down exactly how these trysts were set up at the hotel, so I asked him about it. He said he didn't know about the other guys, but after his first 'date' there, a man with a thick southern accent called him to arrange another one. I asked if he ever met him or learned his name. He said no, he didn't. But he said it was an unforgettable voice. The guy contacted him a few times. He said he would recognize it easily if he heard it again."

Darrel and Mercedes exchanged a look of disgust. Rand had played them. The avalanche of bad news just kept coming. Mercedes felt sick.

"He's absolutely certain it was a southern accent?" Darrel queried, his eyes flashing with anger.

"Yes, and I said nothing about the accent before he brought it up. Is there anyone it could be, besides Rand?"

"I doubt it. Keep digging and see if anyone else corroborates this. We have to know everything, Tony—no holds barred."

"Understood."

Darrel ended the call and jumped to his feet. "God damn it. God *damn it!*" He roared. He rubbed the back of his neck and paced back and forth in a fury.

Mercedes's thoughts turned immediately to Jack—to what he must have known and when he knew it. As if reading her mind, Darrel said, "I really must talk to Jack."

"Darrel, there's just no way. He's unconscious. You can go see for yourself," she offered.

"Then we have to call Rand, immediately. If he's culpable, we can't waste another minute on this case."

Darrel summoned Stuart, who appeared in the doorway.

"Take a seat," Darrel told him. "We're getting Rand on the line. He's got some explaining to do."

Mercedes kept her silence. She knew she was about to learn more than she wanted to know. Again.

"Mr. Crenshaw?" Rand asked in surprise, after Darrel greeted him.

"Rand. I'm here with Stuart and Mercedes, and we have you on the speakerphone. We have a few questions we need to ask you."

"Why certainly, counselor," he drawled. "How may I be of assist-ance?"

"For a number of months our private investigator has been pursuing leads on your behalf. As we get ready for trial we want to make sure there will be no unpleasant surprises. We want to see our case as much as possible through the defendants' eyes, so we can anticipate what they'll do and be ready for it. Does that make sense?"

"Perfectly."

"Good. And in order to represent you most effectively we have asked you to be completely forthcoming with us from the start, have we not?"

"You have, and I have been."

"Good. Our investigator just called with some unsettling information that we'd like you to clarify."

Rand was silent. Stuart looked at Mercedes with a quizzical expression. She shook her head at him.

"An informant we have at the escort service just disclosed that his contact at the hotel for assignments in the executive suite had a thick southern accent. What do you have to say about that?"

"Oh my."

"What does *that* mean?" Darrel's face was flushed.

"I discussed all of this with Mr. Soutane."

"So it's true? It was you?"

"It was my job to see to my employers' comforts. That is precisely what I did. I did not participate in the activities, as Mr. Soutane is well aware. I merely made a few phone calls."

"I'm afraid 'merely' won't cut it with a judge and jury," Darrel said, barely containing his anger. "At what point did you share this with Jack?"

"At the very beginning. Now I would like to speak with him, if you don't mind."

Mercedes leaned forward in her chair and spoke. "Rand, Jack is seriously ill. He's in the hospital with pneumonia and can't talk. He won't be able to participate any further in your case."

Stuart's eyes widened.

"Rand, we need you to tell us everything you told Jack," Darrel said. "We can't represent you if you withhold information. Otherwise, we are playing poker with half a deck. Can't you see that?"

"I see no reason for you to speak in such a tone. I've followed Jack's instructions to the letter. I went to him first and have been doing exactly as he advised."

Mercedes's stomach turned a slow somersault.

"Things have changed," Darrel responded. "Jack's incapacitated. You're welcome to seek other counsel, although at this late date I don't believe it would serve your interests."

Darrel glared at the speakerphone with his arms crossed, and waited.

"Jack said he wanted to see what the paralegals could figure out. He told me I should never admit to any involvement."

Rand paused for a second—long enough for Mercedes to reflect that she was one of "the paralegals" her husband had set up.

"I want this case to be over and I want my money," Rand added.

"We have that in common, at least. I suggest you tell us everything about what went on in the suite and precisely what your involvement was."

"I want to talk to Jack first."

"We've just told you—that's not possible. From now on you're dealing with us. Better spill it, Rand. What was it? Prostitution? Drug deals?"

"The former only, as far as I know, but minor boys were involved. Please be assured that I was only the messenger. I only conveyed my employers' preferences."

"That's not going to get you much sympathy," Darrel said curtly.

"I am well aware of that. My employers rewarded my loyalty and discretion by relocating and then terminating me."

Mercedes recalled the day she, Lindsay, and Simone had pieced together the evidence of who was in the suite on what day, and how proud they had felt in doing so. Rand had known all along and was the facilitator, yet Jack had silenced him. On top of that, Jack had called her a "genius" for her idea of back-channeling information to the wives, when all along he knew the truth. She felt so imbecilic. How could her own husband have treated her like that? How could he have done this to Darrel?

The Taylor case was a disaster. Her home situation was a disaster. Thoughts of what she would say to Germaine haunted her. Fear of her pending test results crept into her veins, cold and cloying. Her heart jumped into her throat. Her mind leapt from one terror to the next. Her breathing was shallow, leaving her light-headed. She felt completely isolated and trapped.

⚬⟨♥⟩⚬

IN THE AFTERNOON SHE DROVE to Jack's office. She had the tiny key with her and was anxious for the bottom drawer to disgorge its contents.

Melanie was on the phone and waved when Mercedes strode past her desk. Without bothering to put down her briefcase, she walked to the doorway of Emerson's office, where he was squinting at the screen of the boxy white computer monitor. He looked up when she entered and met her serious expression with one of his own. The smirk had disappeared.

"Hi," he volunteered.

"Hi."

"I hear Jack is sick."

"Jack is seriously ill, Emerson."

"I was going to go see him last night, but I got tied up."

"It's better if you don't."

She stared at him, watching the color climb up his neck into the cheeks. "Was this some kind of game to you?" she asked.

No response.

"Certain things have come to light in the last couple of days. It would be better for all concerned if we were to call a truce and start leveling with each other."

"About what?"

"I know you've known all along about Jack's 'other life,' shall we call it, and didn't care to share that information with me."

"Mercedes, it was not my place to do that."

"I can appreciate that, but we're now in a bit of a bind."

"*We?*"

"You and I. Melanie and Germaine. Jack's clients. Janine Reneau. Darrel."

"What are you talking about?"

"It is very doubtful that Jack will be able to work again."

"You're exaggerating."

"I wish I were. Melanie has no idea of what I'm about to tell you, so please keep it in the strictest confidence."

Emerson waited.

"Jack has AIDS, in his brain, and is at death's door with pneumocystis. He cannot speak. He doesn't know where he is or who I am."

Horror splashed across Emerson's face.

"The doctor says that even if he survives this round, he has to stop practicing law at once. I need your help, Emerson. Jack needs your help. He's probably had HIV for a good while for it to have progressed so far. It's entirely possible his judgment has been compromised for months or even years. His legal exposure is—"

"I get it," he interrupted.

"We need to make a coordinated plan for how to handle his clients. We need to let them know he's ill, but not raise suspicion about his—and your—work for them. Eventually we'll need to tell them to find other counsel and take their files with them. For as long as possible I have to protect Germaine from knowing that I've been exposed to the virus, so I want no one else to know. No one at all. Will you help me?"

He nodded. She could see the wheels turning.

"I'll be in his office for a couple of hours, if you want to talk."

"Mercedes, I'm sorry," he answered. He was in shock.

"I know you care for Jack, and I'm sorry for your situation. I want us to be allies."

She walked past Melanie, who was dealing with a delivery man and fielding phone calls. She closed the door to Jack's office and sat in his chair. There was a burgeoning pile of new mail on the desk.

She dug the small gold key out of her coin purse and slipped it into the lock in the bottom drawer. It fit perfectly. She opened the drawer all the way.

Unlike the others, it was in pristine order, with files labeled in Jack's bold handwriting. *Client Trust Account. Disability Insurance. Estate Plan. Income Tax. Legal Malpractice Insurance. Life Insurance. Personal Correspondence. Prenuptial Agreement. Real Property. Reconciliations.*

She began with the disability insurance file. To her amazement and profound relief, there were four substantial disability policies in place. She read the declarations pages and added up the figures in her head. Jack had spoken about wanting to protect her and Germaine before they were married, and he certainly seemed to have accomplished that. In fact, there would be an abundant tax-free monthly income if ever—no, *when*—he was declared disabled.

She pulled out the insurance applications, spread them out on the credenza and compared them. It seemed lavish even for Jack, at age forty-one, to have four policies. Each application was dated months before their wedding and all within a few days of each other. Each one included a question about whether the applicant had applied to any other company for disability insurance. "No" had been his answer on each form. But here they all were, so how could that be true?

She pulled out the life insurance file. Again, there was more than one very large policy on Jack's life and a policy on her life as well, for which she recalled filling out an application before the wedding. The beneficiary for all was the Soutane Family Trust. But why, she wondered, did she not remember there being more than one policy on Jack, or that they were so large? And why would he buy term insurance instead of whole life? He had been working on the estate plan before the wedding, a logical thing for a probate attorney like Jack to do. She recalled thinking how kind it was of him to think of the future in such a pragmatic way. And here she was about to reap the benefits. Tears filled her eyes as she imagined Jack's big arms encircling her.

The estate plan file was full of the legal documents Jack had created. There were medical and legal powers of attorney, advance medical directives, the trust, and their wills. Her hands trembled as she slowly worked her way through the file.

She pulled out the legal malpractice file, and inhaled sharply when her brain registered what she saw. His coverage was in the millions of dollars and was designed to blanket a great span of time. The numbers seemed out of all proportion, even with his propensity for extravagance. Martin Macey's word for Jack—*strategic*—popped into her head. There was a knot in the pit of her stomach.

She stared out the window and watched a turkey vulture circle the brilliant green field next to the office building. A scene from Thanksgiving dinner began to replay itself in her mind. Janine was describing Jack's father to Germaine. Mercedes could plainly see the old lady's sweet face and hear the quaver in her voice as she praised Dr. Soutane. How kind he was to her, how fine and elegant, what an excellent physician. Jack had objected, with a look of bitter reproach on his face. His father, he'd said, was "underinsured and irresponsible." It suddenly made perfect sense. He'd made certain he would never find himself in that position. But at what cost?

She opened the drawer containing all the check registers. She paged through his checkbook to view a few months' expenses. A staggering amount of money was going out the door each month for disability and life insurance. The malpractice coverage must come out of the business account. She'd have to dig into the finances over the weekend.

The intercom buzzed. Melanie announced a call from Dr. Sinclair.

The news was grim. Jack had had another small seizure and had not been conversant since the day before. They had moved him into intensive care. The pneumonia was not yet responding to the antibiotics. He was unconscious and everything possible was being done for him. They agreed that it would serve no purpose for her to visit that afternoon.

She asked about the medication she'd found in the glove compartment. Dr. Sinclair said only that the pills were appropriate for Jack's condition, and that he'd become allergic to one of the antibiotics.

"I'm so confused," she said. "I don't understand why there are so many things he kept from me."

"Perhaps he told you all that he could. None of us ever really knows another person, Mercedes. We can know some of the layers. We can be intimately familiar with another's personality, how they appear in the world, some of what they think, some of their skills, and their family history. But the inner person, the psyche, the child within, is deeply cloaked."

"You sound like a shrink."

"The mind and body are not separate pieces of a puzzle. They're enmeshed in a million subtle ways. In my practice, and especially in treating AIDS patients, I'm always learning about these interconnections. We see layer upon layer peeled away, particularly when the virus is housed in the brain. And as those layers peel away, an entire universe shows itself: loveliness, cruelty, altruism, fear, a lifetime of memories, a person's sense of time, his identity—everything."

"I see."

"If you love Jack, have compassion for his flaws. You will surely see them all before this is over. Right now let's concentrate on bringing him back so you and he can talk. Let's concentrate on helping *you*. Did you take an HIV test?"

"Yes. The results will be back in two days. I'm trying not to think about it. But now I have another question. Did Jack go to you for the HIV test before we were married?"

"No, and there's nothing in his medical records here about a test prior to the one we gave him when he was admitted. Did you investigate the insurance situation?"

"Yes. There's quite a bit of disability, life, and malpractice coverage."

"Smart man. I'm very glad to hear that. I'll help you get the disability claim going."

After hanging up, she stared out the window while some of his words sank in. How could she have been so blind? She'd been too busy to see the truth, busy looking for what she had wanted to see. She had wanted to believe so many exalted notions about Jack, but most of all that they were each other's true love, destined to be together, to bring out the best in each other, unafraid to reveal all and share all. And from these recent revelations she had a new context for understanding other things she'd seen and not grasped— his supposed patience with her for waiting until they were engaged before having sex, that shocking night in Florence when she'd first met the frightening side of him, their weirdly inconsistent sex life, his mysterious late-night meetings with "clients." It had never occurred to her to question those. Now she questioned everything.

She opened the top drawer and pulled out the photos Jack kept there. *The good old days. The good old carefree days before a woman entered the picture.* She propped them up around the perimeter of the desk. It was clear that Jack and Damon had been in love. She could stop pretending she didn't see it. Damon was such a charming man and a good friend to Jack. Who could not love Damon?

Melanie knocked on the door and entered. She was anxious for any news of Jack.

"They've just taken him to intensive care. They're discouraging visitors. He's unconscious and the antibiotics are not showing any signs of working."

"How are you holding up?" Melanie asked.

"I'll be better when Germaine's back. I'm trying to understand our budget, or lack of one. How are you doing?"

Melanie shrugged; her eyes were very sad. "I keep imagining he's just out of the country on one of his trips, and he'll walk in the front door full of energy, with three new deals to work on."

"I suppose he *is* in another country. We just don't know when or if he's coming back. This pile of mail is rather intimidating. Is there anyone Jack has talked to about the accounting?"

"Only Rose, before she quit."

"Do you have a phone number for her?"

"Sorry, I don't."

"Maybe I can figure it out on my own. What about all this corre-spondence from insurance companies? I'm seeing an awful lot of past-due notices. Doesn't Jack pay his bills on time?"

"Sure he does—when he can."

"What does that mean?" Her tone of voice was sharper than she wanted it to be.

"He always makes payroll first."

"But don't payments for client bills come out of the client trust account?"

"They should."

"But sometimes they don't?"

"It's a cash-flow situation."

Another uneasy feeling had taken root.

"But I'm not involved with that," Melanie added quickly. "Jack handles the money."

"Not now he doesn't! I need to figure this out, and fast."

Melanie fidgeted with the edge of her cardigan. "I'll get you a box for those files." She left to go find one.

Much of the correspondence on top of the desk was from insurance companies addressed to Jack as the trustee of various family trusts. Mercedes recognized the names of many of the guests at their wedding.

Emerson knocked lightly on the doorjamb. He seemed more relaxed and conciliatory.

"Any news?" he asked.

"Nothing good." With her eyes, she signaled the direction in which Melanie had left. "Do you think you can manage Jack's court appearances for now?"

"I'll get continuances for those I can't." He saw the photos arrayed around the top of Jack's desk and stepped closer.

"Do you mind?" he asked tentatively.

"Go ahead. I'm the last to know, evidently."

He picked up the photo of Damon resting his head on Jack's shoulder to get a better look.

"Emerson, do you know anything about these trusts and insurance policies?"

"I do."

"Would you mind sharing it with me?"

He sat down and began to explain, "Jack has a lot of clients who are exceedingly wealthy and in their late eighties. For many of them, the estate taxes that would be owed upon death are quite substantial. To avoid the heirs taking a big hit and having to sell off assets to pay the taxes, Jack creates a trust into which the assets go. Then he purchases a sizeable term life insurance policy for the client. When the client dies, the insurance proceeds pay the taxes. The premiums are high, but the life spans of the clients are not long, so the actual amount paid out to cover the premiums is far less than the taxes would be without them."

"Sounds ingenious. But why do the bills go to Jack and not the client?"

"It's a service he provides, as trustee. The family pays him a lump sum to cover the premiums. When the bills come, he pays them. That's why he's the trustee—to keep it simple for the families and ensure that no one forgets to make a payment. The elderly are forgetful, and often their children know nothing of their parents' actual holdings or how the estate will be divided after they pass. The clients prefer it that way."

"And what happens if Jack forgets? I'm seeing quite a few past-due notices."

"If those payments aren't maintained, the policies could lapse, and the estates would be exposed to substantial tax liability—exactly what the plans are designed to avoid."

"And if Jack isn't able to write those checks?"

They exchanged a look as the realization of what might be lurking in the pile of correspondence struck them simultaneously.

Melanie entered the room with a box and saw their expressions. "What's the matter?"

"Oh, we're just working out a few things. It'll be fine," Emerson deftly replied.

Mercedes grabbed the remaining files out of the bottom drawer and locked it.

"I'm taking all the ledgers and checkbooks home except this one," she said, handing the Soutane & Associates check register to Melanie. "Since you're the only one who can write checks on that right now, it's all yours."

Emerson watched Mercedes lower the files into the box, then empty two of Jack's desk drawers into the box as well. He chewed the corner of his mouth and said nothing.

Melanie nimbly sifted the mail, setting aside the bills and any envelopes from clients that contained checks. She placed them in a manila envelope, which she added to the box.

"What are you going to do?" she asked Mercedes.

"Pick up Germaine, try to figure out what needs to be done next, and go to work in the morning."

Emerson looked from Mercedes to Melanie and back again. Mercedes regarded him warily. The crisis had done nothing to bolster her trust in him. She recalled the annoying high twitter of his laugh and how he'd begun clinging to Jack while still working for Darrel. Now she had no choice but to rely on him to cover Jack's cases.

Emerson said good-bye and briskly returned to his office. Melanie walked with her to the front door—faithful Melanie, Jack's right hand all these years.

"Mel, I really appreciate all that you're doing to hold the fort. I don't know what Jack or I or this law practice would do without you. I wish the antibiotics would kick in, and we could talk about his coming home."

Melanie kissed her cheek.

MERCEDES LOCKED THE BOX IN the trunk of the Alfa. It was just as well that Dr. Sinclair had encouraged her not to visit the hospital. Her heart felt so heavy it was a miracle it could still beat.

When Jack had made his wedding vows, she wondered, what had they meant to him? What had his intentions been? Had fidelity entered into his equation at all?

What if Jack had gotten HIV from another woman? The thought sobered her for a moment. If she'd found out he had a mistress, she would be livid and ready to take any necessary steps to free herself, but she felt none of that. She was going to lose everything, and there was no way to fight it. There was nothing to fight *with*, and fighting would serve no purpose. She'd been deceived; she'd deceived herself.

He was *terminally ill*. The phrase reverberated in her head, like bats storming a cave. She could hear Eleanor's shrill voice: *For God's sake, Mercedes, your husband is terminally ill!*

SHE DROVE HURRIEDLY BACK TO the house. It was time to pick up Germaine, time to hear all about her adventures in Yosemite and watch her beautiful face light up in the telling—time to turn another page in the book. It was time to sow some seeds of joy in this wasteland.

What she could not yet face was Germaine's future. *My precious, gifted child, what will it mean to lose your father, then your stepfather, and finally your mother, all before you're an adult?* There would be many days together yet, and each one must count for ten.

THE NEW MATH

Germaine sat solemnly eyeing her mother, who labored over the accounting ledgers and checkbooks arrayed on the dining room table. With all that was on her mind, she couldn't concentrate on schoolwork.

Mercedes had a pencil behind her ear, a notepad covered with calculations in front of her, and a perplexed look on her face. She punched numbers into the calculator, but no matter how many different ways she added and subtracted, the numbers refused to balance.

"Oh, I don't understand this," she said in exasperation. "I wish I had your head for figures!" she exclaimed to Germaine, who did not respond. Her gray eyes were focused on her mother, who looked drawn and short on sleep.

"What happens if you can't figure it out?" she asked.

"I don't know, Sweetness. But I'm not giving up."

Germaine sighed. All the lightheartedness she'd brought back with her from vacation was gone. She'd returned to disastrous news about her stepfather, although Mercedes had tried to put the most positive spin on it. She saw past her mother's smile to the fear in her eyes. The fact that she had not been allowed to see Jack was scary enough, but to see her mother involving herself in the finances of his law practice left no doubt that matters were dire.

She knew the set of Mercedes's jaw, the way she pursed her lips when she was wrestling with a problem. It was no use interrupting her with questions. Without saying a word, Germaine got up and went into her room. She lay on her bed and looked out into the trees.

Mercedes redoubled her efforts. Jack's personal account showed a generous income overall, but funds were low, and she had yet to figure out how he paid himself. There was no identifying information in the register where deposits appeared and no matching debits from other accounts—at least not with any regularity. Before the mortgage was paid each month, a deposit greater than the mortgage was made, but she could not find its source. To make matters worse, the client trust account funds were insufficient to cover the premiums due on the clients' insurance policies. Even after she deposited the checks Melanie had given her, there would not be enough. She sighed and rubbed her temples. Perhaps, if she just took a break, some understanding of how it all worked might come to her.

⁓

THE HOUSE WAS TOO QUIET. She was sick of struggling with the numbers and trying to map Jack's financial labyrinth. She scooped up all the papers and put them back into the box. She'd done all she could with what she'd brought home. There was no use trying to squeeze blood out of a turnip.

She thanked God again for the news she'd gotten on the HIV test. The nurse had taken her into a private room that morning and informed her that the results were negative. But the nurse had also urged her to "remain realistic" and take another test within six months.

At this moment I'm still healthy. At this moment a full life is still ahead of me.

She walked back toward the bedrooms and found Germaine, who did not stir. She lay down and curled around her, throwing an arm over the young girl's side. Germaine grabbed her hand tightly.

"Mom, is Jack going to die?"

"We're all going to die someday, darling. We just don't know when or how. We go through life pretending otherwise, acting as if we'll be young and healthy forever, but it isn't so."

"What will happen to us if he dies soon?"

"We'll carry on. We'll be very sad, but we'll carry on."

"What will happen if he's sick for a long time?"

"I know some smart lawyers who will give us good advice about what to do. I will take care of everything, so don't you worry about it."

"I hate this. Can't we please call Grandmother?"

"Let's wait just one more day. Maybe there will be better news tomorrow."

"She's going to be very upset. She loves Jack."

"That's why I've been waiting."

"She has a right to know."

"Honey, your grandmother will be fine."

Germaine tightened her grip on Mercedes's hand and soon the girl's hot tears were running down it.

◦◦◦

THE NEXT AFTERNOON MERCEDES RETURNED to Jack's office, eager to inspect the files she'd left behind. They had to contain the answers that were so markedly absent from what she'd already read. She arrived to find Melanie in a swivet.

"Emerson missed a court appearance this morning. He hasn't surfaced all day. I've called his home phone three times, but there's no answer."

"Did he have the file with him?"

"No, it's on his desk where he left it last night. And all his personal effects are gone. He must have taken them home last night. He was still here working when I left."

"Great. That's all we need."

Her mind turned toward their conversation the previous day, his oddly conciliatory behavior in Jack's office, his explanation of the term life insurance policies.

She went into Emerson's office to see for herself. His diplomas were missing from the walls and his drawers were cleaned out. There was no doubt he'd flown the coop.

Before she could settle in at Jack's desk, Melanie put a call through from the hospital. It was Paul the nurse, with good news. Jack was regaining consciousness. He seemed somewhat lucid and was asking for her. The antibiotics were kicking in and his fever was down. Her heart leapt into her throat. She told Paul she'd be over as soon as possible.

Melanie walked into the room, buoyed by the expression on Mercedes's face.

"Is there good news?"

Mercedes smiled at her, but it was the grin of someone carrying a dagger. What she had to say would devastate Melanie, but there was no use holding back any longer. She repeated the good news from the hospital and then carefully said: "There's more you need to know. You'd better sit down, Mel."

Melanie did so, looking uneasy.

"Jack has pneumocystis and AIDS. The virus is in his brain. He may be rallying now, but it won't last. He's dying, Melanie. He's a dying man."

The words fell like stones from her mouth and struck Melanie forcefully.

"He has to stop practicing law. The doctor says he shouldn't be giving any legal advice. He's mentally incompetent. Even if he sounds reasonable, his judgment is no longer sound. He has AIDS dementia."

Melanie stared at her in astonished disbelief.

"We have to close down the practice. He has five years to live at the most."

Melanie swallowed hard. "What about you?"

"I'm expected to be in the same boat, although it hasn't shown up on a test yet. Germaine must be protected from worrying about my fate for as long as possible, so I haven't told her. Nor have I told my parents or Darrel or anyone else at work."

"And Janine?"

"She doesn't even know Jack is sick, let alone in the hospital."

Melanie's face was pale, her expression stunned. "Did Emerson know?"

"Yes. I had to tell him why when I asked if we could count on him to carry the ball on Jack's cases. I also had some questions about the clients' insurance policies."

"You'd think he'd want to help Jack, as much as he admired him. And you'd think he'd have a more professional sense of duty to the clients. What a nightmare!" Melanie exclaimed.

Mercedes watched her sympathetically. She was a few days ahead of Melanie in catching onto things and she knew Melanie would now start to put together some of Jack's incongruities.

Ironically, Emerson's disappearance fit perfectly with the cavalcade of calamities. Sometimes everything in one's life must fall apart.

Mercedes returned some of the files to the bottom drawer and took out others. It was no use trying to work that afternoon, but at least she'd have material on hand for later. She felt desperate to see

Jack, with a noxious mixture of lovesickness, fear, and anger boiling inside. It was as if someone had placed a drop of some lethal drug on her psyche and it was slowly spreading throughout her consciousness.

She had another talk with Melanie. They decided to ask Matthew Spencer, the forensic accountant whose office was upstairs, to go over the accounts and advise them. They would find other probate attorneys to take Jack's cases. They would call clients together. Then Mercedes took off for the hospital while Melanie stayed behind, left alone to contemplate a future without Jack.

The sight of Jack awake and making sense, and the rich sound of his voice, were the two things Mercedes craved. While he still breathed, she felt an urgency to cling to the love they had, and to be reassured that it had not all been a charade.

⚬⚬⚬

THE WEATHER OUTSIDE WAS BREATHTAKING. Fruit trees were in blossom, filling the warm breeze with their heady fragrance. Flower beds packed with impatiens lined the walkways around Jack's office building. The sky was lapis blue with billowy cumulus clouds. The glorious sun beamed life onto all quarters. Mercedes felt its warmth on her neck and back. She raised her eyes in order to memorize the color of the sky and watch the clouds change shape. She slipped on her sunglasses and took a deep breath. In spite of everything, she felt as she had when she was first enthralled with Jack. The prospect of seeing him soon made her heart race, and made her crazy with desire to forget her misgivings.

She found him in a new room, no longer under an oxygen tent. Instead, tubing connected to an oxygen tank ran up his nostrils. Faint color had returned to his cheeks. His intense blue eyes drank in his wife when she entered the room and followed her long strides toward him.

She took his hand and bent over to kiss his grizzled cheek. He squeezed her hand weakly.

"Remember me?" she asked, eyes filling with tears.

"Do I ever," he whispered between wheezes.

"It's so lovely to see you awake! Have you spoken with any of the doctors?"

He nodded. "Hard to talk," he whispered. "So tired."

Paul entered, took Jack's temperature, and adjusted his bedding, rewrapping his long feet in a warm blanket. Jack's eyes remained glued to Mercedes.

"Beautiful," he whispered.

She sat down close to the bed and stroked his arm. It seemed impossible that soon he would no longer be in this world.

"Jack, do you understand why you're here?" she asked.

He nodded. "Sick," he said. "Lungs."

She glanced at Paul and back at Jack. "Pneumonia almost got you."

"Getting better." He said softly.

After a while, when fatigue forced him to close his eyes, Paul motioned to Mercedes. She let go of Jack's hand and followed the nurse out of the room.

In the hallway, Paul explained to her that the pneumonia was in retreat. Jack's oxygen levels had come up significantly. He was relatively coherent, but remembered nothing about collapsing at home or coming to the hospital. He'd been told he had AIDS, which he took rather well.

"What you're seeing is his first rally. He could be back on his feet fairly quickly, if everything goes well. He's lost weight, so anything that can be done to help him regain it is very important."

"Our daughter is back from her trip. She wants to see him."

"Tell her he's quarantined. That usually works."

"Has he been this lucid since he woke up today?"

"No. It comes and goes. He asked for you and he asked why he's here. But don't be surprised by rapid changes in behavior. He really can't help it."

When she reentered the room, Jack turned his head and looked at her with surprise.

She approached the bed. He stared at her with suspicion. The affectionate smile was gone. She attempted to take his hand, but he pulled it away and slid it under the covers. She touched his arm under the blanket, but he glanced at her hand and up at her face as though she were a stranger, and shrugged off her touch.

"Jack, Honey, it's me—Mercedes."

He considered the words.

She lifted her handbag off the chair where she had placed it. "Remember this? You gave it to me last Christmas."

"Okay," he said, without conviction. His brow furrowed slightly. He watched her every movement.

She pulled an envelope from the purse and took out the photo of him and Damon in their youth.

"Remember this?"

He squinted at the photo and smiled softly. "Damon," he whispered.

She pulled out another. "And this?"

"Janine," he said, without hesitation.

"And this?" It was Germaine's school portrait.

He looked mournful and turned his head away. Then he rolled onto his side, with his back to her and faced the door. She gently stroked his back. He put up no resistance. She felt the weight of their plight pressing down on her. Jack was right here and yet so far away. She missed him. Had the sight of Germaine reminded him of something? Did he realize she was someone he should recognize, but couldn't?

"Mercedes loves Jack," she said. No response. She bent over him and put her arms around him lightly, kissing his neck.

His eyes were open. He curled into a fetal position.

"I love you," she said.

He covered his eyes with his hands. "What is happening to me?"

"You've been very sick, so you've forgotten a lot of things. You may remember more a little later."

His hand emerged from the covers and he pulled at her left hand. He looked at the sapphire ring.

"Do you remember buying this ring?"

He smiled slightly. "Jackie did it."

"How is Jackie doing?"

"Jackie's a good boy."

"Yes, he is." She kissed his cheek and continued holding him, which he seemed to like.

At that moment Dr. Sinclair entered the room in his white lab coat. Jack cringed and clutched the rails of the bed, closing his eyes tightly.

"Jackie's a good boy!" he cried out. He began to shake, and then buried his head under his arms, still clutching the rails.

Mercedes held him tighter. "It's okay, Honey. Dr. Sinclair is here to help you feel better."

"No!" His legs twitched under the covers.

Dr. Sinclair took a step closer. Jack grew more agitated.

Mercedes explained, "His father was a physician and was very cruel to him. Maybe it was your coat that set him off."

"I'll be back in a moment," the doctor mouthed to her before stepping away and drawing the curtain around the bed.

A few minutes passed and Jack opened his eyes. She repeated that she loved him and would protect him, that he was safe. His breathing calmed, and he let go of the side rails. She fought back tears and the tightness in her throat.

Dr. Sinclair returned without the lab coat; he had removed his tie and opened the collar of his shirt. He now resembled a lawyer more than a doctor, despite the stethoscope in his hand, and Jack accepted him without apprehension.

The doctor adapted to Jack's state of mind as much as possible, not challenging the delusions. He worked with them or around them, whatever was necessary. Mercedes's presence was obviously calming, at least to the version of Jack who was present at that moment. At this rate of recovery, the doctor said, Jack might be able to go home before long. He would need to be on oxygen around the clock. He would not be fit to drive and would need a home-care nurse. They would be starting him on AZT, the newest weapon in the war on AIDS. Combined with other drugs, it was the most effective treatment available. There were strong side effects, and it was important for Jack to gain back as much weight as possible. He would need ballast for the days ahead. Mercedes and a nurse must stay on top of his medications and food until he could do so for himself. Dr. Sinclair urged her to make the most of their time together.

He looked Jack in the eye and instructed, "You have to wind down your law practice. You can't be giving people legal advice any longer. Do you understand that?"

Jack nodded, but his comprehension was doubtful.

"I understand, and so does his secretary," Mercedes said.

The doctor looked at her sympathetically. "I'm sorry about all this."

Jack looked from one to the other without speaking, as though they were talking about someone he didn't know.

A tray of food was brought in, and Dr. Sinclair excused himself.

Jack was intent on the food, but his hand shook so much when he held the spoon that he couldn't manage getting it to his mouth.

Mercedes took the spoon and fed him as though he were a small boy. He ate hungrily. Tears filled her eyes and spilled down her cheeks, but he didn't appear to notice. Where had he gone? The Jack who first greeted her just that afternoon, her old lover, had been replaced by a child.

When he closed his eyes, she decided it was time to go and began pulling herself together. Suddenly a voice she had not heard in a long time began speaking.

"Phone Melanie and tell her to be here at nine," the voice boldly ordered. "She can't be taking any more days off. We need her here *now*." Jack gestured toward his valise in the corner. "There are tapes to be transcribed, and I need her to make some calls for me."

Mercedes's scalp prickled.

"Melanie hasn't been off, Jack. She's at the office right now."

"I haven't seen her and I've been here every morning," he retorted hotly.

"Where do you think you are right now?"

"At work, of course."

"I see. And where's your desk? Why aren't you wearing a suit?"

"It's behind that curtain. I just got back from racquet ball."

"Your voice sounds much better. The food must have restored your strength more than I thought."

"Lunch at the club always revives me. Did you check out that hot new waiter?"

"I fed you lunch from a spoon."

His laugh at this was hearty. "Oh, Bella, you're funny today."

"You're pretty funny too, Darling. Do you have any messages for Emerson?"

"He knows what to do. We have a deal coming together, if we can get the client to fund it," he said with a wheeze.

"Which client would that be?"

"Now, you know I can't discuss that with you. Frankly, I'm surprised you would ask." He erupted into coughing.

"Emerson didn't come in this morning. We don't know where he is."

"Court appearance."

"No, he left the file on his desk."

"We can sort that out when he gets back."

"I hope he comes back. When I told him you were sick, he acted rather strangely."

"You shouldn't have done that."

"I thought it was in our best interest for him to understand the situation."

Jack laughed again. "Oh, Bella, you're cracking me up. Emerson is on top of it. He knows everything."

"Such as what?"

"Such as where the bodies are buried."

"What bodies?"

"The rich ones. The old rich ones." He laughed and broke into a violent coughing fit, which forced him to close his eyes.

"Have you given any thought to Janine?" she asked calmly.

"I take care of her and she takes care of me."

"I mean with regard to your illness and what arrangements will be made for her."

"I'm not ill, am I?" His eyes flew open. They darted with horror from the bed rails to the IVs, bed tray, and the catheter bag over the side of the bed.

"What the hell is going on here?" he shrieked.

"Darling, you have pneumonia and you're in the hospital."

He looked frantically around the room.

"How long have you known this?" he demanded, heaving himself up on his elbows in a burst of strength.

"I brought you here a few days ago. You collapsed at home from lack of oxygen while Germaine was away."

"Why didn't you tell me?"

"I have. We have. You've been unconscious and you're a little confused."

He sank back into the pillow, pale now and struggling to breathe.

"I'm afraid I'm tiring you out," she said.

"You did more than that, you bitch," he said menacingly. "You've ruined everything. You kept them all away and you think I didn't notice. Well, I did notice, and there'll be no more of that."

Paul stepped forward from behind the curtain, where he had been listening. He motioned to Mercedes to stay calm.

"Now Jack," he said, "Is that any way to speak to Ms. Bell? She kept you company today and fed you lunch and took time away from her child and her job for you. My goodness, you're forgetting your manners."

Jack seemed puzzled by the sight of Paul materializing from thin air. "Sorry," he said sheepishly.

"I think it's time for medicine and a nap, don't you?" Paul asked pleasantly. "There, there. We do get grumpy without our nap."

Jack responded by slumping farther down into the bed.

Mercedes was frazzled. She gathered up her things and stared out the window. The fog was rolling in and would soon enshroud the trees below. Jack's eyes were closed when she slipped out of the room. Paul followed her.

"Tomorrow he probably won't remember anything he said to you today. At least, it's unpredictable *what* he will remember," Paul said. "Try not to take offense when he acts out like that. I know it's hard on your nerves, but it's the virus."

"I suppose we should just be glad he's regaining strength at this point."

"Yes, that's right. We almost lost him."

"So tell me about the 'periods of lucidity' that Dr. Sinclair predicted. I need something to look forward to."

"He may recover from the pneumonia entirely. Before another opportunistic infection occurs, he may seem almost normal. He'll go through times when he's a child and can't even read, let alone re-member who everyone is; but then he'll also have times when his memory is intact and he will seem capable of making decisions. When he's like that, you'll be able to work with him to take care of business. You will have to manage his behavior as best you can. There's no way to predict how long any particular phase will last. He'll be all over the place in terms of personality changes."

"I can't believe this is our reality now."

"That's quite understandable. But try to be glad you have a little time. And it's not too soon to start getting ready for him to come home."

"*Now?* In this condition?" Panic flooded her. She'd thought Dr. Sinclair meant a few weeks from now.

"As soon as he's stable, we'll be discharging him."

She clapped her hands over her ears. "But I can't let Germaine see him like this."

He tried to reassure her. "Children are more adaptable than we give them credit for."

Her eyes flashed with anger. "Children should not have to adapt to things like this. My daughter has done nothing in her life to deserve this."

"I understand. That's a normal reaction, but it will pass. Every-thing will pass. These are all stages. Try not to get too far ahead of yourself. Just take it a day at a time."

"And in the middle and in the end, and when I get sick too? How will it be then?"

"One day at a time, Ms. Bell."

THE MYSTERY THEATER

John Slayne's office overlooked the lake, too, but unlike Darrel's it was a maelstrom of paper, which lay in drifts on various pieces of furniture and on the floor around his desk. The man sat back in his green leather chair, doodling with a felt-tipped pen and cradling the telephone receiver in the crook of his meaty neck. He was talking to a criminal defense client, who was out on parole. Mostly the subject was baseball. The Oakland A's were looking good, and John had season tickets. He was laughing heartily when Mercedes appeared in his doorway.

She had done very little work with Darrel's partner, who was much loved by the staff for his irreverence and absence of pretense. He had a miniature basketball hoop positioned over his trash can, surrounded by many wads of paper that had missed their mark. Another wad sailed through the air in a high arc and swooshed into the trash. He was delighted by his success and motioned Mercedes to sit down as he hung up the phone.

"I wanted to ask your opinion about a couple things, if you have time," she said.

"Fire away." His friendly eyes smiled at her, and he resumed doodling.

"Here's a hypothetical case: two people get married. Sometime after they marry the wife discovers that her husband has secretly taken out several large disability and term life insurance policies on himself. All the documents are kept in a locked drawer in an obscure place, along with his will, a trust, and other documents of that nature. She reads the policies and the copies of the applications that had been submitted for them. The total amount of disability insurance coverage is immense—enough to purchase a mansion—and the premiums are over a thousand dollars per month, although her husband isn't even forty-five. There's over half a million dollars of life insurance as well."

John whistled at the figures and kept doodling.

"That's not all. The applications contain certain inaccuracies, but they are too consistent to be accidental. The policies were all issued before the wedding date but after they became engaged. What would you make of that?"

"Sounds like premeditation to me. Someone was planning something. How is everyone's health, in your hypothetical?"

"That's just it. The husband has gotten very ill all of a sudden."

"And who are the beneficiaries of the life insurance?"

"A family trust."

"And who is the beneficiary of the trust?"

"A child."

"And is the hypothetical illness contagious?"

"Yes."

"Seems pretty clear what's going on here. He must have known before the wedding, maybe even before the proposal, that he was going to get sick, and he planned the whole thing."

"Is there no other explanation?"

"There could be, but not one that immediately jumps to mind. I've never known anyone who had multiple disability insurance policies. Why would you, unless you knew you were going to need it? Furthermore, the companies would want to know about each other."

"Suppose he grew up in a situation where there was insufficient insurance and the result was the financial ruin of the family? Is it possible he would be a bit paranoid about his finances, and go overboard to protect his own family?"

"For a thousand dollars a month? It's excessive. You'd have to have an impressive monthly income to justify it. Is this person rich?"

"Comfortable, certainly."

"I'd have to ask why there had not been full disclosure to the spouse, if there wasn't something to hide. I'd be interested in his medical history, the representations on the insurance applications, the sources of income for the premiums. In fact, the whole thing stinks—hypothetically speaking."

"What if there were a test for the type of illness afflicting the husband, and that test had been taken prior to marriage by both of them, and the results were negative?"

"According to whom? Did they take the test together and receive the results together?"

"Separately."

"So they reported the results to each other, but didn't actually see the test results or speak to each other's doctors?"

Mercedes shifted in her seat and looked uneasily at Slayne. "Something like that," she said.

He shook his head. "Somebody lied. That's what my gut tells me anyway." He patted his sizable paunch. "As you can see, this gut has a lot to say."

"What would you advise a client who made such a discovery?"

"What is the state of her health at this point?"

"Fine."

"I would encourage her to protect herself, investigate further, and get some distance from the situation, for safety's sake. I would want her to take a cold, hard look at the facts, once the facts were known, and be prepared to act. And of course I would use every means at my disposal to help her get the facts and advise her on her legal rights."

"What about the ailing spouse?"

"That's another kettle of fish. The degree and nature of the disability would obviously affect a lot of things. My client could use that to her advantage, particularly if she has his power of attorney."

"I see."

Another wad of paper sailed into the air and swished through the hoop. John Slayne raised his arms in a victory salute. "Two for two."

"I'd better leave while you're ahead. Thanks for your time."

"Happy to help," he said with a smile.

He watched her leave and kept his eyes on her until she disappeared from sight. There was no longer a smile on John Slayne's face.

⋯⋯

HIS WORDS HIT HER FORCEFULLY as she walked around the lake. Her misgivings about the insurance had been overshadowed by the chaos of Jack's rapid decline. She had avoided facing the nagging questions, but her intuition would not let her rest.

She'd managed to come to grips with Jack's bisexuality, after a fashion. It had become a convenient excuse upon which she could hang his actions. She had no objections to homosexuality per se. People were wired the way they were wired. Motherhood had taught her that. Children came into the world whole and unique.

Jack had obviously been gifted with brains and physical beauty, and he was no shrinking violet in spite of his childhood traumas. He had been a man hungry for adventure, eager to experience the rich tapestry of life, and with the resources to do so.

It was his withholding of facts that unsettled her, along with the vast quantity of insurance. She could no longer ignore the implications. Premeditation, John had said. She had to find out when Jack had learned he was HIV positive. She walked and walked, scarcely aware of her surroundings. Had his love been entirely feigned? Surely not.

She recalled their conversation when he'd been drafting the trust. It was to protect and provide for Germaine when they both had gone. At the time she had thought only of his magnanimity, even in noting how testy he'd been. They were also planning the wedding then. She had chalked up his grouchiness to a groom's jitters and having too much to do in too little time.

But why had he been in such a rush to marry? He said he'd waited all his life to find her, to find happiness, and didn't want to wait a moment longer. Perhaps he *couldn't* wait a moment longer.

Doubt consumed her. If only she could talk to him about it! But he was in no condition for that. When she'd left him that morning, his cadaverous, towering figure had stood over them, drooling. His eyes had leapt from Mercedes and Germaine to the nurse, unsure of who they were, of where he was. He badly needed grooming, he could barely control his bodily functions, and he was too large, even in his weakened state, to be managed like the helpless person he was fast becoming.

Geneva, the home-care nurse, had calmly led him by the arm into the living room, where she helped him onto the couch. She had made him comfortable with kind words, and administered his medicine. He'd become teary-eyed, frightened, and shaky. He was tethered to the oxygen tank by yards of plastic tubing, like an animal on a leash. He resisted food. The medicine's harsh side effects seemed to ravage him as much as the virus that now controlled his mind. He lived in a twilight of confusion and nightmare, his identity shattered by a fragmented memory, his past kept from him behind a partition in his own brain. From time to time, the doctor had assured Mercedes, the partition would lift. He would reappear, unaware of the madness from which he had emerged. Once again he would be interested in the world, capable of making some limited decisions or actions. But even then he was not to be trusted with responsibilities or adult judgments—and certainly not with the keys to a car.

When she'd left the house, he was vomiting violently into a bowl held by Geneva. That was a frequent occurrence, and perilous in its own right. All his bodily fluids were potentially lethal. Geneva had taught her how to clean up after him, to wear plastic gloves, to protect her eyes from splattering vomit when she dumped it into the toilet, to scrub his dishes and flatware, to segregate household linens that might be subject to his bodily excretions. He was a walking contaminant, a creature that bore little resemblance to the man they had known a few short weeks before.

The nurse's care provided Mercedes with her only respite from the chamber of horrors. She juggled work at her office and his, keeping her job alive and winding his down. She'd been foolish to think she could shield Germaine. Mercedes had not given a name to the illness, but Germaine watched and heard and withdrew. What she saw didn't need a name.

Now a new specter loomed, one that threatened the very foundations of their relationship. What more could be added to the macabre theater her life had become? She kept walking. She must keep up her endurance while she still had the use of her own faculties.

She stopped in a deli for some minestrone soup and a piece of fresh focaccia. She took the food back outside to eat by the lake, unaware of others.

"Mind if I join you?" a male voice inquired. It was Darrel, with his own lunch in hand. He sat on the bench beside her. "I was behind you in line, and I have some good news."

She looked up at him earnestly. No news he had could possibly assuage her torment, but it was welcome nonetheless. She managed a smile.

"I was just on the phone with counsel in the Taylor case and I think we may be close to a good settlement."

"That *is* good news. Have you talked to Rand yet?"

"Yes. He knows we can't refuse the offer, but he wants to talk to Jack first."

She put down her soup. "I don't think that's possible."

"He's home from the hospital, though, right? Do you think I could call him or perhaps come over? I know you said the recovery would be slow."

"Jack is very ill, Darrel. He has a nurse with him at all times. He'll be collecting disability soon and he has to close his law practice."

"I had no idea. I—"

"No one has any idea. I've kept it that way for a reason. I can bring you a copy of the doctor's orders if you need proof. I can appreciate that it's just my word you have to go on, but Jack is in no condition to be consulted about anything."

"What's the prognosis?"

She shook her head and stared straight ahead at the lake. "There isn't one. Please settle the case without him, and please keep this conversation confidential." Turning to Darrel, she saw the question in his eyes. She couldn't bear to hear it or to lie to him, either, so she looked away again.

They finished their lunches in silence.

GERMAINE FOUND WAYS TO KEEP herself busy at school and afterward for as long as possible to minimize her time at home. Mercedes was glad to see her building a fortress of her own life independent of her parents. She would need it. They were lately in the habit of going out for dinner together at the end of the day, as long as Jack had a nurse present to care for him. It was their time together, as it had been in the days before him.

⚬⚬⚬

HE WAS IN BED WHEN they arrived home that evening. According to the nurse, he'd been speaking more coherently in the afternoon and had rallied enough to sit on the deck and eat a small meal without assistance. These were baby steps, but light-years of improvement from two weeks earlier.

Germaine went straight to the master bedroom to see her stepfather, who seemed to be asleep. Mercedes stepped past her, turned on a lamp at the writing desk, and kicked off her heels. The long plastic tube snaked through the house up the hallway from the dining room where the big tank resided, and across the bedroom floor. It encircled Jack's head, looped over his ears, and went up his nostrils, streaming oxygen into his troubled lungs. His color was no longer ashen, but his breathing was raspy. Germaine's curiosity drew her to the foot of the bed.

"He looks better," she whispered. Mercedes stood behind her, wrapping her arms around her growing daughter, feeling Germaine's silky hair fall against the front of her dress. If only there were some way to shield her. If only she didn't have so many if-only's on her mind.

His eyes opened sleepily and gradually focused on the figures at the foot of the bed.

"Hi," Mercedes said.

He raised a hand and waved.

"My girls."

Germaine remained where she stood, wary but interested. Mercedes kissed her head and walked over to Jack's bedside. She knelt on the carpet beside him to assess his condition. A stew of emotions boiled inside her. And still she felt great longing and love for this enigmatic man.

She patted his arm. He looked into her eyes with recognition. Unexpectedly he asked, "How was your day?"

"Full of surprises. How was yours?"

"Okay. Nice afternoon."

"I heard you ate lunch outside."

He smiled faintly. "Big achievement."

Germaine climbed onto the bed and sat beside him. He regarded her tenderly. "And you, young miss?"

"Are you getting better now?"

"You bet."

Mercedes averted her gaze. She got up and left the room, saying over her shoulder, "That's good."

"Could you get me a glass of water?" he asked his stepdaughter.

She left the room promptly, keen to help him. Mercedes was washing her hands in the bathroom when Germaine returned to Jack with the glass.

"Where have you been?" a shrill voice demanded. Mercedes turned to see Jack pushing himself up onto his elbows. His eyes were open wide in terror, darting all around the room as if it were a torture chamber. Germaine nearly dropped the glass.

"You left me here for days! I've been tied down to this bed for days!" he shouted. The exertion drained his energy and he fell back into the pillows.

"No, Jack," Mercedes interceded. "You haven't. You've had a nurse with you all day, and Germaine just now went to get you a glass of water." She took the glass from the badly frightened girl and put it on the marble top of his bedside table. "Thank you, Honey," she said to Germaine.

Jack glared at the girl and then at her mother, as though he were under attack.

"No nurse has been here," he uttered in a deep, accusatory voice. He narrowed his eyes intensely, as if to bore a hole into Mercedes. Then a demonic leer broke across his face. "You think you can trick me but you can't. I just untied the ropes and now I'm free."

Germaine looked at her mother in terror.

Mercedes kept a firm grip. In a tone straight from Eleanor, she commanded: "Get hold of yourself, Jack! Look around—there aren't any ropes. This is your home, for heaven's sake! You're safe, and people are here to take care of you morning, noon, and night."

She stood behind Germaine and put her arms around her. "Germaine is your stepdaughter. She was very kind to bring you water. You should say thank you."

He stared at both of them, perhaps reevaluating his accusations.

"Drink your water." She pointed to the glass. "You probably need it."

He stared at the glass, which he seemed to be seeing for the first time. He picked it up shakily and took one sip, then another.

"Thank you," he said, in little Jackie's timid voice. "Sorry."

"You're welcome," Germaine said meekly, shifting her weight from one foot to the other. Her mother whispered into her ear, and she hurried out of the room.

Mercedes sat down on the edge of the bed. She could hear Germaine on the phone talking to Eleanor; that would occupy her a good long while. Deciding to take advantage of Jackie's compliant nature, she led him into the bathroom, where, like a most unusual five-year-old, he was showered, shampooed, shaved, and then wrapped in two bath sheets. He sat on a chair at the sink while his wife helped him brush his teeth. The ordeal seemed to exhaust him.

She combed his silvering hair. He had acquiesced entirely, and now he put his arms around her, leaning his head against her abdomen. She fought back tears and held him to her for a long moment. He was lost; but in spite of their unraveling circumstances, the love she felt for him was not.

She helped her big child into clean pajamas and settled him in bed, gave him his medication, and turned out the lamp. She sat beside him and rubbed his back, wondering which of them she was really trying to soothe. Until they could have a frank, adult conversation, there would be no answers to her nagging questions. It was only Jack who knew what he had done—only Jack who could explain why. As of now she was trapped in a twisted reality, as if she had stepped into an Escher illustration where the stairs that seemed to go up really went down; where the doors that seemed to open to the outside really opened inward, into dark places of suspicion and fear.

⸙

NONE OF THE LEDGERS BALANCED. Jack's law practice was fraught with obfuscation, a maze of insurance policies, elaborate estate plans, complicated real estate transactions and tax matters no one could decipher. Emerson had disappeared. Matthew Spencer grappled with the bookkeeping. Melanie was working her way through the client list, calling one by one to tell them that Jack was ill and would be unable to represent them any longer. Mercedes was immersed in documents and photographs, delving into Jack's past and keeping the household bills current.

The monster she kept chained up all day strained to be released. Here lay Jack, the master of the disability policy, disabled. He was clean, fed, medicated, and surrounded with comfort, even with love, in a beautiful home. He was financially secure. Soon, tax-free money would begin pouring in the door from all his insurance policies. Everything was working perfectly—for Jack, and for as long as he lived.

As he slept, she felt strangled by doubt and confusion. The need for secrecy was pushing her fear into a tiny corner.

Germaine was in bed with her nose buried in a book. Mercedes lay down beside her, thoroughly drained by the day and wanting to escape into Germaine's book with her. She closed her eyes. Germaine began to read aloud the enchanting story of Anne of Green Gables. She read for a long while, then stopped. Mercedes took the book from her and resumed where she had left off. This was their world, and no one could spoil it. She read another chapter and put the book aside. Germaine had curled up in a ball next to her. She turned out the light.

"Mom, why is Jack going crazy?" Germaine asked.

"He's still very ill, darling. Some of the germs are in his brain. He can't help it."

"He's so weird and scary now."

"I know. The doctor said he'll soon get more clearheaded. We just have to be patient."

Inside she felt like screaming. Patient was the last thing she wanted to be.

After kissing her daughter goodnight, Mercedes carried Jack's soiled laundry downstairs to the washer. Although she knew that AIDS could not be casually transmitted, she had a horror of Germaine being contaminated by anything Jack touched. She felt like boiling and bleaching every cloth that touched his person.

The basement lighting was poor. Dark blanketed the room save for the circle of light in front of the washer and dryer. The pipes made their comforting noises in the blessed quiet of night. She saw the shelves, laden with banker's boxes, where the history of Jack's law practice and much of his personal life was incarcerated. She strained to read the labels, but it was no use in the poor light. She walked slowly up the wooden stairs, poured herself a glass of wine in a crystal goblet, and ran a bubble bath in Germaine's bathroom.

Each hellish day had its pockets of light. John's candor, Darrel's faith in her, dinner and reading with her daughter, a glass of wine, and a bath: those were six things to live for. Sufficient unto the day are the joys and sorrows thereof.

UNMASKED

His fine blue pinstriped shirt hung on him like a sack, the collar too loose around his neck to support a necktie. But Jack enjoyed donning his fine clothes now more than ever. He examined the blue of the stripe and picked out lapis cufflinks from his jewelry case. He pulled on starched khakis that were now so baggy he had to cinch up his belt to keep them on, and his belt needed another hole. Unconcerned, he slid his feet into polished loafers.

Despite the brilliant summer sunshine, he was cold, so he retrieved a cashmere sweater from the shelf and pulled it on. The effort made him light-headed, and he slumped in the boudoir chair that Mercedes had moved into their closet for this purpose. Many accommodations had been made throughout the house, starting with handrails and a sturdy bench chair in the oversized shower stall.

He had managed to groom himself after a fashion and put on cologne. He got up unsteadily, and put on his Cartier watch and his new diamond ring. He had bought it on one of his recent forays into the city, which Mercedes knew nothing about. He saw no reason to tell her since they disagreed about whether he should be driving. The ring sparkled and made him smile. Once again, he could have whatever he wanted.

He had the house to himself. He had discharged the nurse the previous week, after demonstrating his independence. He could count his many pills and take them on schedule; he could feed himself again. But being able to dress properly was by far his favorite accomplishment following those many dark weeks.

Mercedes was at work and Germaine was away at summer camp. The day was at his command. No one was aware of his intention to drive to his office for the first time since he'd gone to the hospital. He gathered up his wallet and keys and put on a sport coat. He looked into a full-length mirror. The man who returned his gaze startled him. His were the hollow cheeks, long thinning hair, and the confused eyes of a stranger. He stepped closer to scrutinize the face. Then he summoned his most charming smile and lightly rearranged his hair with his hands.

⚬◖◗⚬

MERCEDES WAS BUSY FACT-CHECKING a legal brief for federal court. Now that Jack was beginning to recover his mental faculties, she was able to sleep better and concentrate on her work. The harder the work, the happier she was—anything to keep her mind off the situation at home or the news she was facing. Tomorrow was the red-letter day on which she would get the results of the second HIV test. At least Germaine was out of town. She would have a few weeks to adjust to the bad news before her daughter's watchful eyes were on her again.

The secretaries were congregated in the kitchen when she went there to refill her water glass. One was reporting that her neighbor's husband had just been diagnosed with AIDS. He'd received a blood transfusion after surgery a few years earlier, before the blood banks were testing their inventory or their donors for HIV. After two years of declining health and much illness, he had just learned the truth. All the neighbors were in an uproar about it, she said, and were prohibiting their children from playing with the sick man's daughter. To make matters worse, the young girl was being ostracized at school.

"But that's so unkind," Louise said. "The poor child hasn't done anything."

"Easy for you to say," Lorraine replied. "Your kids are grown and gone. I wouldn't want mine playing with anyone whose parent has AIDS. Nobody really knows how it's transmitted. Why take a chance?"

"But they do know," Louise contradicted. "It's from an exchange of body fluids, right? And not a casual one either. How could a little girl get it from her father?"

A look went around the table.

"Yes, we all know how that works," Lorraine cut her off, with a disparaging expression on her face. "It's disgusting!"

Mercedes filled her glass. None of them knew her circumstances. Lorraine's was the type of thinking that Germaine would be up against as soon as word got out. Unsuspecting, Louise's eyes met Mercedes's, and she smiled. She and Mercedes were like-minded about most things.

Mercedes was glad she'd kept Jack's condition buttoned up, and wondered how much longer she could do it, now that he was getting about. As soon as people began to see him in public, the jig would be up.

⁂

WHEN SHE DROVE UP THEIR street toward the house that evening, she saw from half a block away that the garage door was standing open and Jack's black car was parked half in and half out of it at a bizarre angle. Jack had been driving. She would have to find his keys and hide them before she went to bed that night. She wondered what catastrophe awaited her inside the house, or which version of Jack would greet her, if he greeted her at all. Before facing the madness, she stopped for a moment in their courtyard to commune with Athena, who was serene as always.

In the living room, magazines and newspapers were everywhere, as if scattered by the wind. The day's mail was partially opened and strewn in a number of places. Envelopes addressed to Soutane & Associates had been tossed around. Papers were on the floor, on the couch, on the telephone table.

"Jack?" she called out.

No answer.

He was not in the bedroom, which was a jumble of sheets and blankets. His bureau drawers were open, as was his jewelry case. The bathroom was a disaster, with towels and clothes littering the floor, whiskers and globs of toothpaste dotting the sink.

She found him out on the deck, resting on a chaise with a highball in his hand.

He noticed his wife, with a start, and nodded. He looked haggard, with dark shadows below his eyes, and his Adam's apple protruding from his skinny neck.

"You're all dressed up," she said, bending over to kiss his forehead politely, "and you went out today." Confronting him about his driving would serve no purpose. She would simply have to prevent a recurrence. And he definitely wasn't supposed to drink while on AZT.

He patted the cushion of the chaise next to his, inviting her to sit. "I think we may have found an attorney to take over the practice," he said. "I surprised Melanie today with a visit."

Mercedes wondered how Melanie had felt seeing a scarecrow replica of Jack show up at the office unannounced. She sat back, stretched out her legs, and eyed the lush landscape, recalling the moment a few months before when the pheasant had so proudly fanned his plumage for her.

"Well, that's big news. Who's the lawyer and how is Melanie?" Jack was ignorant of the frequent communications between the two women, or the depth of Mercedes's investigations into his practice and his life.

"He's a sole practitioner that Matthew knows and recommends, so we're going to proceed. Melanie interviewed for a position in his office and she's going to work for him. She seemed very happy to see me," he smiled, "but I couldn't stay long. I brought the mail home."

He laid his head back on the cushion and closed his eyes.

Her eyes suddenly fell upon his hand. The enormous diamond glinted in the sunlight.

"Where did you get that ring?" she asked in astonishment.

He sat up with a start, realizing he'd forgotten to take it off before she got home.

"Oh, that. It's a recent purchase. What the hell, right?" He flashed what would once have been a dazzling smile, his charmer's smile, but now it flashed from sallow cheeks beneath sunken eyes.

"You bought it for yourself?' She was dumbfounded.

"I thought it suited me." He stretched out his hand and admired it.

"What did you buy it with? We're not exactly flush at the moment. There's been no income from your practice to speak of, and the disability payments haven't started."

"I have my resources," he said dismissively.

"Evidently so." She didn't have the energy for an argument, especially one that was doomed from the start.

His tone was repellent to her, so she left to change out of her work clothes and take further stock of the house. A day of Jack being home alone was tantamount to a toddler being home alone all day. A giant toddler who thought he could drive, and who felt entitled to any bauble that caught his fancy. Everything he touched was left wherever he felt like dropping it when he was distracted by the next thought or attracted to the next object. The sight of the mess everywhere made her feel even more tired than she already was. Her work would never be done. There would never be any peace.

She pulled on her shorts and a tee shirt and straightened up the closet, then cleared the floor of the bathroom. She ran hot water in the sink to clean it out. His keys were on his bedside table, so she scooped them up and walked out to his car. The interior was a mess. Out of curiosity she opened his glove compartment. There were no bottles of medication in it this time. All those were now out in plain view on his dresser. But, to her surprise, she found Janine Reneau's checkbook and some of her bills. He must have collected them when he went to the office.

She reparked his car properly so the garage door would close, and locked it. He should be more careful with Janine's affairs, she thought, and not leave her so exposed. Anyone could have stolen her checkbook that afternoon.

As she walked back into the house, a sense of dread overwhelmed her about the pending test results. Was this how she would be next year?

Out in the living room she pushed Jack's paperwork into piles and sifted through the day's unopened mail, which included an envelope on heavy bond paper bearing Matthew Spencer's business logo. It was addressed to both of them. She poured herself a lemonade and opened the letter. It concerned the valuation of Jack's accounts. He proposed a meeting of the three of them and provided a list of items he wanted them to bring.

Those items touched on matters she'd not been able to figure out from the documents she'd examined, including Janine Reneau's affairs—all of which would have to be sorted out before Jack was incapacitated again. It was a good list, and she was glad that she and Melanie had thought of going to Matthew. The time had come for Jack to face facts, and for her to know what they were. She wondered, ironically, whether Jack would wear his new ring to the meeting.

Jack shuffled in from the deck. He had lost so much weight, it was hard to connect this incarnation with His Majesty. But there was no time for sentiment. She went into the kitchen to see what sort of rich meal she could concoct for him.

He stopped at the dining room table, which was in his path, and spied the letter lying on its glossy surface. He picked it up and began to read. Mercedes, who was pulling ingredients out of the refrigerator, watched him inconspicuously from behind the refrigerator's open door. For so many weeks he'd been unable to read, it was a relief to see his mind working better. Concern crept over his features and he scowled. His face registered a number of emotions, none of them pleasant. He looked outside momentarily, then resumed reading. She could see that some grim realization was dawning on him. When he finished reading, he let the letter fall to the table and left the room.

He stayed out of the kitchen while she cooked and remained withdrawn throughout the evening. They ate dinner in silence. She could see him brooding and was happy, for once, not to know the cause. She was deeply tired from the day, and from the constant battles against clutter, against mystery, against things she didn't understand and didn't have enough information to figure out. She savored her food and ate it slowly, staring out at the trees.

Jack ate hungrily for the first time in a long while, then abruptly pushed away from the table without a word. *Fine,* she thought, *be that way.* By the time she was done cleaning up, he'd gone to bed.

When she left for work the next morning, he was still asleep, or pretending to be asleep, his clothes on the floor exactly where he'd dropped them.

⋯

"IT'S GOOD NEWS," the nurse said. "You're lucky so far. The results are negative, again."

Mercedes had steeled herself for the worst. The moment she heard the news, whatever had clenched around her heart let go, and she took a deep breath. She and Germaine now had a little more time. Every increment was a gift.

"Congratulations," the nurse smiled, "but come back for another test in six months, please. And enjoy yourself in the meantime."

They both knew what her odds were. Nevertheless, the immediate future had cleared. Whatever problems she had to face were manageable as long as she could have just a little more time to take care of things for Germaine.

⋯

THAT EVENING JACK MADE THE unprecedented effort of greeting her at the door when she arrived. He put his arms around her and gave her no choice but to hug him and feel his bony rib cage. He smelled fresh and clean and of fine cologne. For a moment she rested her head on his chest and closed her eyes. She listened to his heart beating. If only their last months could be like this, she would be so grateful.

"Bella," he murmured and held her close, stroking her hair. "I'm sorry things are so difficult for you."

She almost laughed at the understatement. It was the first time he'd expressed any kind of empathy since becoming ill, so she had to give him credit for that. She looked up to see his eyes, but he was staring out the window.

"Here, put your stuff down. Let me pour you a glass of wine," he said.

He lifted the bag off her shoulder and hung it on the back of a chair. He looked down into her face and smoothed her cheek. She wondered at the change in him since yesterday. Whatever it was, whoever he was tonight, was a great improvement over the big baby of recent weeks. She looked around and noticed that he'd picked up the living room and straightened the cushions on the couch. There were even flowers from the yard in a vase on the coffee table.

She followed him into the kitchen. His dishes from lunch were in the drainer. He'd eaten a real lunch on a real plate and actually cleaned up after himself. Could he be coming around? He poured her wine and led her out onto the deck where they could sit, as they had tried the evening before, to enjoy the soft summer air and the fading light of day.

"I want to explain something that you should know before we meet with Matthew," he said. "I would like you to listen to everything I have to say without judging until you've heard me out. Can you do that for me?"

"Of course I can." *At last, an explanation.*

"Do you remember, when I was drafting our prenuptial agreement, how we disclosed to each other the details of our assets and liabilities?"

"Yeah, I had nothing and you had everything," she quipped.

"And I told you that I took care of Janine, managed her money, and paid her bills?"

She nodded.

"I don't know if I told you then, but I'm her sole heir," he said, gazing off into the distance.

"It's obvious she thinks of you as a son."

"Janine's investments have done very well—so well that she'll never be able to spend all her money even if she were physically able to do so."

Mercedes recognized the tone of voice. She'd heard it when he was cajoling opposing counsel or schmoozing a potential client at a party or dealing with Eleanor.

"As you well know, Janine is very elderly and frail and I've made sure she has every comfort, a full-time attendant, and the best possible medical care."

"That's true."

"From time to time I've also borrowed funds from her, as a son is apt to do. I may have neglected to tell you that. I don't recall." He turned to make eye contact.

She watched him with sphinx-like impenetrability, not moving a muscle.

"The thing is, I haven't always paid the money back. Nevertheless, Janine and I have an understanding." He waited for her to react, but she didn't, so he continued. "And that understanding is this: as I'm like a son to her, and I'm her sole heir, my repaying the loans, which is what they really are, is not a priority."

She said nothing.

"So, of course, when Matthew questions us about this, I don't want you to be surprised."

"How nice of you," she lied. "When you said that about 'repaying the loans, which is what they really are,' did you mean that Janine isn't aware you've been borrowing money?"

"I think that's a fair statement. I saw no need, given the extent of her assets."

"I see," she replied sweetly. "So when did you first 'borrow' from Janine?"

"Well, that's the thing. Quite awhile ago."

"So, like right after you started taking care of her money?"

"Uh-huh." He looked quickly at Mercedes again.

"What kind of money are we talking about?" she asked, frowning. "And why would this be of concern to Matthew?"

"I'm not sure—maybe $500K, give or take. Matthew will notice the debits from her accounts and the deposits into—"

"Half a million dollars? Or more?" She nearly choked.

"Yes. But it's really my money, you see. I'm her sole heir."

"So you keep saying. But if it's your money, why are you telling me they were loans that you neglected to repay?"

He did not answer.

"And didn't *you* prepare her will?"

"Of course. I'm a probate attorney," he said proudly. "Who better to do it than I?"

She took a sip of wine. "Someone who didn't have a conflict of interest."

"I think Matthew will see the logic of my taking care of Janine and her taking care of me."

She had to admire his gall. "What about the small matter of ethics—you know, right and wrong?"

"That's relative. It's not anyone's business but our own."

"No, that's not quite true."

He seemed calm and oddly receptive, the lawyer in the middle of negotiating with the other side, his eyes on the prize.

"I can see a couple of scenarios," she continued, her temperature rising. "Let me break it down for you. You have AIDS. Or did you forget that? So there's a high probability you'll die before Janine. She will need someone else to take care of her when you're gone, and it won't be me. I'll probably be quite sick myself—or have you not considered that either?"

He studied her face.

"And when that someone hires a lawyer, or if that someone *is* a lawyer, he or she will go over all of Janine's accounts and invest-ments. And what, Jack darling, will this person see? Enormous holes where the money should be. Don't you think this person will wonder where it's gone and try to recover it? Where will this person look first? To her previous lawyer—to you. But you won't be here, will you? So the next place will be your estate—meaning me, if I'm alive, or Germaine and whoever her legal guardian is when she's orphaned. You're going to leave *us* holding the bag to pay back Janine all the money you *stole*. You've just confessed to multiple counts of grand larceny and legal malpractice over many years."

Although she had not raised her voice, her pulse was raging.

"Oh, now don't get carried away," Jack said smoothly. "It won't come to that, Bella. I'm going to live a good long while. Janine's in her eighties. You worry too much."

"Do I? I suppose it's easy not to worry if you don't have a conscience."

He chuckled. "No one has done anything wrong here. It's *my* money pure and simple. No one needs to know about those accounts. I don't have to make them available to Matthew."

"There's an even better way to handle it . . . pay her back."

"With what?" Now he was the incredulous one.

"Sell off your real property." She quit gripping her chair—the side he couldn't see—and took another sip of wine.

"It's not quite that simple. Especially since there's no need." He was beginning to sound irritated.

"Of course there is. Unquestionably, emphatically, there is. Why can't you sell your properties?"

"They're encumbered."

"With what?"

"Tax liens. Really, Mercedes, I expected more loyalty from you."

She shot a look at his new diamond ring. "And I expected more integrity from you. Did you buy *that* with Janine's money?"

"What difference does it make?"

"Did you buy my engagement ring with Janine's money?"

"It's *my* money. When you understand that fact, Bella, your apprehensions will be dispelled. You enjoy our lifestyle as much as I do. Germaine certainly does. She's at summer camp right now because of it. Didn't you ever cheat on a test in school?"

"Not once."

"Didn't you ever pilfer anything from a store when you were a kid?"

"No, I didn't."

"Let's not argue. We're in this together. Just let me handle Matthew at the meeting."

She regarded her formerly debonair rake of a husband, enjoying a drink on his deck—at whose expense?

She got up and went into the kitchen to start dinner. Cooking relaxed her and helped her dial in on her mission.

Jack's face was beaming when he sat down to the candlelit table, taking the scene before him as a victory. With his newly redeployed charm, he complimented her cooking and her hard work—but she could see his artifice and the ease with which he turned on the charisma when necessity dictated.

He ate a big dinner. He talked about vacations they should take, the traveling they would soon have the money to do. He shared the details of the day he'd driven into San Francisco and purchased his ring. She nodded politely and forced herself to eat.

She was thinking of tiny, white-haired Janine and the complete trust she had in Jack. Then there was the puzzle of Jack's law practice. Hadn't there been a lot of money coming in every month from legitimate business? Why had he felt the need to steal? How could there be tax liens on his properties if he had so much money at his disposal? It didn't add up. Emerson must have known that the house of cards was about to collapse. No wonder he vanished at the first sign of trouble.

After dinner he cleared the table and helped her with the dishes for the first time in their marriage. *You must really be desperate. You're laying it on so thick.* If she were not so intent on her purpose, she would have walked out and let him do all of it. It was high time he cleaned up his own messes and it was her turn to be "strategic."

Although he seemed to have made miraculous progress in the last two days, he tired quickly. He tried to lure Mercedes to come to bed with him, no doubt to seal the deal he thought he saw—a grotesque prospect. She assured him she would be in as soon as she finished up a few things. He had no idea of the revulsion she was stifling—the outrage building inside her.

She ran a bath in Germaine's bathroom and lay in the deep water by the light of a candle. Now her mind raced from memory to memory —his shopping sprees, their storybook wedding, the honeymoon in Italy, the dark side of him she had first glimpsed there, his purchase of the Alfa, their trip to Hawaii, and his callous disregard for her that afternoon when she got so badly sunburned. She pictured the ocean off that beach, and the oceans of money that had been going in and out of Jack's bank accounts, credit card accounts, and law practice. How much of it had been Janine's? She wanted to know, and at the same time couldn't bear to find out. She focused on the present. Jack was waiting for her, if he was still awake. She would never have a better opportunity to ask the ghastly question that had been eating away at her.

She slipped into bed beside him. He was lying on his side facing away from her. He seemed to be asleep, but then he reached back with his long arm to give the back of her thigh a proprietary squeeze. She bit her tongue and snuggled up to him, putting her arm around his waist and burrowing her head against his back as she used to do when they first became lovers.

"Bella," he said in his deepest, most affectionate tone.

She smoothed his pajama top over his heart with her hand. She could feel it beating underneath her palm. The black heart of her lover.

"Jack?"

"Yes, Bella?"

"Why did you marry me?"

He paused a moment, then said thoughtfully, "You have the perfect combination of qualities. I knew I would never tire of you, and we would be a ready-made family. And I knew I wouldn't have to die alone."

"Because you knew I would take care of you."

"Yes, just as you've been doing. You're the perfect wife."

"But weren't you afraid of giving me the virus?"

"It was a calculated risk."

The words detonated in her consciousness like a bomb. John Slayne had been right.

After a moment she said, "You could have protected me."

He chuckled. "That kind of sex isn't any fun at all and you know it." He cupped her buttock in his hand. His meat. She struggled to keep her voice calm.

"But what about Germaine?"

"What do you mean?"

"I mean, giving me the virus will make her an orphan."

"I thought about that," he said, matter-of-factly. "But my mother died when I was young, and I turned out okay. Besides," he added, "she'll be rich. She'll inherit all the life insurance proceeds and everything in the trust—maybe just in time for college. She'll be all set."

Except for the small matter of being an orphan. But then she can turn out like you. And you sure turned out "okay"!

SHE WITHDREW AND PUSHED HIS arm off of her. She rolled over away from him and stared into the dark. After a moment of silence, she got out of bed and put on her robe. She was aghast that she had ever allowed such a monster to touch her.

She went into Germaine's bathroom and locked the door. She ran water in the sink and immersed her hands in it, then her face. She wanted to wash the touch of him off her. She wanted to scream, throw up, smash the mirror with her fist—*something, anything.*

She went into the living room, where moonlight streamed through the windows onto the carpet. For a while she sat on the couch staring at the quadrangles of light on the floor. She tried to grasp the full significance of Jack's admissions, the cold premeditation of his actions; she reeled under the horror of knowing that someone who'd purported to love her had consciously plotted her extermination for years through uncountable occasions of unprotected sex, the very act designed to bring life.

He'd made the ultimate fool of her. She must have been the easiest mark in the world, with her ratty raincoat, her battered old car, her impoverished neighborhood, and her sweet, sad daughter.

Images of Germaine's face filled her mind. Germaine as a baby. Germaine as a toddler. Germaine missing her front teeth. Germaine learning to read. Germaine learning to roller skate. Germaine broken-hearted after Eddy's death. Germaine immersing herself in books and studies. Then her transformation after Jack had entered their lives.

Mercedes thought of their simple life in the pink palace and wished with all her being that she and Germaine could rewind the clock and go back there. As fragile and imperiled as that existence had been, it was infinitely safer than the present. Then the dam broke, and she began to cry. The illusion of Jack was finally shat-tered. She lay down on the carpet in the moonlight and rocked herself back and forth, sobbing. She curled up in a ball on her knees and held her head in her hands. She couldn't do it. She could not face the life before her. She couldn't bear it. She no longer had the strength. Her humiliation was complete.

Please help me, she prayed. *Please help me protect my child. Please let me find a way out of this mess. If I am to die of AIDS, let me live with Germaine in some semblance of honor and peace until then. Show me the way out.*

Another wave of tears surged through her, and she cried again. Never had she felt so used, so dirty or worthless. She crawled into Germaine's bed and buried herself under the covers.

⋄

IT WAS HER BIRTHDAY, and she'd just awakened in her bedroom. It was a small room with beige wall-to-wall carpeting. Light shone through an eight-paned glass door to the right of her bed. Sleepily she looked outside through a small window. A brown sparrow sat on a branch, chirping and cocking his head this way and that. She heard footsteps. Germaine came stumbling in, her flannel pajamas rumpled from sleep. She had braces on her teeth, and her hair was in a messy ponytail. She smiled as she climbed into bed, her eyes twinkling with merriment. She threw her arm around her mother and hugged her.

⋄

IT WAS SUCH AN INTENSE HUG, packed with so much love, that Mercedes felt it still when she awoke to the dawn of a new day.

Jack was sitting at the kitchen table reading the newspaper by the time she was ready to leave for work. When she entered the kitchen, he watched her like a cat waiting outside a mouse hole. She was calm and collected, in a sleeveless black dress and low heels. As always, he found pleasure in the way she moved.

She ignored him. He watched her pack a lunch, rinse out her coffee cup, and leave it in the sink. When she was ready to leave, she let the front door shut soundly behind her.

CHAPTER THIRTY-TWO

June 1988

THE DARK STAR SHINETH

Roadwork had slowed traffic to a near standstill on Mercedes's route to the office, so she turned down a side street to avoid the crush. Camphor trees formed a bower over the middle of the road, which was lined with nice single-family homes. She rolled down her window and leaned her elbow on the window ledge. A cool summer breeze blew through the car. No children were out yet, but their toys and bikes were scattered here and there. A woman walking a small wirehaired terrier waved as she passed.

A sign peeked out from the greenery in front of a pale blue house with white trim. She strained to read it, but couldn't. Something made her stop the car and get out. The house was nestled in the bushes at the bottom of a slight incline, framed by a row of mature sycamores in the back. The sign read, For Rent.

She walked down the eight stepping-stones to the uninhabited house. *The eightfold path,* she thought, and smiled. The house had large windows into the living room on the left, an attached one-car garage to the right, and a breezeway between the garage and the front door in the center. The wind in the trees sounded like waves rolling into shore. She cupped her hands around her eyes and looked in the windows of the empty house: wood floors, a kitchen with a skylight, a small brick fireplace with a painted wood mantel in the living room, and a doorway that must lead off to a bedroom or two—all in all, a very pleasing configuration. She wrote down the information on the sign and took a minute more to check out the yard.

She imagined living there with Germaine through her high school years. She daydreamed about watching her daughter turn into a young woman. She would attend her school events, watch her learn trig and calculus, read the papers she wrote for English and history. She could picture Germaine getting ready for dates and the prom, preparing for the SATs, filling out applications for college, heading out the door to go babysitting—all in this little blue house. Was it possible?

As she drove away she noticed neither large houses nor rundown ones in the neighborhood. The yards were reasonably well kept and the few cars she saw were economy cars, plus an occasional pickup truck or van with a business logo on it. Nothing fancy. The neighborhood was midway between Germaine's school and the office, and close to a good public high school.

⁊⁊

SHE TRIED TO SETTLE IN at her desk and focus on the chart she was supposed to be making for Darrel, but her mind was like a bird in a cage, hopping from one perch to the next. Jack's confession had upended everything. She couldn't process all of its implications and felt a wild urgency to do something about it, but had no idea where to begin or what to do. She went to the conference room and closed the door behind her. In a few seconds she was speaking with Dr. Hand.

"Is everything all right?' the perceptive doctor asked.

"No, far from it, and I need your advice."

After hearing all that had happened the night before, Dr. Hand said, "I think you should speak with a lawyer as soon as possible. You're in jeopardy legally *and* financially and you need to move quickly. And as far as Matthew Spencer goes, you might reconsider whether to go to that meeting at all. I don't see any advantage in your being there—only danger."

"What do I do about Jack at home?"

"Keep calm and don't engage him until you figure out exactly what you need to do."

"He changes so much from one day to the next, I never know what he'll be like."

"Then don't anticipate. Concentrate on Germaine and yourself and what you need. Call and let me know what the lawyers tell you, please."

Exiting the conference room, she nearly ran into Caroline.

"Hi, stranger," Caroline said cheerfully.

"Caroline, you're just the person I need to see. Can we talk?"

"Hmm, that doesn't sound good. Follow me." They closed Caroline's office door behind them.

"Sit," Caroline ordered. She'd never seen Mercedes so agitated.

"I'm here as a client."

"Okay."

She explained the truth of Jack's illness, his dementia and bizarre behavior and the doctor's advice to her. She talked about her discoveries at his office, the disappearance of Emerson, and the confusion of their finances.

Caroline interrupted only once. "Mercedes, are *you* all right? Are you HIV positive?"

"It hasn't shown up yet. But the odds are next to nil that I will remain this way."

"I see." Caroline's eyes filled with concern.

She continued describing Jack's state, his personality changes, his dependence on her, and having to stop practicing law. She spoke about Darrel settling the Taylor case, Melanie contacting clients, Matthew Spencer evaluating the practice. She recited the history of Jack and Janine, and some of what she'd learned from Emerson about Jack's probate cases. Finally, she described Jack's behavior and admissions of the previous two evenings. Caroline, who was normally stoical in her response to her clients' sad stories, clapped a hand over her mouth in shock.

"Caroline, what should I do? Germaine's away at summer camp and doesn't know any of this."

"Distance yourself immediately. Your therapist is exactly right. Even though you have a prenuptial agreement, it may not protect you completely. The less you know about his business dealings, the better. I want to see a copy of the prenup, the estate plan documents, and anything else you can dig up. Have you kept your money separate?"

"My pay goes into my own checking account, if that's what you mean. The house and cars are in Jack's name. I pay for the groceries and most of Germaine's and my expenses. Jack pays for everything else."

"Good. Keep it that way. I want you to keep yourself as far as possible from Jack's practice and his affairs with Janine. You should separate physically, too. From a business standpoint, you should get a divorce. I don't know how you feel about that, but you have only a small window of time before word gets out. If Melanie has been calling clients for the last two weeks, time may be very short. If Jack's been embezzling from Janine, there's no telling what else he's been up to. Stop investigating. Go to his office and get copies of all the insurance policies, the trust document, your will, whatever pertains to you and Germaine personally, whatever will give me a picture of

Jack's assets. Don't say anything to Melanie about this. We don't know what she knows or how she may be involved. If there are legal malpractice actions, she could be a key witness."

"What about Jack's clients? Don't they have a right to know?"

"Yes, but it's not your responsibility. And it's not in your best interest for them to hear anything until you're in the clear. My job is to protect you."

"It may be too late for that," Mercedes said.

"Legally it isn't. Financially it isn't. And we don't know about the other, really, so let's not borrow trouble."

"I went to see Mr. Slayne about some of this a couple of weeks ago. I didn't know about Janine then, but the disability insurance policies were bugging me."

"As well they should. What did he say?"

"I presented it as a hypothetical case. He said the policy holder must have known of his illness before buying the policies. Otherwise it made no sense that such a young person would spend so much money on premiums."

"There's a reason John's a rainmaker. He doesn't miss much."

"Listen, another odd thing happened that I haven't told you. I took a different route to work this morning and stumbled upon a charming house that's for rent. I even wrote down the realtor's name. I keep thinking about it."

Caroline looked at her friend, wondering if she had any idea of the firestorm she might be facing. "Call the number."

"I just can't believe this is happening."

"There will be plenty of time to sort it all out later. Right now it's time to get busy. I want you to copy the documents as soon as you can, especially now that Jack knows you know. Is he driving?"

"Yes, but he shouldn't be. I hid his keys."

"Go to his office today, okay?"

They exchanged a look of stunned understanding.

Taking leave of Caroline, Mercedes walked down the hall to John Slayne's office. He had just come in from court and was taking off his suit jacket. He motioned her in.

"You were right—about that hypothetical case," Mercedes said.

"I'm sorry to hear that. One always hopes."

"The hypothetical case may soon become real."

"Let me know how I can help."

"You already have. Caroline is working on it now."

"Keep me posted."

Her heart was racing. She thought of Caroline's alarmed face and Dr. Hand's voice. She ducked back into the conference room and closed the door. She dialed the number on the slip of paper in her pocket. A real estate agent said the house had been on the market for three months and was still available. They agreed to meet that evening after work.

⌘

WITHOUT CALLING MELANIE, she drove hurriedly to Jack's office. Her insides were in an uproar. She found the front door of Soutane & Associates locked and all the lights turned off. She fished Jack's keys out of her purse and let herself in. Melanie's desk was completely devoid of paper. Perhaps she had already started working for the new lawyer. Mercedes locked the front door behind her and nearly ran back to Jack's desk.

She sat down. The blood was rushing in her temples. There was no way of knowing if Jack or Melanie would appear at any moment, and she hadn't considered what she would say if they did. Time was of the essence. She unlocked the bottom drawer. All the files were just as she'd left them. She collected an enormous stack of files and papers from the drawers and the credenza, and hauled everything to the copier. She told herself to be calm. A paralegal on her own case now, she worked as quickly as her fingers would allow. Her mouth was dry with anticipation. There would probably never be another opportunity such as this, so she had to capture as much information as she could. She prayed that the machine wouldn't jam, and that no one would walk in.

Miraculously, she managed to complete the task, return the files, and lock up behind her without interruption. She had parked the Alfa in a remote area of the lot near the dumpster. Exposed as she was, leaving the building laden with documents, she practically ran to the car to secure her cargo in the trunk. No sooner had she gotten into the driver's seat than she spotted Jack's big black Mercedes careen into the parking lot from the far lane of the busy thoroughfare.

She held her breath. He must have found his spare keys. She watched him stop the car in front of the building with a lurch, taking up two spaces. He got out with considerable effort and shambled toward his office. He wobbled to the left and the right, mercifully oblivious of the Alfa.

When he was out of sight, she exhaled a sigh of relief, put the car in gear, and tore out of the parking lot as though her hair were on fire. She could just make her appointment with the realtor if she hurried.

⁓

DESTINY WAS FLYING TO THE RESCUE. The landlord had lowered the rent a whopping $300 per month only that morning, the agent told her, because of the lack of interest in the house. As it turned out, the realty office had mistakenly classified the property as a potential sale instead of a rental. The office had also failed to register it with the Multiple Listing Service or advertise it at all. Meanwhile the For Rent sign had become obscured by foliage.

The agent extracted the key from the lockbox. Mercedes was the first potential tenant to set foot in the house.

"We didn't realize our error until after the owner contacted us this morning, and then you called."

"May I see the master bedroom first?" Mercedes asked. "I have a funny feeling."

"Of course," the agent eagerly replied.

They walked through the small living room, past the fireplace, across polished wood floors, down a short hall into the master bedroom. A sensation came over her as though someone's arm were caressing her shoulders, comforting her. She walked into the center of the room, which was carpeted wall to wall in beige. A door with eight panes of glass opened out onto a small curved patio. Opposite the door was a small window, outside of which was an oleander bush. Her scalp prickled. It was the room in her dream.

There were two more bedrooms, one of them perfectly suited to Germaine. It had room for her lovely old bed, a large closet, and built-in drawers and shelves, which would help greatly with their impending furniture shortage. Across the hall was a second bathroom with plenty of room for a teenager's toiletries. The kitchen had been recently remodeled and had an open dining area. There was even a small laundry room. The attached garage would accommodate one car. They walked out into the backyard, which was enclosed by a wood fence and bordered by a row of towering sycamores.

If this was going to be the house in which she spent the end of her life, it could not be more perfect. It was walking distance to good public schools and the rent was affordable. She filled out the application and wrote a check for the deposit. The real estate agent promised to call promptly with the landlord's decision, but she was confident it would be affirmative.

After the agent left, Mercedes stood on one of the stones in front, listening to the wind in the trees, watching cars return to the neighborhood at the end of the workday. The house had been waiting for a tenant since the day she first took Jack to the hospital. She looked up at the heavens, drank in the beauty of the mackerel sky, and again felt a great calming presence. Things were happening for a reason.

⚬⚬⚬

WHEN SHE RETURNED TO JACK, she found him stretched out on the couch, reading the newspaper with his shoes off. Roxy Music's "More Than This" was on the stereo: *It was fun for a while. There was no way of knowing . . .*

She avoided his eyes when he looked up, and when he roused himself to greet her she watched his movements with reptilian wariness. She avoided his touch, said nothing in response to his greeting, and fled to Germaine's room, which she had commandeered. He followed. He tried to engage her in conversation, but she kept her back turned toward him.

"Go away, please."

"What's the matter? Why are you home so late?"

"So *now* you're concerned with my welfare?"

"Of course I am."

"You're probably just hungry and want dinner. Well, you have a *long* wait ahead of you."

"Bella—"

"Don't call me that!"

He seized her elbow.

"What did I say? What do you mean?" He seemed sincere, but then he always seemed sincere.

"Let go of my arm."

He did so.

"Jack, go back to the living room. I need some time to myself."

He gave up and returned to the couch.

She walked across the hall to the master bedroom. She removed the little gold key from her purse and put it back in Jack's dresser drawer. She was no longer his caregiver, his cook, his errand girl, his personal shopper, his messenger, or his patsy. She returned his car keys to his bedside table. He could drive all he wanted. It was no longer her concern.

Except for the documents in her trunk, she had now divested herself of Soutane & Associates. *The less you know, the better,* Caroline had said. It certainly made things simpler.

What would she and Germaine need to start over? Their extraction had to be swiftly executed. She pictured the new house and how it would feel to walk through the front door with Germaine. Soon they would have their own world again, and with no gunshots in the neighborhood. Her star was shining. It might be a very dark star, but it was hers and it was shining.

⊸⣫⊸

JOHN SLAYNE REACHED ACROSS HIS messy desk to hand her a news clipping when she went to his office the following morning. He watched her while she read it. The story was about a lawsuit for emotional distress damages brought against the estate of Rock Hudson by his former lover, Marc Christian. Hudson had knowingly exposed Christian to HIV without disclosing that he had the virus. Adding insult to injury, Christian had learned of his lover's illness from an evening news broadcast. During an interview in France where he had collapsed with AIDS, Hudson had revealed that he had known he was HIV positive for over a year. Mercedes knew exactly what that moment had been like for Christian; it was inexpressible to anyone who had not experienced it. The jury had awarded a whopping $14.5 million to the plaintiff.

When Mercedes looked up, Slayne said, "It's not nice to do that to somebody."

Understatement was not usually Slayne's MO. His comment struck her funny, and then hysterically funny. She began laughing and was soon convulsed with laughter, laughing so hard that tears were streaming down her face.

Watching her made him laugh, too. But once she was quiet again, he said, "It's food for thought—perhaps something to consider . . . later."

She wondered how he knew so much about her predicament. "It wasn't too hard to figure out," he said, as if reading her mind. "But don't worry, this is just between you and me."

Mercedes pondered the situation for a moment. A multimillion-dollar award for damages would certainly be welcome, but the prospect of spending the end of her life embroiled in litigation would just be piling on more misery. Anyway, she had more pressing business.

"I brought you something as well," she said, "some business, perhaps." She pulled out a few pages from a file and handed them to him. "The people whose names and contact information you can see there were clients of Jack's, all very wealthy and very old. Jack drew up their estate plans. Now that he can no longer practice, they need new attorneys."

He looked at her curiously.

"I know you don't do probate. That's not why I've brought you this. I have reason to think that Jack 'has done some things in business' he's 'not exactly proud of'—that's how he puts it. I don't know the extent or nature of those things, but I *know* these people are victims. I think they will need not just new probate attorneys but an attorney like you to help them recover what may be owed to them."

His interest perked up.

"If you're interested in pursuing it, you could call a forensic accountant named Matthew Spencer. Another attorney is taking over Jack's practice, and Matthew knows his name. I daresay that by now Matthew is acquainted with some of Jack's Machiavellian accounting methods, which probably included embezzling from his clients. Perhaps Matthew would have a conflict of interest in talking to you. I don't know how that works. But I believe Matthew is an honorable man."

John's wheels were turning.

"I wasn't involved in any of this mess and I'm getting as far away from it as I can. I want to try to help these people on my way out, though. They've been hustled by my husband, and they aren't the only ones." She paused. "Emerson was also involved in this somehow."

"In what way?"

"I'm not sure. But when I let him in on the nature of Jack's illness, he promptly took off. I don't think it's a coincidence."

"Probably not. I bet Tony can find him."

"Another thing—in the basement of our house, which I plan to vacate shortly, there are sixty-seven boxes of Jack's business records. I haven't been through them, but they could be a gold mine for future lawsuits. Jack has no idea how much I know."

Slayne was perusing the papers she'd handed him. One of his eyebrows shot up.

"What do you think of those documents?" she asked.

"They're probably explosive," he answered.

"Good—because you're the munitions expert."

"Mercedes, take care of yourself. And thank you."

Caroline, already drafting the divorce petition, was keenly interested in the documents Mercedes had to show her. She said the separate property agreement "was worth its weight in gold." It went a long way toward shielding Mercedes and Germaine from possible fallout from any claims against Jack. What was hers was hers, separate. It also meant that what was his was his; but his assets, which on paper looked to be vastly greater, were entangled in a web of deceit.

How ironic, she thought bitterly, that Jack had bothered to protect her with a prenuptial agreement, at the very time they were having as much unprotected sex as their two bodies could bear. But then she realized the prenuptial agreement also protected him in case she left. He would have everything and she would have nothing.

The coldness and brutality of his actions hit her afresh. What did any of the money matter? What had he been thinking? *Germaine'll be fine. My mother died when I was young, and I turned out okay. Besides, she'll be rich.*

⸰⸫⸰

LATER IN THE MORNING SHE picked up the phone to hear a cheerful voice telling her she'd passed the credit check with flying colors. The landlord had accepted her application, and she was the new tenant of the blue house. She could have the keys as soon as the rent was paid and could move in any time.

That afternoon Mercedes called the summer camp to reach Germaine. The girls had just returned from a long horseback ride in the Sierra foothills. While waiting for Germaine to come to the phone, Mercedes pictured her daughter climbing off her horse, her hair in pigtails, a straw cowgirl's hat pushed back on her head, freckles popping out on her tanned face. They'd been sending each other picture postcards daily, with no mention of Jack.

After hearing about Germaine's adventures, Mercedes asked what she would think about coming home to a new house.

"Like what kind of a new house, Mom?"

"A new house for just you and me with no Jack in it."

Germaine let out a whoop of delight. "Just you and me? Really? That would be so cool, Mom!"

"Yes, really. I found a great house with a nice yard in a good spot. It's time we were happier, don't you think?"

"Wow! That's so rad. Have you told Jack?"

"No. I wanted to be sure how you felt about it."

"When are we moving?"

"When I come get you from camp, we'll drive home to our new house."

"I can't wait! Oh, thank you, Mom."

When they got off the phone, Mercedes was filled with Germaine's exuberance and, for the first time, the feeling that things might be okay. At least until she got sick.

Until she got sick. It was the tornado on the horizon. Until she could no longer function. Until she could no longer care for Germaine, keep a job, drive, keep food on the table, or think properly. Would that be next year? This time next year, would her eyes be sunk into a sallow face, with her hair falling out? Would she have Kaposi's sarcoma with its blotchy discolorations covering her body, or would the virus be eating away at her brain and laying her reason to waste? Would Eleanor go on another cruise, or would she swoop down to assess the damage and take Germaine away from her?

The thought of Eleanor bringing up Germaine was like a plunge into ice water. She shook her head to expel the notion. Next year would be next year. Right now she had a happy daughter, a new house waiting for both of them, and plenty of work to do.

◦◦◦

IN A MATTER OF HOURS, she met with the realtor, signed the lease, wrote the first rent check, and shook hands on the deal. As in a waking dream, she walked across the threshold, closed the door, and stepped out of her shoes. Afternoon light bathed the house in gold. She walked through each room slowly, feeling its serenity, noting the placement of cabinets, windows, closets, and shelves, mentally placing furniture and imagining how it would all look.

She walked into the master bedroom and sat down in the center of the carpet. Waves of sorrow, loss, and fear crashed inside her. She was afraid of what people would say when she left her sick husband. And yet here she was, in the room she had dreamed, in the house that had been waiting for her.

How could she despair? With so little time left, there was no time to waste on despair—or on self-pity either. There never had been, but she'd failed to realize it. She'd been asleep, sound asleep, in the illusion that life would go on and on without ever being stymied by illness and death. Now she faced it: she would never see gray hair or wrinkled skin or the natural decline of age, and death was a certainty.

Losing the illusion of permanence, she felt lighter, as though she had shed the ultimate armor. She sat quietly in her new room and felt great relief and the first moments of peace in many, many months.

⁕

THE HOUSE WHERE JACK LIVED had reverted to a state of chaos when she returned that evening. It had ceased to be her home. It was where her possessions were temporarily stored, in the company of a madman. She found him wandering around in the backyard, barefoot, unshaven, wearing stained sweatpants and his bathrobe, untied and open, with his bare chest exposed. He was searching for something in the ankle-high grass.

He jumped with a start when he saw her standing on the deck. He squinted at her, neither waved nor spoke, then returned to his task. He must have lost something, or imagined he had. She wondered if he'd taken all his medications—then reminded herself that his medications were no longer her problem. If he was not back in the house before sunset, still nearly two hours away, she would do something about it then.

She had lost all sympathy for his plight. Twenty hours had relieved her of that. She missed what she'd *thought* they had; she missed the illusion. *And what was the point of it? Just what the hell was the point?*

She got to work. Many of her belongings had been relegated to the basement storage area when they moved in, since they were not up to His Majesty's standards. The old couch from the pink palace was still there, along with a small dresser, her desk, and other items. She would get those things to the new place, along with most of the contents of the kitchen and the few antiques she'd inherited. She could pack it all up in a few hours. What they did not have, they could live without, as they had done before.

She got on the phone and dialed Gabe. She could hear his surprise that she was calling, and the clinking of ice in his glass. Though Jack had told Gabe he had AIDS and was closing down his practice, Gabe had no grasp of his old friend's deterioration. No one did, except for the medical staff and perhaps Melanie.

Mercedes asked their best man if he could come by on Saturday, and maybe take Jack out for a day in Belvedere. She explained that she had some work to do that day and a break from caring for Jack would be most helpful.

Gabe was delighted she'd thought of calling him, he said, and would be happy to take Jack off her hands for a day. He knew she'd had a "rough time of it," that she had "a lot on her plate" and it was time Jack got out of the house, now that he was "better."

She peeked out the French doors into the backyard. Jack appeared to be mesmerized by the grass and was only a few feet from where she'd last seen him. She wondered if he even remembered what he was trying to find, but put it out of her mind. She got to work packing Germaine's room. As she filled each box, she carried it downstairs to the basement.

Jack headed for the house when the fading daylight made it too difficult to see. He stopped twice to catch his breath and slowly ascended the stairs. By the time he reached the top, he was panting. Mercedes was in the kitchen and had just closed the door to the basement when he walked into the dining room from the deck. He caught sight of her in the kitchen and brightened. He hadn't eaten all day, and seeing her made him suddenly eager for food.

"Jack, what were you looking for?"

He was confounded.

"Out in the yard just now."

"I wasn't out in the yard. I've been here."

"Look at your feet. See the grass on them?"

He looked down and inspected his feet.

"You seemed to be searching for something."

He shook his head. She noticed the ring was gone from his right hand.

"Did you lose your diamond ring?"

He examined his hands, squinted, and frowned. "What diamond ring?"

"The fat one you just bought yourself the other day."

He didn't know what she was talking about.

"Never mind," she said and laughed to herself. *What were a few thousand more dollars of someone else's money?*

He sat down at the dining room table. She knew what he was doing. Instead of cooking dinner, though, she had other plans. She poured them each a glass of water and sat down. He stared at the glass and then at her.

"Expecting dinner?" she asked.

He nodded. "You always cook it."

"Well, there are going to be a few changes around here. You'd best hire yourself a new cook. This one is quitting." She took a long drink.

"What?"

"You heard me. No more cooking. And you'd better find another housekeeper, too. I've resigned that job as well." She waved her arm at the living room, covered with the papers, clothes and clutter that follow in the wake of a demented mind.

His eyes followed her gestures, and he glowered.

"You're going to face the future without me. I know you had a different plan in mind, but things don't always work out the way we plan, do they? Sometimes life gives us surprises. Just like when we met. That was a surprise for both of us—one that you tried to make the most of, didn't you?"

He stared at her in disbelief.

"You were so sure I'd stay that you confessed everything to me last night. You thought I'd stick around no matter what. That took some nerve, I'll give you that. But I do have one question."

"What?"

"Just *how* stupid do you think I am?"

"You don't understand." He was beginning to get worried. First no dinner, and now she was mad.

"Oh, I think I do. I understand plenty. I don't want any part of your lying and stealing from Janine, your cheating on taxes, and whatever you've been doing to your clients. I don't want another cent of your filthy money. It's over."

She had not raised her voice, but the intensity of her glare was frightful. He'd never seen her like this. She got up from the table, feeling lighter still, and went into the kitchen to make herself a sandwich. While in there, she opened the cabinets to determine what needed to be packed. When Jack got up to leave the table, she ignored him.

⸎

THE NEXT MORNING HE WAS already up when she got out of the shower. By the time she was ready to leave for work, he'd shaved and dressed and was reading the newspaper. She wondered how much he remembered from the night before.

She sat down across from him just long enough to fasten the buckles on her sling-back heels.

"You know," she began, "of all the people you could have picked to marry, it's pretty ironic you picked me."

"How so?"

"You could have told me everything and I would have understood. I would have helped you. You could have admitted you owed Janine money and I would have helped you pay it back. You could have admitted you were behind on your property taxes, and I would have stood by you while you made amends. Of all the people you could have chosen, you chose someone you could have leveled with. If you'd just been honest, Jack, I could have loved you until the end and helped you make things right."

He listened with mild concern.

"You could have told me you were bisexual and HIV positive, and I would have loved you anyway. I might not have married you, but I would have helped you when you got sick, which is really why you married me anyway. But you miscalculated. I'm leaving you and filing for divorce."

"Aren't you forgetting a few things?" he asked.

"No, I don't think so. It's all pretty clear."

"You'll be getting sick and you won't have any disability insurance. You won't be able to get it once you test positive, and you won't have the means to get help at home."

"That's not your concern anymore. I have insurance at work—or did you forget that I support myself?"

"I'll be getting ten thousand dollars a month, tax-free. I can take care of you if you stay."

"Oh, like you've been taking care of me these past two months?"

"You know what I mean—financially. If you leave, I'll cut you both out of my estate plan."

"This isn't about money, Jack. Don't you get it? You've knowingly exposed me to HIV for several years now. You planned for Germaine to be an orphan without batting an eye. You've been stealing from Janine even longer, although she's both your client and the closest thing you have to a mother. Yet apparently you don't see anything wrong with what you've done."

He was quiet.

"Those are grounds for disbarment, civil and criminal prosecution, and imprisonment. No amount of money is going to make any of it palatable to me. You'll be lucky if I don't sue you myself. I'm not afraid of you. You're pathetic. There's nothing you can get from me any longer because it's over."

Without hesitation he said, "We'll see how pathetic you think I am when you're sick and you can't work and you're broke. You'll be begging for help."

"You'll be dead, and I'll have a clean conscience. What could be better?"

With that, she got up and walked out.

WAR *and* ROSES

A chill wind rattled leaves from the aged sycamores, sending them down on Mercedes and Germaine in a fluttering shower of bronze and gold. They worked ankle-deep in the crunchy drifts that had fallen since they last raked the yard. Six full leaf bags sat near the back gate. Germaine was cheerfully chattering away about the upcoming holiday break from school and the pending visit of her grandparents. She held the bag's mouth open for her mother, who scooped great piles into it. Their cheeks were red from the cold and their exertions.

Mercedes grinned at Germaine, whose speech was altered ever so slightly by her mouthful of silver braces. Seeing her so excited cheered Mercedes, even if it meant spending a few days under Eleanor's microscope. Eleanor *was* the only mother she had, and this might be their last healthy Christmas together, so she'd invited her parents to share it with them. Awareness of her mortality had softened her. Eleanor had taught her many things about being the queen of her own realm, and those had served her well these past few months.

Germaine cinched the top of the black plastic bag and applied a twist tie. She hauled the big bag over to the others. Storm clouds were gathering, and they hoped to clear the yard before the rains began. Mercedes wiped her calloused hands against her fleece jacket and renewed her efforts with the rake. She remembered the previous Christmas with Janine, watching Jack dote over the old lady when all the while he was stealing from her. A shiver went up her spine. She wondered how Janine was and who was looking after her, but let the thought go with the strong breeze that was scattering the final pile of leaves.

Germaine returned with a broom and began sweeping piles of pine needles and debris from the patio. She loved the fragrances of fall nearly as much as those of spring. Since they'd moved into the new house, she had many more chores to do, but she didn't mind. They worked in harmony, and the time passed quickly. Home was peaceful again, despite Jack's calls and the long rambling messages he left on the answering machine.

She hated how he upset her mother, although Mercedes tried to conceal it. Germaine could see the strain wearing on her, but it did nothing to undermine her mother's resolve. She looked at her mom working across the yard, her long braid moving this way and that, her eyes dark with private sorrows she did not share.

The pale sun slipped behind thick gray clouds and the temperature continued its steady decline. Just as the last bag was filled, the rain began, dotting the concrete patio with black circles. Mercedes piled dry firewood near the back door, then pulled the tarp over the wood pile. No sooner were they inside than the heavens opened up and let loose a steady, driving rain that pounded against the skylight in the kitchen.

"I call that perfect timing," announced Mercedes. The house smelled of the smoked ham shank flavoring the split pea soup in the

Crock Pot, and of bread rising in a bowl on top of the stove. Germaine's stomach growled. Mercedes cooked a lot of food on the weekends to carry them through the workweek, and Saturdays were notoriously mouthwatering.

The rain intensified, soaking the ground and washing down the empty patio. The red light of the answering machine blinked sleepily. They stared at each other, knowing it was probably another message from Jack. Since they'd left, he called often, usually under some pretext related to the divorce proceedings, the division of property, or an imagined wrong. The messages ranged from whiny and petulant to threatening and angry. They were a source of misery for Mercedes and anger for Germaine. Anyone who hurt her mother was her sworn enemy, especially someone who had pretended to be so nice when, in hindsight, he so obviously was not.

Mercedes's arms were full of firewood, so she stepped carefully past the answering machine into the living room and gently laid the wood on the hearth, brushing the splinters off her jacket. She pulled aside the screen and laid a fire for later that evening, wadding up newspaper and nestling kindling and small logs on top. As soon as the newspaper noise subsided, Germaine punched the playback button and waited with her arms crossed in front of her, glaring at the machine.

"Bella," Jack began in a whine, "please call me when you get this. I really *need* to talk to you"—Germaine sniffed her disapproval —"about visitation rights with Germaine. I've been talking to Caroline and there must be some mistake. I'm willing to stipulate to your terms, but not unless I get my own time with Germaine. I'll be home all afternoon, then I'm going *out*," he stressed, as if to inform her that a retinue awaited him.

"Mom!" Germaine protested.

"I know, I heard. You have nothing to worry about, Sweetness."

"Why does he think he can see me?"

"God only knows."

"Eeeuuuw! He makes me so mad! Who does he think he is?"

"Someone he isn't. Now, young miss, how about finishing up the chores before dinner? As I recall, you're losing at Scrabble, so if you want to regain your former glory, I suggest you get on with the housework."

There was no reply. Instead, Mercedes heard the touch-tone keys of the telephone clicking as a call was being placed.

"Jack, it's Germaine. My mom and I just got your message. I am *not* going to spend time with you *ever*. You're not the boss of me and you have no right to me! You're not my dad, okay? You can't make me come see you! Even if my mom were okay with it, WHICH SHE'S NOT, I REFUSE!! So stop calling here and stop bugging us! If you call here again, I'm calling the police *and* Caroline. Good-bye!" She slammed down the receiver and put her hands firmly on her hips. Her eyes were fierce with anger.

Seeing her mother standing in the doorway to the kitchen, Germaine shook her head and proclaimed, "He just makes me so mad. I'm sick of him!"

"So I noticed."

⟞⟊⟝

THE NEXT DAY THEY CAME home from the store to find Jack sitting on the step by the front door. He was growing a beard, which was white and gray. He reminded Mercedes of Ichabod Crane with his gauntness, rounding shoulders, and sunken eyes. His hand trembled as he stroked his whiskers. She parked their Jeep, which she'd bought after selling the engagement ring.

"Wait here," she instructed Germaine. "I'll deal with this."

Germaine stared in horror at Jack, whom she had not seen since going to camp. He looked like one of the homeless men in San Francisco, but with clean clothes. His eyes had a wild expression that she could never have imagined on her stepfather. It scared her to think that someone could change so much.

"Hi, Jack," Mercedes said as she strode toward her front door.

"Bella," he stood up on uncertain feet, holding onto one of the posts that supported the portico. He took a step toward her. "I think there's some misunderstanding." She took a step back.

"The only misunderstandings we have are yours, I'm afraid," she began. "First, you can't come here. We have restraining orders against you, as you know. You must stay one hundred yards away from the premises, so I suggest you make yourself scarce before I call the police. Second, don't call me. I'm represented by counsel. I have nothing more to say to you now, and whatever I have to say in the future will be said by Caroline."

He reached out his arms to touch her. She took another step back.

"Bella, I think when you left you took the crystal goblets Damon gave us for a wedding present. Also, there are some tools missing. And I want to see Germaine. I need to come inside."

"You need to *leave*. I assure you, I didn't take any crystal, or any of the other gifts from your friends. I don't have any of your tools, either. I'm not the thief, remember? That's *your* specialty." With each sentence her voice increased in volume. "Moreover, you have enough money to buy yourself a boatload of crystal and a hardware *store*, okay? So this is just an excuse for you to harass me. We're not going to discuss Germaine."

He flinched as though she'd slapped him.

"You've *lost* me. You've *lost* her. You're a cold-blooded liar and a crook and a ruthless, self-centered bastard! *Now go to your car and drive away! GET OUT OF HERE!*" she roared.

He looked down and fumbled with the zipper of his jacket, as if to buy more time, then tottered up the stepping stones to his car and left.

⋅⊂⊃⋅

THE NEXT MORNING SHE REPORTED the incident to Caroline, who called Jack to reaffirm that he could be arrested for violating a court order. A hearing in the dissolution proceedings had been calendared, she reminded him, and until then, any issues he cared to raise must be discussed with her alone.

No matter how much anger and disgust she mustered, it did nothing to ease the sorrow and grief Mercedes sequestered inside. She had to keep plodding forward and let the events that had been set in motion continue along their trajectory. After lunch, she went by the reception area to check for messages and was there when Darrel and John Slayne exited the elevator. They were in dark suits, carrying briefcases and talking animatedly. When Slayne spied Mercedes, he fell silent and looked at her with his big brown eyes.

"We've had quite a morning, Mercedes," Darrel said. He glanced at his partner, saying, "We might as well tell her. She's going to find out sooner or later."

"Find out what?"

"Follow me," Darrel said, and the three marched through the suite into Darrel's office, where Mercedes took a seat.

"We just served Jack with another lawsuit. That makes three so far," Darrel began. "We've taken possession of the boxes in his basement, which Stuart has been going through with Simone. As you predicted, there's plenty of evidence."

"I'm surprised he didn't have everything shredded," she said. "But then he's not quite on his game these days."

"Actually, his friend Gabe facilitated everything when we served him with the subpoena. He has Jack's power of attorney now and he seems to be an honest enough fellow. I don't think he knows what Jack's been up to, at least not where his law practice is concerned."

"So this morning I was taking Jack's deposition in the first case," Slayne interjected, "which is on behalf of one of the family trusts he defrauded, and we thought it would be an opportune time to serve lawsuit number three, since we knew where he'd be for a few hours."

Darrel was watching Mercedes's expression, wondering how she could remain so calm in the midst of her apocalypse.

"At the break," Slayne continued, "we let the process server into the conference room. He marched up to Jack, handed him an envelope, and told him he'd been served. Jack opened the envelope, saw the summons—and lost it. He stood up, grabbed one of the conference room chairs and hurled it at the process server. The young fellow jumped out of the way, and the chair crashed into the glass wall that partitions the conference room from the hall. The glass shattered. You never heard such a racket! Shards flew everywhere. Fortunately, the insurance reps and the court reporter weren't in the room at the time, so no one was hurt. Counsel got Jack under control. We postponed the deposition and left."

Mercedes listened with a deadpan expression on her face. Nothing Jack did could surprise her. She longed for the day when she wouldn't hear his name or think about him. Would that day ever come?

"I'm surprised he had the strength," she remarked. "I saw him yesterday, and he was rather feeble. But I guess it depends on which Jack shows up. So you said this is lawsuit number three?"

"Here's another," Darrel said with a hint of a smile. "Jack has sued me over fees in the Taylor case. He thinks he should have gotten a larger share of the settlement."

"We're not done yet," Slayne added. "Stuart's been contacting the families on a growing list. Jack won't be the only defendant, either. There are insurance agents and at least one carrier at fault. They had quite a party going on for a few years."

"Until Mercedes crashed it," Darrel joked.

"Very funny," she said. "I know the name of the company. It was all over the documents I saw. What did they do that was illegal?"

"Never you mind," Darrel said. "Don't bother yourself with it. Anyway, now we know to wear flak jackets to the next deposition. We located Emerson, too, by the way. He's beyond subpoena range but he's going to cooperate, thanks to 'The Hammer' here," he said wryly, pointing his thumb at Slayne.

"There's nothing quite like the threat of criminal prosecution to soften the heart when you're still paying on your law school loans," Slayne said.

"How did you find him?"

"Tony found him in about ten minutes."

She wished she could wash off all the taint of Jack and the people who had worked with him. It was a noxious feeling that clung to her, no matter what she did or where she went. She wished she could rinse every thought of him from her mind. She wished she could purge all cellular memory of his kiss, his scent, his lethal love-making. She wished she could shed her skin like a snake and lose his touch. Even so, the paralegal in her was curious about the campaign against him. At least Jack's former clients were getting good legal representation.

"Thank you for the business," Darrel said gently. "I should have said this earlier. I hope you know that we're glad to help you regard-less, but also know that I do feel responsible for having brought Jack here in the first place. He charmed me just as he did everyone else. You won't owe the firm anything for your divorce. It's the least we can do."

"Good will come of it," Slayne said reassuringly. "And now counsel will get to redecorate his office at Jack's expense."

⠿

A FEW DAYS LATER, Julie, the receptionist, paid a visit to the paralegal office carrying an enormous vase filled with long-stemmed red roses. She placed them on Mercedes's desk, handed her an envelope, then left. Without opening the envelope, Mercedes knew the flowers were from Jack. They were flawless and came from the same florist he'd used after their first date.

She closed her eyes and put her face into her hands. The music to "One More Night" played in her head. For a moment she was once again in his arms, swaying to the slow song, feeling the heat of his body, the size of his hand wrapped around the small of her back. She recalled the feel of the lovely crimson dress that Eleanor had sent her when she'd heard she was being courted by a wealthy young lawyer.

Simone came into the paralegal room and lit up at the sight of the roses.

Mercedes saw her and asked, "Would you do me a favor?"

"Of course."

"Take these flowers and put them in the war room where you're working on Jack's boxes. I don't want to see them again."

"Gladly," Simone replied, and carried them away.

Mercedes opened the envelope and saw Jack's bold scrawl on his fine stationery. The writing was very sloppy, the lines crooked, his penmanship erratic. He had changed pens in the middle of the page from blue to black, neither of which had the blunt nib of his good pen. She supposed he'd misplaced it by now. For a moment she wondered whether he'd ever found his diamond ring, if indeed that's what he'd been searching for in the grass, and how he was managing his daily life. Why couldn't she just let it go?

Dear Mercedes, the letter began. *I want us to be friends. I want to be at peace with you.* The letter went on to offer additional terms for the divorce:

> *It makes the most sense for each of us to remain liable for our separate debts and to pay for our own insurance policies. I would like to give you the house in exchange for your waiver of any interest in my other properties, and I relinquish all visitation rights concerning Germaine. Why would I want to harm someone who has brought me so much love and joy?*

Mercedes sat quietly and contemplated the letter. The last sentence made the hair on the back of her neck bristle and prompted her to read his words again. Nothing from Jack was ever free. What was she missing?

The subtext suddenly jumped out at her: I want you to agree to submit to my terms, in spite of the fact that you told me last weekend not to communicate directly with you again. I'm sending you flowers and writing you a personal letter because what I'm about to propose would never fly with your lawyer.

It makes the most sense for each of us to remain liable for our separate debts and to pay for our own insurance policies. Subtext: our debts are separate anyway, because of our separate property agreement, but perhaps you don't know that, so I will put it under your nose to distract you from the second clause of this sentence. I will no longer pay premiums on the life insurance for you. The Soutane Family Trust will be extinguished, and Germaine will not be a beneficiary of any insurance other than what you pay for, despite the fact that I have done my best to give you HIV.

I would like to give you the house in exchange for your waiver of any interest in my other properties, and I relinquish all visitation rights with Germaine. This was a particularly rich sentence. The house, heavily encumbered with tax liens from years of rolling over property taxes on previous properties, had no equity left in it, according to Caroline, and was also laden with debt from remodeling and repairs. Jack was willing to give her all this in exchange for her agreement not to make any claims against his other properties, which were less encumbered and actually had some equity! Germaine's voice message had disabused him of any notion about visitation, so he was now willing to relinquish a right he never had anyway.

She read the letter one more time, wondering what else she was missing. *Ah yes,* she thought, *any mention of spousal support.* No wonder he'd sent flowers.

⋘⋙

IT HAD BEEN RAINING ALL morning that December day, and the sky was thick and dark. She drove in silence, listening to the tires on wet pavement, feeling the damp air on her skin, smelling the rain-soaked earth. Cyclamen was blooming red and pink all around the entryway to the clinic. A long-haired Sylvester cat paused in his hunting under a nearby tree, a white foot suspended in the air, when he spotted Mercedes. A robust robin was his target, but in the half second of his distraction the bird flew up from the hedge to a higher perch in the redwood. The cat crept over the wet bark chips into a hedge.

The doctor ushered her into her office and asked her to be seated. After preliminary pleasantries she said, "You're here for results from your HIV test, your third one—is that right?" They both knew it was. "And how is your husband doing?"

Mercedes could sense that the doctor was just trying to soften the blow.

"Not well. We've separated."

"I'm sorry to hear that. It's always sad when a marriage is stressed like this."

Please just get on with it and tell me the bad news.

"Your test is negative, Mercedes. There's no sign of the virus."

The words took a moment to register. She was shocked speechless.

"And honestly, I don't think follow-up tests are necessary. I think you should go on with your life and put this all behind you. If you want, have another test in a year, but I'm convinced it will be negative too. Your immune system has defended you perfectly."

"How is it possible? Are you sure the test results weren't mixed up in the lab?"

"I have no explanation. There's no reason to think there was an error in the test. I think you're very, very lucky. You have some natural immunity that I haven't seen in this epidemic. Maybe there will be others. I certainly hope so. It makes me so happy to be able to tell you this!"

The doctor shook her hand, and Mercedes left in a cloud of astonishment.

Outside, the clouds were dispersing. She got into the mud-spattered Jeep, looked in the rearview mirror, and noticed the top of her head. With a start she realized she would live to see her hair turn gray. She was going to have the privilege of aging, along with others in her generation.

She drove out of the parking lot and turned onto the main road. The sun began to peek through the clouds and a rainbow emerged over the road ahead, its arc forming a perfect semicircle of vivid colors, a matinee produced by the gods.

She was free! She would live! She would see her daughter become a woman! Germaine would never be an orphan, and together they would leave all this behind. It was over. The nightmare was over! The dread that had hung over her for months, the tornado of doom on the horizon, had given way to a rainbow and a future.

Tears filled her eyes and streamed down her cheeks. She pulled the car off onto the shoulder of the road, overcome, and wept.

⁓⁓⁓

THAT HOLIDAY SEASON WAS MAGICAL in a way she had never known before. Although she kept her good news mostly to herself, her spirits brightened more each day. She felt like singing when she woke up in the morning. She daydreamed about what she wanted to do years hence. Even the pending visit from Eleanor and Philip was going to be fine.

She strung colored lights along the eaves of their house, like so many others on the street. They bought a Christmas tree for the living room and decorated it, combining new ornaments with the old. They read beside the fireplace each night. They went shopping, wrapped presents, baked cookies and took them to all their neighbors, sent Christmas cards to their friends. They bought special dresses to wear for Christmas dinner and carefully planned the meal they would cook for the grandparents. Germaine didn't know what had come over her mother, but it didn't matter. They were getting over their sorrows one by one.

⁓⁓⁓

IN ALL THE YEARS SINCE she'd left home, Mercedes's houses had been her refuge from Eleanor's drama. But she'd been seasoned by death's hourly companionship. She had stared real madness in the face. No behavior of her mother's could possibly match what Jack had put her through. And finally, she accepted that Eleanor loved her in her way.

All was ready on Christmas Eve when the doorbell rang. Eleanor made her grand entrance swathed in fur, followed closely by Philip, who was laden with bags of presents. Germaine ran to her grand-mother and was immediately engulfed in mink. Philip put down his load and embraced Mercedes. Eleanor drew Mercedes into her overwhelming cloud of perfume, clutched her awkwardly, and released her after a kiss on the cheek.

Mercedes helped her out of her coat. As usual, Eleanor was perfectly put together—tonight in a deep purple cashmere sweater with a cowl neck, decorated with a prominent diamond brooch. Her suede high heels matched the sweater and peeked out beneath impeccably tailored black silk slacks. Eleanor peeled off her long leather gloves and straightened the heavy gold bracelets on her wrists, then looked askance at the oddly furnished room.

Germaine took Eleanor by the hand and led her on a tour of the house, proudly narrating what she considered to be its fine points. She pulled her from room to room, effervescent and loquacious, even turning on the outside lights and dragging Eleanor out onto the back patio to extol the virtues of the backyard. When Germaine loved something, she loved it with every hair on her head.

Mercedes could hear Eleanor trying to echo her granddaughter's enthusiasm, but it was obviously difficult for her to be impressed by the small house and its humble amenities. Eleanor must be finding it impossible to imagine herself in their position, Mercedes mused, or to comprehend why Mercedes had tolerated men who treated her poorly.

Whatever Eleanor thought of the house, she was definitely drawn to the aromas coming from the brightly lit kitchen. As she swept through the room behind Germaine, she snatched an appetizer and slid it into her mouth, careful not to smudge her lipstick.

"Divine!" she proclaimed.

Philip opened the wine. Mercedes showed him all the dishes they had prepared for the holiday feast. Casseroles were warming in the oven and a succulent roast fowl was resting on a platter. Mercedes wore a chef's apron over her dark green Christmas dress, with her thick curly hair pulled back and twisted around the crown of her head in a Renaissance style that became her well. She whisked a steady stream of rich, seasoned stock into the roux and a scrumptious gravy began to coalesce. Eleanor, who was a stranger to the kitchen and had never made gravy in her life, watched in mute wonderment.

Her daughter was an enigma to Eleanor. Mercedes was interested in things completely foreign to her, and indifferent to much that Eleanor deemed vitally important. The result was an introspective, self-sufficient young woman, who lived her life on her own terms and actually seemed to enjoy working. Eleanor watched the playful banter between Mercedes and her father, unable to disguise a twinge of envy.

Philip gave his wife a glass of wine and a wink, and then poured a glass of sparkling cider for Germaine.

"Cheers! Here's to our enterprising daughter and her gracious hospitality," he exclaimed.

Wind blew through the bare tree branches outside, and the full moon ascended. They all joined hands at the dinner table, the candlelight shining on their steaming plates, while Philip said grace, something he never did ordinarily. He and Eleanor seldom ate dinner at home. Germaine, so sweet and appealing, even with braces, had scrunched up her nose, shut her eyes tight, and appeared to be praying with all her might. Mercedes, having walked through the valley of death, had never felt so grateful or so blessed by life.

The meal was exactly what she had hoped it would be. Germaine ate as though she were starving, and had seconds while her grandparents talked about their travel plans for the coming year.

When it was time for dessert, Mercedes brought out a lattice-top cherry pie, Germaine's favorite. The candlelight flickered, and they listened to the wind whip around the corners of the house while she served everyone. Mercedes looked at her family and felt great love. Philip took a forkful of the succulent pie and flavor exploded in his mouth. He was perfectly happy, and that made at least three of them.

As the last bites of dessert vanished from their plates, Mercedes said, "I have something to tell all of you that I've been keeping to myself for many months. It's about Jack and what happened this year."

Eleanor and Philip looked at each other as if to say, "At last!"

"I first noticed a change in him during our honeymoon," Mercedes began. "He was very moody, but I thought that was just how he was, and I hadn't taken enough time to get to know him before we married.

"He began to reveal more of the truth about his life—starting with his childhood. His mother died when he was little, and his father was vicious. Jack was abused and neglected from an early age. His father went bankrupt paying for his mother's medical bills, and they had to sell the family home. Dr. Soutane became dependent on drugs and took out his aggression and bitterness on Jack. He died when Jack was in college. Within a short time, Jack also lost his only two siblings. He was completely on his own.

"Only a short time into our marriage, he seemed to become several different people. There was a child of five or younger named Jackie, a slovenly scatterbrain who couldn't remember anything, a mean guy who was suspicious of everyone, and so on. The Jack we loved made fewer and fewer appearances. The scary Jack, the nasty Jack, and the lost boy were around more and more.

"After months of coughing, one weekend he had a seizure, became desperately ill, and I took him to the hospital. They gave him an MRI, which led to a shocking discovery. In college, Jack was introduced to a gay lifestyle by two fellow students who were very kind to him. For obvious reasons, he could pretty much choose his companions, and he did so with impunity. Somewhere along the way he contracted the AIDS virus. I don't know the circumstances, but it was well before we met. By the time he had the seizure he was really very ill—too ill to practice law any longer."

Germaine reached for her mother, who grasped her hand. Philip's eyes glittered with outrage, while Eleanor, for once, was speechless.

"Before I go on, I want you all to know that I didn't get it. I'm clean. All the tests have come back negative. I've been very lucky."

"Oh, thank God!" Eleanor exclaimed. Philip shook his head, pressed his lips together, and waited for Mercedes to continue.

"Anyway, although there was finally a rational explanation for Jack's crazy behavior, I felt panicky, realizing my own exposure. And there was so much I didn't know—about our finances, Jack's private life and law practice. I scrambled to keep everything afloat while my own prognosis could not have been worse.

"I spent a lot of time in his office trying to figure out how to pay the mortgage and wind down his law practice. I was still getting up to speed when Jack was released from the hospital, which was another kind of nightmare. I'll spare you the details, but Germaine saw a lot of it. It was very, very difficult for us. For many weeks he was tethered to an oxygen tank. He had dementia. He couldn't manage his own bodily functions, read, remember anything, or take care of the most rudimentary things. We had a nurse with him until he was able to wash and dress himself and take his own medicine."

Germaine got up, climbed into her mother's lap, and buried her face in her neck.

"All this time, I myself was facing death. I was told repeatedly that no one who had been exposed to the disease as I had could possibly escape getting it. Yet each HIV test I took was negative.

Jack's doctor told me that less than one percent of the people exposed to the virus do not succumb. It is a miracle, truly, that I am well. But there's more you need to know.

"One night Jack seemed more lucid than he'd been in a while. We had gotten a letter from an accountant we hired to help with the dissolution of Jack's law practice. He was asking us for information. I watched Jack read it and saw his shocked reaction. The next day, he confessed everything to me—that he had known he had the virus when he married me and planned the whole thing. He had prepared an estate plan based on the assumption that I would get the virus and Germaine would be an orphan.

"He admitted embezzling hundreds of thousands of dollars from an old family friend, who was like a mother to him. He also stole from his clients' trust accounts. That money was the source of his lavish lifestyle. He admitted there were tax liens on all his properties and he had no intention of repaying anyone.

"He expected me to go along with all of it. He committed fraud to obtain four disability policies. He thought that the huge amount of his disability income would ensure my compliance. He saw no reason for anyone to know. He was sure I would do nothing to jeopardize Germaine's or my position. He was incensed at my suggestion that he come clean."

"He didn't know you very well," Philip remarked.

"So now I've passed another HIV test and I know I'm going to live. I didn't want to tell you anything until I was sure of my fate. I wanted to spare you if I could."

Germaine curled up even tighter in her lap.

Philip's eyes had tears in them. "Thank you for not telling us. That took a lot of character, Mercedes."

"We're proud of you," added Eleanor earnestly.

She acknowledged her parents with a nod.

"The doctor told me to go on with my life, to close the door on this chapter. I've told the lawyers at my office what I found out about Jack's law practice, and they're prosecuting him on behalf of many of Jack's former clients. He's embroiled in litigation. I am grateful to be healthy, to be able to take care of Germaine while she grows up, and to be here with you. "

"Thank you for sparing us," Philip said again.

"I couldn't have stood it," Eleanor said. "I would have been out of my mind with worry. Oh, that jackass! May he rot in hell!"

Mercedes fixed her gaze on her mother and said, "So I'm hoping that we can all have a new beginning." Germaine looked at her grandmother and at her mother, then sat up and wiped her eyes.

"I've learned that anything really *is* possible. It's not a platitude. I've learned that the truth is incontrovertible. It is there in plain sight. Mostly we look for what we *want* to see. We don't see what *is*. Most people live as though they're immortal, leaping from one desire to the next, trying to manipulate other people and circumstances to their advantage. We bypass so much of life in the rush to achieve our own ends. We waste so much time and energy.

"I don't want to do that anymore. I've been given the best possible gift by being forced to think my death was imminent. I want to live my life in the slow lane. I don't want to be manipulated or controlled, and I don't want to do that to anyone else either. There are ways for people with great differences to get along."

Eleanor was quiet and appeared to be turning some things over in her mind.

"You cannot change another person," Mercedes said. "Except perhaps with a little orthodontia," she added humorously, patting Germaine's head.

Germaine caught her mother's jest and laughed, then grabbed her arm and held it tightly.

ONE LAST WISH

I t was a Saturday afternoon, and Germaine was at work. Mercedes had just finished yoga and was sitting in the quiet, meditating. Although nearly four years had passed since she had seen Jack, images of him paraded across her mind's eye. The phone rang.

"Mercedes, it's Gabe," a familiar voice said through the receiver.

"Hi, Gabe." She knew what he was going to say.

"It's Jack. He doesn't have long."

Her pulse quickened.

"I thought you should know, in case you want to say good-bye or anything."

"How much time do you think he has?"

"Maybe a day or two. He's not able to communicate at all, but he does open his eyes. Anyway, there's a nurse with him." He gave her the address. "Just ring the bell, and she'll let you in."

GERMAINE WAS WORKING IN A café and had recently learned to make cappuccino on the massive copper Italian espresso machine. Mercedes came in and sat on a stool at the counter. The braces had worked wonders; her daughter's smile was radiant with her straight white teeth.

"A cappuccino, please. Quality control."

Germaine was now Mercedes's height, but her hair was straight and glossy, like Eddy's, and pulled up into a ponytail. Her glasses had been replaced by contacts, and she wore silver hoops in her recently pierced ears. She wiped her hands on her apron and set about making the espresso drink. Mercedes admired her daughter's form in the black slacks and tucked-in white shirt required by her new job. It was not hard to guess she was on the high school track team. She was lithe, long-limbed, and quick on her feet.

Germaine placed the frothy drink in front of her mother with satisfaction.

"Perfect!" Mercedes exclaimed. She took a long sip. "And delicious. It's about time we had a barista in the family."

"So what's happening?" Germaine asked as she cleaned the milk-frothing spigot with a wet rag and buffed the front of the machine with a dry one. Business was slow at the moment. Even so, her big hands worked quickly.

"Jack is dying."

Germaine's hands stopped moving.

"How do you feel about that, Mom?"

"Not the way I expected to feel. It's rather disconcerting."

"Really? I'm surprised he lived this long."

"He had the best care money could buy."

Germaine looked at her, irritated. "Yeah, and he almost took you with him. It could have been *you* dying."

"*Almost* doesn't count."

"It most certainly does! I'm glad he's dying. I wish it had been a lot sooner."

"I was wondering if you'd like to go with me to see him one last time."

"No way! And why would *you* want to see him?"

"I don't want to regret that I missed the opportunity to . . . finish something. Does that make sense?"

"Nothing about this makes sense. Well, stick a pin in him for me." Germaine gave her a devilish grin.

Mercedes took another sip of cappuccino and swallowed. "Listen, you don't ever have to worry about getting even with anybody. Life will do a much better job of it than you could ever imagine. I'm living proof."

⚬⚬⚬

THE FOLLOWING AFTERNOON, Mercedes opened the iron gate outside a house just off Castro Street in San Francisco. The flower beds on either side of the walkway were well tended and full of luxuriant red dahlias. A vibrant fresco covered the stucco wall around the property. A tiled walkway led to the imposing double doors at the entrance.

A female nurse in uniform answered the door. "Yes, Ms. Bell, we were expecting you. Come in, please."

She was led over a familiar carpet into a spacious bedroom full of windows. Outside she could see the garden of fruit trees, flower beds, and a sitting area beneath a bower of morning glories. Athena stood amidst the flowers, serene as ever.

Jack lay in a hospital bed, curled up on his side. But for his eyes, she would never have recognized him. He was bald and had shrunk by more than a hundred pounds. He stared straight ahead. His withered hands were curled one on top of the other, with no resemblance to the big, beautiful hands she had known so well. He lay mute and motionless, his brow creased in an expression of perpetual worry.

She stood by the side of the bed and looked down, shocked by the totality of AIDS's ravages. She wondered if Jack's spirit knew she was there and whether her words would register in his consciousness.

She picked up one of his bony hands and held it. It was cool and dry, more like a claw than a hand.

The nurse said, "We think he's been waiting for you. I'll be in the next room if you need anything."

She spoke his name and began talking. He turned his blue eyes in her direction and stared incoherently at her face—his mouth hanging open between concave cheeks.

"Jack, it's Mercedes."

Staring up at her, he moved his jaw but made no sound. The cloudiness in his eyes seemed to recede, and some faint semblance of recognition crept into his face.

She leaned closer. Tears welled up in her eyes. She pictured him as he had looked the first time she'd seen him—kingly, refined, impeccable, and captivating. She remembered the deep timbre of his voice and his thick, glossy salt-and-pepper hair, all of which was now gone. He stared at her intently, his breathing very shallow.

"I want you to know that Germaine and I are fine. I never did get the virus. I'm healthy and everything is working out. It's a miracle."

He looked into her eyes without blinking, as though he wanted to beam his thoughts to her.

"Thank you for all that you gave us. I bear you no hard feelings anymore. I loved you and I don't regret that.

"Jack, be at peace. Whatever unfinished business you have is between you and God. You showed Germaine and me some of the finer things in life. You exalted us and made us feel treasured, for a while. You helped us to regard ourselves in a completely different way. It is a great gift to have your horizons expanded.

"Germaine's nearly grown. She's as big as I am, smart and spirited and pretty. She's going to do something worthwhile with her life and that is partly because of you.

"I learned invaluable lessons as a result of knowing you. Some of them were painful, but I really did love you."

Heat was building up inside her, and she felt as though she couldn't breathe. She let go of his hand and stepped away from the bed. He did not move, but his eyes followed her. She felt her words settle upon him like a shroud.

She looked around his room, full of familiar things. There were photos of her and Germaine on his dresser directly across from where he lay. There was the writing desk she had used in their bedroom, the chairs on which she had sat, the rug on which she had walked and practiced yoga and begged for help. There was the king-size bed where so much of their drama had played out.

She walked out into the living room. She would have known Jack had created the room, even if no one had told her. The furniture, art, and colors were all his taste, arranged for the comfort of a guest, pleasing to the eye and reflecting all his travels. There on the coffee table was one of the beautiful Senegalese baskets he had brought back, identical to the smaller one that had been his first gift to her. The pain of being there was suddenly sharp and intolerable.

She returned to his bedside. His blue eyes had gone cloudy again. He had retreated to that place where only a veil separates this world from the next. She looked at his hands again. He still wore his wedding ring, resized to fit a much smaller finger.

"Good-bye, Jack," she said. "Go in peace."

She walked out of the room in a daze. The nurse showed her out —out of his life and into the day. She stopped among the dahlias to compose herself. They were splendid and velvety and intensely colorful. A plump black and gold bumblebee buzzed among them. Life went on, enriched by all that had gone before, whether good or ill. Nature endured all things.

⊱⊰

EARLY THE NEXT MORNING, the phone rang.

"Jack passed away last night at sundown," Gabe's voice said. "He was in no pain. I think your visit helped him let go."

"Oh," was all she could say. Instead of the relief she had hoped to feel, a big hole opened up inside her. She'd been managing quite well without him, especially in the last year, but now a piece of her was suddenly missing.

"The world just won't be the same without him," Gabe said. "For all his grandiose illusions and foibles, there was never anyone else like him. He was a man of great extremes. And Mercedes, for what it's worth, he loved you as much as he ever loved anyone."

⊱⊰

THE DAY OF THE MEMORIAL service was overcast with the June gloom that so often blankets the Bay Area in early summer. Germaine had already left for work. Mercedes moved robotically through her morning routine. She had taken to running with Germaine in the early mornings for the past few months; but this morning, instead of feeling energized by their exercise, she felt tired and full of dread at the prospect of seeing Jack's friends all in one place.

She had had no contact with any of them, but had heard about their reaction to her abandonment of Jack in his hour of need. Her reasons were no one's business, and she had felt no desire to explain. She had found out who her friends were, and who held her in contempt. Now she faced another day of reckoning.

She dressed in black from head to toe and ran her fingers through her very short hair, which now had a shock of white in it. She wore no jewelry and wrapped a black shawl around her bare arms. Her joy and sense of self-containment had sprung a leak and were trickling down the black hole in her heart.

Cars lined the street on both sides of Jack's house. She felt apprehensive, but worked her way through the throng of young men, past tantalizing platters of food tastefully arranged on the table and the flowers from Jack's gardens, which were everywhere.

Of those present, she knew only Gabe, Martin Macey, and Damon Vanderveer. Damon looked like a phantom already. With a walker and an oxygen tank, he barely resembled the love-smitten, robust young man in Jack's photos. He obviously had AIDS and had expended tremendous effort to be present. There were men from the Castro District, whom Jack had befriended since he moved there, but no one else from the past. She was the only woman, save for the two nurses who had attended Jack at the end, and only she was dressed in black.

Gabe kissed her cheek and poured her a drink.

"I don't know anyone here, really," she said.

"They all know you. You're a legend."

"You mean a jezebel."

"Not at all. Jack showed his hand to all of us before the end. No one knew why you left at first, but that didn't last long. The lawsuits, his treatment of Janine, the liens against his assets, all the estate plans he had drawn up with himself as trustee—it all came out. Jack had legal dealings with most of his close friends over the years, and we've all had unpleasant surprises as a result. You never told anyone what you knew, and you could have."

"I saw no point. What became of Janine?"

"She passed away two years ago and left everything to Jack."

"Who took care of her affairs?"

"I did. It wasn't that arduous. She was a sweet little old lady."

"So Jack got away with it, embezzling from her all those years!"

"He told her everything he'd done—all the money he'd taken from her. But I don't think she really understood. She had dementia herself by then. It didn't seem to matter to her."

"The lawsuits all settled. I know that from the office. None of the insurance companies ever contacted me, though, if there were even any investigations."

"It's just as well."

One by one, people began to toast Jack. Since most of them had only met him in the last three years, their speeches rang hollow in her ears. But everyone had heard about Mercedes and recalled Jack's oft-repeated praise of her. She stood quietly and listened, feeling more depleted with each eulogy.

The group moved outdoors to the garden, where the sun was now shining. Gabe guided her to the bench under the bower, and someone else brought her a plate of food. Each guest came by to shake her hand and to pay his respects to the woman Jack Soutane had loved; the woman, as he had told them, who showed him what love was supposed to be. She could barely speak. The black hole inside stole her breath.

Damon shuffled over and sat down on the seat of his walker beside her.

"Mercedes, I have a confession to make. I owe you an apology," he panted.

"I can't imagine what that could be," she said.

"I judged you after you left Jack. I thought he told you he was gay before you were married, so I assumed you knew the risks. And I'm not the only one who thought that."

"I know, Damon. It doesn't matter anymore."

"I need to say it, Mercedes. None of us knew about Jack's financial improprieties. We didn't know he'd concealed so much about himself from you. I only found out in the last few years that he knew he was HIV positive before he married you and kept it secret."

"How did you find out?"

"He told me, in a lucid moment. He felt very guilty. He said hurting you was what he regretted most."

"It's generous of you to tell me. I'm sorry you're sick too, Damon."

"It was bound to happen, the way we carried on."

"I found pictures of you and Jack in his desk at the office when he was first hospitalized. That's when I realized he had another life I knew nothing about. I'm glad I found out, but I wish he had leveled with me. I could have helped him straighten out a lot of things. He must have loved you very much, Damon."

"Jack was the love of my life, but he was damaged goods. We can't help whom we love, though, can we? Love strikes, and you're toast! I'm not too far behind him now," he said, gesturing at his emaciated body. "We've lost so many friends to AIDS, nearly everyone in our old group. Well, this is good-bye."

She squeezed his hand before he slowly got to his feet. He shuffled toward the door and was soon out of sight.

Martin was next. He sat down by Mercedes on the bench.

"I tried to warn your friend Caroline about Jack before you were engaged. I don't know if you remember that."

"I do. You said Jack was 'strategic.' That was the understatement of the decade! I guess we didn't take your warning seriously. By then I was too much in love. I only saw what I wanted to see."

"I'm glad to see you're healthy. How's your daughter?"

Mercedes's face softened into a smile. "She's doing well. She's just about ready for college."

"Jack used to talk about the two of you as though you were twin angels. You brought him a lot of happiness."

"For a while. With conditions."

"Yes, there were a lot of conditions, weren't there? Many, many people were drawn into Jack's orbit. He attracted everyone. And once you were in, his charisma kept you there. But he didn't fool everybody. Many of us found out what he was up to after it was too late, when we were too entangled with him to extricate ourselves gracefully. I had to move my law practice away from his, at some loss, but even then I continued to see him socially. I never met a more appealing man." Martin took a deep breath. "It was most difficult for you, but you showed great decorum in how you handled it."

Gabe filled her glass again. All the guests had left; only the three of them remained. "And now we have the business of settling Jack's estate," Gabe said.

"Who's handling that?"

"Martin and I will be, with help from Matthew Spencer."

"I don't envy you."

"I don't envy us either. But there are a few things we can tell you up front," Gabe said. "Jack maintained the premiums on the life insurance policies, and kept the trust. There's no reason to think the policies won't pay out, so you and Germaine will be well provided for. He also left you a few items in his will—a lot of his household furnishings, his car, some U.S. Treasury bonds, and this."

Gabe reached into his jacket pocket and pulled out a sealed envelope, which he placed in her hands. She saw the Soutane & Associates return address, engraved on Jack's fine bond stationery, and slipped it into her purse.

"Things will be a bit easier for you now, at least financially," Martin said. "As soon as we get the title to the car straightened out, I'll drive it over to you."

"I wasn't expecting anything," she said. "I don't know what to say."

"No need to say anything," Gabe said, "except maybe to Germaine. She'll be able to afford the best college she can get into. Jack would like that. He always said she was going places in life."

Mercedes stood up and shook Martin's hand. She walked slowly through Jack's house one last time, feeling his presence and appreciating the harmony of the environment he had created. Gabe accompanied her to the door and kissed her again.

"Still got those yoga sutras?" he asked.

She smiled. "Yes, thank you. They've served me well these past few years."

"I'm glad. Take care of yourself, Mercedes."

She drove home the long way, taking back roads at a leisurely speed. She drove with the windows rolled down and the radio off. The greenery of the hills and side streets was soothing and the fragrance of eucalyptus leaves and evergreen needles filled the car.

⌒⌘⌒

GERMAINE HAD FINISHED HER SHIFT and was sprawled on the couch in her shorts and tee shirt, barefoot, deeply immersed in *Les Misérables* when Mercedes came through the door.

The girl bounded to her feet and threw her arms around her mother. They were matched shoulder to shoulder, head to head, foot for foot. Mercedes's eyes filled with tears, her arms around Germaine's shoulders.

"Who said you could grow up?"

"I didn't know I had to get permission."

"You did. I must have neglected to tell you."

"It's your fault, Mom. All that food."

"I'll put *Les Misérables* on your head. That will deter you."

"Nothing will deter me."

"That's my girl."

Germaine loosened her embrace, and Mercedes moved a strand of hair out of her daughter's face.

"How was the service?"

"Rather enlightening. I'm glad I went, but I'm very tired now. I think I'll go lie down."

Germaine kissed her face and said, "I'm glad it's over."

Mercedes went into her room and kicked her shoes off. She pulled the envelope out of her handbag. She lay on her bed and held the envelope to her breast for a few moments before opening it. There was one page, folded in thirds, with three words on it. He had found his good pen.

Please be forgiving.

ACKNOWLEDGMENTS

⚬⚊⚭⚊⚬

This book has been many years in creation, so I am thankful to a great many people for help along the way. I am profoundly grateful to Brooke Warner and her team at She Writes Press for bringing Mercedes Bell into the light of day. Crystal Patriarche, CEO and President of SparkPoint Studios, and Brooke Warner have an inspired business model and level of respect for writers that I hope more PR companies and publishing houses will adopt to set more writers free.

I am very grateful to my editor, David Landau who, with such a generous spirit and unflinching wit, challenged every phrase to be its best or to disappear. I was also extremely fortunate to work with Carol Staswick, a Latin scholar and grammarian, whose line edits were brilliant and terrifying. I am grateful to Kathy Beaudoin for her technical expertise, proofreading and friendship through many years in the trenches.

I am indebted to my writing mentor, Spencer Beasley, and my mother, Nancy Bartron Dwight, the original English language maven, for teaching me English usage and showing me that grammar is the elegant skeleton upon which the body of words lives. I thank my father, Donald Stearns Dwight, for introducing me to the creative life through his own, for empowering me as a young person, and for continually pressing me to write this book.

I humbly bow to Dr. William W. Foote for his wise guidance over the past 30-odd years. Without the insights and perseverance his questions sparked I could not have come to understand my characters or my purpose well enough to do them justice.

The following people read drafts and offered in return the great gift of their perceptions: Bethany DeRuiter, Kate Arsenault, Laurel Brandstetter, Kathryn J. Brown, Marcy Ayanian, Jeanne Marlow, Janine Orendain, Evan Michael Sinclair, Judy Brown, Laura Arago, Mary Howell, Chet Paulinellie, Kaitlin Duffey, Karin Larkins, and Trish Bare. They helped me strengthen the book and boosted my persistence.

This book truly owes its existence to my husband, Robert W. Duffey, whose devotion, forbearance, cooking, and encouragement nurtured me through the entire process. With an exacting eye he read many drafts of the manuscript. He was my sounding board and was present at every milestone, including the glorious day on which it was accepted for publication.

May we all remember that every moment in this lush life is a gift.

Namasté

photo credit: Mark Bennington

JENNIFER DWIGHT was born into a U.S. Air Force family who was stationed throughout the U.S. and Asia during her youth, before settling in Colorado. In Asia she was first exposed to ancient cultures and eastern religions, which sparked her lifelong interest in how peoples' beliefs shape their lives.

She attended The Colorado College where she graduated with a B.A. in Religion. Ms. Dwight worked as a litigation paralegal, writer, and trainer for 33 years in the San Francisco area, while rearing a family. During that time she also wrote and published numerous articles, short stories, and three nonfiction books, as well as a 60-segment weekly fiction serial for a newspaper.

The Tolling of Mercedes Bell is her first novel. She lives with her husband, Robert W. Duffey, and their little black dog, Jackie Beane, in Northern California. When she is not writing or outside working in the garden or walking, she enjoys spending time with friends and family, live music, yoga, knitting, puttering, and pondering.

CPSIA information can be obtained at www.ICGtesting.com
Printed in the USA
BVOW03*1352210416

444989BV00001B/1/P